Devil's Thumb

Books by Dan Jorgensen

Devil's Thumb
And the Wind Whispered
Rainbow Rock

**For more information
visit:** www.SpeakingVolumes.us

Devil's Thumb

Dan Jorgensen

SPEAKING VOLUMES, LLC
NAPLES, FLORIDA
2025

Devil's Thumb

Copyright © 2025 by Dan Jorgensen

All rights reserved. No part of this book may be reproduced or transmitted in any form or by any means without written permission.

ISBN 979-8-89022-275-6

For their ongoing support and encouragement, I dedicate this book to my wife Susan; my daughter Kari and her family Obie, Teo and Cyrus Diener; my daughter Becky and her family Evan, Josh and Nolan Yeager; and to my high school English teacher Mrs. Clarke Hoover, who recognized and nurtured my writing skills and started me along the writing pathway that has shaped my life. I will always be grateful.

Acknowledgments

Thank you to my wife Susan for her expert reading/reviewing eye and help in researching the historical background for this book. Author E.L. Doctorow once noted that a historian tells us "what" happened, but historical novelists tell us what it felt and looked like when it was happening. My ability to do that is due in no small part to Susan's expert assistance.

Thanks also to Joe & Karen Muller for their help in tracking down information about Hot Springs people and places. And thanks to Dave and Cathy Sorenson and Carolyn Amiet for their manuscript review. And thanks to many Lakota friends who provided assistance with Lakota historical and language details.

Thank you to Rick Mills, Curator/Historian of the South Dakota State Railroad Museum in Hill City, and to Casey Sullivan at the Keystone Historical Museum for information about the Hill City-Keystone area in the mid-1920s. And, finally, thanks to the Fall River Historical Society and its director Dawn Johnson; and *The Hot Springs Star*, whose archives provided valuable background information.

This is a work of fiction, but many of the locations and people in the story are based on real individuals, places, communities and events in the Black Hills and its surrounding prairielands during the mid-1920s. More about the "factual" and "fictional" events, people and places in the story are expanded upon in the book's *"Afterword"* section.

Prologue

The boy approached the base of the mountain and gazed up at the eagle he had been following. The big bird glided onto a rock outcropping and perched there eyeing him intently before swiveling his great white neck far to the right, looking west. Then he raised his head toward the south, slowly turned 180 degrees to the north, and finally tilted back his entire body and spread his wings toward the sky, framed by the puffy clouds floating above him.

The boy stood frozen in place. His feet suddenly feeling very heavy as if they were planting him where he stood.

"Anunjkasan! Brother!" he cried, raising a hand in salute. The eagle lowered his head to stare back at him and then screamed as if scolding the boy for daring to speak. He ruffled his feathers and looked east toward a rapidly brightening sunrise. Before the boy could make another move, the eagle flapped his powerful wings, rose up and soared westward across a deep ravine and on up toward the next big mountain. Settling there on another rocky ledge, he looked back toward the boy and jerked his head skyward and emitted a second shrill cry.

As if responding to the bird's call, the rocks in front of the boy rumbled, shifted and started coming to life. The boy shrank back in fear as the jagged rocks began to reshape into the forms of six old men—six grandfathers—each clothed in the finest regalia of the boy's Lakota people.

"Thunkasila! Grandfather!" the boy called out toward the shapes. He respectfully moved his eyes from image to image, repeating his greeting before sinking to his knees, his feet still feeling like stone and still holding him firmly in place. "Hear me!" he implored, sweeping his eyes across the images and raising both arms. "I am your grandson.

I am Heȟáka Sápa—I am Black Elk." He looked over his shoulder to where a cloud hovered and pointed toward it. "Wakinyan—the Thunder Beings—have brought me on that cloud to you so I can hear your wisdom and share your words with my people! Tell me what to say."

And one-by-one the Grandfathers began to speak.

* * * * *

"So, is that why the Lakota people call the mountain The Six Grandfathers?" Thirteen-year-old Lincoln Borglum leaned away from the campfire as he asked the question. "I thought it was just a name, from that medicine man; that Black Elk guy?"

Harold Swanzey, who had been narrating the story and who Lincoln considered to be infinitely wiser and more knowledgeable since he was both 19 years old AND a Black Hills resident, nodded. "Nicholas Black Elk. He is the boy in this story," Harold answered, his blue-grey eyes sparkling in the campfire light.

He took off his hat and wiped his brow, pushing back at a thatch of wavy sandy colored hair that added at least three inches above his already imposing six-foot-two-inch angular body. He looked around at the group of men and older teens sitting by the fire, and added, "But that's only part of the story.

"It was my good friend Ben Black Elk who shared the story with me and Nicholas is his father. It was Nicholas who had this great vision when he was a young boy. And in his vision, he saw the mountain come to life—I mean, he saw the Grandfathers emerge and come to life on the mountain."

"How did he have a vision?"

"The story is that the boy had become very ill and was near death and in a coma. But after a Medicine Man treated him he recovered and told of being carried on a cloud to this mountain to hear the Grandfathers' great wisdom."

He pointed off to his right and then behind himself to indicate the big granite mountain that he was referencing.

"Ben said in his father's vision each part of that mountain turned into a Grandfather figure, representing the six sacred directions: west, east, north, south, above, and below." He touched the ground as he said the final word. "But why Grandfathers?" Lincoln asked, perplexed by the response.

Before Harold could reply, another man's voice interrupted them. "Because MY father said the Great Spirit spoke to him and told him that Grandfathers represented the human traits of kindness, love, wisdom, strength, courage and protection, not just for the Lakota people but for our sacred Black Hills. They would stand as mighty sentinels for our people."

Lincoln and Harold both turned to see who had spoken, and a young Indian man moved out of the woods toward the campfire.

Swanzey smiled and nodded in his direction. "Hello Ben," he said. "Didn't see you arrive. Did you hear what I was telling the others about your father's vision? I hope I was I telling the story correctly."

Ben Black Elk moved further into the campfire's glow carrying a thin stick in his left hand and a dried tree branch in his right. He waved the stick in Swanzey's direction and nodded, cautiously observing the rest of the group as he walked up and dropped the branch into the fire.

"You tell the story well," he replied.

"Lincoln, give Mister Black Elk your seat," Borglum's father said as he stood up from the sawed-off log where he was seated across from his son. "Or you're welcome to mine," he added, gesturing toward the now empty spot on his own log. "Glad you could join us tonight, sir. Will your father be coming too?"

Lincoln jumped up and pointed toward the spot where he had been sitting. "Oh, I'm sorry. Yes. Please. Come and sit here."

Black Elk nodded respectfully toward the elder Borglum before accepting the teenager's offer, dropping down onto the log and reaching out with the stick to stir the fire as if to make sure his tree branch offering had been properly accepted. "My father sends his greetings," he answered, "but he will not be coming."

Lincoln shifted nervously and edged around toward where Harold was seated in front of a small aspen tree. The boy reached out and grasped one of the tree's limbs for support and stood quietly waiting to see what would transpire. But after several seconds, he broke his own self-imposed silence. "What Harold was saying, that's really the story from your father?" he asked.

"Yes," Black Elk replied. "It was his vision when he was a boy even younger than you. The Grandfathers appeared to him as both our people's guardians and as the protectors of the Black Hills." He looked across the top of the fire toward where Gutzon Borglum was still standing. "My father and our people, they are worried about this NEW vision that you have for our mountain, Mister Borglum. We don't want your carving to take our Grandfathers away."

Borglum turned and looked up at the mountain. "Mister Black Elk, when I'm finished with my carving, your Grandfathers will still be there, but they will be joined by other great leaders of our nation. It will be a shrine that honors all our people and every belief."

Chapter One

The sound of the gunshot—at least Al Twocrow thought it was a gunshot—came from far down in the valley to his east, reverberating up the rocky hillsides toward him. Twocrow reined his horse to a stop, lifted himself up in the stirrups and listened carefully to be sure that he had, in fact, heard something that sounded like a shot.

It was the second time in the past few minutes that he had heard what he thought might be a gunshot and just like before, he tried to keep as still as possible to pinpoint where the sound was coming from. But now, other than the wind blowing through the ponderosa pines and a Stellar Jay's rasping call off to his northwest, there were no other noises.

Twocrow shrugged and spoke to his horse. "Probably just some tree branches popping after being weakened by all the wind from the past few days." The horse flicked his ears back and forth as if listening, too, then made a little snort and looked back uphill toward where the edge of the plateau met the large expanse of blue sky that stretched out above them.

Settling back in the saddle, Twocrow clucked encouragement as they continued their climb. The animal was sweating profusely in the mid-morning sun as they steadily moved up toward the flat area fronting the base of Harney Peak, the Black Hills' tallest mountain. He leaned forward in the saddle and gave the steel grey mustang a gentle pat on the side of his neck just below his thick, jet-black mane. It had been that mane accenting the animal's icy grey color that had been the impetus for his naming the muscular little horse Black Ice. "You got this Ice," he said softly into the horse's right ear.

"Come on old man, you can do it!" Twocrow further encouraged as Black Ice heaved himself on out of the narrow, rubble-filled draw that they had been following for much of the past hour. The marshal gave a sharp cry of relief as the horse clambered out onto a flat-topped mesa that marked the halfway point to their final destination. Quivering, Ice stood blowing and grunting from the effort.

"Good boy! Good boy!" Twocrow patted his horse again and the mustang responded with a low whickering sound, almost as if saying, "You're welcome."

He leaned back in the saddle. At 6-foot-1 and just 180 pounds, it had taken all his strength to control Ice's ascent up the steep mountainside and now, like his horse, he felt his body quivering as he rolled his neck and shoulders to take away the tension that had been building up during their climb. He blew out a long breath of his own. Removing his grey Stetson and holding it on his lap, he sighed as the breeze wafted across the top of his thick wavy hair that was starting to show speckles of gray in its otherwise solid black color. He patted Ice once more, put his hat back on and climbed down. Loosening a large canvas water bag that was attached to his saddle, he opened one end of the bag and held it out like a feedbag for the horse to drink.

"Just look at this view, partner. Makes the trip up here worth every ounce of energy, doesn't it?" Ice continued drinking as Twocrow stared out across the expanse of the Black Hills' rugged beauty, the rock formations and craggy hillsides blanketed by the deeply dark green stands of ponderosa pine trees that gave the Black Hills their name.

He pulled out his pocket watch and flipped it open. Still too early to stop for lunch, but he might rest for a while anyway and have one of the sandwiches he'd packed before starting out this morning.

A buzzing noise interrupted Ice's drinking and the horse raised his head, water dripping off the corners of his mouth as he flicked his ears forward. He nervously stamped one foot and softly whinnied.

Twocrow refastened the water bag's top and hooked it back into place, quickly swinging up into the saddle while looking off toward the northwest side of Mount Rushmore. While the sound seemed to be coming from there, nothing seemed to be causing it. The sun glinted off the silver U.S. Deputy Marshal's badge pinned to the right side of his leather vest as he turned back one more time to try to determine the spot where he thought the buzzing noise might be coming from.

"Now what in hell is making a noise like that? Is that an airplane?" he asked aloud as the buzzing intensified. Ice snuffled in response and once more stamped his foot.

Suddenly, a brown and white biplane appeared just above the mesa's northeast corner and cut hard in their direction. As the plane roared past the horse and rider, the pilot, who was operating the aircraft from the rear of the two front-to-back seats, dipped its wings as if to say "hello" as it flew past them. Circling back to the north, the plane banked east then once more swung around in their direction. Re-approaching and rapidly descending, it nearly snagged a wingtip on one of the ponderosas that jutted out just above the plateau's eastern edge and jerked up quickly to avoid the treetop.

Safely clear of the hazard, it dropped even faster onto the mostly flat hard-rock surface and began bouncing on its two oversized wheels—splayed about four or five feet out from the fuselage and just ahead of the empty front seat. As the plane rolled along toward Harney Peak, the earlier buzzing was replaced by a low growling noise as the pilot throttled back on the engine to slow it down.

Ice stamped for a third time and whinnied anxiously as the noisy plane rolled from east to west in front of them. "Take it easy old boy,"

Twocrow reassured his mount even though he wasn't sure if he was right to hold his position or should be turning back toward the cover of the draw. The marshal lightly rested his right hand on top of the handle of his Smith and Wesson .38 revolver while tracking the plane's progress.

As if sensing both the horse's and his rider's unease, the pilot angled away from them and out toward the mesa's northern edge before fully cutting the engine's power and continuing more quietly along the surface, finally settling in place about a quarter-mile away, the smaller rear wheel settling quietly onto the surface.

As Twocrow debated whether to ride out toward the plane or stay put, its engine suddenly revved again, and the pilot brought the nose around to face in their direction. With its engine noise once more growing louder the plane picked up speed as it headed toward them. Ice snorted in alarm and shied backward before skittering to one side.

Twocrow pulled hard on the reins while holding up his right hand to signal to the pilot to stop. The engine noise immediately began to abate until it finally shut back down, but the plane's momentum caused it to roll forward for another 50 or 60 feet. The wheels and fuselage sharply creaked before it finally came to a complete stop about seventy yards away from them.

Now, the only sounds came from the light breeze blowing through the ponderosas, Twocrow's deep breathing, and the renewed nervous huffing from his horse.

The marshal gave Ice another reassuring pat and clucked to him to advance to where the double-winged plane had rolled to a stop. Reluctantly the muscular mustang complied while keeping his ears cocked forward to let the lawman know that if anything out of the ordinary happened, he was more than ready to turn and make a run for it. Sensing the horse's concern, Twocrow double-wrapped the reins around his left hand and wrist to better stabilize himself and his control over Ice's movements.

As they edged closer, he could see each of the two seats had its own protective windscreen curving across in front of it. The front one protected that seat from the wind created by the propeller, and the back one ran between the two seats in front of the pilot.

He could see the top of the pilot's head jutting up just below the top edge of that windscreen anchored between the two seats. The screen stretched straight up to just miss connecting with the center of the top wing to provide the pilot with a good amount of protection from the elements whenever the plane was in flight. And, with the outside edges only reaching about halfway up, the pilot also could easily look over them for a sharper view of the front if needed.

Twocrow reined in, re-resting his right hand on top of the revolver handle as he waited to see what was going to happen.

The figure rose up from behind the windscreen and slowly pulled off an oversized pair of goggles that were tightly strapped around a heavy leather helmet. Draping the goggles' strap onto a small hook protruding from the screen's upper edge, the pilot grasped the helmet with both hands and lifted it straight up. As the helmet rose, a mass of Mary Pickford-style dark red ringlets were released from its confines and started cascading down either side and onto the pilot's shoulders.

With the thick, ringleted hair now swirling around her face, the female pilot continued her climb out of the cockpit and out onto the surface of the bottom wing. Then she turned and pulled the goggles off the hook and stuffed them inside the helmet before tossing it onto the seat that she had been occupying just seconds before. She looked up, her face bright with pleasure at seeing the marshal and his horse.

"Hey, is that you Cochise?" she called out with a broad grin. "You're about the last person I expected to find today riding around up here in the clouds!"

Chapter Two

The pilot shook her head to further settle her mostly disorganized ringlets and nodded toward Black Ice. "See you brought old Ice along with you too." Her voice took on a suspicious tone. "How the hell'd you get Ice way up here? You didn't ride that poor animal all the way from Hot Springs, now did you? That's gotta be at least 70 or 80 miles."

Twocrow blanched at the accusing tone in the woman's voice, but before he could say anything in response, she broke into a throaty laugh and continued her progress sideways out along the plane's bottom wing. She was so petite she barely had to duck her head as she moved along between the plane's two wings.

"I know you wouldn't do that, Alvin. Just messin' with ya." Halfway out, she sat down and scooted forward. Reaching the wing's front edge, she pulled her feet together and dropped straight down to the ground. Her knee-high dark brown engineering boots making a loud "thwack" as she landed on the hard stone surface.

At about five-foot-two inches tall and encased in a lightweight leather jacket that reached well below her waist over loose fitting tan pants that were tucked into the heavy boots, the woman looked more like a young teenager than a pilot. As if to dispel any doubt that she was in charge of the formidable aircraft she'd just landed, she stepped forward and placed her hands on her hips and gave Twocrow a defiant glare. Then she broke into a little laugh and unwrapped a white scarf that was around her neck and left it hanging across her shoulders.

Twocrow grinned back at her and gave her a little wave. "Kallie Sinclair! I'll be damned! Guess I should be asking the same thing from you, because you're about the last person I expected to see dropping out of the sky into the middle of the Black Hills. So right back at ya. What brings you up here to the Harney Peak area?"

Kallie backed up against the biplane's bottom wing and waited to answer as Twocrow dismounted and took his canteen off the saddle's pommel. Taking a quick drink, he waggled it in her direction. "It ain't tea, but it's pretty refreshing if I do say so myself. Wish it was tea," he added as he eyed the container. "I love that stuff."

"Oh, hell yes!" Sinclair exclaimed, waving him forward. He led Ice with him and extended his arm toward her. Accepting the canteen, she pushed a dangling clump of hair back behind her right ear, wiped her free hand across her brow and took a long drink. The corners of her dark green eyes crinkled, accenting the satisfied look on her face from the taste of the water as she lowered the canteen.

She yawned and grinned again. "I probably shouldn't be flying up here or anywhere else today," she said. "Haven't gotten much sleep the past few days with all the wild winds we've been having. But, with a calm day like today, I figured I'd better fly while the flying was good."

"See you still got that farmer's tan going on," Twocrow said, pointing toward the top half of her pretty face as she brushed a hand across her brow for a second time. "Tanned face with big white circles around your eyes and a stripe across the top of your forehead." He chuckled. "Don't you wish you had that 'natural' tan like I have so you wouldn't have to put up with that?"

He jabbed his thumb toward his own bronze features before pushing the front part of his hat back on his head to show her that his skin was the same even color from top to bottom.

She waved her free hand back and forth as if to say she wasn't sure that his "natural look" was all that great either. Accented by yet another laugh she held the canteen up as if to toast him before taking one more small sip and passing it back.

"So, you weren't expecting the world's number one female pilot to drop in on you . . . literally," Sinclair said. "Especially alongside Harney Peak, eh?" She held her arms wide as if to encompass the entire mountainous area around them. "Like I said, I wasn't expecting to find the world's only known Lakota U.S. Marshal hanging out up here either."

"Oh, good, so you remembered I'm Lakota and not Apache," he said, the sarcasm in his voice coming through loud and clear. "I know you white folks think all us Indians look alike, and I'm happy to accept being compared to one of the greatest Apache warrior chiefs ever, but . . ." he grimaced. "But Kallie, really? Cochise? How'd you like it if I started calling you Amelia?"

At the reference to renowned pilot Amelia Earhart, Kallie made a face of her own. "Okay, okay, no offense intended. Although, you know, you probably truly are the ONLY Lakota U.S. Marshal. And I truly am the world's GREATEST woman pilot, despite everyone and their dog thinking it's Earhart. Sorry sister." She looked toward the sky as if expecting Earhart to suddenly fly into view. "You're good, but I still think I'm better."

"Well, no one could fault you for lacking confidence in your abilities," he laughed. "Your flyin' and my marshalin'. Guess we're both plowing new ground these days, ain't we?"

"When they write the history books, this can be OUR contribution to the Roaring '20s," Kallie answered. "You know, seven or eight years ago when we first met who'd a'thought either one of us would be where we are today? And I don't just mean meeting up here on top of this mountain."

She looked around. "But seriously Alvin, we probably should stop meeting like this, or people are going to talk." She grinned again as she stepped forward to give Ice a friendly rub on the side of his nose. "How ya doin' there big fella?" she asked. "Sorry I haven't been around the Southern Hills lately to give you some love." The horse responded to her soft touch and mellow voice by leaning in closer and nickering as she patted him again.

"When WAS the last time you were down our way?" Twocrow asked. "Seems like forever and a day."

"Six months . . ." she paused. "No, probably five. It was when they were starting the grading work on that new runway out on the west side of town. I sorta 'dropped in' uninvited on THAT landing spot, too, if you recall?" She chuckled. "But you have to admit we had a fun couple of days hanging out before I flew back out of town."

Twocrow took in a deep breath. "Whoo, that's for sure. Probably lucky I still have my job." He pointed at her. "You know you never did keep your promise to fly back down and give me a plane ride." He pointed at her plane. "And this one has two seats, so no excuses on that count."

"Well, I wanted to make sure the runway was properly finished."

"Uh huh." He waggled a hand. "Been done for at least a month and I'm still waiting."

Kallie ignored the dig and pointed toward the horse. "So, how DID you get Ice up here?" she asked, changing the conversation as she once again swung her accusing finger around toward him. "If you rode him all the way from Hot Springs, that's pretty tough going for a horse, even if he is a Mustang."

"Naw, I wouldn't have Ice do a long ride like that," Twocrow responded. "I brought him up to Keystone yesterday in one of those fancy new horse trailers. The Fall River County Sheriff picked one up a few months back and I got the marshal's office to spring for a new Ford Double T pickup truck to help pull it. That's the advantage of sharing headquarters' space with both the sheriff and the Hot Springs Police

Department. We're able to pool our resources and buy more equipment. Easier on everyone's budget."

"No kidding? So, how'd old Ice like ridin' in a trailer?" She gave the horse another friendly rub and he reacted by pulling his head back and giving a little whinny.

"If that's his official response, I'd say he didn't much care for the bumpy road or the engine noise, but otherwise the drive was okay. Just hooked the trailer up behind the truck, got Ice on board and drove it on up. Still took us about two and a half hours, though, because we had to take the Fall River Canyon Road out to Maverick Junction, drive north to Hermosa and follow that new dirt road into Keystone from there.

"Gonna be real glad when they get some new gravel roads laid out and built into Keystone. I can't imagine trying to negotiate that road from Hermosa if it was raining."

Kallie nodded her agreement.

"Anyway, we spent the night in town before riding up here this morning." He pointed off toward Harney Peak. "Ultimately we need to get up there, but thought we'd take a little break here at the halfway point before moving on."

She shook her head as she looked up at the mountaintop then back past the edge of the plateau and down the steep hillside behind him. "Even riding him from Keystone up to here must have been a challenge. And you're right about the roads. But I hear through the grapevine the Army Corps of Engineers will be building some new roads real soon. Both the State and the Forest Service have given them the okay."

She waved her hands in a circle. "So, what've you got going on that brought you up here in the first place? I take it you ain't on an all-day straight up the hill pleasure ride."

He shrugged. "Well, it might or might not be anything, but the fire spotters working up on Harney reported some suspicious smoke plumes between their location and Mount Rushmore. Said there have been streams of smoke coming and going, so they know it isn't a wildfire. Since we've had some reports of bootlegging, the Big Marshal in Sioux Falls wants me to check it out."

She chuckled at his "Big Marshal" reference to the U.S. Marshals regional headquarters in South Dakota's largest city, located across the Missouri River on the eastern side of the state.

"Don't know if you know this, but there's some abandoned tin and silver mines around here, and if someone's using them as a location to make bootleg whiskey, the Big Marshal wants me to shut them down. Problem is, those mines are mostly only accessible on horseback. So, it had to be either me or John Rooks from out of the Deadwood office checking into them." He sighed. "Lucky me, I drew the short straw. And, besides, Rooks is sort of semi-retired anyhow."

"Bootlegging. Geez, I hope that's just a rumor and not really a thing!" She scrunched up her face as she said it. "Something like that sure would throw a monkey wrench into that Mount Rushmore carving project, wouldn't it?"

Twocrow nodded. "Yeah, no way a major project like that can move forward if there's a criminal gang operating in the area. And since all the state's Bigwig politicians seem to be signing on to this Borglum fella's mountain carving plan, we'll be under a lot of pressure to clean things up . . . IF that's what's really happening."

Kallie nodded knowingly before pointing to where Twocrow and Ice had been standing when she flew in. "By the way, I was really glad to see you two when I flew up over the far edge of the plateau."

"Oh yeah? Why's that?"

"Well, I hate to delay your ride up to the top of Harney, but I think I spotted another problem that you're going to have to turn around to check on first. I was just debating with myself on how to report it without having to fly all the way back to Rapid City. That would have been a huge bother to say the least."

"What kind of problem we talkin' about here?"

She pointed off toward Mount Rushmore. "Well, I'm not positive Alvin, but I'm pretty sure that when I flew across the west side of the Rushmore ridgeline, I spotted a body down in the valley just below the treeline."

Chapter Three

"A body!" Twocrow's response was so intense that Ice jerked back and shifted sideways. The marshal used both hands to pull the reins tighter before speaking again, this time in a quieter voice. "A body? Where do you mean? The west side of the Rushmore ridgeline is a pretty big area."

"Well, okay, on the southwest corner of Mount Rushmore out along the east side of Pine Creek, just where it merges into that other creek."

Twocrow took his right hand away from Ice's face and thoughtfully stroked his chin as he looked in the direction Kallie was referencing. "But you can't be certain?"

"No, I can't be absolutely certain," she said, looking back toward the northeast. "I only made that one pass and was still trying to figure out if I should turn around and try to get a closer look or head back to Rapid. Or maybe just continue on my way and report it when I got to Custer. That's when I spotted you."

Kallie pointed at her plane. "My ride was supposed to be installed with the newest version of the military's two-way radio before I flew out this morning. They took the old one out yesterday but then they didn't get it done before I needed to take off. So, with the old one gone the only way to communicate is face-to-face when I'm on the ground. And that's a fairly major inconvenience to say the least." She gave a little exasperated groan to accent her statement.

"Any chance that body might've just been someone injured from an accident or something? Maybe a hiker who took a fall?"

"I don't know," she answered. "Maybe. But I kind of doubt it. Didn't see any movement and the body seemed like it was way too far down the hillside for something like that, even if it rolled for a ways. It was down in a flat spot, a little glen alongside a big growth of aspen trees. That's kinda why I didn't try dropping down lower for another look right then and there or even swinging around for another flyby. Too many chances of snagging a wing on one of those trees."

She drew an imaginary map in the air as if diagraming it for Twocrow. "It was just off that old dirt trail that runs alongside that weird wrap-around rock formation. Like I said, where Pine Creek intersects with that other smaller creek that runs south to north. You know the spot I'm talking about, don't you?"

"A weird wrap-around rock formation?" He paused. "You mean Devil's Thumb?"

"Yes, that's it! Devil's Thumb. Isn't that the formation overlooking the spot where those two creeks come together?"

Twocrow tried to picture the location in his mind. "Sure. Maybe? Devil's Thumb's probably the one you're talking about. It juts out right above where Pine runs into Horse Thief Creek."

"Exactly! Horse Thief Creek! That's the other one I was thinking of."

Twocrow nodded. "Then you're right. It's not likely someone could've fallen from any high-up spots over there. But, like I said, maybe it's not a 'dead' body, but just someone who got hurt and can't move." He paused. "Which means, of course, I still probably should get my butt back up on old Ice and ride over there to check it out before going all the way up to Harney."

He sighed. "It'll definitely have to be my new top priority, so thanks for setting down here to let me know. Kind of a tough place to land, so I appreciate it."

He held out a hand to the pilot and she grasped it firmly before leaning in to give him a quick hug.

"Sure thing Alvin. And sorry to put a damper on your day, especially one as pretty as this." Kallie pointed toward a couple of golden leafed aspen trees accented by the dark ponderosa pines. "Really beautiful up here, isn't it? I mean look at those gold leaves. Nothing like the colors changing during leaf season to restore a person's soul."

"That's probably true. But I'm not sure Ice would agree with you after the ride we just made . . . despite the beauty of it all."

Kallie walked around and climbed up a little stairway onto the rear of the wing, close to the dual cockpit. Reaching into the back seat, she pulled out the helmet, then sat back down on the wing and slid forward to drape her feet out over the wing's front edge. Swiveling her body around to look at him, she swung her heavy boots back and forth as she spoke. "I assume you got someone in mind that might be doin' that bootlegging, or the Big Marshal wouldn't have sent you up here in the first place? Anybody I might have heard of?"

"Maybe. Even before the reports from that fire watch crew came in, the marshal's office had been notified that a couple of Verne Miller's cronies might be setting up a still somewhere west of Keystone, with plans to transport the booze over to the East River. There's even been some chatter about Miller sending hooch all the way over to Minneapolis and St. Paul for distribution by the Chicago mob. I don't know if that's true, but it does go along with a memo we had last month that Al Capone's gang is looking to expand into Minnesota and the Dakotas."

"Capone's gang?" Kallie gave a little whistle, and Ice's ears pricked up. "Now, THAT would be a bad problem, wouldn't it?"

"Ummmm," Twocrow half-hummed and half-grunted his reply. "There's also talk of some sort of connection to the Garrison gang. It's a family-owned business if there is such a thing in the 'gang world.' But who knows? Anyway, here I am 'checking' things out. Haven't seen anything suspicious yet but thought I might've heard a couple of rifle shots when I was still riding up in that draw." He pointed over behind him toward the gap where he'd ridden up onto the plateau.

"Didn't hear anything more, though, so it could've just been some tree branches popping from all that wind you were talking about." He looked around. "It's a pretty big area to try and cover, so I'll probably be hanging out around here for at least a couple more days. But that's why I was headed up to the Harney Peak fire hut. Their fire spotting equipment should help me zero in on any possibilities so I can just ride right over to check them out."

He pointed up at the mountain. "I was already thinking I might have to spend tonight up there, so I sent a message up to the Spotters that I was riding their way. Hate to leave them in the lurch not knowing one way or another if I'm even going to show up."

"Well, since you have to turn around to check on that body, do you want me to let 'em know your situation? Like you say, they're probably already keeping an eye out for you. I could be in touch for you as sort-of a courtesy thing. Right?"

Twocrow nodded as he looked up at the peak. "Thanks. But how do you propose to do that?" He nodded at her plane. "I don't think you'll be able to land this thing on top of Harney Peak, even if you ARE the greatest female pilot in the world." She rolled her eyes at the sarcastic tone in his voice. "Maybe you could put down over in Hill City? That's where they have the hookup to their phone line."

"I don't think I'll have time to land in Hill City now that I stopped here, but once I'm on the ground down at Custer I could ask the Custer County Sheriff's office to relay your message. They can call the Forest Service office in Hill City and have them call your message up to the Spotters. That way they won't be wondering what happened if you don't get up to their place until tomorrow."

"A three-way phone relay. Modern communicating at its best, huh?"

Kallie laughed. "Right. Just another one of those thoroughly modern Roaring '20s things, huh? And to answer your earlier question about why I'm up here in the first place, I'm flying back and forth between Rapid City and Custer City almost every day—weather permitting—from now through mid-October. So, I can definitely keep my eyes peeled and let you know if I see anything unusual. Can I telegraph you? Or call it in to your office?"

"Yes, that sounds like a deal," Twocrow answered. "And much appreciated. Like I said, if there's something illegal going on, we'll be under a lot of pressure to get it cleaned up quick so that nothing gets in the way of the Rushmore project. I heard they might even be dedicating the carving next month."

"Seriously? You think that's really gonna happen, even if you do give them the all clear?"

"Yeah, I think it will. Why not?"

"I heard talk that the Lakota tribal leaders don't much like the project and might try to put a stop to it. Plus, ain't there some big anti-carving group formed up down there in Hot Springs?"

"I'm not sure about the Tribal leaders." He paused. "You might think I would've heard something, but I haven't. And you're right; there IS an anti-carving group in the Southern Hills, headquartered in Hot Springs. I just don't know how big it is. Cora Johnson—she and her husband own the *Hot Spring Star*—she's been writing anti-Borglum carving stuff in the paper ever since word first got out that he might try carving The Needles. Even though he's switched the project over to Mount Rushmore, she's still got folks stirred up to stop it if they can.

"They're saying some other area newspapers have come out in her favor, too. But you'd need to check in with Minnie for the details. She'd know for sure if Cora's efforts are getting any legs."

"Minnie? Thompson? Why her?"

"Well, she's the *Star*'s primary feature writer these days."

"She is? I thought she went back out to run her dad's paper in Buffalo Gap after the two of you broke up?"

"Umm . . . "Twocrow stopped and swallowed hard. "Our so-called breakup was just for a short time. She and I got things sorted out . . . about what our relationship was going to be, I mean . . . and now she's back at the *Star*."

"Relationship, huh?" The crinkly corners of Kallie's eyes expanded, accented by a twinkle as she said it. "You know ever since I first met the two of you, I thought you might end up getting married. 'Course I've only known you for SEVEN OR EIGHT years, so I suppose you can't rush into things like that, huh?" She grinned as she accented "seven or eight."

Twocrow slowly shook his head. "I think brother and sister might be a better way to describe our relationship, just like it's been since we first met as kids." His tone turned somber. "I don't think it's the right time or place for an Indian man to marry a white woman—even an Indian man who's a Deputy U.S. Marshal and whose aunt was married to a white rancher."

The twinkle in Kallie's eyes dissipated as she studied the forlorn look on Twocrow's face. "Sorry to have to agree Alvin, but you're probably right." They were both quiet for a minute until Ice snuffled and gave an impatient shake of his head, breaking the silence and causing both of them to laugh.

"Listen, I appreciate your watching out for anything suspicious while you're flying, especially since I'll have to spend who knows how long riding over to check on your body." He stopped as she blushed at that and quickly added, "THE body. Come on, you know what I mean?

"And, like you said, we don't need anything putting a fly in the ointment for whatever ends up happening up at Mount Rushmore. Whatever we find—either a body or a bootlegging operation—needs to get cleaned up and out of here. Sooner rather than later." He gave a firm nod as if reinforcing it for himself as well as for her.

Chapter Four

Kallie crouched on top of the wing, helmet in hand. Turning with it in her hands she gave another low whistle. "So, Verne Miller and Al Capone, huh? Wow!"

She climbed into the cockpit's rear chamber and stood leaning against the back of the seat as she continued talking. "You know? What if . . .?"

"What if . . . what?" Twocrow asked.

"What if MY body has something to do with that bootlegging operation? Could that be a possibility? Is it possible the body belongs to a bootlegger?"

Twocrow made another of his little humming sounds as he digested her words. "Well, shit. Guess I better be keeping that in mind when I'm riding over there to check it out. If there's a still around there and the operators are guarding it, I don't want to end up making myself into a target now do I?"

"Agreed. So, whatever you do, be careful."

"I will, and you too. Thank you, Kallie." He gave her a little salute and pointed to the plane. "By the way, how come you're flying this route back and forth to Custer? What's going on down there?" He reached over and tapped the propeller. "Really nice plane, by the way. Don't know if I've ever seen one quite like it before."

"It's a Kinner Airster. Flies like a dream compared to that old Flivver I was flying before. And . . ." she pointed to the other seating area ahead of her, ". . . like you pointed out, it seats two so I can take a passenger, so just let me know if you need a ride anywhere."

"Yeah, right."

"No, I'm not kidding. If you need a quick ride somewhere I'll be there. Just say the word." She grinned. "But we might have to do it on the sly, since this little beauty ain't mine. Not yet anyway. Army owns it. I'm just their Pony Express rider, hauling dispatch pouches for them from Rapid City down to their bivouac camp in Custer Park every other morning and then back the next afternoon.

"Gonna be doing three trips a week, down on Monday, Wednesday and Friday, back to Rapid on Tuesday, Thursday and Saturday. Which leaves Sundays wide open for some pleasure flying if you want that ride." She grinned and held her hands wide.

"Sounds like you've got yourself a good gig," Twocrow said with a smile. "And I do appreciate your being willing to give me a ride sometime. I tease you about not getting one, but to tell you the truth I'm a little nervous about flying. You think you'll get hired on full time once this part-time thing is over?"

"Hope so. I figure if I play my cards right, flying these dispatches might get me on the short list to do one of those full-time Mail Service routes. My friend Kitty Stinson's been doing that, and she loves it."

She tapped the plane. "Can't let Kitty have all the fun. And I'd love to show you the Hills from the air; it would be good for my resume. Even Kitty hasn't ferried around a U.S. Marshal." She grinned. "So, like I said, you just call and I'm your ride."

She tapped the plane's stick. "And when I'm at the controls it's smooth as silk, so no need to be nervous." She pulled the helmet down over her curls and then pushed at the stray ones to get them back inside. "Oh, and to answer your other question, the fastest route from Rapid City to Custer is right over the top of Mount Rushmore, bank left at Harney Peak and then straight south through the center of the Hills. It's a natural air corridor."

She rested her right arm on the edge of the cockpit as Twocrow turned to get back in his saddle. He settled onto Ice's back and looked up toward her. "Okay. If you see anything that looks suspicious—like another body or a bootleg whiskey operation for instance—just call the marshal's office in Hot Springs or send me a telegraph if it's after hours. I should be back in my office by the end of the week. Until then, the Fall River County Sheriff is taking messages for me, and he'll know how to reach me."

She acknowledged his request with a little wave.

Twocrow turned back toward the spot where he and Ice had first come up onto the plateau.

"Hey, Twocrow!" Kallie called out as she finished re-tucking her hair under the helmet and pulling her goggles back into place. "Keep me posted on my body, too, won't ya? I mean if there even IS a body? I'll be getting most of MY messages down at the Alex Johnson Hotel until mid-October thanks to Uncle Sam."

"Alex Johnson!" He gave a little whistle. "Nice. Your Uncle Sam must have deep pockets?" He pulled one of his coat pockets inside out and watched as a piece of lint floated free. "Mine sure don't."

He looked up to her for a response, but Kallie had already strapped herself in and was cranking up the engine. He waved in her general direction, then clucked to Ice and guided him back down into the rocky draw.

Chapter Five

Minnie Thompson looked out of the Model T's window toward the boardwalk in front of the Keystone Hotel and pulled a gold-plated pocket watch from her bag to check the time. Not yet 9:30 a.m. She'd made good time despite having to beg a ride in the government car going up from Rapid City where she'd spent the night.

Her fact-finding mission on the proposed Mount Rushmore carving project was about to begin in earnest, and she was more than a little nervous about the prospect of face-to-face meetings with leaders of the effort both here in Keystone and neighboring Hill City. She also hoped—but wasn't sure it would happen—for a meeting with the sculptor Gutzon Borglum himself. After that, she would write a series of articles to explain the project more clearly to her Southern Hills readers.

It was already well known that her newspaper, the *Hot Springs Star*, was firmly in the anti-carving camp and she expected to get some major blowback from both Keystone and Hill City officials during her upcoming visit to the community. And Borglum already had made it abundantly clear that he wanted nothing to do with either the *Star* or the group the newspaper represented.

As they had rolled through the streets, she was surprised to see that much of the downtown area was still charred, not yet fully recovered from a devastating fire that had destroyed many of its businesses a couple years earlier.

But some new buildings, like the hotel, a haberdashery, and the newspaper office, sharing space with a printing shop, were open and doing their part to revitalize the little mining town. And that was due in no small part to the woman who stood smiling on the Hotel's boardwalk after catching sight of her peering from the car's window.

The woman waved and Minnie waved back before bouncing sideways and falling onto the open part of the hard leather seat as the car hit a deep rut in the gravel road. She righted herself and held on tight to the seat's edge as the car's young military driver guided the vehicle toward the boardwalk and screeched to a stop alongside it.

Minnie grabbed her shawl, took her overnight bag and a folder full of papers she had put between the driver's seat and the back seat and then stuffed a couple of loose papers into her bag. "Thank you!" she reached ahead and tapped the driver on the shoulder. "I really appreciate getting the ride."

He turned off the car's engine and swung sideways in her direction. "No problem, ma'am. Just hope it wasn't too bumpy, and you didn't think you were going to go flying through the roof. At least with this new touring model you get the bigger wheels to help soften the blow."

"Uh, yes," she said staring at the roof of the car. "I don't think I'd want to experience that 'flying through the roof' version of the ride."

He laughed lightly. "I think every time I drive up here from Rapid there are more loose rocks and ruts in the road. I'll be really glad when the Corps of Engineers gets their road equipment in here and starts the new grading project. Got a buddy working on that and he thinks they'll be going full bore by next Spring once they start that carving work on the mountain."

He opened his door, jumped out and hurried around to her side, pulling open the back passenger door and nodding down at the running board. "Careful when you step out. There's a lot of dust on this thing and it might be slippery." She handed him her bag and then took his hand.

"You going to be needing a ride back down the mountain later today? I'll be heading back about 3; 3:30 latest."

"No, and in fact I still need to figure out how to get over to Hill City. Do you think I can get a car to take me there?"

The young man gave her an incredulous look. "To Hill City? No ma'am. One of them new pickup trucks might work okay, but none of the roads are good enough for a car between. Not from here to there. I think your best options would be by horseback or carriage. It's probably an all-day ride either way."

Minnie stared glumly off to the west, the general direction of Hill City. "I had no idea there wasn't a good road between here and Hill City. What about the train?"

"Well, there's a train but it usually only runs freight and livestock and loads of ore from some of the mines on occasion," the young military man answered with a shrug. "But as far as I know it don't take no people."

Minnie frowned. "Can't believe I didn't know that." She shook her head in disbelief and then gave the driver a little smile. "Well, regardless. Once I get over to Hill City—however that happens—I figured I would just take the train from there back to Hot Springs."

He nodded. "Now THAT you can do. There's a train runs regular between Deadwood and Custer, and it always stops in Hill City. And once you get to Custer, I think you can switch over to the Hot Springs spur line and head on home."

"Yes, that's true. Thank you." She started to turn away, then turned back. "But, if I can't find a way to Hill City, I guess I probably will have to take you up on that offer for a ride back to Rapid later in the week. What would I have to do to make that happen?"

"Just show up here in the hotel lobby," he replied as she stepped out onto the boardwalk and turned to face him. "I can count on one hand the number of passengers I've taken up and down during the past couple months, so I'm pretty sure there'll be plenty of room for you to ride with me whatever day you choose. Besides, I enjoyed your company and the conversation—when I could hear you over all the road noise." He grinned and she patted his arm again in thanks.

"Driver! You bring along that government pouch?" The harshly shouted question came from a large man with a walrus mustache hurrying toward them from the nearby depot. Barely acknowledging Minnie's presence, he strode past her and banged impatiently on the car's front fender. "You're late!"

The driver rolled his eyes at Minnie, then reached back into the car and pulled out a leather bag sitting on the front passenger seat. As he handed over the bag, he held up a hand for the big man to wait. "Got a couple more things that you'll need to put onto the CBQ freight train once it gets in. And there's a packet full of stuff from the sheriff's office inside the boot that you're supposed to deliver over to Major Goodman."

He pointed to a boxy structure attached between the rear window and the spare tire on the back end of the vehicle. "I'll need a few more minutes to get them out for you."

The big man looked annoyed at having to wait before grunting his okay and plopping down with a heavy sigh on a nearby bench as the driver started walking to the back end of the car.

"Well, thank you again young man," Minnie gave the young driver one more friendly wave and turned toward the hotel's entrance as the woman who had been signaling to her before hurried over to greet her. Giving the big man on the bench a perfunctory nod as she passed him, the new arrival half-screamed the name "Minnie!" as she rushed forward to throw her arms around her.

Minnie dropped her bag, and both women laughed and excitedly hugged one another. "I'm so glad you could come! How long can you stay? Oh, my heavens! It's so good to see finally see you again."

Chapter Six

Welcoming words and questions cascaded from the woman's lips leaving Minnie no room to respond as she leaned back to catch her breath and continued to grin.

"Oh, and here's Paulette's daughter Maxine," the woman bubbled on. A young woman dressed in a bright green version of the new "Flapper" style dress, its skirt reaching just below her knees, came out of the hotel's doorway and walked quickly to join them. Both the walrus-mustache man and the young driver turned to watch as the attractive woman approached, but she ignored them and kept her focus only on Minnie.

"No!" Minnie exclaimed. "This beautiful young woman?" She smiled broadly as Maxine reached the two older women and held both hands out in Minnie's direction.

"Welcome to Keystone, Miss Thompson!" Maxine gushed. "It's so good to have you here, and we have so much to talk about."

"I can't believe it," Minnie said, holding Maxine out at arm's length. "You've grown up!"

Maxine laughed. "So I have Miss Thompson. I'll soon be 21 and . . ." she paused and smiled shyly toward the older woman. "Well, I'm married now with a little girl of my own."

"Married," Minnie gasped. "And with a child. Who's the lucky man?"

"His name's Matthew Grimalski," Maxine said. "We've been married two years. Mrs. Swanzey tells me you're back working at *The Star*. When did you return to Hot Springs?"

"A few months ago; early summer," Minnie said. "I was only out in Buffalo Gap for a short time. Trying to figure out what Alvin and I were going to do and whether I wanted to take over *The Gazette*—that's my family's newspaper out there in The Gap—or sell it. But ultimately, we both wanted me to be back in Hot Springs even though we've decided to just keep on being friends. Nothing more. Simple as that."

Her face sobered. "I was saddened to learn of your mother's passing. I always treasured her friendship."

Maxine stepped forward and gave Minnie a hug. "Thank you," she whispered in her ear. "She thought highly of you, too. Her death was a shock to us all, especially Mister Senn, the owner of *The Recorder*." She smiled again. "But, when Mister Senn asked Carrie . . ." she paused. "I mean Mrs. Swanzey, to step back in to help run the paper for a while and she agreed, I was so happy. Now I'm able to continue Mother's editorial legacy. Ink runs through the family veins, you know? Just like in your family I'm sure."

"That's definitely true," Carrie said. "And as I told you before my dear, you CAN call me Carrie or—as close of a friendship as we have—you can just call me Car'line," she said as she said the name as CARE-Lynn. "After all, that's what I like to call myself."

She looked back to Minnie. "When Paulette died and the Senn family asked if I could give Maxine some help in running the paper, I was honored to give her a hand, especially now that our children are grown. I'm good on the business side, and she's a fine writer. We make a good team. But I've still got responsibilities at our home, so I definitely have to keep that in mind."

"I thought you just said your kids were grown?"

"Yes, but as you know, Mary has moved in with us now and . . ."

She paused in mid-sentence as the burly mustachioed man noisily jumped up from his bench and took the leather pouch and a couple of smaller bags from Minnie's driver. As he moved past them and headed back in the direction of the depot, he gave the younger woman another appreciative look before seeing that both Carrie and Minnie were watching him and noting his reaction.

"Hello Floyd. How are you?" Carrie said with a disapproving note in her voice.

Looking embarrassed, Floyd just frowned and nodded before continuing on toward the station.

Carrie pointed toward the man's back and then at Maxine. "I don't know how you feel about these new fashions?" she asked Minnie. "But I think it's scandalous the way young women and girls dress these days. Even the young mothers like Maxine. Did you see the way Floyd Marston was ogling you, Maxine?"

"Oh," the young woman laughed lightly. "Floyd probably would ogle his grandmother. It IS 1925 and this IS a perfectly everyday style now. Just because I'm married doesn't mean I don't want to stay up to date on the new fashions. Besides, Matthew thinks these new styles are the berries."

"The berries," Carrie scoffed. "That's another thing. Whatever happened to ordinary English?"

Minnie pulled the girl back in and hugged her again. "Since I haven't been here for so long, I'm just glad to see you AND hear what you have to say no matter what slang you use. And congratulations . . . on everything!" She planted a kiss on the younger woman's cheek. "I'm sure the paper will thrive." She looked over to Carrie. "Despite what old grumpy Gertie over there says I like both your fashion sense and your word choices.

"Carrie, if you'll recall, I'm sure you and I were trying new styles and language choices of our own when we were her age." Minnie paused as if thinking about that further. "And even beyond as far as that goes. Our language in some of those stories we wrote after setting up 'Black Hills Women in the News' was considered pretty scandalous." She chuckled. "Especially by older women like your mother."

She turned to Maxine. "We had quite the scathing letter from Carrie's mother Caroline Ingalls after one of my editorials showed up in your Keystone newspaper."

Carrie reddened slightly as Maxine gave her a questioning look. "Well, that was a long time back, even before I married David," she said, clearly flustered. "Let's talk about something else." Carrie grabbed Minnie's arm. "So, you mentioned Alvin. How is he? Is he still a lawman? Sheriff's office or with the Tribal Police? Something like that?"

"He's a United States Deputy Marshal," Minnie said, a hint of pride in her voice. "Twenty years now. And he's actually supposed to be somewhere in the mountains around here today and tomorrow. Not sure why, but that's what he told me he was planning to do when I told him I was coming up here. I thought he might take the hint that I could use a ride, but I guess it didn't register. Typical Alvin. Oh well." She shrugged. "And how's David?"

"He's great. I've said it before and I'll say it again, marrying him was the best thing I ever did, and I'm so happy with the ready-made family that came along with the deal. I'm just glad Harold and Mary Elizabeth accepted me as their new 'Mom.'"

"Oh, for Heaven's sake," Maxine chided. "There was never any doubt." She turned back toward Minnie. "Mary Elizabeth and Harold have both told me that they'll be forever grateful that you brought their father and Carrie together, Miss Thompson."

"It's Minnie, or Aunt Minnie, and I won't have it any other way. I've known you almost since you were born, even before I met Carrie." She turned to face Carrie. "And you. Matching you and David has to be one of my best achievements. Along with starting our Women's News Group, of course."

Minnie's reference to the "matchmaking" and the women who shared reporting and newspaper editing in and around the Black Hills elicited a broad grin from Carrie.

Minnie wrapped an arm around Maxine's shoulders. "As for your dress, Maxine, I like it!" she said warmly. "I just wish I wasn't too old to wear something like that myself." She gave Carrie a mischievous look. "Carrie, you know darn well you'd wear a dress like that in a minute if you were 20 years younger. Don't tell me you wouldn't."

Carrie registered a dismayed expression as she glanced over at Maxine. "W-Well," she stammered, "I might . . . maybe . . . if I looked as good in it as she does." She gestured toward her own clothing, tastefully in fashion for a middle-aged woman. "But these styles are just fine."

"Yes," Minnie snorted, "and fine for me, too." She took her arm off the younger woman's shoulders and pulled back her shawl to show off her traveling suit, a style being worn by most women who were in their 40s and 50s. "But I'd love to be able to trade this old model in for one of those glamorous travel outfits I keep seeing in *Leach*'s or *Vogue*. I'm afraid I'm just too old to get into something like that now. And," she added quickly as the other women started to protest, "too fat."

She held out her hands, displaying her slightly plump figure. "I mean, look at this. My butterfly fashion days are long gone."

"Oh, come on Miss . . . Aunt Minnie. You're anything but fat. You, too, Mrs. . . . Carrie. I mean, after all ladies you ARE in your 50s." She stopped as a somewhat shocked expression crossed Minnie's face. Maxine gulped. "Um . . . aren't you? I mean, I just thought you and Mrs. Swanzey were the same . . ." She stopped. "I think I should just close my mouth now."

Minnie laughed. "Fifty is close enough dear." She gave Maxine another pat on the shoulder. "I'm 48. And isn't that how old you are, too, Car'line dear?"

"Maxine already knows that I'm past the 'middle' of middle age. My 55th birthday was in August. I know you don't remember, but back when David and I were married, I was just two days shy of turning 42."

"THAT was a great day for everyone—Harold and me as well as Father," a joyful voice interrupted them. The women turned to face Carrie's stepdaughter Mary Elizabeth hurrying toward them. "My brother and I couldn't have asked for a better mother." She turned back to Minnie. "I'm so glad you saw the possibilities."

Minnie bear-hugged the newest addition to the group. Like Maxine, Mary Elizabeth was decked out in a flapper style dress. "Look at you," Minnie said, taking a step back and appraising the younger woman. "I would've known you anywhere. Mary Elizabeth Swanzey, you never change."

"Except for getting older, getting married, having a couple of babies," she paused to let that all sink in. She laughed. "And it's Mary Elizabeth Harris now. My husband Monroe and I have a two-year-old daughter and a baby boy. Other than that, I guess I haven't changed a bit!"

"Oh my gosh! Married with TWO children!" She shifted her gaze to Maxine and back to Mary Elizabeth and finally over to Carrie. "You think there's something in the water up here?"

The younger women half-choked on the comment while Carrie turned even redder than she had before. She grabbed Minnie's arm and started pulling her toward the hotel entrance.

"Why are we standing around here when we should be over at the house sharing a cup of coffee or tea?" Carrie asked. "As I started to say to you earlier, my sister Mary now lives with David and me and she's probably baked a cake to go along with it, too. She can't wait to see you again." She paused. "Well, you know what I mean. To talk with you again."

"How is your sister?" Minnie asked. "I was surprised to find out she had moved here."

"After mother died, she stayed in DeSmet with my sister Grace and her husband for a time, but it just wasn't working out because Grace was having some health issues of her own. And for some reason Mary thought only I could understand the special needs that a blind person might have." She shrugged.

"I remember Mary being kind; and gentle," Minnie said. "I'm surprised she's remembered me. I think the last time I saw her was at your wedding. And your sister Laura too. "That's another thing we share," she said to the younger women. "We both have sisters named Laura and they're both writers."

"What's YOUR Laura up to?" Carrie asked.

"Living out east and working for a newspaper there."

"My Laura's writing regularly, too," Carrie said. "She works for a magazine down in Kansas and her daughter Rose is living out in San Francisco. She's a journalist out there. She's been encouraging Laura to write down some of her childhood memories. They're my memories, too, of course. She's thinking of doing a series of stories or maybe even try writing a book or two."

The women had made their way to the hotel and Maxine hurried forward to pull open the main doorway leading off the street.

"Who knows if anything will come of it, but I wouldn't be surprised if she does," Carrie continued. She nodded toward Maxine. "Like Maxine said, there's definitely ink flowing through all our vei . . ." But before she could finish the statement, she was interrupted by the blaring "Ah-oo-gah!" of a car horn's blast.

Chapter Seven

A flashy four-passenger yellow Packard Roadster convertible came roaring up from the east, emitting a second loud "Aa-oo-gah" as it headed toward them. Churning up dust as it sped along Keystone's 1st Street—past both scorched open land and the charred remains of several burned-out buildings on either side of the street—the automobile rolled to a halt alongside them.

Minnie coughed and all four women turned their faces away as a cloud of dust and ash kicked up by the speeding car's tires wafted over them.

As the dust settled, the car's young driver removed a large Stetson hat, leaned across the top of the door, and slapped it on the side of the car. Dust puffed off both the hat and the door from his action and he pulled the hat back inside, swung the door open and stepped out. Firmly grasping the hat in his left hand, he reached back into the vehicle with his right and pushed the seat forward to allow two backseat passengers to disembark.

On the opposite side of the car, a distinguished-looking man wearing a three-piece suit and soft felt fedora opened his own door, got out and started around the back end of the vehicle.

"Mrs. Swanzey, great to see you again!" The driver exclaimed before looking at the others and then focusing most of his gaze on the two younger women. "Ladies." He swept his hat forward with a flourish. More dust flew off the hat and he slapped it one more time, this time alongside his leg, before refitting it on top of his head. Maxine and Mary Elizabeth looked at each other and giggled at the young man's antics.

"Ray Sanders!" Carrie said. "What on earth?"

"We just drove up on that new dirt road leading over from Hermosa," he said as he now began brushing the dust from his clothing. "I think I brought about half the road into town with me."

"Hope not. I still have to drive home on that road," Mary Elizabeth said with another little laugh.

"Where'd you get this fancy car?" Carrie interrupted. "And who's that riding with you?"

The cowboy stepped to one side as a middle-aged man and a teenager pulled themselves out of the back seat. His front seat passenger had now reached the driver's side door and reached out to hold onto it and ensure that it didn't swing back shut onto the other passengers' legs. Assured that they were safely getting out of the vehicle, he turned and removed his fedora, giving the women a little nod.

Sanders nodded respectfully toward the older man. "Ladies, this is the car's owner. Have you met Senator Peter Norbeck?"

Norbeck's broad face, accented by a thick, dark-brown mustache, lit up with a smile as he nodded to Carrie and held out his hand toward hers.

"Yes," she said, accepting his hand. "We met a couple years ago. I'm Carrie Swanzey. I work for the *Keystone Recorder*."

"Pardon my dust," the big man said, interrupting himself to put his hand over his mouth as he made a small cough. "Of course, Mrs. Swanzey. Always good to see representatives from the local newspaper." Norbeck's smile widened, and his sharp nose bobbed down toward her. "How are you?" He turned and looked expectantly toward Minnie and the other women.

Seeing he was waiting for introductions, Carrie reached out and touched Minnie's arm. "Well, I'm doing fine. And this is my good friend and fellow newswoman Minnie Thompson from the *Hot Springs Star*," Carrie said. "She's visiting here and hopes to also get over in

Hill City for a couple days, trying to get the inside story on the carving work being planned." She pointed toward Maxine and Elizabeth. "This is Maxine Grimalski, my friend and co-worker at *The Recorder*." She touched Elizabeth's arm, "And my daughter Mary Elizabeth Harris."

Norbeck held out his hand to each of them in turn as they continued to admire his bright yellow convertible and check out the other passengers now standing alongside him. The man from the back seat, who was wearing a heavier leather fedora, removed his hat to display a rapidly balding head and intense dark eyes that were accented by bushy black eyebrows. His own full mustache continued off the corners of his mouth, drooping down to points about an inch below his bottom lip.

"I've met both Mrs. Swanzey and these younger women," the bald-headed man said with a booming voice as he stepped forward past the Senator to take Carrie's hand while nodding to Maxine and Mary Elizabeth. "As for this other distinguished woman, I don't believe I've had the pleasure."

He turned away from Carrie toward Minnie. "Gutzon Borglum," he said, starting to offer his hand while nodding over his shoulder at the boy who had been sitting in the back seat with him. "And that's my son Lincoln." Suddenly he pulled his hand back, looked back at Carrie and frowned. "Wait! Did you say *Hot Springs Star*?"

Minnie had moved forward to shake his hand but also abruptly stopped at the sharp tone in Borglum's voice at his question about the newspaper's name. She nodded. "Yes. I'm the feature reporter there."

"Do you work for that Hot Springs woman who keeps trashing my project? That agent of evil?" He glared at her.

"If you mean Mrs. Cora Johnson, why then, yes I do and I'm proud to work for both her and the *Star*. And I'll thank you to not take that tone with me since we've just barely met! As for Mrs. Johnson she's a fine, upstanding woman who only has the best interests of our Black Hills at heart. She is NOT an agent of evil."

Borglum shook his head. "I'm sorry and I apologize for being sharp with you. It's just that Senator Norbeck, Doane Robinson and I have a great vision for Mount Rushmore, and she hasn't even looked at my plans. She just lashes out against my proposal and causes trouble."

"She's just worried about the integrity of our sacred Black Hills," Minnie retorted. "And that's why I'm here, Mister Borglum. I'm here in Keystone to see exactly what it is that you have planned, hear from the locals—not only here but over in Hill City—and then bring that information back to Mrs. Johnson and the others who think you might be misguided. I'm here for you to convince me that what you have planned is going to be a good thing for our mountains."

The sculptor eyed her with suspicion and slowly nodded again. "All right. I'll do just that. You come over to my studio today after lunch and I'll both show you my plans and answer any more questions that you might have." Now he extended his hand, held back before. "And if you find yourself unable to understand my vision, then **I** will listen to what you have to share with me. I'm willing to listen and consider compromise on this—even if your Mrs. Johnson does not seem to be. Agreed?"

She took his hand and gave him a little bow.

"All right, agreed, and . . ."

Pounding hoofbeats and a horse's huffing and grunting, followed by a whinny filled the air, cutting her off in mid-sentence. Everyone who had been captivated by the exchange now turned toward the noise as a fast-moving rider rounded the corner about half a block to their southwest. He reined in his horse as if trying to assess who was standing there before quickly galloping on in their direction.

"Mrs. Swanzey! Mrs. Swanzey!" It was a young man's voice calling out as the horse approached. The bareheaded rider was dressed in the rough clothing of a miner and wildly swinging a broad-brimmed big-domed hat from his left hand as he urged the horse toward them.

"Now who in the world is this?" Senator Norbeck asked as the man drew nearer, his horse panting hard as if he'd been running for quite some time.

"Why it's Clifford Barkley. He's a friend of my son Harold." A cloud passed over Carrie's face. "They went up into the hills together overnight to do a little exploring for feldspar and tin in some of the old ghost mines on the west side of Mount Rushmore. We weren't expecting them back until the weekend." She took a few steps toward him as he pulled his lathered horse to a stop and jumped down.

"Clifford? What is it? Where's Harold?"

The rider gave her a panicked look in return. "I don't know!" He gulped hard and let his horse's reins drop. The animal took a couple steps back, still huffing and blowing from the run. "We split up this morning to each check on a mine. I went up along Pine Creek and he went down past Devil's Thumb to look at a mine we'd heard rumors about over along Horse Thief Creek. We were going to meet back at that grassy area out alongside Devil's Thumb to have some lunch and share whatever discoveries we might've made.

"I was riding back to wait for him at the meeting place when . . ." he paused and took a deep breath.

"When what?" Borglum asked, stepping up between Carrie and Minnie.

"When I spotted Harold's horse coming down from the old dirt path that runs up into the trees alongside Horse Thief Creek. Not Harold. Just his horse. So, I rode up a little closer and saw someone . . . or something . . . lying on the ground a hundred feet or so ahead of me in the open glen there. I had just started to ride over and check out if it might be Harold when someone took a shot at me!"

"What?" Carrie pushed Borglum aside and grabbed Barkley's arm.

"Someone shot at me and tried to kill me!" He held up his hat to show a bullet hole clean through the top part of the big hat he was clutching in his left hand.

The women gasped and Borglum and Norbeck exchanged a concerned look as Carrie tightened her grip on Barkley's right arm.

"So, I pulled up and rode out of there as fast as I could." The young man dropped the hat and reached out to embrace Carrie.

"And you're sure it was a body?" Senator Norbeck asked.

"No sir, I'm not sure. I tried to get another look back when I reached one of those crossing points on the creek, but then a woman with a rifle came running down from the hill behind where I saw that body was at and she took another shot at me."

"A woman?" Minnie asked. "A woman? Are you sure?"

He gulped. "I'm pretty sure, but with those bullets whizzing past my head I didn't hang around to see for sure, or to see who that body might be. I just got across the creek and rode back here as quick as I could."

Chapter Eight

The women were talking quietly outside the split entryway that led into both the *Keystone Recorder* newspaper office and the Keystone Print Shop when four men, led by Maxine's husband Matthew Grimalski, rode up on horseback. Trailing him were Matthew's brothers Howard and Merle and their friend Otto Anderson, who preferred to go by the nickname "Red." The riders' saddles were weighted down with ropes and rifles.

Matthew dismounted and gave his wife a quick hug. Mary Elizabeth stepped forward and hugged him too. "They still inside?" he asked.

She nodded to the left. "They're meeting on the Print Shop side."

"Talking strategy," Carrie said as she stepped over to hug him as well. "Matthew, what if it WAS Harold that Clifford saw out there? I mean, what if what Clifford saw was Harold's body?" She stifled a little sob.

Before Matthew could answer, Lincoln Borglum, who had been pacing up and down on the boardwalk in front of the office doorway, interrupted. "Will you all be riding up in the hills to find those shooters Mister? Maybe my father and me could ride along? We could help you!" The men, all seasoned miners and riders, exchanged a bemused look at the thought of the boy and his city slicker dad riding with them.

"We'll just have to wait and see what the major says," Matthew answered, gesturing back toward the doorway. He turned toward Carrie. "Did David say anything more when he and Major Goodman got here?"

"Just that there was a telegram from the sheriff's office in Rapid City instructing him to go get the major and bring him along." She turned to Minnie. "The Army Corps of Engineers has been asked to check out what might be needed to build or improve the roads around here once they get the carving project started. They sent in Major Jeremiah Goodman to lead a surveying crew to check the options," she explained. "But he's also a former military policeman, so the sheriff down in Rapid wants him to take charge and help us out since we don't have a town marshal."

The office doorway swung open and Major Goodman strode out, trailed by Swanzey, Sanders, Norbeck and Borglum. A few seconds later Barkley, who still looked exhausted and slightly in shock from his ordeal of being shot at and then making his frantic getaway ride, edged out and stood solemnly waiting behind the others.

Matthew stepped forward to put a reassuring hand on Swanzey's shoulder while Carrie moved over to her husband's side. "I'm sure Harold's okay," Matthew said to David as Carrie worriedly looked up at her husband. Matthew stepped back to wait with her alongside the others.

Before anyone could ask what was happening, the major, who cut an imposing figure with a full head of wavy brown hair capping his six-foot-four-inch frame, started speaking. "All right, listen up!"

He held up the telegram that Swanzey had received. "The sheriff over in Rapid has put me in charge for now and gave me the power to deputize those of you who want to go along." He nodded toward Anderson and the Grimalskis and glanced across at Swanzey to include him, too. "Senator Norbeck, I don't expect you to ride with us. First of all, it's a dangerous ride and second, I know that you are expected back in Rapid City before the end of the day."

Norbeck removed his hat and nodded. "Thank you." He looked at the others. "I do want to help find your son, sir," he said to David, "but I must be in Rapid City in order to catch the train east. I'm expected back in Washington by the weekend for a crucial vote, and also to extend a special invitation to President Coolidge to consider a visit to the Black Hills next summer; or by the following summer at the latest."

He turned toward Borglum. "We really need the president's support if this project is going to succeed, and I think if he comes to the Black Hills, spends some time here and personally sees what you have planned, well . . ." He let the sentence trail off as if no other explanation was necessary.

Turning back to the rest of the group, he added, "I wish all of you Godspeed in finding young Swanzey and returning him safely back here to Keystone." He motioned to Sanders. "Raymond, I know that you want to help your friends, but I'm going to need you to drive me back down to Rapid City now."

Ignoring the upset look on his young driver's face, the senator moved person-to-person shaking their hands and wishing them a safe excursion up to the mountain, ending with a hug for both David and Carrie. He gave Major Goodman a little salute and started back toward the hotel, Sanders plodding reluctantly behind him.

The major turned to face Borglum. "Gutzon, I know you and your boy would like to go along on this rescue mission, but you're neither a seasoned rider nor do you know the landscape . . ." he held up a hand as Borglum started to object, ". . . despite those earlier rides you took up to the top of that mountain with Major Tucker. We're going to be riding through some rougher terrain now and moving fast, so you are NOT welcome."

He looked back at the others. "As for the rest of you. Do you men all have your rifles?" Each one nodded or answered yes. "I hope we won't need them, but better safe than sorry." He swept his hand across the group as if he were a priest giving a blessing. "Okay, by the power given me from Pennington County Sheriff's Office all you men are hereby deputized."

Reacting to the disappointed look he saw on both Gutzon and Lincoln Borglum's faces, he added, "I'm sorry Borglum, but you and your son need to stay here. The carving of this mountain behind us is extremely important to Senator Norbeck and Mister Robinson and I don't want to be the one responsible for it's not staying on schedule. Especially if you were to be injured from the ride . . . or worse . . . because whoever is up there decided to take his next pot shots at us, or you."

Clifford Barkley nodded in agreement and moved out from his spot behind the major to go get his horse. But now the major stopped him as well. "You need to remain here, too, young man. You're in no shape to ride back up there. David can guide us."

Barkley looked shocked but also somewhat relieved as he stopped, unsure of what to do next. Then he stepped over and stood by the Borglums.

"Now, just before we heard about the shooting, I received some other information from the sheriff in this morning's government dispatch pouch." Minnie thought back to her arrival with the military driver and his telling the walrus-mustachioed man that he had some important messages to get to Major Goodman. Now she looked expectantly back up to hear what the major had to say.

"It might mean nothing. But it might be a very big something that we need to worry about when we ride up there," Goodman continued. "Yesterday, when the Borglums and Sanders rode up to the top of the mountain with Major Tucker, the major reported back to me that he had spotted some suspicious smoke over to the northwest of the rail line. At first he thought it might be a forest fire, but then it seemed to die down and even disappear for a time.

"After getting his report, a couple of my men and I rode back up there just to check into it, and we also saw smoke coming from over that direction. But it seemed like it was much further north, not to the northwest—maybe a couple miles beyond the Hill City to Keystone railroad tracks. And Tucker was right, it didn't seem like a forest fire, more like something you'd see coming from a campfire."

"So, it was up north and west of Old Baldy?" Anderson interrupted. His deep, gravelly voice immediately drawing everyone's attention. "Sorry," the big, raw-boned man with fiery red hair said, speaking more softly. "Shouldn't have cut you off like that Major Goodman."

Goodman gave a dismissive wave. "No problem and, yes, out in that direction, west from Old Baldy.

"Normally, seeing smoke like that wouldn't be too much cause for concern, especially with the fire spotters still on duty up on Harney. I figured if it WERE a wildfire, the spotters would be right on top of it. So, when we got back down here I checked in with the Forest Service office over in Hill City just to see if their spotters had reported it, too.

"And sure enough, they said they HAD received a report of intermittent smoke, not just yesterday but on a fairly regular basis from the west side of Mount Rushmore. They had already called it in to the sheriff."

"Why the sheriff?" Matthew asked.

"Well, there's been reports that there might be a gang of Bootleggers operating a still or even several stills around these parts. The U.S. Marshals asked the sheriff to be on the lookout for just that sort of thing—since any off-and-on smoke might be coming from a Bootlegger's cooking operation. The Marshals are involved because all the land around here is part of the Black Hills National Forest—federal land."

"Last week Harney Peak's crew reported a number of smoke trails over near Devil's Thumb, and then yesterday—just like Tucker and me—they saw that other smoke over to the northwest of Old Baldy."

"So, they were thinking that might be a bootlegging gang?"

"Yeah, maybe, but unfortunately it might be something or someone even worse."

He pulled an envelope out of his pocket and held it up. "I didn't give that campfire smoke much more thought until this morning when the military driver delivered the dispatch pouch from Rapid. One of the letters in the pouch was this joint report sent overnight to all area law enforcement offices from the Pennington Sheriff's Office and the U.S. Marshal's Office down in Denver.

"When I read it, it definitely changed my thinking about what might be causing that campfire smoke."

He opened the envelope and took out several sheets of paper.

"Do any of you remember hearing about that Federal Reserve Bank getting robbed down in Denver? Happened about ten days ago?" Matthew, Carrie and Minnie all nodded. "A guard got killed and the robbers escaped. Everyone thought they were headed east toward Kansas or maybe even southeast toward Oklahoma. So that's where most of the searching has gone on trying to locate them and that missing money.

"But a couple days ago, a rancher in western Nebraska filed a report with the sheriff over in Cheyenne saying that he and his wife were held hostage by four people—a woman with blonde or platinum colored bobbed hair and three men, one of them pretty badly wounded. He said that they holed up at their ranch for a couple of days while his wife treated the wounded man, bandaged him up, that sort of thing.

"He said that whoever those four people were, they just up and took off about three days back. He was out in the barn feeding his stock when he heard them drive away, and by the time he got over to his driveway they were headed down the road. And he said he could see by the dust their car was kicking up that they didn't take the main road east toward North Platte but instead turned north and headed off toward Scottsbluff.

"Now there are three main roads going out of Scottsbluff, I know because I helped build them a few years back. The main one goes east but I'm guessing that they probably had no intention of trying to take that one, especially since they didn't go east from that ranch in the first place. If I'm right, that would leave them with the two other options—one going west toward Wyoming and . . ."

"And the other one going straight north into the Black Hills," Minnie said, her nearly breathless but clear voice making a dramatic interruption of the major's authoritative narrative. Everyone turned to look at her and she took a step forward. "Major Goodman, I'm Minnie Thompson from the *Hot Springs Star*. I think I know the route they could've taken."

Goodman nodded. "Yes. I do too. It's a straight shot going north. Right up past Fort Robinson between Hot Springs and Edgemont and straight on toward Custer and Hill City. Once they got up here they could ditch their car and pick up some horses to ride through the Hills over to Rapid City."

"Why would they do that?" Carrie asked.

"Because no one would expect them to be on horseback nor would they be suspicious of a group of riders taking their sweet time riding around in the Hills, especially with hunting season about to get underway. You know, they could just be some Black Hills hunters or visitors enjoying nature. Then after a few days they could make their move into Rapid City, sell their horses and pick up a train ticket to almost anywhere they might want to go. And no one would be the wiser."

He nodded as if reaffirming the scenario to himself. "You have to admit it's a pretty good get-away plan."

"So, you think that it might've been their campfire smoke that you, Major Tucker and the fire spotters saw? And that one of them might be the person that took a shot at Cliff up there this morning?" It was Anderson speaking again, his gravelly voice taking on a more concerned tone.

"That's exactly what I think," Goodman answered. "Especially with this rancher's report that one of the shooters is probably a woman. There's a regional gang being led by a guy named Charley Garrison and his sister Clara—who styles herself after that so-called 'Bobbed-Haired Bandit' back in New York. They've been operating all around this region for about 6-8 months now. Up to now they've mostly been doing small time or small-town robberies, but this latest one in Denver, especially with the guard getting killed, takes it to a new level. And I'm thinking this might be them."

"But wouldn't it be hard for them to ride horseback? I mean this ain't the Old West anymore," Red said. "I heard about the Garrisons, but all I've heard is that they come in and out by car, not on horseback."

"That's true, but I did a little more research and found out that they got their start out on the Powder River Ranch and they're all pretty damned good horseback riders—especially the woman, Clara. She's supposedly a champion barrel racer and a hell of a shot. So, they'd have no problem switching over to horseback to ride through the Hills. It'd be the perfect camouflage," the major replied.

"The only drawback for them is that they probably never rode through the Hills before, so they'd need to find a guide to lead them from Hill City through the backwoods and then on down to Rapid. But it's a pretty small drawback. A bigger one for them might be that one of them has been wounded, so that could slow them down. In fact, it might be the reason they've been camped out for a few days. I mean, IF that's who's making the campfire smoke."

"Oh no!" Minnie looked stricken as she interrupted.

"What's the problem Miss Thompson?" Goodman took a step closer to where she was standing, concerned by the distraught look on her face.

"My friend Marshal Alvin Twocrow is also riding around these hills somewhere between here and Hill City for the past couple days. But you said you just learned about the robbers being around here and he wouldn't know that, would he? He's not anywhere he could get a message like you got this morning."

"Marshal?" Goodman said. "You mean he's a U.S. Marshal?"

"Yes! Deputy marshal, actually," she answered. "His office is down in Hot Springs, but he told me a few days back that he had to come up here on some sort of mission for the 'Big Marshal's' office. That's what he calls the headquarters over in Sioux Falls. As far as I know he's out there right now and probably doesn't have any idea that this gang might be around here, too. Like I said, he wouldn't have been anywhere where he could've gotten that message that you saw earlier today."

She turned and gave Carrie a panic-stricken look. "He could have ridden right into them not knowing that they were there. Oh my gosh! You don't think that body could be Alvin's, do you?"

The major gave her a concerned look. "Look, I'm not going to sugarcoat it, Miss Thompson. That body might be Harold Swanzey and it might be the marshal's. But more likely it's somebody totally different who we know nothing about. Like I said before, there's a good chance that those Bootleggers are operating up there, too, and they might have had a shootout with that other outlaw gang.

"Dollars to donuts I'd guess that whoever that body might be it's connected to one of those two gangs. And young Barkley here just happened to stumble into the middle of it." He walked over and clapped him on the shoulder. "He's very, very lucky that he didn't become another one of their victims."

Chapter Nine

Twocrow reined Ice to a stop in a clearing at the base of the long draw and dismounted. He led the horse over to where a small stream was gushing down from the rocky hillside before it turned to the northeast where it would eventually connect with the much larger Pine Creek.

He pulled a map from his saddlebag and studied it. "Pretty sure this is the east branch of the Tenderfoot Creek according to this map," he said to Ice, who seemed more interested in getting a drink of water than hearing Twocrow's report.

"From this point we can either turn to the right and wind our way south back around Mount Rushmore on the trail back into Keystone, or we can continue to follow this stream over toward Pine Creek." He tapped the map. "It's just about where we need to go anyway because that's where Pine joins up with Horse Thief Creek below Devil's Thumb."

Ice gave an impatient shake of his head, bobbing it up and down in the direction of the stream. Taking the hint, Twocrow pulled one of the reins forward over the horse's head and held it loosely to one side, allowing Ice to drink his fill from the clear, cold stream. After a couple of minutes, the horse raised his head, water dripping from his muzzle as a pair of bluebirds flew into a small bush just across the stream. The birds settled onto the bush and erupted into a series of high-pitched "tink tink tink" calls, sounding the alarm that intruders had arrived. Further downstream a Stellar Jay's raspy call replied.

Annoyed by the birds' reaction, Ice snorted in their direction and shook his head, water spraying everywhere from his muzzle. Then he returned his nose to the water running in front of his feet and resumed drinking. Letting the rein slide through his hand but still keeping it under control, Twocrow knelt on the horse's upstream side and noisily slurped several handfuls of water for himself.

Seeming to realize that the horse and rider were not a threat, the birds flitted away with a series of their normal "tew, tew, tew" calls to each other. The marshal looped the loose rein back up onto Ice's neck and remounted.

Ice started to step into the stream in the direction of the main pathway to Keystone, continuing toward the route they had taken earlier on their way up the hill. But the marshal gently pulled him to a stop and turned the reins to his left, guiding his horse into the untrodden grass and underbrush alongside the stream's northwest bank.

The horse hesitated as a couple of branches from the thickening stands of kinnikinnick shrubs brushed up against his legs, but Twocrow insistently pushed his knees into Ice's flanks to assure him that this was, indeed, the new path they needed to follow.

The underbrush grew heavier and the grasses taller as they slowly descended alongside the gurgling stream, which narrowed to just feet across in some places and then flattened out into a ten-to-twelve-foot-wide streambed in others. The red-berried kinnikinnicks remained a constant impediment to their movements, but Ice gamely trudged through them until they reached a point where the stream widened even further, running up against granite boulders and solid rock walls that jutted up alongside its banks.

Twocrow pulled the horse to a stop and took the map out of the saddlebag once again. He eased Ice forward to the water's edge and loosened his grip on the reins, a signal to the horse that he could drink again if he wanted. He did. And while the horse was drinking, the marshal opened the forest service map and studied it carefully.

"Okay old Ice, we've got two choices here, partner. Go out in the water and move downstream or cut up through these trees and shrubs until we reach that flat area up there." He pointed toward the boulder tops and Ice whickered as if telling the marshal that he might want to veto such a climb.

"Yeah, I agree," the marshal said. "Let's take the stream. Besides," he tapped the map and then refolded it. "Map says there could be one of those abandoned mines cut into the hillside just before this stream empties into the Pine. Might as well check that out, too. Then we can cross it off our list of Bootlegging possibilities. Right?" Not waiting for Ice's response, he added, "Okay then, let's go."

Pulling back on the reins, he clucked to the horse and Ice stepped gingerly out onto the sand and rock streambed and started walking downstream. The water was running near the middle of his pasterns, about six to eight inches above his hooves as he moved out near the middle. After half-a-dozen steps and seeming to realize that the streambed was solid and the water not too fast, Ice settled into a steady downstream pace. Twocrow unsheathed his rifle and laid it across the saddle in front of him while keeping a vigilant eye out for any potential hazards—both man-made and natural.

For about a hundred yards the stream squeezed between ever-growing rock walls before fanning back out as they followed it around another rock outcropping on their left. From that point they descended into a fairly gentle rapids that Twocrow figured would be much more intimidating during rainstorms or snowmelt runoffs. After a steady decline, dropping 50 or 60 feet in elevation, the stream wound back to the right, looped around yet another sharp rock formation and emptied into a small pond.

Facing them along the pond's righthand bank was the deteriorating framed opening of an old mineshaft that had been cut into the side of the rock wall. Out in front of the mineshaft's opening, a ten-foot-wide sand beach ran for about 30 to 40 yards between the pond and the boulders, trees and a mixture of flowers and weeds that pushed up against the wall.

Twocrow turned Ice along the western edge of the pond until they could step up onto the coarse grey-white sand beach. Then he pulled the horse to a stop and took the map out again, laying it on top of his rifle as he traced the stream's route and pinpointed where he thought he was located.

"Ghost mine." He read the words aloud and stared at the map. Beneath the words in very tiny print inside of parentheses was another line reading: Calendar Mine. "What the hell?"

He turned the map over and unfolded the end panels that had explanatory writing about the map's designations. On one flap were the map's terms written in alphabetical order. Seeing "Ghost Mine," he read: "A mine that was once said to exist in this area, but official records and coordinates cannot be verified. Further exploration or study is needed to confirm. The possible name of each ghost mine is listed in parentheses."

"So, this MIGHT be the Calendar Mine," he touched the map with his thumb. "Never heard of it. But I don't see any other old mines listed near here Ice, so there's a good chance that this would be it." He clucked to the horse, and they slowly advanced toward the granite wall's framed-up square opening. It was about 9 or 10 feet tall and 12 to 15 feet wide. Several large branches lay criss-crossed out front of the opening, one jutting partway into the entrance. The branches were surrounded by chunks of rock that had rolled or broken off from the hillsides above them.

A pyramid of debris, maybe left over from when the mine had been operational, rose up along the left side of the opening. Numerous small ponderosa pines had started to re-establish themselves in the dirt-rock mixture as well as on top of the opening where the solid rock wall sloped back toward a dense, tree-covered hillside.

At first glance, the mine looked completely abandoned, but Two-crow reined in anyway and dismounted. He tied Ice to a small tree about 15 feet from the right-hand side of the opening, took his rifle and walked over to the entrance, carefully surveying the ground for any sign of footprints. As far as he could tell, there were none, but the fallen tree branches appeared just a bit too neat and organized. And right in front of the entry the ground appeared "swept," as if someone had picked up one of the branches and swished it around to eliminate any evidence of movement in and out of the shaft.

He dropped to his knees and inched forward while keeping the rifle at ready. The only sounds were being made by a light breeze blowing through the pine boughs and causing the pond's water to lap lightly against the shoreline just behind him.

He could see about 30 to 40 feet into the opening and up to a point where a solid wall appeared to be blocking the way. That seemed way too soon for a mine with this elaborate of an entryway to come to an end. He studied it for another minute then backed out and walked over to where Ice was patiently waiting.

"Need a little more time partner. Just gotta check it out with the torch." He reached into the saddlebag and extracted a long, slender fiber tube capped by a solid brass cover on one end and a bulls-eye glass lens at the other. It was stamped with the words "Ever-ready" on one side and topped with a sliding on-off switch on the other. He flicked the switch to check that the batteries inside were working and grunted with satisfaction when the light shone out through the lens.

"Back in a flash," he said with a chuckle as he waved the hand-held torch in front of him and started back toward the mine. Ice stamped impatiently but stayed quiet, stretching his neck to snag a mouthful of drying grass near the tree's base.

Dropping to his knees, Twocrow crept into the entryway's right-hand side and advanced toward the solid wall at the far end of the shaft, keeping the light turned off as he moved. He slid over to one side, moved his rifle into position and snapped on the light's switch. Now he could clearly see that while the wall stopped a head-on advance into the tunnel, it also served as a dividing point for two other shafts, each leading off at a 45-degree angle.

The one going to the left was the taller of the two, perhaps 6½ or 7 feet high and 6 feet wide. It's pathway also showed signs of being disturbed by somebody or something and there were scrape marks and gouges in the corner of the wall at the spot where it cornered onto the main entryway.

Getting to his feet, he aimed the light into that side, took a few steps forward and started down the passageway. Reaching yet another solid wall, he turned a corner to his right and instantly jerked his arm up to cover his nose. He gave a little cough and stepped back; his advance stopped cold by an intense odor.

It was the sickening, rotting smell of something dead.

Chapter Ten

Coughing, Twocrow scrambled back out of the mine's entrance, took several deep breaths, and made his way over to Ice's side. He cleared his throat and spat, then pulled a bandana out of the inside pocket of his leather vest. Shaping it into a triangle, he walked over to the pond, thoroughly soaked it and wrapped it across his nose and mouth before tying the ends into a tight knot at the back of his head.

The horse gave him a curious look and shifted nervously as Twocrow came walking back toward him. The marshal pulled the bandana down to show Ice that it was still him, then reached up and unhooked his canteen, swished some water in his mouth and spat once again. He took a deeper pull on the water and swallowed.

Looking around to be sure he was still alone, he gave the horse a reassuring pat and headed back to the opening, dreading what he might find waiting at the front end of that terrible smell.

* * * * *

David Swanzey held up one hand and the line of riders trailing behind him halted. They were nearing the top of the ridgeline now after more than an hourlong steady climb out of Keystone. He dismounted and the others followed suit; a chance to give their horses a blow after the tough ride.

They had climbed past the top of the tree line and now rode along on mostly bare ground as they approached Mount Rushmore's summit. The imposing mountain's highest point loomed on their right while farther to the north and slightly downhill they could see the round clear dome of Old Baldy poking up through a bank of gathering clouds. The long grey-white line of the Eagle Ridge formation framed them off to the southwest.

"Barkley said they shot at him when he was down where the Pine and Horse Thief Creeks come together," Swanzey said. "But I'm not sure if taking the regular trail over there from the south is fastest, or if we'd be better off going on across the top of the mountain and looping back in from the northeast." He paused and pointed behind his companions. "Rider coming."

The men reached for their rifles and Major Goodman pulled a pistol from his belt. A man wearing a buckskin fringed jacket and floppy leather hat guided his horse up onto the spot where the posse had ridden, then continued riding toward them as the Army officer took a few steps in his direction.

"Hold on there . . ." the major started, but Swanzey walked past him with a careless wave of his right hand and gave the newcomer a warm smile.

"Hau kola! Howdy Ben. You just out for a ride or what?"

Ben Black Elk pulled up near them and dismounted. "Hau kola Mister Swanzey. I was in Keystone and saw your wife," he answered. "She told me what is happening, and I wanted to help." He reached out and put a hand on Swanzey's shoulder. "Harold's my friend."

Swanzey put his own hand on top of Black Elk's arm, gave it a little squeeze and nodded. "I know. Thanks, Ben. You're more than welcome." He turned toward the others. "Major, this is Ben Black Elk from the Pine Ridge. He's the son of Nicholas Black Elk, the man who gave this place its Indian name, The Six Grandfathers. Ben's also a friend of Harold's."

The major gave him a curt nod in response.

"The rest of you know Ben, right?" They all nodded or said a quick hello to the newcomer.

Swanzey turned back to Goodman. "Ben can be a big help to us, major. He knows this landscape better than any of us, especially the hills and streams running between Keystone and Hill City. He probably even knows other ways for us to get down to where that man took a shot at young Barkley."

"That true?" Major Goodman asked. "We need to find both a quick and safe way to get down to where those creeks come together—the Pine and Horse Thief Creeks. David thinks maybe we could go across the top of Mount Rushmore and approach from the northeast. Maybe save us some time and not be spotted as easy if we came in from that direction?" He pointed off to his right. "Or do you think we'd be better off taking the regular Hill City trail alongside Eagle Ridge on the south?"

Black Elk pointed in the direction of Old Baldy. "Mr. Swanzey is right about staying along the edge of the mountaintop to where it flattens out going west. But there's a faster way down to Devil's Thumb than either of the ways you said."

"Devil's Thumb? No, I want to get to where the two creeks converge," the military officer had an impatient 'We're wasting time here' sound to his voice as he interrupted Black Elk.

"Devil's Thumb's a rock formation near the two creeks' convergence point," Swanzey explained. "It's just below Eagle Ridge." He turned back toward Ben and nodded to him to continue.

"There's an old, abandoned bear's den just below the lip of The Six Grandfathers' backside rim that most people don't know about," Black Elk continued. "And beginning from that point there is a natural runoff area and pathway leading down through the trees. The bigger animals like deer and elk use it to get to the water. I've only walked down it a couple of times, but I know we can follow it to just above the Devil's Thumb."

Swanzey nodded with a determined expression. "And if that yahoo that shot at Cliff and maybe shot my boy is still down there, he won't know about the forest trail, will he? We can surprise him."

"Is that the black bear cave where Ted Brockett got that big trophy skin of his?" Red Anderson asked. "I never got to meet Brockett myself, but my old man said he was a hell of a shot and got that trophy bear when he was on a ride up here with Charles Rushmore himself. I saw that bearskin once when I was a kid, and we were picking up some supplies over to his place. Never seen a bear's hide so big."

Swanzey nodded. "Yeah, it's one and the same. Brockett got him when he and I, and I think Bill Challis too, were coming back from one of our rides with Rushmore. Not sure if it was on that particular ride or the one right before then that we started calling this place Mount Rushmore." He walked over to his horse.

"Funny, but I remember more about Ted taking down that bear than I do about giving the mountain its name. Who'd a'thought?" He shrugged and mounted his horse, a signal to the others to mount up and get ready to move again.

Major Goodman turned in his saddle toward Black Elk. "You said you 'walked down' the path before. Do you think it's a 'rideable' path or are we going to have to lead the horses once we get over there?"

"We'll be able to ride," Black Elk answered. "But stay in sight of each other behind me. There are steep drop offs in two or three spots, and you could go over the edge if you don't keep your horses under control. Just ride with care and no one will get hurt."

The men all shifted nervously in their saddles as Black Elk swung back up onto his blanket-covered horse and started forward. He stopped and looked back. "I think everyone here is a good enough rider to handle it, but if you are at all worried, then just those who feel okay about

Devil's Thumb

it can ride behind me. The rest of you can take the southside trail. We can come back together at Devil's Thumb."

Not looking back to see who would follow, he made a little clicking noise to his horse and continued on.

And one-by-one, starting with Swanzey, the men clucked to their own horses and turned them into a line behind their Lakota guide.

Chapter Eleven

Minnie's arrival at Gutzon Borglum's studio followed a quick lunch with Carrie, who was in no mood to eat but had implored Minnie to come to her home and meet with her sister Mary before going over to visit with the famed sculptor.

But with Borglum's invite on the table, Minnie had begged to leave immediately after, not wanting to miss the chance for this coveted one-on-one opportunity. It was, she explained to Carrie, one of the main reasons she had come up to Keystone in the first place.

"No sense in putting it off," Minnie told Carrie. "Much as I want to spend time with you all again, talking to Borglum is one of the main reasons I came up here after all. I promise to return with a full report as soon as we're finished."

Mary Elizabeth had volunteered to bring Minnie to the studio and told her on the way that while she was desperately worried about her younger brother's fate, she also needed to drive home to check in with her husband and children since they did not have a telephone at their rural location.

After a very bumpy ride across town, the young woman pulled the car to a stop in front of what appeared to be an abandoned office building sitting alongside a couple of warehouses fronting a gigantic freight yard. The open space behind the buildings stretched out alongside the Chicago, Burlington and Quincy Railroad's Keystone to Hill City rail line, which ran west from town out toward Hill City.

"THIS old building is Mister Borglum's studio?" Minnie gave it an incredulous look as she stepped down from the passenger side of the car.

Devil's Thumb

"It's not the place that matters for the artist, Miss Thompson, it's what he's able to create inside of it that counts!" The sculptor's booming voice responding to Minnie's comment filled the air before Mary Elizabeth had a chance to say anything.

"So said Jules Verne," Minnie replied, jerking around to face the building's front door where the sculptor and his son had emerged.

"What?"

"That's a saying from Jules Verne when he met Nellie Bly at his little writing hut in France, when she stopped to see him while on her 'Around the World' trek. I know that because Nellie herself told it to me."

Seeming to be slightly taken aback by her response, Borglum gave her a little smile and nodded. "Well, so it is, but it still applies to me and MY studio as well."

Borglum and his son strode across the gravel-covered area between the old building and the car to greet them. He extended his hand to Minnie. "I apologize again for my earlier boorish behavior and thank you for coming here where I can both show AND tell you about my sculpting plans."

He looked up at the car's driver's seat. "You're welcome to stay, too, Mrs. Harris."

"No, I'm sorry," she said. "Thank you, but I need to get back to my home out near Hermosa." She looked back to Minnie. "Unless you need to have me stay to take you back to the house?"

"I'll be happy to drive Miss Thompson back to your mother's," Borglum said. Minnie nodded her approval, and Mary Elizabeth gave them both a grateful smile.

"It's a few miles drive, so it's good that I can get going." She looked past Borglum to where Lincoln stood listening. "We actually live out near where I heard you might be building a spot for your own family to live. Although I think we'll be moving away sometime soon. My husband found a very nice farm-ranch location for us out near Scenic."

The sculptor gave her a blank look at the name.

"It's a little town out east of Rapid City," she added.

Borglum just nodded.

"Anyway, my husband and children are expecting me home and I've no way of letting them know what's happened without actually driving out there. No phone lines yet." She gave them a little laugh. "We don't even have electricity out at our place yet. I'm learning how to be a pioneer."

He smiled at that and nodded again. "Yes," he agreed, "Lincoln and I have been dealing with the 'no electricity' setup ourselves. Like you say, 'pioneering' it. Not sure how my wife's going to adapt to that once she arrives. Time will tell, I suppose."

"I'm sure she'll be fine," Mary Elizabeth said. "Women are pretty resilient, you know?" She smiled. "Well, I'm grateful to you for ensuring that Miss Thompson gets back to my parents' house when you're finished with your meeting."

"Yes. It's not a problem."

She gave him a little wave and held out her hand to Minnie. "Once I make sure everything is going okay with my family I'll be back. I can't sit around out there without knowing what might be happening with Harold. I hope to see you again this evening—at the house." She shifted the car into gear. "And I hope this meeting answers some of your questions, too."

"Yes, so do I." Minnie gave Mary Elizabeth's hand a squeeze and turned to face Borglum as the noisy old car pulled away.

"Well, shall we?" He gestured toward the old building's front door and then escorted her toward it.

Minnie gave a little gasp as she walked into his so-called "temporary" space. As run-down looking as the building was on the outside, it was the exact opposite inside. Not only did the "temporary" studio look "permanent," but it also was adorned with a large plaster model of the planned sculpting for the mountain.

She stopped and stared up to where the model jutted seven or eight feet above the top of a large, ornately carved wooden table that filled the center of the room. And just beyond the model's topmost edge, the upper one-third of nearby Mount Rushmore itself—towering 6,000 feet above them—could be seen framed inside a floor to ceiling window.

Minnie nodded appreciatively toward the window that took up most of the studio's west side and Borglum gestured to her to walk over to get a closer look. "This is quite a 'temporary' space you have here Mister Borglum," Minnie said with just a hint of sarcasm in her voice.

He shrugged. "Yes, I suppose it will have to do until I can complete a new studio I have planned just below the mountain itself—once the carving gets underway," Borglum said as Minnie walked with him toward the mostly glass wall. "But for now, since I'm still settling in, this place is going to serve. I will need a good base of operations here in town to properly plan for the project's logistics; something I really can't do from the place out by Hermosa that Mrs. Harris was talking about.

"But first I need to secure more funding. Contributions have been . . ." He paused. "Well, financial contributions have not been strong, let's just leave it at that."

Lincoln had been waiting for his father and Minnie by the doorway and now he gave Minnie a shy wave hello as she turned back to acknowledge that he was there. The boy smiled and walked over to a much smaller plaster image that he was shaping at a worktable in the corner while his father led Minnie away from the window and back to the large tabletop model.

The plaster sculpture depicted the four presidents he was planning to carve into the mountain—starting with Jefferson on the left followed by Washington, Roosevelt and Lincoln. The model, sitting on top of the table like it did, towered over both of them. It showed the Presidents from head to waist in the clothing styles that they probably would have worn while still alive.

After walking halfway around it, Minnie turned back and pointed toward it as she spoke to Borglum, while in the background his son tried to look busy. But she could see he was only going through the motions as he listened intently to what the adults had to say.

"So, Mount Rushmore as we know it will no longer be just a mountain? It will just be these four bodies carved out of it?"

"Well, four faces and partial bodies. But the carving will only be along the top and face of the southeast half." He paused and pointed out the window toward the peak that he planned to carve. About one-third of the mountain—the mostly treeless part—could be seen from their viewing location. From bottom to top the dark ponderosa pines not only filled up the landscape between them and the peak but also almost completely covered up the front of the mountain as well.

"I know it's not the way nature gave the mountain to us, but nature also gave us a granite surface here that's almost as perfect a carving palette as any sculptor could ever ask for," Borglum said as he shifted his gaze from the mountain to the model. "It's not only ideal for carving the faces at the top of the peak, but the bodies all the way to its base. That's why I'll be able to depict each of these men as they actually appeared to their fellow citizens.

"Modern day people will forever 'know' these past leaders of our great nation. Not just their names, but the way they looked to others in their own lifetimes."

He walked over to the model, placed a hand on the figure of Lincoln, and turned to face Minnie. "What I'm going to share with you now is off the record for public consumption. Do you agree?"

"Yes, of course. Off the record."

"Good. Well, then once I transform the front of Mount Rushmore, I am contemplating building some type of permanent Hall of Records beneath the faces; beneath the heads."

"You mean like an entryway down below them?"

"No, no. If I do it, it will come in from the back, behind the figure of Abraham Lincoln, which I'm planning to be over on the north end as you can see by my model. I haven't widely shared this yet and that's why I must keep it off the record.

"Just know that if I do build such a Hall, it will not only tell more about each of the men themselves and their achievements, but it also will serve as a repository for copies of all the great documents and stories from our nation's history. It will be a permanent historical record to supplement my carving of the mountain."

Minnie stared back up at the mountain's peak. "You know, the Lakota people call this mountain The Six Grandfathers," she said. "They look at the mountain as it now stands and see six great figures standing there dressed in the finest clothing of THEIR people. And they don't need to have those figures carved into or out of the rock in order to see such a vision."

"Madam, while they may see a vision, I am creating a visible monument that will still be standing for ALL people to see 500 thousand years from now. These presidents I've chosen to carve here represent the most important events in our great nation's history. Washington, Jefferson, Roosevelt, and Lincoln represent the birth, growth, preservation and development of America, and what better place to showcase these things than here, the place that the Lakota call the Center of the World?"

"Well, I can't argue with you about that depiction," Minnie said. "And since I know you have powerful friends both here in South Dakota and in Washington who are going to help you move this project forward, I'm under no delusion that your carving effort will be stopped. I know it is going to happen.

"As for me, I just want to write a couple of stories that fully explains to our readers what you've got planned and how people who live here feel about that plan."

She walked back to the window to look out again at the top of the mountain. "One of my lifelong best friends is Lakota. When we were younger, both still teenagers, we lived for a time with Chief Yellow Feather's Lakota Band, and I learned much more about how and why the Lakota revere the Black Hills and this mountain. You need to know that your monument is going to be built on the place they believe The Great Spirit—Wakan Tanka—God himself, if you will, lives.

"So, when you carve away part of the mountain, in their minds you won't be creating a new monument. You will be changing one of their most sacred places." She cleared her throat and pointed back at the model. "Unlike my boss Cora Johnson down in Hot Springs," she paused as he made a derogatory grunting noise at the name.

"As I was saying. Unlike Mrs. Johnson, my editor and publisher, I KNOW that your carving is not going to be stopped. So, all I and others who love the Black Hills ask is that you be respectful in how you do it, because you will not just be carving a monument here. You will be carving away a piece of Wakan Tanka; carving away a piece of the Great Spirit himself."

Chapter Twelve

"Wakan Tanka, send me a sign that you are with me." With his bandana still pulled down, Twocrow extended his arms and spoke toward the direction of Eagle Ridge, a long, greyish-white line of small cliffs looming out over the west side of the Rushmore valley.

He pulled his mask back over his nose and prepared to re-enter the mine to confront whatever death awaited him there. But before he could take another step, a shrill cry came from his right and he turned to see a red-tailed hawk soar down the length of the stream, swoop low across the pond in front of him and settle onto the top of the tallest ponderosa pine directly across from where he was standing.

The bird sat there in silence blinking at the deputy marshal as Twocrow tried to calm his rapidly thumping heart.

"Chetan!" He tilted his rifle in a half-salute as he called out the Lakota name for the hawk. He turned in the direction of Eagle Ridge where he had just spoken to the Great Spirit. "Pela-Maya! Thank you Wakan Tanka! You have heard me, and I have seen your messenger, Chetan. Wopila-epi. Thank you."

Shifting his rifle over to his left hand he cradled the flashlight in his right hand as he lifted the bandana back into place over his nose and mouth and walked back inside. This time he walked briskly toward the solid wall where the trail split. Once again turning down the left-side corridor, he followed the increasingly powerful smell of death while training his torch on the pathway as he moved forward.

After 50 or 60 feet, the narrow pathway widened and made another sharp left turn directly into a room that was about 20-feet square with some sort of faint backlight coming from the far side. From the light's tone he decided it must be another exit from the old mine.

Faintly visible in the center of the room was a two-to-three-foot-high brick and rock structure built to support a bell-shaped copper container that had two pipes coming out of it. One seemed to be serving as a smokestack of sorts because it disappeared into the ceiling toward some unseen chimney. The other pipe jutted out sideways from just below the top of the copper container and directly into the top of a 50-gallon barrel. From the bottom of that barrel a third pipe continued on out in the same direction before making an L-shaped downward turn into the top of an even larger barrel that was partly buried into the floor of the old mine.

Stacked against one of the rock walls were about two dozen 5-gallon kegs, obviously brought in to receive the bootleg whiskey that was being distilled, then funneled into the much larger half-buried barrel. Twocrow nodded as he picked one up. A barrel this size would be fairly easy to load up onto a horse or mules to transport out.

Centered beneath the bell-shaped container, Twocrow could see the remnants of a burned-out fire and a stack of firewood piled alongside. But while he could detect the faint odor of the now mostly burned wood, it was almost fully overpowered by the smell of death. Sprawled just beyond the stack of firewood were the rapidly deteriorating remains of a very large man.

He swung the light around to the other side of the room and spotted a pair of kerosene lanterns with a container of kerosene fuel sitting against another of the walls. Switching the rifle back to his right hand to keep it at the ready, he followed his torch's light over to the lanterns, examined them and lit first one, then the other. With their glass chimneys lowered into place, the lamps immediately filled the cavern with their light. Twocrow snapped off his torch and stuck it in his back pocket.

Devil's Thumb

Leaving one lamp in place, he picked up the other and walked back to the body. From the decomposition and smell, he guessed the man had been dead for at least a couple or maybe even three days. That meant this couldn't be the same body Kallie had seen while flying over Devil's Thumb.

"Great," he muttered. "Two bodies, and I still gotta go find that other one." He studied the big man lying before him. The man had several bloody spots on his clothing, the largest two formed from a mass of dried congealed blood on his left shoulder and the second making a large, dark circle on the right side of his stomach. Either one, Twocrow figured, could've caused the man to bleed out.

"Shot," he said aloud, his muffled voice making a hollow echo in the space. "No doubt about it." He looked around. There was no blood spatter or anything else that he could see that would lead him to believe the shooting happened in here. The man must've been shot outside and either carried in here or somehow made his way back inside to seek shelter or help, or both.

He turned toward the still and pulled the sideways pipe free. A small stream of condensed liquid ran out and he put his fingers into it, pushed the mask up and tasted an intensely acrid alcohol. "Whoo!" he said in the dead man's direction, puckering up and spitting it out. "That's some extra heavy-duty hooch." Maybe the man had come back here to try to use the whiskey to sterilize his wounds? He pulled his mask back in place, but the decaying body's smell was so intense it barely filtered it out.

Now that the room was fully lit, he could see at least a dozen bags of grain, probably malted barley, wheat and corn along with another small barrel marked "yeast." A water pipe with a faucet jutted from the wall directly across from the copper kettle. He tried the faucet, and clear cold water ran out of it.

"All the comforts of home," Twocrow muttered. He glanced again at the dead man. "But somebody wasn't happy with the living arrangements, were they?" Now he looked past the man toward the faint natural light on the wall behind him. Setting the lantern down on top of the half-buried barrel, he started walking toward the wall and could see that just like at the other end of the mine, where he had entered, this rock wall also ran floor to ceiling and divided two new continuing passageways, each with its own walking path.

He edged around the right-hand side to find that the two passages almost immediately came back together to form a single corridor leading at a 60-degree angle up toward an outside light, which was much more intense on this back side of the wall.

Once again taking out his torch, he started moving up this new pathway, and as he climbed the natural light's brightness grew exponentially. The light's intensity continued to increase with every step as he made his way toward an opening that he could now see was even larger than the one he had entered on the other side of the mountain.

He reached a flat area that stretched out for six to eight feet toward the opening, which was draped with vines—a "natural" camouflage covering. Now feeling a cool breeze, he pulled his mask down and took a deep breath as he pushed the vines aside to step out onto a flat rock shelf.

Like the other entry, this opposite side also had a pond fronting it, but unlike the other one this pond was not being filled by a stream. Instead, a small waterfall splashed down from the hilltop behind him and bubbled into the pond's upslope side. On what he figured was the southeast side of the pond he could see the beginnings of a stream taking some of the water away. He took another long deep breath to clear out the smell of death and decay that still seemed to be clinging to his clothes.

Looking back to the northwest side he could see the beginnings of what looked like an old logging trail that started on top of a small mesa and then wound through the trees beyond.

Off to his right a small footpath branched off from the mine's opening before quickly disappearing between the edge of the pond and into the woods. The rest of the pond was surrounded by very heavy foliage. Stands of trees and shrubs butted up against the shoreline, some branches actually spreading out over the water and providing shade and effectively making the pond invisible to anyone who didn't know it was there.

Despite the tree branches, shrubbery and grass that was partially dipping into it, the water in the pond was so clear that Twocrow could easily see the spot where the intake end for the water pipe he had discovered inside was anchored.

"Genius," he said softly.

Twocrow stood in the opening looking around. Unless you had some sort of background knowledge about this place even existing, it seemed like it would be almost impossible to find. So, whoever was running the still must've first known about the old abandoned mine with its two-sided entrance, and then the fact that a no-longer-used logging trail ran nearby, making transport of the finished products easier to carry out.

And if it hadn't been the need to vent out smoke during the still's cooking process, the illegal operation might never have been discovered—or at least not discovered for a long time.

He looked back toward the shaft. Had the man inside been shot by a competitor or by someone else who was already involved with the operation? And if not, then who else might it be? And what about that other body that Kallie thought she had seen? Who was that? Was he also involved with the Bootleggers, or had it been some sort of shootout between him and the dead man in here?

On top of that if the shooter was still lurking nearby, either looking for the dead man or coming back here to safeguard the whisky-making operation, Twocrow realized he was going to be an obstacle that needed to be eliminated if he stayed where he was.

Time to get moving, get some help and try to unravel this rats' nest knot of questions that he had uncovered. He blew out a long sigh. He'd have to go back through the mine, get Ice, and ride into Keystone for help. He looked up. The sun was already moving into the western sky.

"Okay," he said aloud, looking first at the sun and then at the pond. "Time to get moving." He stretched and made a giant bellowing yawn that Minnie liked to say sounded like a moose call. He clamped his mouth shut realizing he was making way too much noise—especially if he hoped to avoid someone who might be running around here with a gun.

He jerked the bandana back up over his mouth and nose. His eyes were already watering at the thought of going back into that intense smell. But he had only taken a couple of steps when a voice rang out causing him to drop onto his knees behind one of the rock formations jutting out alongside the vine-covered opening. Pulling the bandana to one side, he brought the rifle up to the ready position and looked around.

"Hey! Is somebody out there?" It was definitely a younger man's voice that called out once again. "Is somebody there? Help me! I need help! Somebody! Anybody?"

Twocrow looked around but still saw nothing.

"Help me! Please! I'm hurt!"

He stared in the direction where the little footpath melted away into the forest. The calls for help were coming from over there.

Chapter Thirteen

Sam Palmer stepped onto the train caboose's back platform and leaned far out to the right side in order to wave a pole with a red cloth attached back and forth. Far ahead, the engineer acknowledged the action with a long steady blast on the train's whistle to verify that they were successfully approaching the loading dock in front of the Keystone Depot.

Engaging the brakes and releasing a cloud of steam as he cut back on the engine's power, the engineer gave another long blast on the whistle. The train cars jerked to a complete stop, many banging together to protest the engineer's action.

Palmer checked his watch to "officially" note the arrival time before jotting down the military time of 1207—for the arrival at 12:07 p.m.—into his conductor's log before he jumped down. Walking forward until he reached the side of the engine where the engineer was leaning out of the window smoking a cigarette, he gave the man a friendly nod.

"Good work." He pointed back toward the depot. "You might as well go get yourself some chow and I'll check in with Floyd and see if we have any freight for the trip back. I'd like to get out of here around 3:30 if that still works for you?"

"Sure does." The engineer gave him a little two-finger salute and turned back to disengage the big Baldwin Steam Engine's control panel. He nodded to a pair of rail workers as they walked up to the water tower and started swinging an overhead pipe into position to fill the water tender hooked in directly behind the engine. The steam engine relied on having plenty of water to keep operating as efficiently as possible without overheating, and that meant keeping the water tender refilled at each stop, regardless of how much had or hadn't been used.

Sam ignored the two men as he hurried back alongside the train cars toward the depot. He had just reached the third car from the rear when he was startled to see a man come running out from between two small sheds on the off-track side. He stopped and gasped as the man leapt up between the train cars to intercept him.

"Holy Shit! Who the hell are you?" The shock of the man's sudden arrival caused Sam to grab at his chest as he stepped back. Then he froze in place as sunlight flashed off the barrel of a gun that was pointed toward his face. "What the hell? What do you think you're doing? Is this some kind of joke?" He pointed at the train cars. "This is a freighter. We ain't carryin' no cash."

Not speaking, the man held his position on top of the steel coupling in between the cars and looked both directions alongside the train to be sure they were alone. Seeing no one else, he waved over to the woods as if signaling to someone, then cupped his free hand toward himself as if inviting the conductor to step forward between the cars to join him.

"I ain't coming over there with you. What's this all about?"

"If you don't want a bullet for your lunch, you get your ass over here and talk to me," the man hissed. He looked out around the cars again. "And if you don't want your brother Billy to get hurt, you're going to want to hear me out."

"Billy?" Palmer stared at the man, who was surprisingly well dressed in what he'd label a "city slicker" style suit jacket and fedora, a clear signal to Palmer that he obviously wasn't dealing with anyone "local."

"What do you know about Billy? You're full of shit. Billy's back in Hill City."

The man reached into one of the pockets on the pinstriped suit jacket and extracted a shiny round object, which he held out toward Palmer. "No, he ain't. This look familiar?" The conductor eyed a silver-plated pocket watch being extended in the man's hand. He reached out and took it as the man thrust it forcefully in his direction. "Open it! You'll see."

He swallowed hard as he saw the initials WP etched onto the watch's top surface as he turned it over in his hands and flipped it open. The watch dial was on the downside in the palm of his hand, and on the flipped out side was a miniature photo of his brother's two children.

The man gave him a lopsided grin. "Billy sends his regards and so does my boss Charley Garrison and a new friend of ours, name of Verne Miller."

Palmer blanched. "Charley Garrison and Verne Miller?" He swallowed hard as he said the names. They were two of the most notorious outlaw names in the region. He knew Garrison and his gang from when he was still down in Denver. As for Miller, he'd heard nothing but warnings about him since arriving in the Hills. And now this man was telling him they were holding his brother hostage.

Palmer stepped forward into the shadows between the two train cars, and the man with the gun slipped back a couple steps to keep some space between them. "I wouldn't recommend you trying anything with me if you want to see your brother alive, or him you as far as that goes." He pointed toward the woods. "One of my good friends is set up over there with a gun aimed at your head and that's a second reason for you to play nice."

Palmer stared toward the woods and even though he couldn't see anyone he nodded. "Okay, what do you want?" He eyed the man suspiciously. "Do you really work for Garrison? Been told he shot up a bank down in Denver a couple weeks ago."

The man nodded.

"Cripes! And what about Miller? I thought he was long gone from these parts? Shit, I heard he moved over to work with Capone in Chicago."

The man just gave him another lopsided grin in response. "That's just wishful thinking from your local law now ain't it? Miller's not only still around but he told Charley that he wants to set up a 'marketing' arrangement with you and your brother regarding that little brewing operation you got going."

"Little brew . . . what the hell you talking about?"

The man re-leveled the gun toward Palmer's face and waggled it from side-to-side. "Cut the crap, Palmer. Both Miller and Charley know all about that still you've got set up in that old ghost mine down near Devil's Thumb, and if you and Billy want to have any share of it at all you're going to have to work hand-in-hand with us from here on out. Mister Miller's got some big plans for those barrels of whiskey you've been producing, and they ain't going nowhere unless they go through us first."

"How'd you . . .?" He stopped in mid-question and held his hands partway up as the man thrust the gun in his direction. Then he nodded. "Okay, okay. So, where's my brother?"

"Well, he ain't at that cabin you and him been sharing in Hill City, I can tell you that. Charley and a couple of our other friends are keeping him company at a little campsite we've got set up north of here. They'll get him back to meet your train tomorrow afternoon. So, tonight, when you get back to Hill City you and Mister Miller are going to talk about what you need to do to get that whiskey away from your still and into our hands."

"But, how . . .?"

"Just consider this an invitation to join Miller and a couple of his boys for a little 'heart-to-heart' discussion tonight. Just a friendly little gathering to make sure you're all on the same page with our new partnership arrangement. Okay?"

Palmer swallowed hard. "So, Miller is waiting for me over in Hill City? But Billy's not there?"

"You got it."

"Look, I don't want no trouble with Miller, or your boss, or whoever the hell YOU are. Okay? Me'n Billy and a few of our friends from Denver just wanted to brew up a few batches of hooch and make ourselves a little extra cash. Whatever happens to that whiskey is a joint arrangement between Billy, me and the three of them. And we already lined up a couple of people down in Denver to help us do that 'marketing' you're talking about.

"If you know what I mean?"

"Oh, I DO know what you mean, but that whiskey you've been brewing ain't going anywhere near Denver."

Beads of sweat started forming on Palmer's brow and he swiped at them. "Look, if I don't take a couple loads south to Denver, I won't be around much longer to make ANY of it for you, me or anyone else. If Capone or his friend Miller are taking this over, then someone needs to be providing protection for me and Billy."

The man waggled the gun. "Then you're gonna be real pleased to hear that that's already being taken care of. Mister Capone runs himself a first-rate, no-nonsense operation over in Chicago and your friends down in Denver and anyone else who might have booze marketing plans have gotten the message loud and clear that they ain't getting any whiskey out of the Black Hills. It's taken!" He swiped the gun across his chest for emphasis and nodded.

"What do you mean, taken?"

"A couple of Capone's boys already dropped in for a visit with them and let's just say your friends are no longer in the picture."

"What the hell! What happened to my friends?" Palmer was nearly wailing the question, clearly distraught over what he had just heard.

The man shrugged. "Well, the long and the short of it is, they're dead. And if you and your brother don't want to join them you need to start cooperating with us. Right now!"

"Look, I—I just can't start dealing with you without talking it over with my partners up here first. There's five of us working together on making this whiskey."

"Not anymore."

Palmer's eyes grew wide. "What . . .?"

"Palmer, none of you should'a thought you could play with the big boys without clearing it first," the man cut him off. "My boss and Miller have themselves a deal going with Capone. So, you can be sure that from here on out anything you and your brother produce up here ain't going to Denver. It's headed back east."

"Jank!"

The name was shouted from the woods across from where the two men stood and a lithe platinum-haired woman cradling a rifle that was almost as big as she was edged into view. Following behind her with three horses in tow was a bedraggled looking Indian who hung back by the trees as the woman advanced.

"What are you doing Jank? For cripes sake, we ain't got all day here!"

"Yeah, yeah," the man with the gun aimed at Palmer muttered, waggling the gun for Palmer to move in the woman's direction. The conductor continued between the train cars and walked across the clearing with his captor trailing a few feet behind. The woman pulled the big rifle into shooting position and Palmer lifted his hands higher.

"Who're you?"

She grinned. "You can just call me the Bobbed Hair Bandit."

Chapter Fourteen

"Bobbed Hair Bandit? That's bullshit," the conductor answered. "Everybody knows she's not from around these parts. That woman's out on the east coast somewhere. Hell, last I heard that Bobbed Hair Bandit chick was on the run down the coast with a passel of U.S. Marshals in hot pursuit." The young woman glared at him, her face turning red as she jerked the rifle up again, looking like she was ready to shoot in Sam's direction. Palmer held his hands higher and took a step back, Billy's watch dangling by its chain from his left hand.

"Quit fuckin' around Clara," Palmer's captor interjected, pushing down on the gun barrel and shaking his head in disgust. He nodded at Sam and then at the watch, which he now took back, snapped shut and slipped into his coat pocket. "Our friend Sam here knows that if he wants to see his brother alive he's not gonna be trying anything foolish." He looked over at Sam. "Ain't that right Sam?"

Palmer nodded weakly as Jank turned back toward the woman. "Clara you gotta quit screwin' around with that Bobbed Hair Bandit crap, tryin' to make yourself out to be someone you ain't. One of these days you're gonna say that in front of the wrong person and they're gonna shoot your ass before you have the chance to explain yourself. There's a big reward on her head, you know?"

Clara pulled the rifle tight against her chest and glared first at Jank, then at Palmer. "Yeah, well, just because she gets all the headlines doesn't mean I'm not at least as good at robbing things as she is. And I'd like to see her try'n ride a horse as good as I do." She smiled sweetly at Palmer. "Born and raised on a Montana ranch so I can ride circles around her or any of the men I'm riding with now, including this yahoo!"

She turned and squared up in front of the other man. "And Jank Kaufman, you might think I'm in love with you and you can say anything you want, but you better watch your mouth around me or Charley's gonna be shooting YOUR ass—boyfriend or not! My brother don't like people disrespecting his little sister."

Sam looked from Clara to Jank and back to Clara. "You're Garrison's sister?"

She made a little mock curtsy with the rifle stretched out in front of her. "At your service. Clara Garrison, rodeo barrel ridin' champion, model, . . ." she stopped and flipped back one corner of her platinum-colored hair adding a quick hand on her hip pose to accent the claim. ". . . And bank robber extraordinaire!" Jank snorted and she glared at him again.

"So did your gang rob that bank down in Denver?" Sam said as he looked over to where the Indian was still standing with the horses. "Heard there was someone killed during the robbery. That Indian your shooter?"

"What?!" Clara was indignant. "He don't know shit, and he sure as hell didn't shoot anybody for us. He's just wrangling our horses."

Palmer shook his head in disbelief. "So, you're saying you're the one killed that guard?"

Clara beamed. "You bet your sweet ass I did. He was mouth'n off about how he wasn't giving up any money to a little woman just because she had a big gun." She shrugged. "I forgot to mention, I'm also a crack shot." She rubbed her hand on the rifle stock. "So, I shot him." She turned the gun halfway in his direction and Palmer stepped back while raising his arms up as high as they would go. "Good," she nodded. "Already shot one of your pals over by that still of yours. Done enough shooting for today."

Devil's Thumb

Palmer bowed his head at her comment. "So, you found our still and shot my partners?"

"We DIDN'T find your still," Clara said. "Yet. But Miller says he's got a good idea of where it's at after one of your boys tried to stop us from looking around for it down by Devil's Thumb a couple days back. He took a couple shots at us, so we shot back, and he ran off into the woods. I'm betting that I hit him." She smirked.

"When Clara and I went back down there this morning we ended up having ourselves another little shootout with a couple more of your friends," Jank added. "Let's just say that if they had behaved themselves when we rode up to talk, they wouldn't of got themselves shot."

"So now all three of them are dead?"

Jank shrugged. "Well, we ain't found that first one from a couple days back but... he looked over at Clara who just nodded. "I'm gonna say 'Yes'."

"Cripes!" A tear formed at the corner of his right eye and then ran down his cheek. He swiped it away before straightening up and cautiously lowering his hands. "Okay. So, what is it you want me to do?"

"Tomorrow we're gonna be riding with you from here in Keystone when you head back to Hill City. But we'll be getting off at Leaky Valley. Our friends and your brother are at a campsite up north of there and they'll be bringing him down to Leaky Valley so he can join you on board. Then the two of you can start arranging for how you're going to get us the first of that booze by this weekend."

"But we don't just stop the train at Leaky Valley. We gotta have a damn good reason . . ."

"I didn't say you had to stop there," Kaufman cut him off. "I said we'd be getting off and your brother'd be getting on. We been watching your train the last couple days and when you reach Leaky Valley it's moving so slow through there that getting on and off will be easy. The hard part for you starts after we get off and he gets on because by the time the train gets back to Hill City you and your brother need to have that booze transfer plan ready for Mister Miller. You understand?"

"And this is your only warning," Clara chipped in. "If you don't want to end up dead like your friends, you'll come up with that plan by tomorrow. So, you might want to start thinking about it now." To accent what she was saying, she reached into a bag hanging from her shoulder, extracted a small pistol and waggled it toward Palmer's chest. Then she crossed her arms. Facing him with the rifle in one hand and the pistol in the other she gave him a menacing scowl. "Understood?"

Kaufman gave Clara a tight smile of support and leaned in toward Palmer, making a cutting motion across his throat with his free hand. "If you don't cooperate, Mister Palmer, then Clara and I and Clara's brother can guarantee you that your railroad is going to be short a conductor." He reached back into his pocket, once again pulled out Billy's watch and tossed it back to Sam.

He signaled to the Indian to bring the horses closer before turning back to Sam. "As for your brother's cute little kids, well . . ." he shrugged. "I reckon they might not just be short an uncle. They might be missing a father, too."

* * * * *

Black Elk's horse, now about three lengths ahead of Swanzey's, disappeared around a huge cottonwood tree. David gave Major Goodman a worried glance over his shoulder and a little hand signal that he was going ahead before urging his own mount to pick up the pace to catch up.

Turning past the tree, he reined in sharply, nearly bumping into the Indian guide's horse now stopped crossways and blocking the trail.

Behind Black Elk and just beyond a couple of smaller ponderosa pines was an open, mostly grassy glen that stretched out for about 40 or 50 yards.

Ben held up a hand in front of his mouth to signal quiet and David turned his own horse around and rode back past the tree toward the major, who came up quickly and also stopped. "Wide open spot." Swanzey half-whispered. "Just beyond this cottonwood. Stop everyone here and I'll go forward with Black Elk to check it out."

Goodman nodded and turned his own mount at an angle to wait while David pulled back onto the trail and once more went past the tree to ride up alongside their native guide. Black Elk swept his left hand over to that side of the glen to show he was going to ride just inside the tree line in order to get around the open area without being seen. He pointed silently to the right to indicate Swanzey should do the same over there. Not waiting for a response, Ben turned quickly into the trees on his left and seemed to melt into them, barely making a sound as he rode.

David marveled at the man's riding skill before patting his own horse on the flank and starting to the right, afraid that his efforts to be as quiet as Black Elk would almost surely be a failure. He reined the horse to a stop. Maybe if he waited a minute or two, the Indian would reach the other side. Then even if his riding noise gave them away, he could draw the focus to himself and away from Ben.

He shook his head. "No, that's dumb," he muttered, once more patting his horse lightly and turning the reins so that the horse would know he should advance. *If I'm going to get shot at, I want to at least give them a moving target,* he thought.

But he had only advanced a few lengths when Black Elk re-emerged from the trees, now on the far side of the glen. "Come on!" he said aloud while waving for David to come forward straight across the open area. "Tell the others. There's another open space just past these trees and I can see a body!" He turned his horse away.

"Ben!" David's call to him caused Black Elk to pause and turn his horse back around. "You can definitely see a body?"

"Yes! But Mister Swanzey, it's not Harold!" the young Indian called back. "Whoever it is, he's been dead for a while. And there's no sign of your son anywhere."

Chapter Fifteen

"Harold—God willing that he is okay—desperately needs the job that Borglum is going to be providing for him, and for so many other under-employed or unemployed miners in our community," Carrie said as she placed a steaming cup of tea down in front of Minnie and sank down into a chair next to her while cradling a cup of her own.

"I know Cora and some of her friends are adamantly against this project, but we really do need it, Minnie. Keystone has closed many of its mines, but the miners are still here, and Borglum says the miners are exactly the people he needs to help carve the mountain. He's going to pay them five dollars a day to get started and then he's promising them up to eight dollars a day once they're fully trained in his techniques.

"It'll be a godsend for the men and their families . . . and for this town and towns around us like Hill City and Hermosa. I'm sure you're going to hear the same sort of stuff from people living there."

"Yes, I know," Minnie answered. "And as I told Borglum, I know this project is going to happen. It's just a matter of time. I'm glad for you and Keystone, and Harold." She reached out and touched Carrie's arm. "I'm sure he's going to be okay."

Carrie nodded and wiped away a tear. "Like I said. God willing."

She stood up at the sound of footsteps on the front porch, followed by a knocking on the door. "Now who could that be? Do you think they've found out something from up on the mountain?" She hurried over to the door and jerked it open. A middle-aged man with a leather bag on his shoulder stood facing her and appeared startled at her abruptness.

"Oh, Joe! It's you. I thought it might be . . ." She let the sentence trail off. "My boy Harold is missing, and David and a group of men went up into the mountains to search for him. Last time he was seen was out west of Rushmore—out toward Devil's Thumb. When you knocked, I was thinking it might be someone with news."

"I'm so sorry. I wish I were the bearer of news about that. Instead, I'm just here to bring you the mail. Filling in again this week for Louie." He held out a package toward her. "And I have a delivery for your sister Mary," he said. He reached into the bag and took out a couple of letters. "Here's your other mail, too." He looked back into the bag. "Do you want me to leave the newspaper's mail here as well?"

"Yes, thank you."

Mary came out of the hallway leading toward the back of the house and smiled at the sound of the postal worker's voice. "Lewis Mills, is that you?"

"No, ma'am, it's just Joe Parker. Louie's on a road trip somewhere and I've got the route for a couple weeks," he replied with a smile on both his face and in his voice. "How are you doing today, Miss Mary? Always good to see you."

"And you, too," she said, and then pointed at her sightless eyes. "Well, you know?" They both chuckled and then he sobered. "I'm sorry to hear about Harold Swanzey being missing."

He turned back to Carrie. "Anything I can do? I'm heading over to Hill City on the 3:30 train to take some packages that need to be hand-delivered from Hermosa—planning to spend the night. Anyway, when the train stops at Addie Camp maybe I could get some of the miners there to help look for him?"

"Oh, that would be wonderful," Carrie said with a grateful expression on her face.

"You can ride to Hill City on the train? Do you think I might be able to catch a ride with them too?" Minnie stepped out from the kitchen as she asked the question and nodded to the man at the door.

"Hello. I'm Minnie Thompson. Visiting from Hot Springs. Does the train come in here every day from Hill City? I thought it was just a couple times a week. And until I heard you tell Carrie that you were going to ride the train over there, I didn't know it carried passengers either. They told me it just hauled freight."

"Well, normally it don't take people," Parker replied. "But they make an exception for me 'cause I'm so dang handsome." He made a little bow in her direction. Minnie gave him a warm smile in return.

"This is Joseph Parker," Carrie hurried to identify him. "Whenever our regular mail carrier Lewis Mills is gone, Joe fills in for him. Hardly misses a beat."

"Good training from Louie," Parker hurried to add.

"Whenever Joe's doing the route, he has come all the way over from Hermosa," Mary said, speaking in the general direction of where Minnie was standing. Whether it's Joe or Louie, they have to meet the train bringing the mail in from Hill City every morning. Make sure that we Keystone country bumpkins stay in touch with the outside world."

Joe laughed. "Funny, but I've heard some of you Keystoners describing the Hill City and Hermosa folks in that very same way."

Minnie walked over to Carrie's side. "Well, it's too bad there's not a regular rail line running out to Hermosa either," she said. "That would've made my trip here today a lot easier." She spoke to Parker. "And I'm sure it must be quite a trip over here for you each day for a temporary job?"

"Oh, I don't mind. And my old T can go through almost any terrain," Parker said with a careless wave. "And now there's a new dirt road from here to Hermosa that ain't too bad. It's not like driving on a gravel highway, but it's not terrible either. But once I get here I either have to have a horse or take the train if I want to get over to Hill City. There's a riding trail but no way for a car to go there. Even a Model T.

It's either a bumpy carriage ride or by horseback." He paused. "Or a really long hike.

"As for a rail line out to Hermosa, I doubt the CBQ will build anything going east anytime soon. More'n likely they'll run their next line north and follow Route 16 on into Rapid City. They're already hauling several carloads of tin out of Addie Camp each week and I'm sure they'd like it to end up in Rapid. Right now, they have to ship the ore back through Hill City and then all the way down to Edgemont or even to Cheyenne. If they could take it to Rapid instead I'm sure that would save them a ton of money."

"Addie Camp?" Minnie gave him a questioning look. "Sorry Mister Parker, but I have to admit I haven't heard of such a place. Is it a mining camp or a camp where people live?"

"Well, it's a little of both," Joe answered. "It's maybe halfway between Keystone and Hill City. They've been digging out tin from an old silver mine there and there's also a campsite set up for the CBQ to house their miners. Tin mining got started there by the Burlington Railroad way back in 1880, and when the Burlington merged with the Chicago and Quincy about twenty years back it became a CBQ property.

"Since the rail line already ran out that far, some of the Hill City businesses got them to extend the route over here to Keystone so they could bring in supplies and then go back and forth with the mail and other special shipments. That's what Louie and I pick up and deliver for them."

"So, the train runs over here in the morning and back to Hill City later in the day?" Minnie asked.

"Actually, the train makes TWO round trips a day now—early morning here and then back to Hill City mid-morning. Then back here in the early afternoon and heading back again around 3:30 or 4, enough time for me to make my mail deliveries and bag up any outgoing mail to send along."

"But they don't have any passenger cars, Minnie. It's just freighters, ore cars and flatcars to haul logs. And they usually hook up a couple livestock cars in case they have to pick up any cattle or horses," Carrie chipped in.

Joe waved a hand in the air. "Yeah, they only take passengers when there's something special to haul like today when I need to personally deliver that load of packages for the post office. Then they make a space for me—or Louie usually, of course—to ride along with the conductor in the caboose.

"They make at least one stop each day at the Addie, too, to pick up and drop things off including those ore cars, both full ones and empty ones. Anyway, if they do stop this afternoon I can take a few minutes to run over to the camp office to let the manager know about your boy. I'll see if he might be able to get a few of his men to help out with the search. Nothing ventured, as they say."

Carrie reached out and patted him on the arm. "Thank you, Joe. I'll write some things down—everything I know—and you can just give it to him. Now why don't you come into the kitchen for a quick cup of tea while I get the note ready?"

Parker smiled, took off his hat and followed her into the kitchen with Minnie and Mary trailing behind.

"I might have a friend missing up in those parts, too," Minnie said. "Would you be able to ask if anyone's seen him around the mines?"

"Oh, yeah? Sure. Who might that be?"

"Alvin Twocrow. He's a U.S. Marshal out of Hot Springs."

"I know the marshal," Parker responded. "So he's up in the Hills, too? What's he been doing?"

"Working on something for the Marshal's Service out of Sioux Falls, but I'm not sure what. Anyway, haven't heard from him and now with Harold missing and the shooting and all."

"Shooting?"

"Yes, where Harold went missing. One of his friends reported that there was a man shot, and he didn't know who it was. That's why I'm worried about Alvin. I'm sure he's fine, but . . ."

Joe nodded. "Based on my knowledge of him, I'd guess he's fine."

"Yes, I'm sure you're right."

"But I'll still alert the miners to be on the lookout."

She patted his arm, smiled and nodded her thanks. "So," Minnie asked, "non-railroad workers DO get to ride the train every once in a while? Do you think they might be open to taking me along? Just this once? I'd really like to get over to Hill City to interview a couple of people there about how they feel about the carving project."

She paused as a look of confusion crossed Parker's face. "I'm a newspaper reporter Mister Parker," she added. "I'm working on a couple of stories for the *Hot Springs Star* to be shared with other Black Hills area newspapers as well. I'm writing one about Borglum's plans for carving Mount Rushmore and another about local reaction to the project– both here and in Hill City since they're the two communities that will be most affected. I originally was just going to do the Keystone perspective, but when I got ready to come up here my editor decided to be fair, we should find out how Hill City folks are feeling about it too."

Joe nodded.

"I thought once I got here, I could just take the train over to Hill City. Then when I got here, I found out that wasn't really an option, so I've been dreading the thought of having to either take a long rough ride by horse and buggy or going by horseback all that way."

"Well, like I said before, there's really not a regular road running between the two towns. It can be a rugged ride with a horse and carriage, too, but quite a few of the locals do it. Usually, though, it's just farm wagons or buckboards on that route. Sorry to say, but the best way over and back—at least in my book—is by horseback."

"And since I didn't realize that I didn't bring along any riding gear, although I'm sure Carrie could help set me up with something to wear." She looked up at Carrie who raised her chin in agreement. "But what I'd REALLY like to do is try and get on board that train."

"Well, I ain't saying they'll allow it, and even if they do it's not very likely you'd be able to go before tomorrow. I'd guess you probably couldn't get on board until tomorrow morning's return trip back to Hill City." Parker sat down at the table. "And just so you know, there's only room for a couple of people at a time in that caboose and the conductor has to be one of them. Although if there happened to be more riders, I suppose they could take turns sitting and standing or maybe even riding in one of the freight cars."

"I'm definitely willing to forego comfort to save time AND avoid that long horseback ride. Do you know where I go to find out?"

"The depot," Carrie joined in. "David maintains an office in there working for both the CBQ and taking care of the telegraph and phone connections between Keystone and Hill City—and he's in charge of the telegraph line down to Rapid City, too. He works about half time as a CBQ rep alongside the station agent. That's Floyd Marston. He's the man we saw earlier when you arrived—the big man with the bushy walrus mustache who was ogling Maxine."

Minnie smiled at that.

"David runs the depot and Floyd's the station agent, scheduling the shipments and making sure that anything needing to get over to Hill City and back—like Joe and his postal packages—get on board," Carrie continued. "If David was here now instead of up in the Hills looking for Harold, I'm sure he'd make all the arrangements for you. But for now you're at Floyd's mercy."

"Yeah, it'd be up to Floyd, and probably Sam Palmer," Parker agreed before taking a small sip of his tea and blowing lightly across the cup to help cool it down. "He's the new conductor and runs a pretty tight ship. So if you do get to ride, just remember you'll probably have a stop at the Addie and that mining crowd's a pretty tough bunch.

"I don't think they'll cause you any trouble. But don't be shocked if you get a few wolf whistles."

Minnie looked startled before giving him a mischievous grin. "At my age getting a few wolf whistles might actually be good for my ego."

Carrie blanched and Mary guffawed at Minnie's response. Carrie reached over and gave her sister a little tap on the shoulder. "Mary? Really!" Mary just shrugged and kept on smiling.

"Is the tin mine doing well?" Minnie asked, as she slid another of the chairs away from the table and reached in to retrieve the mug she had been drinking from earlier. "You say a couple loads of ore get shipped every week? Can the railroad make much money selling tin?"

"I don't know the going rates, but I hear that it's a pretty lucrative deal. On top of that they're doing some logging out around where they dig, so they get a few timber sales too. I know it's good enough that they're scouting out a couple other potential digging spots that might lead to even more carloads going out of there each week. Word is that their biggest drawback is having to take the ore west and south instead of north and east like they'd really like to do. Most of it ends up at the mills in Gary, Indiana, so taking it southwest first costs them both time and money.

"But" he added, leaning back in his chair, "I've heard through the railroad's grapevine that once this Mount Rushmore carving project gets underway a new Rapid City to Keystone rail line will be a done deal. They think they'll need a line to bring in supplies and help transport the financial supporters and sightseers that Borglum hopes to attract. So, if a new line gets built, it'll pay off in spades for the railroad. They can just link their Hill City to Keystone track into the new one and get themselves a huge cost savings shipping ore and timber back east."

Minnie nodded. "And that's probably another good reason to approve the carving project, huh?" she said to the room.

"What do you mean?" Parker appeared confused by her response.

"Oh, Carrie and I had just been discussing how the Mount Rushmore project could be particularly good for both Keystone's economy and the economy of the surrounding area—what with dozens of carving jobs being created and all. But the expansion opportunities for the railroad and mining would be another good reason to get the carving underway. In fact, that would be two more good reasons, wouldn't it?"

"Oh, you bet," Parker said. "And did you see all the Corps of Engineers folks running around here? They're going to have to build new roads and bridges like the one Norbeck had built over by the Needles when he was still Governor. On top of that they're probably going to have to expand that gravel highway—route 16—down to Rapid City." He looked up at Carrie. "I could easily see a combined Route 16 and new rail line running side-by-side, couldn't you?"

He blew across the top of his teacup once again. "That carving is going to do more than just change the face of Mount Rushmore, you know. It's going to change the face of ALL the landscape around here."

Parker took another sip, and reassured that he wasn't going to burn his lip he took a longer drink before pointing out the window. "They're saying the mountain carving is going to bring thousands and thousands of new tourists to the Keystone area in no time at all; even while the carving is underway. And that's going to mean more money in the local businessmen's pockets—even out in Hermosa or over in Hill City.

"Tourists are gonna need places to eat and drink—maybe stay overnight or even for two or three days."

"Imagine," Mary said as she looked sightlessly across the table in Minnie's direction. "Thousands and thousands of new visitors every year. Just imagine."

Minnie looked thoughtful. "Yes," she said. "Imagine that."

Chapter Sixteen

Twocrow stepped gingerly onto a natural rock shelf that was jutting out from the brush-covered hillside that was adjacent to the little pond's upslope side. He took a couple steps and paused just outside a stand of smaller ponderosas.

"U.S. Marshal!" he called out, chambering a round in the rifle and holding it skyward in his right hand while using his left hand to steady himself up against the first of the trees.

"Come out slowly with your hands raised!"

"Marshal?" He could definitely hear now that the voice was a young man's. "Don't shoot me. I can't move. I'm hurt." The voice seemed to be weaker than when he had heard it while he was still standing in front of the mine's opening. And the sound now seemed to be coming from further out in the trees.

"Identify yourself and state your business here!" Twocrow called out. Without waiting for a response, he quickly moved two steps to his left, putting another tree between himself and the direction where the voice was originating while moving out of the line of sight he might have been creating by talking.

"My name's Harold. Harold Swanzey," the young man's voice replied as Twocrow took a couple of steps closer to the next tree. He peered around it until he could see the young man lying in a little clearing. "I'm a miner out of Keystone," he called out again. "Coming to check out that abandoned mine."

"You alone?" the marshal asked, remaining behind the tree.

"Yes. But I was supposed to meet a friend over near Devil's Thumb and he might be around here looking for me." He pushed himself into a more upright position and slid back against a small boulder. Holding up both hands, he said, "I'm not armed." He gestured toward his feet. "I think I might have a broken ankle."

Twocrow stepped out to the right side of the tree, looking around with caution before moving closer. Satisfied that there was no one else, he continued toward the young man and signaled with his rifle that Harold could lower his hands. Coming up alongside him he could see the boy's left ankle was twisted gruesomely over to one side.

He waggled the gun at Harold's leg. "Looks broke all right. Maybe even more than just your ankle. How'd it happen?"

"Earlier this morning, I came up from where I was camping with my friend Cliff Barkley. We decided to each take a different area to try and check out a couple of these old, abandoned mines. I had heard there was one right near here, but I never did get into it. I was riding my horse through the trees when a timber rattler spooked him. He threw me right over there." He paused and pointed to the opposite edge of the clearing where another little boulder protruded above the grass.

"Landed right on the edge of that rock and snapped it. The snake crawled off but my horse went completely crazy and just took off up the trail behind me. Haven't seen hide nor hair of him since. Guess that was a couple hours ago now." He groaned. "Thought I might really be in danger of nobody finding me until I heard you talking to someone and making some sort of weird noise." He pointed in the general direction of the mine's opening. "Came from over there. Is there someone else here with you?"

"No. It was just me. I like to talk to myself."

Harold grinned at that. "Yeah, me too. That way at least I know someone's listening. Although my dad says it's when you start answering yourself that you have to worry."

Twocrow laughed in spite of the seriousness of the situation. "And that 'noise' you heard was just my yawning to clear out my lungs."

Harold shook his head. "Glad you did it, 'cause it definitely got my attention." He looked back toward the mine. "Is there some water over there? I thought I could hear a falls or some kind of splashing, like maybe water going into a pond." He pointed to his throat. "I'm pretty thirsty."

"Yeah, there's water there." Twocrow laid his rifle down and got onto his knees. "I'm gonna have to get a couple of small branches and put a splint on your leg, but let me take your hat and get you some water first. You okay drinking from your hat?"

"I'd take a drink from my boot . . . or even yours right about now. Like I said, I'm really thirsty." He gave the Marshal a weak smile. "Thank you."

Twocrow picked up the younger man's hat, which had blown up against a nearby kinnikinnick bush. Threading his way back through the trees, he knelt at the pond's edge and filled the hat. Then thinking about it further, he dumped the water into the grass behind him, thoroughly swished out the inside of the hat and filled it again. Carrying it back with a minimal amount of sloshing, he carefully knelt down and helped Harold take a few swallows.

"Drink it by sips," he advised. "Otherwise, you'll get a terrible gut ache."

Harold nodded and gratefully drank some more.

"I'm Marshal Al Twocrow, by the way," he pointed at his badge. "Out of Hot Springs. I was just checking on that abandoned mine myself when I heard your call for help. You any relation to David Swanzey?"

"My dad," Harold answered, leaning back further against the boulder.

"Met him once at a meeting in Rapid. You say you're a miner? How old are you, anyway?"

"Nineteen. But I been working part time at one of the old tin mines down by Keystone since I turned 17," Harold said. "Some of the local guys my age are working to clean out the mines now that a lot of the full-time miners have moved on. But I'm hoping to get me one of those carving jobs when Mister Borglum starts work up on Mount Rushmore.

"In the meantime, my friend Cliff and I thought we'd explore some of these abandoned ghost mines, too. My dad says sometimes you get lucky and find a new ore vein, especially feldspar and tin, so even if these old mines are out of gold and silver they might be full of other good things. We had a couple free days and thought we'd ride up here, camp out and take a look."

He gestured toward his lower leg. "Guess that wasn't such a good plan, was it?"

Twocrow gave Harold a sympathetic pat on his shoulder and then pointed at Harold's banged up limb. "Maybe I can temporarily fix you up enough to get you back into town where a doc can take a better look at it. You snapped it pretty good, but if you didn't tear any muscles or tendons and can get it re-set proper it should heal up pretty fast. Had a broken ankle myself a few years back and it only put me out of commission for about five weeks."

He moved over and tried to shift it, exhaling sharply as Harold cried out in pain.

"Hurts like the devil," Harold said. "What you gotta do to it?"

"Now that I'm moving it, feels like you might have a break in your lower leg too, just above the ankle." He shook his head as Harold moaned. "Sorry, but it's going to be pretty painful while I'm working on it. But I'll need to put a branch along the inside part of your leg and then shift your foot back straight up and put another branch along the outside. Then I'll tie them together with my bandana and yours. I'm not gonna lie to you Harold. It's gonna hurt."

Tears welled up in the young man's eyes, but he nodded. "Okay, Marshal. Guess you know best, so just do it."

Twocrow gathered up two medium-sized branches and one smaller one. He started to strip the bark off that one. "You're going to need to bite down on this piece of wood while I tie the other ones in place. "It's going to be painful, but getting it splinted is the only way you'll be able to stand up and get up onto my horse." He offered Harold another drink from the hat.

"Kind of surprised I haven't heard anything from my friend Cliff," the young man said as he took a bigger drink. "We were planning to meet up in the clearing by Devil's Thumb a little before noon and then try'n figure out what to do next."

"Hmmmm," Twocrow responded, thinking about the body he still hadn't located. "He's probably out looking around for you right now."

"Yeah." Harold wrinkled his nose. "It's kind of weird, but I thought I heard what sounded like some gun shots over that direction, too. But that was right about the time I got thrown so I didn't think anything more about it. Haven't heard anything since. So, it might have just been some branches breaking or something, huh?"

"Sure," the marshal said, looking around uneasily as he handed the now bark-free piece of wood to the teenager.

Harold took it, pushed himself up even straighter and looked around.

"Hey Marshal, where's that horse or yours? I didn't hear you ride up."

"Yeah, that's a pretty long story Harold." He touched the piece of wood. "You bite down on that and I'll tell you all about how I got here after we get this splint in place and start our ride."

Chapter Seventeen

Major Goodman stood up from where he had been kneeling alongside the dead man's body but the other members of the posse, who had tied their horses to the surrounding trees and shrubs, stood further away. Most were trying to avoid looking directly at the body, which not only was covered with blood but also was gruesomely twisted across the top of a small boulder.

He reached down, grasped the man's shoulders and moved him onto the flat ground, brushing the dirt and twigs off his face as soon as he was settled in the new position.

"He look familiar to any of you?" The men all turned to take a look at the man's face as Goodman shifted his legs so they, too, were lying straight.

No one spoke until finally David said, "Well, I ain't sure major, but I think I might have seen him with the railroad's weekend crew coming over from Hill City." He looked around at the others, focusing mostly on Matthew and Howard for confirmation. "Ain't he one of them part-timers? One of Palmer's weekend guys?"

Howard Grimalski pulled his bandana over his nose and stepped forward, dropping onto his knees alongside the body and swiping at the hair that had fallen across the top of the man's face. He signaled to his brother to join him and after both had given the man another once over, they backed away from the body and turned toward David and the major.

"Mister Swanzey's right," Matthew said. "When I was doing that weekend shift filling in for Floyd at the depot a couple weeks back, this guy was on board the train for both runs. When I had a couple of boxes to load onto the caboose he gave me a hand."

"Yeah and believe it or not, I had to buy a ticket from him when I had trouble with my horse and asked if we could get a ride back from the Addie Camp," their brother Merle said. "My horse came up lame when the three of us were riding back from Hill City and we had walked into Addie when the train pulled in on their afternoon run and stopped to offload some supplies for the miners."

His brothers both nodded.

"Anyway, I asked if they could just let us get into one of their livestock cars for the ride back into Keystone—but this sucker would only agree to let me ride because my horse was hurt. Then on top of that, he charged me two dollars, one for me and one more for transporting my horse." He gave a little grunt followed by a derogatory wave in the dead man's direction. "No 'milk of human kindness' in him, that's for sure."

"He works for Sam Palmer, then?" Major Goodman asked.

"Is Sam Palmer the name of that new full-time conductor?" Merle asked.

"Yes. Met him just last week. He came up here from Denver about six weeks or maybe two months ago now so he's still pretty new."

"So, he must-a brought this yahoo along from Denver with him because I don't ever remember meeting him before I had my horse problem," Merle added. "Seems like they've added three or four new guys on those part-timer shifts, and I've heard all the new guys came with Palmer up from Denver. Hard to keep 'em all straight. And I don't know what in hell they do over in Hill City during the week when they're not on duty. Must be boring?"

The men's horses suddenly started shifting and whickering, moving nervously about. The men turned to look first at them and then toward the northwest as a saddled, bridled and riderless horse burst out of the woods at the far side of the glen.

"Hey, that looks like Harold's horse, don't it?" Merle looked toward the others for confirmation and started walking toward the animal. The horse immediately snorted at the sight of a man moving in his direction and pranced around as if getting ready to run.

"Something's got him good and spooked," the major said. "And he's staying close to the trees. Definitely ready to take off again so be careful."

"Merle, wait up. Why don't you and me get to our horses and try to ride up on him from both sides," Howard said. The major and David both nodded their approval, and the men started moving toward their horses, walking at a snail's pace to avoid further frightening Harold's horse as it kept snuffling and shifting back and forth in front of the trees.

As soon as the men swung up into their saddles, the action caused the riderless horse to shy away and bolt back into the woods, heading back to the west. "We're on it!" Howard called, and the men urged their horses toward the spot where the animal had disappeared. Ben walked over and climbed up onto his horse as well.

"I'll circle down toward the stream and try to get ahead of where the horse probably will run," he said matter-of-factly. Without waiting for a response, he rode away.

The major and Matthew regained their feet and Goodman turned to face the others. "So now I think the question is, 'What in hell was this man doing out here and who shot him up like this?'"

"And," David added, holding his arms wide. "Where's my son?"

Suddenly, Black Elk's horse re-emerged from the lower edge of the woods and his rider held up his left hand. "Major! Mister Swanzey!" Black Elk called. "Hurry! You need to come over here! I can see another body down near Pine Creek along the hillside!"

"Is it Harold?" David was already mounting his horse as he called out the question.

"I don't know. He's face down and lying behind some fallen logs. And his horse is down on the ground, too, back where I came riding along the edge of the trees. I don't know about the man, but the horse looks like he's been shot dead."

"The man's shot dead?" Swanzey was confused.

"No, not the man, the horse! I don't know for sure about the man Mister Swanzey. Whoever it is, I thought I could see him moving so I'm pretty sure he is still alive."

* * * * *

Harold made a little whistling sound as he exhaled sharply between his gritted teeth. Then he followed that with a little moan as Ice shifted his weight and braced his forefeet to maneuver down the slope. "Sorry," he apologized. "Don't mean to complain."

Twocrow was leading Ice with his left hand on the halter, both reins wrapped tightly around his wrist. In his right hand he still carried the rifle, cocked and ready to fire if needed.

"No, I'm sorry you have to deal with that Harold," the marshal said as he guided the horse onto a wider and flatter piece of ground that stretched out alongside Tenderfoot Creek, the little stream that he had been following earlier and now continued from the pond by the old mine and on out toward Devil's Thumb. Harold's weight shifted back as soon as they hit the flatter ground.

They had been walking along like this now for half an hour, the start of their "moving" process delayed until Twocrow could make his way back through the mine, pick up his horse and ride up and across the top of the hill covering the hidden ghost mine.

Once successfully across, he then had to wind his way back through the trees before coming to the clearing where Harold lay dozing in the sun, exhausted from both his morning-long ordeal and the painful process of having his broken ankle and lower leg put into the splints.

It had been an exhausting process for Twocrow, too, trying to maneuver the 6-foot-2, 160-pound teenager onto the saddle. After tying Ice in between a fallen log and the trunk of a tree, he had to shoulder the younger man over to the log and half-lift, half-shove him on up while the horse nervously shook at the process.

To his credit, Twocrow thought as he looked up at the injured teenager, Harold had endured the pain with only a minimal amount of complaining and then, like now, only when extreme stress had been placed on the injuries.

"This look familiar? You know where we're at?" Twocrow asked.

"Yeah, I think," Harold answered. He pointed off to his right. "If we go through that little gap between the stream and that next stand of trees, we should come out pretty close to Devil's Thumb and Pine Creek. There's a grassy spot over there where I told Cliff I'd meet him at lunchtime."

He removed his hat and looked up toward the sun, which was now further to their west. "That would'a been an hour or so ago, right?"

Twocrow took out his pocket watch. "Yeah. It's already 12:30." He took off his own hat and wiped his hand across his brow to brush away the sweat beads forming there. He eyed his watch again. "Well actually, it's 12:45. If we're lucky we'll find both your friend and your horse waiting for you over there, but I'd settle for just running into your friend."

Harold nodded as he put his hat back on. "Me, too. Kind'a surprised he didn't come looking for me. But then again maybe he did. If so, I hope he went back and isn't out here wandering around." He shrugged and touched the canteen on the side of the saddle. "Okay if I have another swig of your water?"

"Sure thing, and then chuck it on down to me when you're done. Glad we filled it up with that good water from the pond." He reached up and took the canteen from the young man as Harold leaned forward with it in his direction.

"Definitely beats drinking out of my dirty hat." He grimaced as he looked up at the hat's brim now partially shading his eyes. "But I was so damned thirsty I think I would'a drunk from a cesspool if that's all that was available."

"I've had water out of some mud holes, myself," the marshal agreed. "Water's water when you don't have any." He took a long drink and handed the canteen back for Harold to re-secure it. He flipped the reins around his wrist and re-grasped Ice's halter. "Ready?"

The boy nodded and they started moving again, crossing the stream before pulling to an abrupt halt as a riderless horse suddenly galloped out from the same gap that was their destination. "Hey!" Harold exclaimed. "There's my horse!"

Before he could say another word two riders made their way out behind the wayward horse, one carrying a rifle, the other a lariat. At the sight of a man walking toward them and leading a horse and rider, both Harold's horse and the two men approaching him came to a stop. All seemed shocked at what they were seeing.

Releasing his hand from Ice's halter, Twocrow flipped the reins toward Harold and dropped to his knees.

"Harold! Quick! Make yourself as flat as you can on top of that saddle. Stay flat and get ready to ride." Harold winced as he shifted but did what he had been told, waiting for whatever order Twocrow might give.

The two men at the woods' edge continued staring toward them before one of them suddenly rode up and grabbed the halter of Harold's missing horse. He quickly dropped the rope around the animal's neck and pulled the horse over against his own to calm him down.

The second man lifted himself up and called out. "Harold? Hello! Harold Swanzey! Is that you?"

Harold sat back up in Ice's saddle. "Merle? That you?"

The man waggled his rifle toward the sky. "Yeah, it's me. And Howie's here too." Twocrow stayed low but looked back up at Harold then over again at the two men.

"What are you guys doing here?" Harold called out.

"Looking for you!" Howard pointed at Harold's horse. "Found your nag."

Merle sat up straighter in his own saddle as Howard continued to calm Harold's horse while staying up tight alongside him. Merle pointed the weapon toward Twocrow who was slowly getting to his feet. "You okay Harold? Who's that you got there with you?"

Chapter Eighteen

"Your ankle and lower leg don't look so good, son." David Swanzey was standing alongside Ice, checking on Harold's splinted leg as his son sat stoically atop Twocrow's steel gray horse. David's handsome face was smeared with trail dust and sweat, and his normally thick, luxurious handlebar mustache was matted and drooping, making it easy for the others to see how deeply the search for Harold had affected him.

Now he reached out and lightly touched his son's leg. "Sorry to say this, but I'm sure the marshal is right. Looks like you broke the lower part of your leg and maybe tore up the tendons in there too."

Black Elk came over to join them and gave Harold a sympathetic smile. Turning toward where Twocrow and Major Goodman sat leafing through the papers that Goodman had received earlier that day, he said, "Hau kola marshal. I am Ben Black Elk." He nodded at Harold. "Harold's friend. I can help get him to where he can get his leg treated."

"Hau kola." He paused as he saw Black Elk frown. "Sorry, I'm Lakota but not real good with the language? So, Black Elk, huh? You the one who had the vision about Mount Rushmore being The Six Grandfathers?"

"My father," Black Elk replied.

"Sure, you'd be way too young." Twocrow pointed again at Harold. "If you or someone can get him to help, that would be great. He needs to see a doctor for that sooner rather than later."

"And staying on my horse ain't doing him much good either." He looked over to the other younger men. "Maybe one of you could go back into Keystone with Black Elk to bring help? I don't think a ride up over the mountain will work for Harold, especially once you get over the top of Rushmore and start on the downslope into Keystone. That would put a lot of pressure on his leg."

He pointed to where Merle and Ben were tending to the other man they had found. Black Elk had been correct. The man's horse had been shot dead, and the badly injured rider had a gunshot wound to his stomach but was still breathing. "A long ride, hell even a short one, is definitely not gonna work for that guy."

As if on cue the man groaned. It was obvious that he was in a lot of pain from his stomach wound. He had drifted in and out of consciousness and for the short times he'd been awake he had just moaned, not telling them how or why he'd been shot. "Whoever the hell he is, he's going to need some special attention. That wound on the right side of his stomach looks pretty bad."

"We ain't' got no doctors living in Keystone," Red Anderson said as he and Mathew Grimalski came over beside them, each giving Harold a reassuring pat on the arm in the process. "Nearest Doc is all the way over to Hill City. That'd be a ride-and-a-half for Harold with his bad leg."

David nodded at the wounded man. "Yeah, we can probably control his bleeding. So bad as it is, that wound ain't gonna kill him as long as he stays still. He definitely ain't ridin' anywhere without treatment." He pointed to Harold. "Maybe we should just get Harold down off the marshal's horse and try to make him comfortable, too?

"And Marshal Twocrow's right. One of you can ride back into Keystone while the rest of us stay here and take care of Harold and this other guy. Once you get into town, head over to the depot and let Floyd know that we need to get the doctor to come out here from Hill City. Tell him I said call the Hill City depot and ask them to bring the doc over to Keystone on the first train in the morning."

Devil's Thumb

Twocrow gestured toward the pathway leading out to the Calendar Mine. "That body I found over in the mine's been there a couple days. When do you think these two men were shot?"

"Hard to say," the major replied. "But Harold's friend Clifford, who was shot at this morning, said it was coming from someone with a rifle who came down the hill toward that other dead man that we found out in the open. He thought the shooter might have been a woman."

Twocrow looked up at that. "A woman? He sure about that?"

"No, not really, but as you can see by that report we got from the sheriff's office, there was at least one woman in that Denver gang and some are sayin' she's the one killed that bank guard. So, if they did come up this direction, well . . ."

"You think she might be our shooter?"

"Yes. I'd say it's a good possibility. And it might be that body you found in the mine was an earlier victim. And young Barkley was almost another one." He nodded at Harold. "Plus, if Harold hadn't been thrown from his horse over by your abandoned mine, he might be lying here dead now, too."

"Well, if the shooter here also shot my guy in the mine, then he's . . . or she's . . . been takin' shots at folks for a couple days now because I'm pretty sure the body over there is more than a day old," Twocrow said.

Major Goodman took off his hat, ran a hand through his hair and sighed. "None of this makes any sense. Unless there's two gangs and they had some sort of shootout." He looked around at the others. "You sure you don't recognize either one of these guys? They're not from around these parts, right?"

David moved over to the wounded man and knelt beside him. "You know Matt, I keep thinking that I might've seen this guy somewhere before. You think he could be another one of Palmer's new guys from Denver? Take a closer look at him, would you?"

Matt turned and walked back, kneeling alongside the wounded man. "I'm not sure major," David continued, "but this guy might be another one of Palmer's boys."

"Now that would be kind of strange, too, wouldn't it?" Major Goodman mused. "Two part-time rail workers shot out in the middle of nowhere."

Before David could respond, Matt interrupted, standing back up as he spoke. "I think David's right. I sort of remember this guy from when I was filling in at the depot a couple weekends ago." He looked down at the fallen man and back to David. "And speaking of the depot, won't the afternoon train from Keystone to Hill City be heading out pretty soon?"

"Sure by 3:30 or 4 if they're on schedule."

"Couldn't the marshal try'n get Harold over to Hill City on that train yet today? If they can stop the train and get on board, he could get Harold looked at by the doc yet tonight. Then Harold could just stay there until he's able to ride again. Meanwhile the marshal can bring the doc back here in the morning to take a look at this other guy."

"You keep talking about the CBQ train carrying passengers and horses. I thought they just hauled ore from their mines and logs, not horses and people," Goodman said.

"Well, it used to be that way, but they've added a modified car to carry livestock back and forth," Matt replied. "Ain't that right, David?" He turned toward Swanzey for confirmation and got a nod in return.

"Drovers been bringing beef cattle, sometimes sheep too, up from Hermosa so they can take them over to Hill City without having to drive them all the way through the hills and worry about runaways or wolves," David explained. "They don't need the special car every day, but they usually keep it hooked up to the train just in case."

"So, you could put both the men and their horses on board?"

Swanzey nodded again. "I'm sure Palmer would let Harold and the marshal ride in the caboose with him. Not a lot of room, but he's got a cot in there that Harold could lay down on and he and the marshal could stand."

"And you could tell him about these men of his getting shot," the major said to Twocrow. "You'd think he might be real interested in finding out about something like that, right?" He turned from Twocrow and spoke to Matthew. "But how can they stop the train? And where can they stop it?"

"Well, there's an old logging trail somewhere near here. Hasn't been used for years but my dad said they used to take loads of lumber and trees on it up to where the rail line crosses—not that far north of here," Matthew answered.

Twocrow nodded. "I think I might've seen part of that when I came out of the Calendar Mine. Looked like a grown-over trail starting on a little mesa north or northwest of the opening and moving off into the trees."

"Gotta be it," Matthew said. "We picked it up closer to the tracks when we were out hunting." He pointed at Harold. "Harold's been up there before. Remember when we were hunting, and Merle's horse came up lame? We got on that trail through the trees and ended up stopping the train over by Leaky Valley? You remember that spot don't you Harold?"

Now it was Harold's turn to nod in agreement.

"Once you get up there you can pick a spot to stop the train. Best place is probably where Pine Creek empties out into Battle Creek," David added. "I rode with the train crew over and back about a month ago and then again about two weeks back. They had to slow the train almost to a stop at that river crossing over there. So depending on where that logging trail comes out when you ride north from here, there'd be that spot and then the one at Leaky Valley. So, Leaky Valley or that river crossing point to try'n get them to stop."

"There's a third spot where you look out toward Hardesty Peak to the northeast," Matthew said to Harold. He looked north then back to the others. "You know the place I'm talking about?"

Harold nodded again and shifted to face Twocrow. "Yeah, that's a great spot, too, marshal, but I think it's further up. You definitely should be able to get the train to stop for us by Leaky Valley because it's a wide-open location; flat with lots of grass on all sides. And you wouldn't have any trouble loading up the horses there either. That might be a problem at the river crossing area."

David pulled at the right corner of his handlebar mustache, running it up between his thumb and forefinger as if hoping to re-curl it. "You're right. That's what you'll need to do. Marshal, if you start out now you and Harold should be able to get up to those tracks in plenty of time, even riding slow because of Harold's injury."

He pulled out his pocket watch. "I don't think the train will leave from Keystone for at least another hour. Might even be later than that if they're putting on any freight. You should have plenty of time to make it up to the tracks and scout out just the right spot to try'n get them to stop." He put a hand on Twocrow's shoulder. "You okay with that?"

The marshal turned to look at Goodman.

"I'll go major, but I'd like David to ride with me, too. He ought to be the one to take care of his boy and get him on the train. Plus, David knows everyone—both on the railroad and over at Hill City. Nobody's met me and they might not recognize Harold either. If you and the others don't mind taking care of things here? I think David should go along." He directed the question and the comment to all of the other members of the posse.

Goodman looked around at the rest of the men and seeing their nods of approval, he turned back to where David and Twocrow were waiting. "Agreed," the major said. He looked up at Harold and pointed at David. "Like the marshal said, your old man shouldn't have any problem stopping the train. I know if I saw a scary looking bastard like him standing out in the middle of the tracks I'd stop, that's for sure."

"Or speed up," David said with a little grin. Despite his pain, even Harold had to laugh at his father's droll pronouncement.

"Well, scary looking or not I'm sure the engineer'll be way more inclined to stop for Swanzey than he will be for me," Twocrow said matter-of-factly. He touched his badge. "Star or no star."

None of the others said anything but from the looks on their faces it was clear they understood the Indian lawman's meaning. A train stopping for an Indian was not as likely to happen, even if he did wear a marshal's badge and have an injured white man riding alongside.

Black Elk grimaced at Twocrow's pronouncement but said nothing.

"I think we better get a move on, just in case that train leaves early," Twocrow added. "Are you all okay with me taking one of the other horses? I doubt Harold's horse is ready to ride after all the running around he's been doing. But if you give him another couple hours or so, he should be calmed down enough. Especially once he knows he's on his way back to his own stable."

"Take my horse, marshal," Red walked over to where his horse was stretching his neck to reach for some tufts of grass and untied the reins from the small tree where he had tethered him. He led the animal over to the lawman, gently patted the horse on the side of his face and handed Twocrow the reins. "He won't give you any trouble. You can bring him back along with the doc on tomorrow morning's train after he gets Harold taken care of tonight."

"Appreciate it, Red," David Swanzey said, clapping the big man on his shoulder. "And if Harold's horse still won't ride by the time you get ready to head back to town, I'm sure Matthew will be glad to share his ride with you, won't you Matt?"

"Actually," Major Goodman interrupted, "I think most of the rest of you men are going to need to hunker down here for the night." He signaled to Ben, who walked over to join them. "Mister Black Elk, if you're okay coming with me, I'd like to make that ride back into Keystone myself to report what's going on out here. And we can pick up some pack mules to bring back tomorrow. You other men can stay here to watch over the wounded man and make sure the dead men—both the one out here and the one the marshal found over in the Calendar Mine—aren't disturbed."

"Yes," Black Elk replied. "I can ride with you and come back with you tomorrow." He held a hand up to Harold. "Whatever I need to do to help my friend Harold."

Harold gave him a weak smile in response.

"And like we been sayin', that gut-shot guy ain't going nowhere until he gets seen by a doc," Goodman added. "We need to do everything we can to keep him alive because right now he's our only source about what actually happened out here. Maybe we can bring him back into Keystone after the doctor fixes him up tomorrow morning. Hopefully once he recovers we'll be able to get a few answers. Meanwhile we'll at least get him and these dead men off this mountain by mid-day tomorrow. And who knows, maybe someone in town will recognize them, even that body starting to fall apart inside the Calendar Mine."

Seeing the distasteful look on the other men's faces, he said, "Don't worry, I'll make sure we load up some canvas to completely wrap up both dead bodies before we try and move them. Okay?"

"You know, Major Goodman, if you're right about these men being shot by that bank robbing gang out of Denver, it might be a good idea to deputize a few more men and send them out here to help guard this place tonight," Twocrow said. "Whoever did these shootings obviously doesn't have any qualms about shooting at anyone who they think might be getting in their way."

Goodman nodded and turned to Ben. "Mister Black Elk, would you be willing to lead my men back here if I send some from my engineering unit out to do that overnight support? If you can do that, I can round up a couple more locals to help me wrangle those pack mules up here in the morning."

Black Elk nodded and the major reached out to give him a thankful handshake. Then he turned back to Twocrow.

"Listen marshal, once we get the two bodies and the wounded man on their way over to Keystone, we can take the rest of the men on a look-around to make sure none of the shooters are still holed up anywhere nearby. Although I have to admit I'm a little skittish about just riding around willy-nilly when there's a gang of shooters who probably won't hesitate to take some shots at us. What do you think?"

Twocrow looked to the northeast. In the far distance, just barely visible, the bare rock face of Old Baldy reflected the afternoon sun. He turned and looked back over his shoulder toward Harney Peak.

"Earlier today I was on my way up to Harney to meet with the fire-spotting team and check on the exact spots they've been seeing that intermittent smoke for the past couple weeks. Originally my plan was to check out those spots for a possible bootlegging operation. Now that

I've found the whiskey still in the Calendar Mine, I'll just need to verify that their smoke sightings match up with that mine's location.

"But if some of the recent smoke they've been seeing is from more than just this old ghost mine's coordinates . . ."

"Like that smoke I saw yesterday, for example," Goodman interrupted, seeing where Twocrow was going. "Then it's probably a good bet that smoke's coming from our shooters' campfire, and you can pinpoint those coordinates too."

"That's what I was thinking." Twocrow looked north again. "Listen, if everything goes okay with our getting over to Hill City on that train, I think I'll let David take charge of bringing the doctor back here in the morning and I'll ride on up to Harney to check on those smoke locations. All of them. That'll give us specific places to look instead of you and your deputies just riding around blind.

"After I check in with the fire spotters and leave Harney, I'll head back into Hill City to see if I can catch a ride back to Keystone on the afternoon train. Then we can talk strategy tomorrow night. If you're in agreement, we'll take the posse back out to those smoke sighting locations first thing the next morning."

"And even if it's not from the bank robbers, any other smoke sightings they've had still might be coming from whoever shot these men—and took those shots at Harold's friend Barkley," Goodman agreed. "Robbers or not, I think we still need to try to catch the shooters, too. Don't we? I mean, I can't imagine they'll let the Rushmore carving project get started until we do."

Twocrow nodded. "Okay, we've got a plan, but even when you're just poking around here, be careful. Whoever these shooters are, there's no doubt that they're dangerous. So, if you don't find anything right away, I think you should just pack up and head back into Keystone and I'll meet you there."

Devil's Thumb

He turned back to David. "If we make that train we should get into Hill City by late afternoon, right?" Swanzey nodded. "Okay, then I'll have time to have the Forest Service call up to Harney and let the spotters know I'll be riding up there first thing in the morning. And I can let them know that I need to get the location of ANY and ALL of their smoke sightings from the past couple weeks. Especially any sightings they've had over in this general direction during the last few days."

He looked to the west where the craggy top of Harney Peak jutted above the surrounding hills. "Listen, if for some reason I can't get back to Hill City in time to catch that afternoon train tomorrow, I'll have the spotters call down to the Forest Service office to send a message over to you in Keystone to let you know. If I don't make the train, Ice and I will ride back to Keystone on our own."

"Really? That's a hell of a ride, marshal."

"True, but it'll be mostly downhill, and old Ice here is pretty durable." He reached over and patted the rugged little horse on his flank. "He's a mustang, you know? So, I'm either going to get to Keystone by mid-afternoon by train, or by mid-evening by horseback at the latest. Either way, we should have time tomorrow night to plot out where we're going to take the posse to search and how we're gonna go about doing it."

"Okay, sounds good," Goodman said. "And maybe by the time you get to Keystone I'll have a handle on who these dead men are, if there's any connection to the robbery down in Denver and what it is that killed them. Although I'm pretty sure it was a rifle bullet or two that got this one AND wounded his friend over there."

"Yeah, same with the guy in the mine."

"So, you and David keep a sharp eye out while you're making that ride up north to catch the train."

Twocrow nodded and climbed up on Red's horse, which was a couple hands taller than Ice. Just as Red had told him, the big animal seemed unperturbed at having a new rider.

"Look, if for some reason I DON'T make it back to Keystone by tomorrow evening, just wait until at least mid-morning the next day before you go looking anywhere else. Okay? Safety in numbers. Especially with an outlaw gang like this."

The military man reached up to shake Twocrow's hand. "Okay." He swung around to do the same with Swanzey before pointing to where Harold was still sitting quietly waiting on Ice. "Better get moving and get that boy of yours fixed up." He walked over and shook Harold's hand too. "Listen to your elders on this ride son." He stepped back. "And that's an order!"

"Yes sir," Harold said weakly before adding a little salute and clucking to Ice to get moving as Twocrow and Swanzey turned their horses off toward the pond and the trail they'd be following back to the north.

Chapter Nineteen

"Hey Sam!" Joseph Parker called from across the lobby as he wheeled a cart loaded with packages into the Keystone Depot's main waiting room, Minnie and Carrie trailing behind him. "Ready for me to get these boxes on board?"

Palmer had been impatiently leaning against the corner of the counter where he was closely watching stationmaster Floyd Marston make painstakingly slow entries onto a lading sheet. He looked up with a scowl. Responding to Parker with a halfhearted wave, he turned back toward Marston and began drumming his fingers on the counter's mahogany surface. His action resulted in an irritated growl from the walrus-mustachioed Marston.

"Can you stop that? The more you do those irritating things the longer it's going to take for me to get these lading sheets ready for you. I need to concentrate." Marston glared at the conductor, who lifted his fingers and slowly moved them over to his side. The stationmaster pointed back to the lading sheet. "Rewriting these figures off the transit book onto your lading sheets ain't as easy as you think, you know?"

Palmer just responded with an exasperated grunt as he turned to face the rapidly approaching trio. He pointed toward Parker's cart.

"All of those boxes need to get over to Hill City?"

Parker nodded. "You bet. Want me to just wheel them on through?"

"More than I expected, but yes. You'll find a spot on the freight car just ahead of the caboose, or you can stack them in the horse car since we won't be using that today." He looked over at Floyd. "We should be ready to roll as soon as Floyd gets me the manifests for the REST of the freight." He sighed loudly to emphasize his ongoing impatience and pulled out his pocket watch to check the time.

He paused in his actions as Floyd made a "hold up" signal with his hand, raising his ink pen straight up in the process.

"Now what?" Sam frowned, a definite irritable tenor to his voice. "For cripes sake Floyd, we're already 15 minutes behind schedule!"

"I know, I know. But seeing the ladies reminds me that I got some dispatches in the government pouch from Rapid City this morning and they'll need to go along with you, too." He started searching beneath the counter while still talking to Sam as he looked. "You should be happy to wait because the dispatches say they're looking for a gang of robbers that might be in our area. I'm sure once your boss sees that he'll want to have plenty of guards riding along with you for the next few days."

The conductor paled at Floyd's proclamation; cleared his throat and shrugged as he looked back at Parker and then toward the two women. "Yeah, maybe. But ain't it kind of a 'Boy who cried wolf!' thing? Seems like lately there's been a weekly 'Beware of the outlaw!' cry going out. I figure you have to take these alerts with a grain of salt, or you might as well stay home."

"I think this one might be the real thing," Carrie spoke up.

"Oh yeah, why's that?" The conductor gave her a closer look. "And what might you know about it, Miss?" He turned back to Floyd. "I thought you said it was in the government pouch. How would this woman know what's in there?" He said it with an accusing tone and then swung back around toward Carrie.

"Do I know you? I haven't been working this route too long, but it seems like we might've crossed paths?"

"Carrie Swanzey," she said, walking over to shake his hand. She pointed over her shoulder. "And this is my friend Minnie Thompson from Hot Springs. We're actually here to ask YOU for a favor."

"Me?" He seemed taken aback as he glanced from the women over to where Floyd continued writing. He looked back toward her. "Swanzey? That's how I know you. You're David's wife, ain't you?

"Seen you in here talking with him a few days ago and when you left, he said you was his wife." He tapped the top of the counter. "That's why you know what was in that government pouch, I suppose? You should tell your husband he shouldn't just go sharing those reports no matter who you are," he admonished.

She gave him a grim smile. "Yes, I'll be sure and let him know. Thanks for the warning."

"Well, then, how can I help you Mrs. Swanzey?"

"It's actually me that needs the assistance," Minnie spoke up. "I'm in need of getting over to Hill City and don't really relish the idea of having to travel by horseback—especially since I just found out that was my primary option." Palmer looked confused at her remark.

"I thought there might be a stagecoach or buggy route between here and there," she went on, "but Mister Parker says it would have to be by horseback, and I haven't been on horseback for quite some time now."

"So you're wanting to ride on my train instead?"

"Yes."

Palmer started to shake his head but stopped at the downcast look that crossed Minnie's face. "Why's it so important for you to get to Hill City? And, by the way, there'd be no way you could go today, no matter what."

"Actually, I was hoping to ride over tomorrow anyway," Minnie said. "I'm working on a story for the newspaper that I work for down in Hot Springs, and I think it's important that I include the Hill City folks' perspective too." She pointed at Palmer's name badge with the formal CB&Q logo. "And the Railroad's too, now that I think about it.

So, when I'm over there maybe I could talk to your bosses?" She gave him a bright smile. "Perhaps you could even introduce me?"

"Well, um, that would be highly unusual . . ." He started to respond just as Parker came walking back from where he had wheeled out his cartload of mailboxes and loaded them onto the train.

"Oh, come on Sam," the postman interrupted. "You could let her ride just like you let me or Louie ride. Ain't no big deal."

Palmer glared at Parker.

"And," Joe gave the conductor a little wink, "I'm sure Miss Thompson here would be more than willing to pay you a few dollars for the convenience and maybe even quote you in her story." He turned to Minnie. "Or am I being too forward in saying that."

"Oh . . . Uh . . . No! Absolutely!" She exclaimed. "And on top of that I'd be buying a CBQ ticket from Hill City to Edgemont. You can be most assured that I'll be telling everyone in Hot Springs about the convenience of riding your rail line, whether it'd be up to Hill City, or even all the way up to Deadwood. I don't think a lot of our readers are aware of that."

The conductor leaned back against the counter as if digesting the possibilities of this new information. "Okay, listen," he finally said. "I'll need to clear it with my boss back in Hill City when we return there tonight, but I can talk to him about it AND see if he might be willing to talk with you for your newspaper story when you get there tomorrow."

Both Minnie and Carrie reached out their hands to shake his and started to thank him profusely.

He held up his other hand to stop them. "But" he said, "I can't make no promises." Parker gave him a questioning look and he added. "Okay. I promise I'll ask."

"And Joseph here can be a witness to vouch that I keep that promise." He turned to Parker. "Meanwhile, I hope YOU can vouch for her, too. Right? I mean, I don't want her writing something bad about the CB&Q once she finds out that a freighter ride from here over to Hill City ain't even close to the ride you get on the passenger train route from Hot Springs up to Rapid City."

Parker grinned at the two women. "What do you say Miss Thompson? Sound fair to you?"

"No bad stories. That's a promise," Minnie said, re-extending her hand, which Palmer now shook.

"Lading sheets are ready!" Floyd slapped a small stack of papers down on the counter.

"Thank God," the conductor responded. "Come on Joe, get your butt on board and let's get moving!" He turned back to the women. "Meet me back here at 9 o'clock tomorrow morning and I'll have a response for you one way or another. And if you're approved the train heads back to Hill City by 9:30 sharp. No exceptions!" He turned back to the postal worker. "Sometimes I'm too nice for my own darn good."

"Yeah, Louie told me you're a prince all right." He laughed and both of the women and Floyd joined in as Palmer's face turned beet red. He made another "harrumphing" noise, spun on his heels, and started quickly toward the depot's doorway.

Parker shrugged. "Or not. Guess I better hurry up and get on board and hope he don't toss me off halfway there." He chuckled again as he hustled after Palmer with a little wave to Minnie and Carrie as he left.

Chapter Twenty

"We must be pretty close to the tracks now," David said as the trio rode across the top of a small hill they had decided to take to save time after the logging trail made a sharp turn to the west. Threading their way between two rocky outcroppings, they urged their horses up to the ridgeline where they had a view of the trail resuming a couple hundred yards straight north.

Now they also had a clear view of Pine Creek, which had been running adjacent to the trail most of the way.

"I think we'll reach the tracks just beyond where Pine Creek cuts off to the left," he pointed as he spoke. "I'm pretty sure that's the place where the Pine and Battle Creek join and makes sense because they could offload logs there, too, and float them on Battle toward Keystone.

"That's the train's river crossing I was talking about before. From that point Battle runs right out into Leaky Valley and that's a much easier place for us to get the train to stop."

"Yeah, it would probably be pretty hard for them to try and stop by the river crossing, especially if they have a bridge to go over before they can pick up speed again."

"Leaky Valley will be perfect—flat and grassy—and then when they start moving again it will be toward a downgrade so the train can pick up speed again before the tracks veer north and back to the west. Do you know this area, marshal?"

"I know OF it but never been. I took a ride out to Old Baldy once, but otherwise I've mostly just ridden the main trails and up in the back country between Mount Rushmore and Harney Peak." Twocrow pulled the map he'd been using earlier out of his inside vest pocket and held it up. "But I saw Leaky Valley listed on this map when I was looking at it earlier today. Figured I might be riding up that way tomorrow after I made the trek up to Harney to talk with the fire spotting team.

"So, being flat and open, you're saying it should be a good spot for us to get on board?"

"If we can get them to stop."

"Oh, they'll stop," Twocrow had a determined glint in his eyes. "I didn't want to alarm the major and have him go all 'Government Control' on us, so I didn't tell him that if the engineer didn't want to stop, I'd be firing a couple warning shots to convince him."

Harold half-laughed and half-snorted at Twocrow's statement, but David looked alarmed. "I'm sure the engineer will pull over when he sees it's me standing there with you." He pointed at Harold. "And Harold, too. We've all known each other for years." Eyeing Twocrow's weapon, he added, "No need for any shooting; especially when we're all on the same side." The marshal just nodded and pulled out his pocket watch.

"It's nearly 4 o'clock," he said. "We better keep moving and get into position or it won't make any difference one way or the other because we won't even be there when the train rolls by."

"I think it'll be less than a half hour to get to Leaky Valley and if it don't look like the right spot for them to stop, we'll just keep riding on toward the Addie Camp. It'll take us a while but at least we'll be indoors before it gets dark."

"Okay." Twocrow rode closer to Harold and held out a hand to Ice who shifted his head and neck toward him and nuzzled his arm then snuffled at the big horse now carrying his owner. "Good boy," he said, rubbing Ice's neck and giving him a little tap on top of his head. Twocrow looked over at Harold's leg. "So how you doing? How's the leg?"

"Numb." Harold replied. He shrugged. "Ice is a good horse, but I'll be glad when we get to Leaky Valley and I can get down." He looked over at his father. "And Dad's probably not going to like hearing this, but I'm gonna need his help going to the bathroom." David looked over his shoulder and grimaced as Harold added, "Sorry dad, but I really gotta go. So, if you don't want to clean up a mess on the marshal's saddle . . ."

David grimaced again and waved his hand forward. "I get the picture son; let's get a move on." He clucked to his horse and headed back toward the creek. Harold grinned at Twocrow and added in a lower voice, "Actually, I can probably hold it a little longer, but I wanted to see if me sayin' that might rattle his cage."

* * * * *

"It's almost 4:30," Palmer closed his brother's pocket watch and slipped it back inside his vest, stretching out his legs from the wooden chair he had bolted into place near the front end of the caboose. Joseph Parker was sitting on a much smaller jump seat directly opposite him and just beyond a canvas cot that took up about a third of the car's wall on the right-hand side.

"I don't think there's any reason for us to stop at Addie Camp this afternoon," Palmer added. "We can make up some of our lost time if we just roll on through. We'll pull in there on the trip back first thing in the morning."

Joe pulled Carrie's handwritten sheet from his own pocket, read it and then handed it across to Palmer. "Mrs. Swanzey was hoping we could have her note here posted over in the Addie Camp office," he said. "Her boy's missing somewhere up around these parts, and I told her maybe we could get the miners to help keep an eye out for him when they're going back and forth to the dig."

Palmer read it and handed it back. "Sure, but we can have them post it first thing tomorrow. Gonna be dark here in a couple of hours and I can almost guarantee you that none of them are gonna be lookin' for anyone at night."

In the short time Parker had known Palmer he'd already learned that once the conductor made up his mind, it probably wasn't going to be changed. "Okay," he said, folding up the sheet and tucking it back into his coat pocket, looking off to the window side of the car to avoid Palmer seeing his expression of disappointment.

He shifted back around to facing the conductor. "So, what time you planning to head back tomorrow morning?"

"Six sharp, and . . ."

His voice was suddenly drowned out in mid-sentence as a blast from the train's whistle erupted around them, sharply cutting over his words and causing the conductor to leap to his feet. Giving Parker a questioning look, he jumped over to the window. Slamming it open, he leaned out and looked ahead toward where steam was rolling back in waves from the big engine. The whistle erupted again with another extended and deafening blast.

"What is it? What's happening?" Parker exclaimed.

"Emergency stop!" Palmer half-shouted as if trying to talk over the whistle even though it had stopped its sharp sound. As if to emphasize the "stop!" part, the train shuddered and began screeching in protest as the engineer applied the brakes. "Two long single horn blasts 15 seconds apart when you're not near a station means an emergency on the tracks! Usually needing a stop." Palmer leaned out further. "Don't know why, though. Can't see a damn thing with all that steam!" he grumbled as he pulled his head and shoulders back inside. He hurried toward the car's rear platform so he could get ready to jump down from the caboose and try to get a better look at what might be causing the emergency.

"Stay put!" he directed to Parker as he stepped through the rear door.

Ignoring the conductor's order, Joe got up and replaced him at the open window, leaning out for a look of his own just as the front of the train hit the track's bend where the rail line turned toward Leaky Valley. The engine and then the boxy water tender shifted to the right of a flat, grass-covered field where three men were waiting.

"Look, there's two riders and someone down on the ground, right alongside the tracks!" he exclaimed. "Can you see them?"

"Yeah, I got 'em!" Palmer responded as he climbed out onto a wrought iron ladder that was hooked sideways onto the back platform. The iron ladder was bent outward in the shape of a reverse modified L with a couple of steps that nearly touched the ground.

He took in a deep breath. "Listen to me," he admonished the postal worker as he stepped off the ladder and hurried forward alongside of where Joe was leaning out the window. "You can stay there but don't get down just yet. Okay?"

Parker nodded.

"I'm going forward to see what we've got." He moved past where Parker was still leaning from the window and waved toward where the riders were now much easier to see with the two largest train cars no longer blocking their line of sight and the engine's steam dissipating. They could both clearly see that three men, two on horseback, were waiting for the train to come to a complete stop.

"If I run into trouble, I'll try'n yell a warning," he said to Joe. "But if I don't yell and you can see I'm in some sort of trouble get your butt off the back end and hightail it for the woods." He pointed across the train coupling on his right. "If you cut across that hill on our north side,

Devil's Thumb

you'll be on line to get to the Addie Camp's main building. So just keep moving on a line to the northwest. Got it?"

Not waiting for Joe's response, he started forward again but only had gone about half a car length when suddenly one of the riders turned his horse around and started riding toward them. Seeing the man's action, Palmer stopped and looked beneath the car as if contemplating going under it.

"Be ready Joe! One of 'em is coming to get us!" Parker jerked his head back to get inside and stopped abruptly as the right side of his forehead banged into the corner of the window frame. "Ow!" He saw stars, closed his eyes and dropped his face forward. With his eyes still closed, he rubbed gently at the side of his temple as the horse's hoofbeats grew louder. Opening his eyes, he turned for one last look at the rider before trying to make his getaway.

"Oh," he shook his head slightly, paused and breathed a sigh of relief as the rider reined in next to Palmer and sunlight flashed off a lawman's badge pinned to the upper right side of the man's chest. "Joe Parker?" the rider called in his direction. "Ain't you supposed to be in Hermosa? Wasn't figurin' on seein' you out here."

"Hello marshal." Joe gave a weak nod toward where Al Twocrow was sitting sideways in his saddle looking in his direction.

"What you doin' hanging out of that window and why you even on board the train anyway?" The marshal sat straighter in the saddle and gave him a little wave, his silver U.S. Marshal's badge now shining even brighter as it reflected the late afternoon sun.

* * * * *

The train eased its way up alongside the railway platform that was fronting the Hill City Depot and creaked and groaned slowly ahead until all the cars from the engine all the way back to the caboose were butted up against it and easily accessible.

"Okay," Palmer said to Twocrow and David Swanzey as he popped open the back door and leaned inside, nearly striking Joe Parker on the other side of his head as he came barreling back in from the caboose's rear platform. "Oh, sorry, Joe," he apologized. "Forgot you were still behind there."

The conductor's body filled up the door's frame as the train shuddered to a complete stop and a new blast of steam came wafting back from the engine. The steam rolling along behind him gave Palmer an eerie halo look in the early evening sunlight. Parker glared at Palmer, gave him a cursory nod and scrunched back up against the wall, saying nothing.

On the other end of the car, Twocrow and David Swanzey stood holding onto leather straps attached to the roof of the car, not only maintaining their balance but also making sure that Harold Swanzey didn't roll off of the cot where they had placed him. The whole process of getting him into the caboose and then loading up their horses had used up the better part of an hour and now it was nearly 6:30 as they were pulling into the Depot.

"Engine'll be powering down now so you shouldn't have any problems getting your boy or your horses off loaded," Palmer continued. "I'll head inside and let them know why we're running so late and send somebody up to get the Doc. He started out then turned back. "Oh, and I'll try'n get someone to come down from the Blacksmith's to help unload your horses, too. They've helped us get livestock on and off before. They even got a little portable loading ramp they can move into place on the track side."

"Is the Doctor's office nearby?" David asked.

"Yes. Name's Amundson. Heck of a nice guy. His place ain't too far from here." He turned to face Parker. "Why don't you come with me Joe and we'll see if the Doc can help us rig up some sort of litter to make it easier to carry the boy. Then he won't have to try'n walk or shift around to get through the doorway."

Parker looked back toward David, got a quick nod of approval and hurried to exit and catch up with the conductor who was already climbing off the back ramp and onto the Depot's boardwalk.

"Look, marshal, I'll wait here with Harold if you want to get over to the CBQ's office and make your call up to the Harney Peak Fire spotters. The phone line from the lookout cabin connects right there, and there's also a connecting line running over to the police station next door. So, if there isn't anyone still around in the CBQ Office, just go into the police station. Somebody's in there 24 hours a day."

"Yeah, I better try to let them know I'll be heading up first thing in the morning. You know how long a ride it is from here up to the top of Harney?"

"It'll probably take you at least a couple hours. Probably about two or two-and-a-half if you get good weather," David said. "Only went up there once myself and that was a few years back. But I remember the trail being a good one and I'm sure it's only gotten better with all the hikers and other visitors who go up and back these days."

Twocrow reached over and gave Harold a pat on his shoulder. "I'll come by to check in with you at the Doc's office once I get everything arranged and make sure my horse is doing okay. How you feeling?"

"Kind of hot and really tired," Harold answered. "Think I must be getting a little sick from the injury, plus all the moving around."

"To be expected." He turned to face David. "I'll see you at the Doc's."

"Thanks, marshal. Don't know what we would've done without you."

Twocrow just shrugged and gave him a small smile before hurrying to the back of the car and out the door.

Chapter Twenty-One

"Your boy's going to be fine, but it'll be a couple more days before he can take the train back over to Keystone," Doctor Amundson said as David Swanzey looked anxiously past the doctor's shoulder toward the sleeping form of his son inside the doctor's office recovery room.

"So you'll just keep him here until then?"

"Yes. No sense in moving him around again. He's probably had enough of that."

Twocrow, who had been standing in the main office waiting area, walked over to join them. "Doc, you still okay to go with David back out to treat that wounded man we found on the west side of Mt. Rushmore?"

"Yes. Actually, I'm curious to see what that's all about. We don't get much excitement here on a day-in, day-out basis you know?" He chuckled but quickly sobered as neither Twocrow nor Swanzey joined in.

"Well, that's good. Good," Twocrow said. "You'll have to ride out first thing in the morning—on the early train. I'll help you put the horse I borrowed on board. He's big but pretty easy to ride. David, you'll need to arrange with the conductor to stop the train and let you off out by Leaky Valley. From there the two of you can ride down to Devil's Thumb to meet up with Major Goodman's posse.

"David knows the spot—but for your information, it's out on the west side of Rushmore. That's where they're waiting with the wounded man I told you about earlier.

"Your police chief has been very helpful too. He told me he'd send a couple of his men along to keep you and David company. Not that we're expecting any trouble," Twocrow hastened to add, "but I say it never hurts to be completely safe. Right?"

"Well, I'll be ready to go bright and early," the doctor said. He turned back toward David. "As for Harold, I've got someone coming over to be with him but you're welcome to sleep in the extra room here tonight, too."

David nodded and gave him a grateful smile.

"Just so you're prepared, Doc, you need to know that it might be the better part of two days before you're all through and get back here to Hill City," Twocrow added. "But whatever it costs you—time, medical supplies, whatever—either I or Major Goodman will make sure you get compensated."

"That's much-appreciated marshal, and like I said, it'll be something completely different from my usual routine so I really am looking forward to helping in any way that I can. Do you want me to ride with the posse back into Keystone after I patch up the guy that you found out there?"

"Yes. And then you should be able to come back on the train day after tomorrow."

"What about you? Sounds like you're not going with us. Where you planning on spending the night?"

"The Police have offered to put me up in the jail, since all the beds are unaccounted for. A bed's a bed, right?" The doctor nodded but grinned at the marshal's response. "And first thing tomorrow morning, soon as we get your horses on board, I plan to ride up to Harney to meet with the Fire spotting team." Noting the look of confusion on the doctor's face, he added, "It's all related to this." He expanded his arms as if that would explain everything. Still seeing a look of confusion on the doctor's face, he added, "Sorry Doc, but that's about all I'm able to share with you for now."

* * * * *

Sam Palmer checked the pocket watch and took a slow deep breath. It was already past 7:00 and he'd been warned that he would be putting his brother and everyone else in their family at risk if he didn't meet with Verne Miller by that time. He only knew Miller by reputation, but that reputation was a deadly one.

He was hopeful he could make his case about being stopped by a U.S. Marshal and being forced to transport an injured man into town. Miller would have to be understanding about something like that, wouldn't he?

He walked down a narrow alley leading off Main Street and emerged onto a street running along the back side of the now closed Hill City business district and fronted by a row of homes—the former now with darkened windows and the latter lit up for the night. He could see people moving about in the homes, settling in. Ignoring them, he turned down behind the business row and continued until he reached the last of the darkened buildings. Locating the back door, he knocked sharply.

Nothing.

He knocked again. Still nothing. "Cripes! Come on!" he said aloud. "It wasn't my fault! Miller, you gotta talk to me. Come on!"

He froze as a gun barrel pushed up against the back of his neck.

"That so? What ain't your fault?" Palmer shuddered and sucked in a sharp breath as the gun was cocked and moved from his neck down to the center of his back.

"Me bein' late, Mister Miller. I'm Palmer. Sam Pal . . ."

"Stuff it!" the man's rough voice cut him off. "Whatever it is you've got to say, you can say it to Mister Miller himself once we get inside. He's been waitin' and he don't like to be kept waitin'." The gun barrel moved up and down on Palmer's back as if urging him to step forward. And almost on cue the door in front of them swung inward to reveal an average-sized blond-haired man stepping into view, his head angelically haloed by the backlight of the ceiling bulb behind him.

Palmer blinked and sucked in sharply, taking an involuntary step backward even though his captor's gun's barrel was digging even further into the center of his back.

"Mister Miller, I . . ." Palmer started. He stopped and swallowed hard as the man suddenly came closer, the two or three-day growth of stubble jutting out from his chin as he leaned past the conductor's shoulder and looked beyond him and the man with the gun to be sure they had not been followed.

"Inside," Miller hissed, his voice quiet but imminently threatening.

The gun barrel in Palmer's back dipped slightly and the conductor glanced over his shoulder. By the look on his captor's face, it was clear to Palmer that the gunman also was cowed by the clearly dangerous man standing before them. Miller took a couple steps back to let them enter and as he moved further into the room's light, Palmer reacted with another slight shudder and thought he detected a similar reaction from his captor.

Now fully bathed in the light coming from the ceiling bulb, Miller stood glaring at them both. "We need to talk now about how you're planning to get me that whiskey, and tomorrow you better have a good plan to share with my friends when they join you on the train—for your sake AND for your brother's." His heavily lidded, large round eye sockets accented by very dark, very heavy eyebrows made it seem as if his eyes were about to pop out of his face.

The conductor swallowed hard and gave a little shudder. He thought they were the cruelest eyes he had ever seen.

* * * * *

"Oh, thank God! That's such great news."

Carrie was standing behind the counter in the Keystone Depot speaking into the wall telephone's mouthpiece while holding the receiver up against her right ear.

"Harold's alive," she gushed in Minnie's direction. "David is with him over in Hill City and he'll spend the night at the doctor's office," she said to her friend.

"Oh, that's Minnie I'm sharing the good news with," Carrie said back into the phone while reaching out to squeeze Minnie's hand as her friend came around the counter to stand beside her. "What? Oh, David, that's really great to hear. I'll share it with her."

She put her hand across the mouthpiece. "Alvin is there, too. He met up with the posse, and then went with David and Harold over to Hill City."

Minnie gasped and her eyes filled with tears at the news. Carrie reached out and patted her on the arm and gave her a warm smile before speaking again into the mouthpiece. "Will you all be coming back on the morning train?"

She listened intently before nodding an affirmation at what she was being told. "Oh, okay, are you sure? Yes, I understand." She breathed out a long sigh. "And I think the doctor is right. Harold should stay there a couple days at least. You can take the train back over to get him on Monday or Tuesday. What about Alvin?"

She listened again and nodded toward Minnie. "I'll tell her."

"He says Alvin needs to go up to Harney Peak in the morning. He'll come back to Keystone later tomorrow. Probably on the afternoon train."

Minnie brushed away her tears and nodded, then reached out toward her friend. "Can you ask him about my riding back on the train tomorrow?"

Carrie listened intently; the receiver pressed up tight to her right ear. "Oh. You already knew that Minnie was hoping to ride the train over to Hill City in the morning. How'd you know about that?"

She put her hand over the mouthpiece again and spoke across it toward her friend. "He said Conductor Palmer told him and asked if he would okay it so that he—Palmer—wouldn't have to go through all the hassle of talking to the management folks in the morning. Sounds like they arrived there too late today for him to ask permission." She brightened at what she continued to hear as Minnie anxiously leaned toward her, trying to listen in on what was being said. "Oh, that would be wonderful David. Thank you so much."

She turned to speak to Minnie, her hand across the mouthpiece for a third time. "He said it's okay for you to ride. He'll take full responsibility."

Minnie grabbed her friend's shoulders and grinned before leaning toward the mouthpiece. Pushing Carrie's hand aside, she said, "Thank you dear David! You're a great friend and I really, really appreciate it."

She leaned away and Carrie smiled as she listened again. "He says, no problem, but you owe him big time. Maybe a dinner at the Evans Hotel in Hot Springs."

"Anytime. Anytime!" Minnie half-shouted at the mouthpiece. "Besides, it's about time the two of you got back down to Hot Springs for a visit. It's been years, you know?"

"Oh, he knows," Carrie continued to smile, and then sobered as she spoke again into the phone. "Listen, I'll be here with Minnie when the train comes in tomorrow morning so if you need me to send anything back to Harold just write me a message and give it to conductor

Palmer." She listened intently and smiled again. "I love you too. Be safe."

She cradled the receiver back onto the side hooks on the boxy telephone, gave a long sigh and started to cry. Minnie grabbed her friend's shoulders, and they stood in a long embrace before she held her back out away from her. "Come on, let's get back to your house and I'll get my bags ready to go. I am so very grateful for everything you've been doing, for David's approval of the ride, AND to know that Harold and Alvin are both safe."

They turned to where Depot Manager Floyd Marston was fidgeting with some papers, trying not to look like he'd been listening in.

"Thank you, Floyd, for coming right over to get me and for setting up this call. I know it's a pain to make all these connections and I'm very grateful." Minnie walked away from Carrie over to the big man and gave him a big hug. Looking embarrassed and turning slightly red in the face, Floyd just made a harrumphing noise and pointed toward the door.

"I'll give you a ride back home then," he said. "This has been a very long day for you," he nodded toward Minnie, too, and then touched his chest. "For all of us, as far as that goes. Thankfully, the worst is over, and things are going to get back to normal."

As he locked up the Depot's front door, Minnie and Carrie walked over toward his car just as a young woman with platinum colored blond hair, her arm firmly latched onto a rough-looking man's right arm, rounded the corner of the Depot walking along the boardwalk that connected between the Depot and the nearby Keystone Hotel.

"Evening ladies. Gent," the man tipped his bowler style hat with his left hand and pulled the woman up tighter to his body with his right arm. Then he gave them all a little grin as the young woman giggled at their shocked faces. He looked at Marston again. "Keeping pretty late hours here, ain't you? Didn't realize the Depot was still open or we'd a come by sooner."

Floyd frowned at the couple. "Oh yeah, what for?" He eyed them suspiciously. "You two must be visiting in our fair community? Can't recall seein' you around before."

"Just in town for a couple days. Came in by car this afternoon. We were just talkin' on how we need to send a telegram on over to Rapid City, but figured we was way too late for today." He looked at the key in Floyd's hand and then over at the door.

"Sorry, but you are," Floyd said, reacting to the man's look. "Can't help you tonight. I'm closed." Marston slipped the key into his coat pocket. "Now if you'll excuse me, I need to get these ladies back to their home." He pulled out his pocket watch. "So, you come back first thing tomorrow—I'll open by 8—and I can take care of you then. That's the best I can do for you Mister . . ."

"Kaufman." He didn't make a move to shake hands, and an angry look flashed across his bobbed haired companion's face. She started to pull her arm away to reach for a bag hanging from a string on her right arm, but Kaufman held her in tighter and gave her a slight shake of his head. She made a sharp little gasp at his sudden reaction and then looked up at him with a tight smile before leaning back into his side.

"That time'll work just fine for us, now won't it Clara?"

The woman glanced over to where Minnie and Carrie were standing by Floyd's car watching the exchange and then looked back at the big man. "Yeah, I suppose it'll have to," she said with a little growl in her voice. "But we'll be back here at 8 a.m. sharp. You can count on it."

Chapter Twenty-Two

It had been a picture-perfect early morning when Twocrow and Black Ice started their ride up the trail from Hill City to Harney Peak. But shortly after 8:00 the wind speed had started to rise and clouds moved in, and now dust was swirling around them as they followed the rocky trail ever upward.

Their destination was a small cabin, constructed of rock, native pine and heavy-duty glass and serving as the U.S. Forest Service's Harney Peak Fire Spotting Station. Despite talk by the Forest Service that it planned to build a road up to the structure, horseback and hiking were still the only ways up. For the past hour the little structure had been in their sights, but the trail's seemingly endless twists and turns had slowed their pace, and now they were hampered even more by the wind.

Twocrow had been up and around since dawn, first arranging for the horses that David Swanzey and Doctor Amundson would need and then meeting with Conductor Palmer and the two Hill City police officers to make sure that they and their horses also were on board. Finally, he had signed off on an authorization verifying that the U.S. Marshals Service needed the train to make a stop for the 4 men and the animals to disembark at Leaky Valley.

Once all that was completed, he had bid them a safe and successful trip, saddled Ice and embarked on his own trip up to the top of the Black Hills' largest mountain.

Despite the unexpected blustery weather, the ride had gone fairly smoothly, and he anticipated getting to the top in the planned three hours. And despite its many twists and turns, the route from Hill City was a lot faster than the winding trail he had been riding the previous morning out of Keystone. But now, as he rode, Twocrow looked nervously toward another problem—an ever-growing bank of ominous clouds overwhelming the other clouds along the northwest horizon.

"That's definitely not looking real good for us is it partner?" Twocrow gave his horse a reassuring pat. "We need to get to the top before it starts raining and blowing or we're going to find ourselves back down at the bottom real quick." The marshal eyed the shale and clay trail with trepidation, thankful that only last week he had Ice's shoes replaced. He couldn't be positive, but he was pretty sure that trying to negotiate on clay and shale in the rain would be like trying to ride along an ice shelf.

A wind gust lashed at them and the horse turned his head to join his rider in looking at the ominous buildup on the horizon. Ice snorted in alarm as a second wind gust smacked them with stinging bits of sand and twigs. Without any urging the sturdy little Mustang resumed his climb toward the small glass and wood frame structure that Twocrow could now see was anchored by steel cables into the solid granite surface that made up most of the peak's summit.

A figure appeared in front of the building, and despite the clothing being a man's, the long hair blowing in the increasingly strong wind indicated it might be and probably was a woman. She waved her arms, first toward him and then together off to her right and his left. Twocrow and Ice moved forward until they reached a point where they could either go straight or veer left. He returned her wave to show her that the message had been received and turned Ice along the path's left leading branch.

After 30 or 40 yards, the narrow trail switched back toward a gap in the rocks. Ice pulled up, eyeing the gap with suspicion. Twocrow climbed down, pulled the reins forward and wrapped them firmly around his right forearm. Ignoring the wind's noise, he stepped into the rock-walled passageway that was about two horses wide and 10 feet tall on either side.

Inside the natural granite, open-topped tunnel the wind's howl almost immediately dissipated and so did the alarmed look in Ice's eyes.

"Okay old man," the marshal said reassuringly. "Glad we were paying attention. We're definitely on the right path now."

They advanced for another 30 yards, made a slight turn back to the left and were surprised to see the woman standing at the far end of the passageway. "Marshal Twocrow is that you?" She called out toward them and gave a little wave from just above her waist.

"Yes!" He pulled his badge free from his vest and held it up for her to see, then again returned her wave while continuing to move ahead.

"Come straight out the end of this chute and make a sharp right turn!" she called. "You'll find a lean-to up against the side of the cliff over there. You can stable your horse inside it and then come on inside." She started to go but turned back. "Take the backside stairs! They're on the right! Away from the wind!" Her instructions echoed off the side of the walls, which were still sheltering them from both the force and noise of the ever-growing storm.

Then she was gone before he could respond. Seeing the roiling dust filled with pieces of branches blowing overhead, Twocrow turned and spoke to his horse. "Hopefully she didn't blow away." Seeming to be in agreement, Ice bobbed his head and snuffed in response.

* * * * *

Twocrow was halfway up the stairs—which were more like a slightly glorified ladder than actual stairs—when the woman's face reappeared, now leaning out over the edge of a trapdoor style opening that led onto a small platform alongside the cabin's back door.

"Watch your step," she called down, "but hurry if you can. There's a lot more lightning and the last place you want to be in a lightning storm is on top of a bunch of metal stairs."

He nodded in agreement and picked up his pace, scrambling up the last half-dozen steps and through the opening onto the platform. The little square house shuddered as a blast of wind hit it. A flash of light followed by a large bang followed as a lightning bolt streaked across the sky directly above them, clearly visible through the cabin's mostly glass walls. The woman was holding the door open and Twocrow ducked inside.

"That lightning's getting a little too close for comfort," the woman said. "Step on over to the middle of the room and sit yourself down in one of these chairs." She went ahead of him and plopped down into one of three overstuffed chairs that were facing a strange looking circular disc. The contraption was mounted on top of a four-foot-high square table with a topographic map on its surface.

Twocrow quickly took another of the chairs and eyed the device. Its rotating disc was made mostly of glass with two slender sighting towers attached across from each other and connected over the top of the disc by a narrow metal strip.

"This is our Osborne. Part of my daily responsibilities," the woman said, noting the curious look on the marshal's face. She stretched out her hand toward him. "I'm Clarice Byers, by the way. My husband Ralph and I are the chief fire spotters. Got your message yesterday that you were headed our way but probably wouldn't get here before now. And I really appreciated your follow-up call last night. Glad you made it up here safe and sound."

"Me, too," he answered, reaching out to shake her hand. "Al Twocrow. I'm the deputy marshal out of Hot Springs, but guess you already know that. I appreciate your taking the time to meet with me. Didn't expect to be riding into a storm or I might've held off until a little later in the day. Your husband busy battening down the hatches?"

"Nope. He had to go down to Rapid City yesterday afternoon to pick up our supplies. But now with this storm, he'll probably stay over there until it blows over. I'll just hold down the fort and keep an eye out for any flare-ups while he's gone. Always a bigger chance of a fire starting when the wind and lightning together get bad like this. And the pack mules he uses to bring our supplies up here don't much like taking the trail in the wind and lightning either. But who can blame 'em, eh?"

As if to reinforce her statement, the sky above them lit up again, quickly followed by another rattling boom. Fat raindrops started pelting the house's glassed-in walls and the little structure shuddered even more than it had before.

"He takes pack mules all the way down to Rapid?"

"Oh my, no," she laughed. "There's a Forest Service truck that goes from Hill City to Rapid City and back; he loads up the mules there. It usually takes the better part of a day."

Twocrow looked around at the hut's living quarters, which were divided by the big disc dominating the structure's center and east side. On the southeast corner of the device was a small bedroom and to the northeast was a kitchen. The west half, with about a fourth of the machine jutting into it, provided a living room, of sorts, with the overstuffed chairs serving as a dividing line in the center.

Most of the other furnishings were hand-hewn chairs and tables of various shapes and sizes. Even the bed frame was rough cut from the Black Hills' native pine.

"My husband made most of this furniture himself," Clarice said, a hint of pride in her voice as she said it. "Had to bring it up those stairs a piece at a time over the years, but it's comfortable for us and a good summer living space. We both are enrolled in forestry courses back in

Iowa during the school year, but this has been our home from May to October for several years now." She laughed. "Well, our home and a stopping off point for several thousand hikers and tourists who think that anything out here is as much theirs as it is ours."

"You get a lot of tourists?"

"Except on a stormy weather day like this. Had more than 7,000 last year and I think we'll make it to at least 9,000 through October, which is the 'official' end of the 1925 'season' for us. Even though it only covers 6 months, it's going to be a record year for sure. And we're thinking that if that carving project goes through over on Rushmore, thousands more are sure to be coming each season. Maybe even 25 or 30 thousand a year."

Twocrow gave a little whistle. "Wow, must take some doing to get used to working with all those people around and trying to deal with something like this, too?" Twocrow pointed at the swirling storm clouds and shrank in tighter to the center of his chair as more lightning flashed across the sky. He looked nervously around him. "So, all this glass holds up okay in this kind of wind and lightning, huh? Seems a little fragile if you ask me."

"Well, it's heavy duty and triple paned," Clarice answered. "In all our seasons up here, we've never even had a small crack or a chip despite all the hail, rocks and debris that we get hit with during some of these storms. Building's anchored with steel cables so even when we get all this shaking there's little chance anything's going to break or fall down. The Forest Service knows how important it is that we stay operational in all kinds of weather."

"My hat's off to you," Twocrow said. He lightly tipped his Stetson then pointed at the circular disc. "You called that thing your Osborne. Is that official or just a nickname?"

"Official. Every fire spotting site in the country has one and you can find them in some big city fire departments too. Name comes from the guy who developed them. Well, actually, 'perfected' them. William Osborne. Some guy in England first came up with the idea about 75 or 80 years ago and then Osborne adapted them for fire spotting here in the States about 10 years back." She pointed at the taller of the two sighting towers.

"You look through this taller one across through the other one and pinpoint a fire's location in the crosshairs that are on that smaller one." She grabbed a little round knob along the side of the disc and rotated it toward Twocrow. "Once you have the sights lined up to whatever it is that you see—whether it's smoke, flames, or something else—you can 'find' that spot on the topographic map that you see laid out on the table's top. It's really genius. You can pinpoint a fire's location—or anything else for that matter—to within a very close proximity."

"Like unexplained smoke plumes that come and go, for example?"

"Yes, just like that. That's why we contacted you," she said. "It's what we've been seeing pop up for the past few weeks now. So, when we got the message that the Marshal's Service and the Pennington County Sheriff's office were on the lookout for Bootleggers or anything unusual that we might've seen, like smoke where it shouldn't be, it clicked in that we might have at least one answer for you. But you'll have to look for yourself, I suppose, in order to be certain."

Twocrow started to stand to look at it closer, but she waved him back into the chair.

"Not now!" she admonished. "The storm ought to pass over in the next 30 minutes or so. Best to not get too close to metal objects until the lightning has moved away. My best advice to visitors is that you don't want to be the object that 'grounds' a lightning strike, if you know what I mean?"

She chuckled as she spoke, but Twocrow just shuddered and shrank back down into his chair.

Chapter Twenty-Three

"Can you tell me the general area where you've been seeing those smoke plumes?" Twocrow focused on his fire spotter host as he spoke, trying to take his mind off the lightning flashes and thunder that now seemed to be enveloping them.

"Sure," Clarice answered. "The one we started seeing first has been west of Mount Rushmore on a direct line toward where Horse Thief Creek and Pine Creek meet—if we've calibrated it properly." She paused and nodded at the Osborne. "And I can pretty much guarantee you that we've calibrated it properly."

"Good to know."

"But during the last few days we also spotted some smoke plumes off on the north side of the CBQ rail line that runs west out of Keystone, a bit northwest of Old Baldy. That smoke's been appearing off-and-on, too, more like we sometimes see from a campfire. The earlier smoke plumes were more like something coming out of a chimney, although that didn't seem to make any sense since there aren't any cabins over there."

"So, smoke like that—chimney smoke—would be weird coming from that location, I take it?"

"Yes, really strange if you ask me," she chuckled. "And guess you just did, huh?"

"But you definitely viewed two different smoke sources, especially during the last few days?"

"Yes. If you know the Hills, I'm sure you'll know where we've been seeing both smoke sources once you get a look-see with our machine."

"Well, I DO know the Hills, but I can't say I've ever ridden through that back country out on the west side of Old Baldy. I was over near Devil's Thumb yesterday . . . that's where Pine Creek and Horse Thief come together," he hastened to add as a blank look crossed her face. "From there we rode north and got on the train at Leaky Valley but that's about as far north as we got."

"Never been to that area myself," she said. "Was it your search for the Bootleggers that took you over to the Devil's Thumb area, marshal?" She leaned forward to hear him better as the wind's intensity increased and the howling grew louder.

"Well, yes and no. I was riding over to check on the report of a body being spotted in the valley out along the east side of Pine Creek. And then we came across a couple of bodies actually. Two men dead, another one wounded."

"No kidding. Was it somebody local?" She paused. "You said 'we.' I thought you were riding alone?"

"I don't think either of the dead men was from around these parts, but we haven't finished our I.D. yet. And I said 'we' because I met up with a sheriff's posse riding out of Keystone. They found one of the dead men and the wounded one before I hooked up with them. The sheriff's office down in Rapid thinks those bodies might be related to a gang of outlaws who supposedly escaped up into the Hills out of Denver. They don't think they're the Bootleggers, but I'm not so sure.

"The rumor is that the outlaw gang drove up here from Denver after robbing a federal reserve bank's truck and then hitting another smaller bank right after. But I don't think that they were the ones we found shot. I'm betting instead that the gang might be the ones who were doing the shooting.

"And as for the victims, that's a whole different story. I think there's a real good chance they ARE a part of the bootlegging operation, and they had some sort of run-in with the bank robbing gang. And that's probably what got them killed."

"So, the posse found one dead man plus the other one who was wounded. And you? You were by yourself when you found the second dead man?"

"Yes. Actually happened a couple hours before I even met up with the posse. I found the other man's body inside the Calendar Mine. And just like those other two men, he'd been shot."

"The Calendar Mine? I don't think I've ever heard of that."

"It's an old ghost mine alongside the Tenderfoot Creek. That's why I think the dead men might be related to the bootlegging operation, because the mine was all set up to take water in from the creek to run through a still that was being used to brew the whiskey."

Clarice made a little gasp and Twocrow continued.

"I was riding down along the Tenderfoot toward where it empties into Pine Creek to check on a report I'd received about a different body—probably the one the posse found—when I stumbled onto the entrance to the mine. Like I said, after seeing the still's setup in there I'm pretty sure that that ghost mine is the location of the bootlegging operation we've been getting reports about."

"Oh my." She shook her head. "So, the smoke we've been seeing over the past few weeks has probably been coming out of that mine." She brightened. "And, of course, it would've been coming out of some sort of chimney, right?" She looked out toward Mount Rushmore. "And that's why it looked like chimney smoke. Makes sense."

"Right." He nodded toward the Osborne. "But I still thought I better check your sightings, just to be sure that they match up with what we discovered yesterday. If so, that would be at least one mystery out of the way."

"One? You mean there are more?"

"Well, we still don't know who killed those two men and wounded the third one? When we found him, he was unconscious, both from being shot and probably from hitting his head when he fell from his horse in the process. His horse was dead, too. When I left the posse yesterday, he hadn't regained consciousness, so we hadn't learned anything about who did the shooting, or why he even got into a shootout as far as that goes."

"But you're thinking it might be that gang that robbed the banks in Denver? You think they might be the ones responsible for the most recent campfire smoke we've been seeing?"

"Yeah, I do. And if I'm right, your sightings could make all the difference in our stopping them before they can do any more harm." He shifted in the chair. "Anyway, I'm sorry about the delay in getting up here. All that stuff happening yesterday put my scheduled check in with you on hold."

Clarice pointed at a telephone hanging from one of the wooden panels next to the little hut's door. "That telephone makes it so much easier to get and send out messages. Like I said, I was glad to get your message yesterday afternoon and know not to expect your arrival until today. We'd been on the lookout for you until that call came in. Appreciate it."

"Sure thing. I have a pilot friend I connected with earlier yesterday and she did me the favor. Glad she got through to you."

"She? You've got a woman pilot friend?"

"Kallie Sinclair. Been flying a regular route back and forth between Custer and Rapid City for a few days now and I guess she'll be continuing it for the next few weeks, carrying dispatches for the Army."

"A woman pilot. If that don't beat all. And I thought being a woman fire spotter was unusual. World's changing fast these days, isn't it?"

He nodded then jumped as another lightning bolt flashed in the window directly behind him. In less than a second it was followed by a deafening crash of thunder that filled the room.

"Was that over by the stable? You think the horses are okay?"

"The rock overhang there is pretty protective, so I'm sure they're fine, although your mount will probably be a lot more spooked about it than mine. Mine's used to it."

A pitch-black wave of clouds washed over them and suddenly the cabin was engulfed in near total blackness lit up only by intermittent flashes of lightning. The cabin's windows rattled from the mixture of hail and debris being lashed across them from the full force of the storm as it passed over them. Then almost as suddenly as it had arrived the storm started to move away. Just like that both the lightning flashes and the aftereffects of the resulting thunder grew fainter as the storm continued moving down along the mountain's southeast side.

Simultaneously the rain and hail began to ease up and the grinding, banging noises on the glass turned to a gentler swishing sound.

Almost immediately the cabin's windows started to brighten as the edge of the sun broke through from beneath the clouds and now the next wave to wash across them turned into one of rain-filled sunshine.

"Holey moley!" Twocrow pointed toward the sunshine and clearing skies to the north and west and back at the lightning flashes and ominous black skies still dominating to the southern and eastern skies.

"I know," Clarice responded. "It's the craziest thing you can imagine. And in a few more minutes after the rain moves further south, we'll probably have the most spectacular rainbow you've ever seen fronting those black skies over to the east. It's nature's way to wrap it all up."

She pushed up from her chair and waved around the room. "Once it's all clear you'll be able to see into four states from up here, counting this one of course. We get a clear shot off toward Nebraska, Wyoming and Montana, and I swear on some days I can see North Dakota too."

"It's no wonder my ancestors called the Black Hills the Center of the Earth," he said with reverence in his voice. "For them, it truly was."

"For most of us they still are," she added.

Twocrow nodded with an appreciative look on his face as he stood to admire the beauty of a double rainbow now fronting the receding black clouds in the southeastern sky.

Chapter Twenty-Four

"So, this is the spot where we've been seeing the regular plumes of smoke two or three times a day. Maybe for half hour and up to an hour at a time," Clarice was reaching down to touch the map as she spoke. "They started appearing about three weeks ago and have been continuing pretty much like clockwork. Early morning, then around noon or early in the afternoon—1 p.m. or so—and then early evening. Could be there has been smoke at night, too, but we couldn't see that, of course.

"At first, we were thinking it might be a group of campers or maybe a surveying team, but they probably wouldn't be in the same dang spot every single day at the same times like that, plus there's the smokestack effect, not just a bunch of smoke. When we were notified about the possibility of a bootlegging operation we knew right away we should call it in as something suspicious." She stepped back and looked across at Twocrow. "So, this definitely might be what you've been looking for?"

"Ummmm, yeah," Twocrow responded. He lifted his head from where he had been bent over looking through the taller tower's eyepiece and then down at the location that Clarice had pinpointed on the map. It showed the topographical outline of the hills and thin blue lines representing the many different creeks and streams running through them.

"And THAT spot looks very familiar. I'm pretty sure that's where I found the Calendar Mine's entrance."

He walked around to where Clarice was standing and pointed to a spot where the Tenderfoot Creek emptied out into Pine Creek. "See that open area there on the map? That's the grassy area on the upslope side along the Pine where the posse' found one of the dead men and the man who was wounded. We think it's the same spot where someone took a couple shots at a Keystone local who was up there doing a little prospecting. That's why the posse was out there in the first place, looking for the person who shot at him."

He leaned in and pointed to a couple of rocky outcroppings between the grassy location and Mount Rushmore. "And this is Devil's Thumb where my friend Kallie thought she saw a body from her plane. You can see on your map how it also overlooks that same grassy spot alongside the creek. Everything comes together near Devil's Thumb."

He reached into his vest pocket and pulled out his own map that he had been using on his search the day before. Opening it, he located Devil's Thumb and then turned it so that it was in line with the bigger one on the Fire spotting table.

Clarice looked in closer at her map and then over at his, and then back to the spot where she and her husband had pinpointed the campfire smoke's location. "So, you think the dead man out near the creek and the one you found in the mine are probably connected to the whiskey still, but that it might be those bank robbers who did the shooting?"

"Yes."

"But why would they shoot at the Bootleggers?"

Twocrow shrugged. "Only thing I can figure is that the Bootleggers thought the gang members were either the law or someone trying to home in on their territory. And the gang members probably thought it was someone after them and they both just started shooting."

"Stupid. So, two outlaw gangs were probably fighting each other."

"Yeah, most criminals aren't real smart about things like that." Twocrow pointed up closer to where Clarice was standing. "Where was the area that you mostly saw the campfire smoke?"

She pointed toward Old Baldy.

Devil's Thumb

"That's up near where they can get onto an old horse trail that goes down toward Rapid isn't it?" She leaned in for a closer look and pointed to where a trail was outlined off to the northwest of the bald topped mountain. Tapping forcefully on the tabletop map she said, "Right here."

Twocrow walked back beside her, turned his map around once more and stared from it to the new location, then held it toward her. "Here, right?" She nodded. "You got a pencil I can circle this on my map?"

She reached into her jacket pocket and pulled one out. "Always carry one, and some paper," she said, holding up a folded sheet. "You never know. Like now." She smiled as she handed the pencil his way.

"It looks like they're in a prime spot to get themselves packed up and moved out on a moment's notice," Twocrow circled the corresponding spot on his handheld map and tapped the pencil down for emphasis. "And now that they've had this shootout, they've got to be thinking that they can't hang around in the Hills too much longer. It'll get too hot, too fast, for them to stay here."

He was interrupted by the jangling of the wall phone, a noise he wasn't used to hearing and one that made him jump. Then he gave a little nervous laugh as Clarice hurried over to answer as the marshal refolded the map and stuck it back in his vest pocket.

"Hello! Who? Oh, yes? Yes chief, he's still here." She gave him a curious look and held out the receiver. "It's the Hill City police chief. He wants to talk to you."

Twocrow edged over, handed back her pencil and took the receiver. Holding it awkwardly against his ear, he leaned in to talk into the mouthpiece. "Hello?" He listened intently, his face growing more concerned. "What? When? . . . And Palmer's going to be all right?" He looked over at Clarice as he continued listening. "What! Are you sure? I didn't even know she was up here!"

His face grew pale as he listened further, nodding. "All right. Well, you try and get ahold of Major Goodman over in Keystone and let him know. He's leading the posse that's looking for that gang. Tell him I'll ride that way to join him as soon as I can. Thank you Chief. Glad you could reach me."

He handed the receiver back to Clarice and she listened for a few seconds, nodded and said, "Yes. Thank you," before hanging up. She turned to face him. "Bad news?"

"Yes. The Keystone Depot got robbed and they're pretty sure it's that gang we've been searching for—the ones who probably are making that campfire smoke. Anyway, they knocked out the stationmaster, got onto the train and then bashed the conductor in the head before jumping off at that slowdown point out in Leaky Valley." He paced over to the window. "Palmer's going to be all right, but he said they took a woman hostage who was riding the train from Keystone to Hill City. And the woman they took is my friend Minnie Thompson. She's a reporter for the *Hot Springs Star*."

Chapter Twenty-Five

"So, we need to track them down soon, because once they start moving on, we'll be hard-pressed to find them again. And, even more important, I'm afraid for my friend's life."

Twocrow turned back toward the Osborne. "Show me again EXACTLY where you were seeing those plumes of campfire smoke during the past few days?"

Clarice walked around and rotated the Osborne's wheel to her left, calibrated the two spotting devices across the top of it and pointed again at the topographical map. "Right there. Like I said, it's just northwest of the Old Baldy Mountain and north of the CBQ rail line. If you look closer, you can see there's a trail that goes out there too. I think it is called the mesa trail because it runs through a spot called the Enchanted Mesa above Moonlight Valley."

Twocrow moved over a few more steps alongside of the map to where she was pointing and ran his finger through the air, tracing an imaginary line from the top of Harney Peak over to the campfire smoke's location.

Then he frowned at the map. "It's probably a pretty long horseback ride from here over to there, ain't it?"

"Yes. You would have to start out now and camp somewhere tonight, because you don't want to ride through that rough terrain in the dark. But if you got going again early tomorrow you could probably make it there by mid-to-late morning. But that's only if the weather cooperates and you don't hit any deadfall blockages across the trails.

"Or you could wait here and start out in the morning. Then you would probably be there before dark tomorrow. The third option is to go back to Hill City and get on board the afternoon train when it goes back over to Keystone."

"Well, like I said, I'm worried that if it is that bank robbing gang, they're probably not going to be hanging around the hills much longer, especially now that they've got a hostage. And they've already killed a couple people, so they definitely aren't against using violence to get what they want.

"I think I have to go get on the train because no matter what time I get there tomorrow they could be packed up and long gone. And who knows what they'll do with my friend Minnie." He put a hand across his face for a few seconds, then gathered himself and looked back at the Osborne.

"Did you see any more smoke from that location today, before I got here?"

"Yes. It was pretty clear earlier, before those clouds started rolling in and covering it up."

Twocrow stared out the window as a flock of birds winged their way past, seemingly celebrating the passing of the storm. "Too bad I'm not a bird. I could just fly over there and find them."

Clarice joined him to watch as the flock continued on a path toward Mount Rushmore. "Maybe you could have your pilot friend come and pick you up? She could fly you over there."

Twocrow contemplated her remark and looked down from the window to where the ground dropped away from them on all sides. "She told me there were no landing spots for a plane up here."

"Not up here at the top, but there's a mesa about halfway between here and Keystone where a plane could probably put down."

"Yes, that's the spot where she landed, and we talked yesterday morning. But it's still a long horseback ride from here down to there.

Devil's Thumb

By the time we connected it'd probably be too dark for her to take off again today. So, I wouldn't really save that much time."

"Well, you COULD ride down on the west side of our mountain." She pointed back behind him. "There's a little unmarked trail that leads to an old sheepherding cabin that the CBQ has converted into a way station. It's right out alongside their rail line that runs between Hill City and Custer, where the tracks cross over the south fork of the Tenderfoot Creek."

"Tenderfoot? You mean like . . .?"

"Yes, it's the same stream you were on yesterday when you found that ghost mine. It also has a fork over on this side of the mountain."

She walked around to join him and pointed to the west. "The trail from here winds through this bit of forest that you can see just below our cabin, and then it turns past those large granite outcroppings you can see down there. Once it crosses the stream you can pretty much follow the stream the rest of the way, even if you get off the trail.

"It's a gradual drop from there to the rail line cabin. With nothing to slow you down, you should be able to get there in about three quarters of an hour, maybe an hour tops. There's a nice grassy spot stretching out between the cabin and the foothills. I'm sure if your pilot is worth her salt, she can easily put down and take off from that location. Do you think your friend could handle it?"

Twocrow pictured Kallie's "devil-may-care" look when she'd popped out of her plane after landing on the grassy field west of Hot Springs, and then the way she'd calmly and coolly brought her plane down on top of the mesa the previous morning. "Definitely. And she told me yesterday that she'd be staying overnight and flying back from Custer to Rapid this afternoon. So, she should still be hanging around down there—probably already gassed up and ready to fly."

Clarice nodded at the telephone. "We can call back to the Forest Service headquarters or the police in Hill City and they can relay a message down to the sheriff's office in Custer. The Custer Sheriff will know where the military units are set up and get the word to your friend that you need to be picked up. That is if you think she'll fly up here and get you."

He thought about her pledge to him the day before and nodded. "Yes, I do. Especially if she hears about Minnie being taken. I know if she gets that message she'll come up and get me, no problem." He paced over to look out the window and then turned back. "But what about Ice?"

"About . . . what?"

"Oh. That's my horse. Name's Black Ice but I call him Ice. What will I do with him while we're out flying around in the Hills?"

Clarice laughed. "No problem, marshal. If your pilot can meet you at the way station, you can just stable your horse out back of there until you return. We've gone down there a couple of times to catch the train to Custer and once we even went on a couple of days' trip out to Cheyenne. They've got a nice little stable and corral with plenty of feed and water. Just give the caretaker a couple dollars for the hay and his trouble."

Twocrow turned back to the window so Clarice wouldn't see him swallowing hard at the thought of getting into Kallie's biplane and flying up and down through the Hills. "Oh, hell," he muttered. "Why not?"

He pointed at the telephone. "All right let's do it. Get back on your telephone and ring them up for me."

Chapter Twenty-Six

The train was scheduled to leave at 9:30. Was that a whistle? Was it 9:30? Was she moving?

Minnie needed to find out. She couldn't miss her ride. She opened her eyes, but everything seemed grey. Her head was fuzzy, and she felt "floaty," but she was pretty sure she was sitting down. She looked around for some sort of verification and realized she not only was sitting but also was tied to a chair in the center of the aisle at the front end of the CBQ caboose.

She groaned as a throbbing pain shot through both her head and her arms as she tried to shift positions. But she could barely move. Struggling against both the ropes that were holding her down and the fogginess permeating her brain, she tried to talk.

"MMMph! Mmmph!" She opened her eyes wider in alarm, realizing for the first time that there was a gag in her mouth.

The bobbed haired, platinum blond woman from the previous evening came walking toward her from the back doorway area of the car, which was bumping along on the tracks with a noisy clack clack clack. As the woman swayed sideways from the train's motion, Minnie could see the Conductor, Sam Palmer, leaning back against the train car's far wall and just off to one side of the rear entry door. Unlike Minnie, he didn't have a gag in his mouth, but his hands appeared to be tied behind his back and latched onto an eyebolt that was anchored into that same back wall.

"So, you're finally awake."

The woman reached Minnie's side and looked back toward Palmer just as the car's rear door popped open and the rough-looking man Minnie had seen with the woman the evening before and again with Floyd

Marston at the Keystone Depot's counter stepped over the metal sill and into the car.

"How's the old bag doing?" The man grabbed a ceiling strap to balance himself against the car's rocking motion and pointed toward Minnie as he spoke.

"She just came to. Side of her head is still bloody. Cripes, Jank, when I said hit her, I didn't mean hard enough to kill her." She swung back toward Minnie and a wave of her heavy perfume flowed along with the motion causing Minnie to cough. "Haven't tried talking with her yet." She reached over to Minnie and pulled the cloth down from her mouth, letting it loosely hang around her neck. "So, you heard Jank. You doing okay?"

Minnie squeezed her eyes shut and then reopened them and tried shifting again in the little chair. "Head hurts," she finally mumbled. She turned her head to the right side trying to see where and why her hands were holding her so tightly against the chair. Out of the corner of her eye she could see she was tethered with a slender rope not unlike what many people used for clotheslines. "My hands and shoulders are really sore. Can you untie me?"

"What do you think Clara? You think you should untie her?"

Jank's voice grated in Minnie's ears, and she closed her eyes again and struggled once more to pull herself up. But the chair wouldn't budge, and she could only move a few inches before the rope cut into her wrists and pulled her back into place.

"You might as well sit still," Clara said. "The more you try'n pull away the more that rope is gonna hurt your wrists. Jank has a special hitch that he uses so no one gets free or even tries very hard to do so." The young woman reached over and unhooked a canteen from a wall mount. "We'll be stopping soon and then we're all getting off. You know you wouldn't be in this mess if you would'a listened to us in the first place." Pulling the stopper loose, she held it up to Minnie's lips.

"Drink?"

Minnie nodded and drank greedily as Clara lifted the canteen's neck toward her lips. After several swallows, she leaned her head back and tried to remember what had happened to her. She was pretty certain that everything had gone as planned for her getting to the depot and preparing for her ride over to Hill City on the morning train, but then what?

She squeezed her eyes shut to block out the pain and to try to remember.

Carrie had brought her to the depot even before the train's 8:30 arrival from Hill City so that she could sign a couple of papers in David's name vouching that Minnie had permission to get on board. And after the train had pulled in and Conductor Palmer had sent Joe Parker away with a bag filled with the morning mail, they spoke briefly to stationmaster Floyd Marston and then to Palmer about her travel arrangements, agreeing that she would ride with Palmer in the caboose. Her bags could be stored out of the way beneath the counter that Palmer used to log in various reports during the travel time for each of the train's runs.

Carrie and Minnie had climbed aboard the caboose, stowed her bags, and tested out the chair—this very chair—that Palmer said would be hers during the ride. But then what? She refocused her foggy brain and remembered walking back through the depot with Carrie. Out front, they had said their goodbyes, and she had returned to the counter area to let Floyd know she was ready to get on board whenever he wanted her to.

Now she remembered. The annoying couple from the night before—the rough looking man and his platinum, bobbed haired female companion who said they wanted to send a telegram—were arguing about something with Marston at the counter. The woman had traded her flashy dress from the previous evening for a stylish cowgirl's outfit—a pair of wide-legged flowing pants touching the tops of rugged looking leather boots and a long-sleeved white blouse accented by a bandana. A nearly circular, broad brimmed hat was draped off her neck and onto the center of her back, held up by a leather cord that could be tightened to hold it in place once she moved it to the top of her head.

The three of them abruptly stopped arguing as if startled by Minnie's arrival, and then the couple turned their backs to her, speaking in a lower tone that made it nearly impossible for Minnie to hear.

The stationmaster's angry face suddenly took on a concerned expression and he glanced past the others in Minnie's direction. She got the distinct impression that maybe she should move away.

As if reading her mind, Marston made a little nod in her direction. "Um, Miss Thompson, you, uh." He stopped as if trying to formulate what he wanted to tell her, then gestured toward the rear of the depot. "I was going to say Miss Thompson that you might want to make use of the facilities before the train gets underway. Not much of a chance once you're on board unless Sam decides to make a stop at the Addie Camp. I haven't asked him if he's planning on doing that."

He gave her a strained little laugh. "Better safe than sorry, if you know what I mean?"

Minnie smiled at the man's seeming unease over talking about something as ordinary as a privy break. "Well, yes, thank you Mister Marston for the suggestion," she said, giving a little wave to indicate that she was going to do just that. The annoying couple remained silent as Minnie left to go to the back of the depot to "freshen up" as they were now saying in polite society.

But when she returned about 10 minutes later the couple was gone and so was Marston. The interior of the depot was completely vacant.

"What in the world? Where'd they all go?" She walked to the front window and looked out. Seeing no one, she started back toward the counter. "Mister Marston? Floyd! Are you in here?"

She started moving toward the doorway leading out onto the loading dock but stopped as the sound of a muffled groan came out from behind the counter. Turning back, she walked to the side of the counter and emitted a little cry. Marston was lying semi-conscious on the floor.

"Floyd! Mister Marston! What happened?"

Marston tried to sit while grabbing at the counter's rear shelf to stabilize himself. "The . . ." he started to speak, stopped to get his bearings, and then went on. "That man and woman. They hit me, took some of my cash and headed out toward the train. You should warn Sam. Warn Palmer! Tell him there's outlaws and they might be trying to get on board." He reached out to Minnie and made another effort to stand before falling hard onto the floor, out cold.

"Mister Marston!" Minnie knelt beside him and felt for his pulse. "Okay." She said aloud as she felt a steady heartbeat. But before she could say or do anything further, the train's whistle sounded, and she jumped. She stood to look out the depot's rear window. And there, in clear view extending a long pole with a green flag on the end of it to signal to the engineer, was Palmer.

"Mister Palmer!" she shouted, but the train's whistle blew again to signal it was about to get underway, drowning out her voice in the process. "Wait! You need to stop! There's danger!" Palmer disappeared through the back door and into the caboose, oblivious to her calls as Minnie ran to the rear door and out onto the loading dock. "Wait! You need to wait!" She rushed from the door across the dock and hopped up onto the metal platform behind the caboose's back entry door. The corner of her travel cape slipped from her shoulder and before she could snag it, it slid away and fell to the ground.

"Oh, damn." She eyed the cape lying several feet below her, then turned back and pounded on the caboose's door. "Conductor Palmer, open the door!"

She grabbed the handle, turned it, and nearly fell onto her face, stumbling forward as someone inside jerked the door inward just as she pushed on it. Gasping in surprise she took a couple of awkward steps before stabilizing herself. Then she gasped again because standing directly in front of her was the platinum haired woman, her left arm holding tightly to Palmer's right as if trying to prevent him from moving. In her own right hand was a gun, which she now pointed at Minnie.

"Stop your shouting old woman and get in here!" She jerked the gun back toward herself as a signal to Minnie to step forward. Instead, Minnie took a step back before stumbling forward again as the train jerked and began to move. The young woman reached out and pulled Minnie further inside.

"What are you doing? Let go of me. I'm getting off now."

The younger woman released Palmer's arm and pushed hard on Minnie's shoulder, knocking the *Hot Springs Star* reporter away from the doorway. "Sit your ass down before I shoot you!" She waved the gun toward the chair.

"No, I won't!" Minnie yelled back. "Who do you think you are? I'm getting off now and reporting you . . ." She grunted in surprise as the young woman reached out and grabbed her left shoulder and forcibly turned Minnie away from the doorway before she could step back any further.

"Miss Thompson," Palmer tried to step in to help her, sliding one arm between the two women and onto Minnie's other shoulder. "It'll be all right. Don't fight her. She's got a gun. Okay?" He had a strange tone to his voice, and she looked away from the young woman into his eyes, which seemed to be imploring her to step back. "Perhaps you should . . ."

Minnie angrily brushed his hand aside and turned to once more confront her young antagonist face-to-face, infuriated by the smirk on the woman's face. "Hit her!" the woman said with a little nod past Minnie's shoulder as she spoke.

"What?" Minnie started to turn to see who the woman was talking to but only had turned about one-fourth of the way before a searing pain erupted just above her right ear. Everything in front of her started turning grey. Then she felt her knees start to buckle, followed by what seemed to be a never-ending cascade of stars before everything in her head went to a deeper grey; then on to black; and finally, to nothing.

Chapter Twenty-Seven

"I can see the Indian over at the edge of the woods. And he's got our horses." Jank had been looking out the window and now he leaned inside. "Have to figure out the best way to take the old lady. She's going to have to ride with one of us."

"Or maybe we should just leave her here. Do we really need to have her along?"

Clara was looking at Minnie as she asked the question, and her partner shook his head. "Yes, we should keep her for collateral, just in case. If someone comes after us, we can trade her for letting us go." He leaned out the window again. "She can ride with the Indian."

"What about Palmer?"

He pulled back again and straightened up. "What about Palmer?" He stared at the conductor who said nothing in response. "He knows what needs to be done if he wants to see his brother again. Don't you?" Palmer gave a short little nod but still didn't speak.

"Maybe you should make it look like I tried to stop you," Palmer said.

"How?"

Palmer pointed to his head and then over at Minnie's. "But not so damn hard. Okay? I need to tell them what happened and maybe get them looking in the wrong direction. And you're right to keep her alive. She's a newspaper reporter and a lot of people will be looking for her. You need someone to hand off so you can get away. She'll be a good one."

Jank nodded and glanced over at Minnie to see if she was listening but saw no reaction now that her eyes were closed again. He turned back to Clara. "We'll at least take her along to the campsite. We can let your brother decide what to do with her, but until then I want to keep her alive."

"Shit, you already half-killed her when you hit her. I say we just shoot her here and get it over with," Clara said with a matter-of-fact tone in her voice. Then she laughed as Minnie opened her eyes with a look of alarm. "Now she's paying attention, huh?"

"No! Clara. Dammit! You know I didn't mean to hit her so hard. And we can't just go shooting people every time we run into some sort of trouble," Jank growled. "Besides, there'd be blood everywhere and it wouldn't take much of a genius to figure out someone on board got hurt, even if we got rid of her body.

"And Palmer is going to have enough to worry about without trying to explain that. He eyed Minnie. "We can take her back to the camp and leave her in the woods before we head down to Rapid. Then if she doesn't make it out alive it'll be her own fault, not ours. We don't need to kill any old ladies."

"Well, I think she's just going to get in our way. Besides we got the Indian to help lead us out of the Hills. We'll be long gone before anyone can track us down so we ain't gonna need any trading bait. She'll just get in our way."

"Maybe. And I guess I don't know if Charley's gonna want her riding with us. Especially if we end up having a meeting with Miller. Although Miller might want to help her. I hear he sometimes fancies himself as a man of the people."

She gave a little shudder. "Personally, I think Miller's a scary ass. And he sure as hell don't strike me as the 'milk of human kindness' type. I think he'd agree with me to just shoot her and get it over with." She gave a harsh little laugh as she said that and Jank shook his head.

"Well, I don't know about the woman, but I think you're right about Miller. He's not the kind of guy you want to piss off, that's for sure."

"You would'a been a lot smarter just to stay out of his business in the first place," Palmer interrupted, startling them by suddenly speaking. "Far as I can tell, he's ALREADY pissed off at you and your so-called 'gang'."

"What're you talking about?"

Palmer leaned back against the train car wall. "I went to that meeting you wanted me to do with him and a couple of his pals over in Hill City last night. All they could talk about was how you screwed everything up for them by killing my friends over at the still that we had set up. He figured he was all set to have us do the grunt work for him and bring out all the whiskey we've been brewing. But now with my men being dead and me not able to do anything to help them, he's got to figure out another way.

"So, trust me, he's pissed! But I think he's waiting on doing something about it because he's heard about that cash that you brought with you from Denver. I might be wrong, but I think that HE thinks a chunk of that cash ought'a be his– you know, as 'just' compensation for all the trouble you've been causing for him."

He glanced over toward Minnie with a little smile as Jank and Clara exchanged a fearful look at hearing what he was telling them. Then Jank coughed, shrugged and gave him a casual wave of dismissal.

"Well, who gives a shit about Miller OR how he's going to deal with that crap whiskey you've been brewing? And now that we know that he's pissed at us it just makes it that much easier for us to break camp and get ourselves out of these Hills and on down to Rapid. By the time Miller and his boys find out we're gone we'll be halfway to the Bahamas."

"Or St. Louis or San Francisco," Clara quickly added, giving Jank a warning look to not give away too many of their plans. "Miller won't know where we're headed now will he?" she said to Palmer with a mean expression followed by a smirk in response to his smile. "So, thanks for sharing that information. Much appreciated."

The train slowed way down, and she moved over to the window to look out. "The Indian's still close by and we're just about to that big slowdown point," she said to Jank. "If you're determined, then you better get the old lady ready to move." She turned to Palmer. "Sweet dreams conductor man." In one quick motion before he had time to react, she pulled up the gun from her waistband and swung it with a thud into the side of his head. Seemingly shocked by her action, he tried to say something before slumping forward, unconscious but still tethered to the train wall by the ropes that had been holding him there.

Jank gave an approving nod and stepped over to where Minnie was looking with disbelief at what she had heard and now had seen happen to the conductor.

Kneeling beside her, Jank cut off her view of Palmer's plight as he fidgeted with Minnie's bindings and pulled one of the knots free. Minnie could feel the tension on the rope easing and for the first time could move her shoulders. But instead of relieving the ache, more pain shot through both her back and shoulders in response to finally being able to move them after so much time.

She groaned again before trying to make a little shrugging motion as Jank released the second knot. But from her shoulders down her arms and hands felt like blocks of wood. She dropped her arms limply to her side and a new wave of pain enveloped her entire body as a result of the action. Jank stood and gestured with his gun for her to stand. But as she tried to do so it felt like an electrical current was ripping through her calves, knees and thighs. She gave a little scream and half-sat back onto the chair as this new wave of pain coursed from her ankles upward to crash head on with the earlier pain moving down from her shoulders and lower back. She gasped again; then shrieked.

"Oh, oh! Oh my . . . aagh! Too much pain!" She twisted to one side and tried to grab her right leg with her half-dead hands, but now that the blood was circulating into them again, they too felt like they were being pricked by a thousand tiny needles.

"Just shut up and get up!" Clara shouted, ignoring Minnie's cries and reaching in to pull the older woman up onto her feet.

Minnie gritted her teeth and rocked back on her heels as Clara grasped her above her right elbow and roughly steered her toward the caboose's rear door. The train's speed continued to dissipate until it was almost stopped and as they moved out onto the rear platform Minnie was startled to see a bronze-skinned rider coming toward them from the edge of the woods. Despite his shabby appearance, dressed in a loose-fitting shirt and pants and wearing a beat-up leather cowboy hat with a feather poking up from the band, Minnie thought something about him seemed familiar.

He was riding on a small brown mustang and leading two other larger horses and now he pulled them up alongside the caboose's rear platform where Jank stood waiting. He started to hand the horses' reins to Jank, but instead of reaching for them, Jank stepped to one side.

"I need you to take this woman!" he demanded, pulling Minnie away from Clara and roughly pushing her in the Indian's direction. "We're going to bring her with us."

Not prepared for the action, the startled Indian rider pulled back on his reins, his reaction not only stopping his own horse but the other two as well. All three horses immediately dropped a few feet back from the caboose as the train maintained its slow but relentless pace.

"Ghost Bear, get closer. I want you to take this woman!" Jank yelled at him. "She'll be riding with you." He turned toward Clara. "Climb down off the back and take the other horses from him." He pointed toward the first one, a dirty grey mare with a white mane. "Get up on your grey and grab my horse's reins too." He pointed at the second one, a larger copper-colored gelding with a deep black mane. "Stay close and I'll mount up after we get the old lady onto Ghost Bear's horse."

She gave him a concerned look but then complied, stepping out onto the angled stair steps and down onto the ground, jogging easily in her flared pants and keeping pace alongside the caboose before letting go. The Indian handed her the reins for the grey mare, and she grabbed them and swung almost effortlessly up onto its saddle. "Hurry up and take my horse's reins, too, so Ghost Bear can help me get the old woman off the train."

Now Clara glared at her companion, but she reached out and grabbed the copper-colored horse's reins. Taking them, she pulled the horse away as Jank lifted Minnie onto his shoulder and out to the edge of the platform near the steps. Ghost Bear once more jerked back on his own horse's reins as if trying to turn away, but this time Jank extended his left arm toward him holding a gun aimed at the Indian's head. "Come up here and take her from me now! If you don't, I'm going to throw her down and shoot you. You understand?"

Ghost Bear gave a little nod and then stared at Minnie with a shocked expression. Flipping his little horse's reins to one side, he slid down off the blanket he was using as a saddle and jumped to the ground, ignoring Jank as the outlaw continued leveling the gun in his direction.

"What in hell are you doing?"

Wordlessly, the Indian pushed his horse aside, ran up to the steps and climbed up onto the bottom rung. Holding onto the outside rail with his left hand, he extended his right to grab Minnie's left arm and pull her down toward him. Jank immediately dropped his own arm away from Minnie and pushed himself back onto the platform. The action caused Minnie's full weight to shift directly onto Ghost Bear.

The Indian released her arm and swept his own around her, half-pulling and half-jumping away from the train car while holding her tightly against his own body. Despite her feeling like she still wasn't in full control of her own arms, she grasped him around the back in return.

Locked in this embrace, the pair tumbled away from the caboose and out onto the grass with Ghost Bear falling flat onto his backside, Minnie plastered up against him. He exhaled sharply as the action knocked the wind out of him. Simultaneously, she gave another little shriek as they hit the ground. Gasping to regain his breath, Ghost Bear continued to hold her in a tight vice grip even as they rolled over once before ending up a body length further out but still together.

For several seconds as the train continued its slow, steady advance they lay there unmoving. Then Jank stepped down onto the iron stairway and out onto the grass just as the train began to pick up speed. Stabilizing himself, he turned and strode over to where Ghost Bear and Minnie still lay tangled. Clara rode toward them, pulling the riderless horse along behind her.

Taking a deep breath, Minnie raised her arms, rolled to one side and started sobbing. Ghost Bear still said nothing as he continued struggling to regain his breath.

"Shit man. All right! Good job." Jank reached down and grasped Minnie's left arm while extending his right hand to help Ghost Bear get stabilized and back onto his feet. "You hurt?"

The Indian pushed himself out of the way, ignoring Jank's outstretched arm as he rolled the opposite direction before getting to his feet. He shook his head before stepping forward toward Minnie. Her first reaction was to jerk back slightly, but then she stopped and gave him a long, searching look now that she had a clearer view of his face.

"Miyelo ca kola. Greetings friend." he said to her in Lakota, then quickly repeating it in English. "Tan yan yahee ya Cuweku Ki—Choo Way Koo Key! It is good to see you again dear sister." He smiled. "My dear Minnie!"

She was transfixed as he translated for her. Finally giving him a little smile she pointed at him. "Hau Kola. You are Lakota? Miyé Cuweku Ki? Do you KNOW me? You call me your sister?" He nodded. "When I was a boy, you were KiKi—Key, Key, yes? My sister. My friend KiKi."

"KiKi? Only my Lakota family called me that." She studied him carefully before finally emitting another little gasp, this time one of full recognition. "My brother? Are you my little brother?" She followed the question with a little squeak of joy. "I AM KiKi. Brother? You are my brother? Wana Gi Saka?" She grinned. "Wait. Ghost Bear. But you . . . you are Ghost Dog?"

He nodded and gave her a warm smile in return.

Seeing Jank and Clara exchanging a suspicious look at the Indian's interaction with their captive, he quickly spoke again in English. "But now I am called Wana Gi Mató, my sister. I am called Ghost Bear."

Minnie pulled away from Jank's grasp and stepped toward the wiry man who was not much larger than herself. "Mató?" She smiled and held her hand up to show she was measuring just above her head. "Bear?"

He shrugged. "Yes, my good sister? Why not?" She threw her arms around him both in thanks and happy recognition, and he responded with a little gasp and groan—a combination of both joy and the pain he was still feeling from their fall.

Chapter Twenty-Eight

"You must be careful Cuweku Ki. These people are Sica. Evil."

Ghost Bear spoke under his breath to Minnie, who was sitting behind him on top of a coarse blanket that served in place of a saddle for her Lakota friend. Her traveling dress was pushed up around her waist to allow for her stocking covered legs to go to each side of the horse's back. And while she thought it must be uncomfortable for a solo rider to ride on just a blanket, it worked perfectly for the two of them riding together, avoiding being squeezed together on a saddle.

They had been riding for just over an hour, winding their way steadily upward along a mostly hidden trail that led north and east through the wooded countryside and away from the spot where they had left the train. Ahead of them but still quite a ways in the distance she could see the barren, rounded top of Old Baldy Mountain jutting toward the bright blue sky.

"Yes," Minnie agreed. "But brother. If they are Sica, why are YOU riding with them?"

"When I met them I didn't know. They came up to me in Hill City and I thought they were going to pay me and my family to guide them through these hills and over to Rapid City. But then after we started our ride, they took my wife and our child and forced me to lead them to a 'safe' place in the Hills where they could camp so that one of their men could heal from a wound that he had. Now they say if I do not lead them safely down out of the Hills and over to Rapid City when they are ready to move again, they will kill my family. And then they will kill me."

"You have a wife and child?"

He glanced back over his shoulder. "KiKi you will know my wife from the time when you and Two Crow lived those years with my family's Band—Yellow Feather's Band—along the Cheyenne River. From those same days when I first called you sister, and you called me little brother."

"I KNOW your wife? Perhaps, but it was so long ago, now," Minnie replied, thinking back to the nearly two years in the 1890s when she and Alvin had gone to live with Yellow Feather's Band so that Twocrow could learn more about his family's roots. "Thirty years ago. Yes, I remember you little brother, but your wife? You say I know her too?"

"Yes. She is Tio-Shlo-win."

Minnie gave another little gasp at hearing the name and leaned forward to hug Ghost Bear once again. "Cricket? She is Cricket?" She tried to keep the disbelief from permeating her voice. "Cricket is now your wife?"

She smiled to herself, remembering again that summer before she had moved back to Hot Springs when a teenaged Lakota girl had become her closest friend, even inviting her to stay and live permanently with their family. The girl had been called Cricket because of her singing ability. And what she remembered of the relationship between Cricket and the young boy called Ghost Dog, who treated Minnie as his older sister even then, was that they never got along.

"But you were always fighting with her," she said incredulously. "I thought you couldn't stand to be near one another? Cricket said you were a pest. Did you know she called you Wana Gi Wablúška?"

"Ghost bug." He snorted the name so loudly that Jank turned in his saddle to look back and see what was going on. Ghost Bear and Minnie said nothing but when Jank turned to look back up the trail, he spoke again. "But you Cuweku Ki, my dear sister, you were kind. You called me brother, not bug. And when you and Two Crow left I was so very sad. And Cricket was also sad, and soon we were sad together." Ghost Bear shrugged. "And then after I came into the Black Hills on my vision quest, I had a great vision and Ghost Dog became Ghost Bear. Cricket was impressed." He smiled. "So, I got the girl."

"You got . . . the girl!" Hearing him use a term that usually was used by white cowboys in Dime novels, it was Minnie's turn to make a snorting sound, this time causing both Jank and Clara to pull their horses to a stop. Minnie erupted into a series of coughs and gasps to try to cover her reaction.

"I'm sorry," she said toward them. "The trail dust is causing me to cough, and I think I just had one of those cough-sneezes." She coughed again to emphasize her malady, and the two outlaws gave her a withering look in return.

"You're lucky we're out here where no one can hear you," Clara said. She rode back and handed Minnie her canteen. "Drink. And then keep your trap shut! That'll keep the dust from getting into your throat."

"Speaking of dust, Ghost Bear, I don't like eating anyone else's dust but you're going to have to move up front to lead us into the camp once we get past that boulder pile up ahead," Jank gestured toward a "stacked" granite outcropping looming about two hundred yards ahead of them, at a spot where the trail made a downhill turn out toward a grassy little valley.

"I'll ride on ahead to make sure it's clear and then the three of you join me there." He turned his horse back and galloped down the trail. Clara retrieved the canteen from Minnie and hooked it onto her saddle. Saying nothing further, she started her horse toward where Jank had ridden.

As they moved back behind her and onto the trail, Minnie spoke quietly again over Ghost Bear's shoulder. "So, they are holding Cricket at their camp?"

Devil's Thumb

"Yes, and our daughter Lela. She is 12."

"Lela? A white girl's name?"

"We all have white names now. If we want to get food or a place to live when we are on the reservation, we must." He spoke straight ahead and while Minnie could not see his face, she could hear the sadness in his voice.

"What is your white name?"

"Now I am called Nelson. Nelson Ghost Bear. Cricket is Lark. She always loved the waki-yela—the meadowlark—and the agent out at Pine Ridge agreed she could take that name." He nodded more to himself than to Minnie. "A small victory."

His horse suddenly reared and snorted as, without warning, a biplane emerged above the trees off to their left and then crossed ahead of them flying in Jank's direction. As the plane roared across the trail and past the rock formation, Jank pulled his mount back and out of view under the overhang created by the bottom part of the rockpile. He looked up the trail and frantically waved to them to move over to the woods.

"Get out of sight!" He yelled as he struggled to keep his own horse from bolting as the plane crossed above him.

Ghost Bear turned his horse off the trail and over to the edge of the forest, but instead of complying Clara did a full 360-degree turn with her little grey mare while watching the plane's flight. The aircraft wobbled slightly before banking sharply off to the right, away from where they were riding. Seeing it moving away, she ignored Jank's order and spurred the grey horse back down the trail to where her partner was waiting.

The plane, wobbling again as if battling the wind currents that were swirling around near the hilltops, finally leveled off and picked up speed before flying straight on and disappearing beyond the hills.

Reaching Jank's side, Clara turned in her saddle and gave Ghost Bear a rapid up-and-down movement of her arm, signaling him to get his horse back on the trail and down to where they were waiting. Without a word, Ghost Bear guided the little mustang out of the trees and looked back over his shoulder at Minnie.

"They say they will let Cricket, Lela and me go free once I safely guide them into Rapid City. I will ask them to let you go with us then, too."

"They won't let me go," Minnie replied. "And I think they won't let you and your family go either. We should start to think of a way to get away. As you say, they are Sica—evil."

"They are Sica, but I don't think they will kill us," Ghost Bear said as he rode his horse around a fallen log and continued down toward where the other two riders were huddled together under the overhanging rock shelf, now fully out of sight in case the airplane returned. Clara moved her arm more rapidly, seemingly irritated that he was riding toward them at such a slow, deliberate pace.

"We have been with them now for many days and the men have treated us well. Cricket has been helping the one who is wounded, and he and the leader—that woman's brother—tell us that they are grateful for his care." He gestured ahead to where Jank was sitting on his horse just below the granite outcropping. "I thought that one might be good too, until he pointed the gun at me to make me take you off the train. I could see in his eyes that he would have shot me if I didn't, and then he would have killed my family. I'm sorry if you were hurt in any way."

She patted his arm. "You did right. I understand."

"I think," Ghost Bear added softly with a small nod toward where Clara was still waving her arm, "if there is anyone who would kill us it would be that woman. She is the most evil."

Devil's Thumb

Minnie eyed the pair over Ghost Bear's shoulder and shuddered. She had no doubt at all that they would soon be dead, and she was pretty sure she'd be the first one to go. She held her arms tighter around her Indian brother's waist as he clucked to his horse to move faster.

Simultaneously the airplane suddenly and silently appeared between the mountaintops on their right side. Even though it was approaching with no sound it appeared to be flying at an angle directly at them and much, much lower, as if determined to get close enough to see who they were.

Alarmed by the plane's soundless sudden appearance, both Jank and Clara hurried to pull their mounts further beneath the rock shelf before Clara jerked her rifle from its scabbard and rode forward. Seeing what she was about to do, Minnie looked up to the plane and screamed as loud as she could in its direction. "Flyer! Watch out! She's got a rifle!"

Irate at Minnie's action, Clara turned her horse and aimed the rifle at the two of them before lifting the weapon skyward, back toward the plane.

"Gun! Gun! Gun!" Minnie screamed skyward toward the silent aircraft just as Clara fired a round in the plane's direction. As if in direct reaction, the plane's engine roared to life and seemed to punch the aircraft forward and into a sideways angle of flight. "You old bitch, you're gonna pay for that!" Clara screamed at Minnie. Then she turned the rifle up again and fired a second shot.

Jank waved frantically toward Ghost Bear to ride faster as he reached across and pulled Clara's arm down just as she fired once more. Her third shot smacked into the top edge of the rock wall behind them and made a whining noise as it ricocheted away.

"What the hell, Jank? We gotta stop them. They've seen us!" She yelled at him as the plane continued its side-angled flight. Then the pilot leveled off and pulled the plane into a rapid climb, clearly aware that there was someone on the ground trying to shoot them down. As the plane continued to increase its power it banked sharply back to the right and skimmed along just above the tree-line down into a gap between two of the hills at the far end of their little valley.

Clara kicked at Jank's horse, spurred her own out into the open and raised the rifle one more time, wildly firing two more shots at the biplane as it dropped over the hilltops and disappeared. "You bitch!" she turned back toward Ghost Bear and Minnie, rifle still raised. "The next shot's for you!"

Chapter Twenty-Nine

Kallie had already landed and was waiting near the sheepherder's cabin when Twocrow rode out from the trail, emerging from the trees beneath the Harney Peak Fire spotters cabin. After getting Ice into the stable, he joined her back at the plane and she immediately began the process of getting him settled on board.

"Don't be surprised if I start sliding around in my seat while we're flying," Kallie said as she helped Twocrow settle firmly into the center of the biplane's front seat. She reached across him to grasp a heavy-duty interwoven cotton and hemp strap that was anchored onto the fuselage just below the top right edge of his seat.

She pulled the strap—fitted on the end with a steel clasp—toward her and then reached back to her own right to grab hold of a similar strap hooked in just below where she was standing.

Like the first strap, this one also had a steel clasp as well as a triple pronged snap designed to slide into the receiving end from the other side. She snapped the two ends together over the top of Twocrow's lap, then reached over to the anchor point on her side and pulled that strap back toward the fuselage's wall. The action took out the slack and tightened the belt snugly against his midsection.

"It's a safety belt—same thing you'd use if you wanted to climb up the side of a mountain or ride around in a race car," she said. "It'll keep you from going anywhere you don't want to go, like falling out of the side of the plane or rising straight up and hitting your head on the bottom side of the top wing, for example," Kallie said with a chuckle as she pointed at the wing looming above them.

Seeing a panicked expression appear on her passenger's face, she quickly added, "Just teasing Alvin. I haven't lost a passenger yet, and even better I haven't fallen out yet either. Always a good thing when you're the pilot." She pointed to the rear seat.

"I like to wear a shoulder harness too. That way I can keep my lap belt a little looser. That's why I said don't be surprised if you see me sliding around. Having the belt a bit loose allows me to slide side-to-side if I need to."

"Why would you want to do that?"

"So I have better rudder control if we hit any turbulence, or I might need to do some sort of sudden maneuver. Gives me a better feel on how I'm banking, climbing and things like that. It's just a 'pilot' thing, I suppose. We call it flying by the seat of your pants because you know when your body turns a certain way the plane's doing that too.

"You can feel every little blast when the air currents strike the fuselage, so even a small amount of turbulence can toss you the wrong way including up against the controls. But the shoulder harness holds me down and also pulls back away from the control panel. Prevents that kind of accidental touch from happening. Meanwhile, the lap belt keeps me centered.

"Basically, I'm using my harness and my seat belt to help me coordinate my maneuvers. Keeps me flying accurately and precisely."

"Good to know." Twocrow looked down at his own belt and she reached out and tapped it.

"As for your belt, it has just one job, keeping you safely inside the airplane. How's it feel? Not too tight?"

"No, it's good."

"Okay. So no matter what, even if you feel like you're going to rise up and hit your head or you might be getting thrown out of the plane, don't worry. That's just a sensation, and not a real thing. As long as you keep your belt just as it is now, you're going to be safe. But if you feel like it's too tight or preventing you from moving the way you want

Devil's Thumb

to move, you can loosen it a little at a time. And, of course, once we land you can unhitch yourself completely."

She reached down and grasped the device that she'd used to pull the seatbelt tight. "Just reach over to your left to this three-point connector. That's where I just tightened it and where you also can loosen it. Once you hit that connector it'll ease the tension, and you can either slide the belt a bit or unsnap the clasp in front of you and take it off."

She moved back onto the wing and pulled open the back seat entry door. "But I'd advise against taking it off if you want to be sure you don't go flying without actually being in the plane." She grinned as he blanched at the picture she was painting. "Trust your safety belt, Alvin. It'll keep you right where you want to be." She tapped herself on the shoulder. "And trust me. I'm the world's greatest female pilot. Remember?"

Twocrow swallowed hard and nodded. "I do. I just hope I don't do something stupid, like unhook the belt by accident or upchuck and send a stream of it back into your face or on top of your head."

Kallie slapped the curved windscreen in between them. "That's why we've got these. The highest point is right between your head and mine. Even if the middle gets covered with vomit, I can slide over to the corners to get a look out the front of the plane." She held her arms wide. "As for looking to the sides—no problem. Plus, my goggles protect my eyes from anything flying through the air. Don't forget to pull yours down before we go."

She finished getting in behind him and he moved to loosen the belt, slid over and then looked around the windscreen's left corner to talk to her.

"Why does the pilot sit in the rear seat and not the front one?" he asked.

"Well, a couple of reasons. When I'm alone it keeps the plane from getting nose heavy; making sure the propeller angles up in the air to where it's supposed to be, especially during landings. And the two main wheels branch out beneath the wings, which are basically even with the front seat. The third wheel is back at the point of a triangle formed from the other two—just behind the rear seat. So, with the wheel located there it's another way the pilot can get a better feel for the plane's balance, especially during landings."

She finished with her lap belt and then grasped at the harness and dropped it into place over her shoulders before hooking it onto the lap belt. Pulling her goggles down, she reached around the arched corner of the windscreen and touched his arm.

"I'll do this if I want to get your attention either to let you know if I see something or am preparing to do something. Okay? Everything will be by both voice and hand signals in case it's too noisy for you to hear what I'm saying. Let's try it once just to be sure I'm getting through to you. Settle in and look straight ahead. When you feel me touching your arm or shoulder, hold your right hand straight up."

She took her hand away, counted to 10 and reached around to touch his arm with her fingertips. Twocrow immediately raised his hand.

"Okay. When I do that, turn and look back over your shoulder. If I want you to look out to your right, I'll point out and away. To the left, I'll go with my arm across my body. If I'm going to bank the plane to the right or left, I'll first point in that direction and then make a circular motion with my hand. When I bank, you should be able to get a much clearer look toward the ground on that side without having to move closer to the side in order to see.

"If I need to climb, either to go over something or get away from any danger, I'll point up and you just lean back and stay as centered as possible. And if I need to dive or glide I'll cut the engine, everything will go quiet, and we'll start going down. If that happens you should be able to hear me okay even over the wind noise, especially if I shout out any instructions. But still watch for my hand signals just in case.

"Same with you to me. Lean as close as you can to the corner gap between the windscreen and the fuselage and yell out whatever you want while trying to look at me. If I give you a thumbs up, that means I understand and I'm ready to give it a try. If I don't do thumbs up that means I'm not ready or I can't do it. If I just can't hear you, I'll point at my ear. Understood?"

Twocrow gave her a thumbs up and she laughed. "Good!" She thumbs-upped him in return.

"I know I shouldn't be scared, but I'm a little nervous," he said. "Kind of wish I had one of those harness things like you've got as a backup to hold me in place."

"Don't worry. It's probably one chance in a thousand of something going wrong and besides, if you come loose from your belt, you'll probably just go straight up, hit your head and get knocked unconscious. You won't even know if something else goes wrong—like your 'flying' outside of the plane instead of in it."

He made a humming-grunting noise in response then added, "like I said before, good to know."

She grinned. "One chance in a thousand." Then she slapped him on top of the shoulder. "Ready?"

"Yes!" He pressed his back firmly against the seat and gave her one more thumbs up as she pushed a starter button on the control panel and fired up the engine.

"Okay," she yelled before revving the engine and starting to taxi the plane out toward the grassy strip where they would take off. "Let's go find some bad guys."

Chapter Thirty

Twocrow felt Kallie's hand on his right shoulder and quickly held his right thumb up before looking around. She was pointing to her left and making a waving motion in that direction. He started to thumbs-up again but she didn't wait and sharply banked the plane to the right and pointed. He could see a trail cutting between two small hills and heading toward an overhanging rock shelf. And just beneath the shelf he thought he could see a horse.

She cut the plane even harder to the right and now as he looked back over his right shoulder, he could clearly see a rider rapidly moving down the trail toward the overhang. Looking away from the controls and up at him, Kallie pointed to her left, then turned the plane back in that direction before leveling off and flying straight ahead. Reaching the end of the little valley they soared into a little gap between the hilltops. As they did so, a gust of wind hit them head on, funneled into the gap from below. The plane wobbled hard before she brought it back under control and veered once more to her right.

Twocrow watched the end of the trail disappear behind them and then they were through the gap and out among several other hills. Kallie cut the engine and went into a glide, pulling back slightly on the stick as she slid further to her left. Then she shouted at him across the opening where the curved edge of the windscreen turned back down toward the seat.

Twocrow also leaned to left to better hear what she had to say.

"You hearing me okay, Alvin?"

He did a sharp thumbs up to which she responded with one of her own before continuing to shout out her next few words.

"Did you see riders on that trail?" He did a thumbs up. "Me, too! I thought there was a rider on the trail moving downhill and maybe one more trying to hide under that rock overhang. I'm going to re-start the engine, make a loop over to the west and then come back around in a straight-line west to east right across that trail. This time maybe we can get a better look at whoever's under the overhang!"

"Yes!" He shouted back. "That's what I thought I saw too. What do you have to do?"

"Once I re-start the engine I'll make a couple sharp turns, both to the right to bring the plane around. Then once I go back across the hilltops, I'm going to cut the engine again and glide down to where we can get a closer view. Once we go quiet, keep an eye out on both sides if you can. When I kill the engine, that's when you should be able to see the trail coming out of the woods on your left side."

The plane suddenly wobbled again, and she pulled the nose up to get it back onto a level glide path.

Twocrow swallowed hard and leaned his head back against the seat. "You doing okay?"

He nodded, started to speak but clamped his mouth shut as it felt for a second like he might vomit. Regaining control of his stomach, he lifted his left hand and did another thumbs up motion. Resettling his head against the seat back but still turned toward the opening he finally added a hearty "Yes! I'm good!" followed by a weak smile.

She reached an arm through the opening and rubbed him on the shoulder. "Okay! Then here we go. Hang on!" She waved as she slid back toward the center of her seat and hit the starter button. The engine instantly sprang back to life, jerking the plane back hard and making Twocrow glad he had kept the side of his face resting against the seat.

Doing just as she had told him she was going to do, Kallie made a sharp right turn and began to climb.

Twocrow felt his stomach moving up to his throat again and he turned his face forward and gulped hard, hoping to get some fresh air and not vomit. He closed his eyes tightly and held onto the seat with both hands as the plane roared ever upward before turning hard to the right. It straightened for about half a minute and then Kallie turned into yet another sharp right turn.

Finally leveling off, the plane started picking up speed as it flew smoothly and evenly straight ahead. He opened his eyes and looked around. They were going back to the east on a straight line toward the barren west face of Old Baldy. "Where in hell did that come from?" he muttered. All this flying around and he hadn't even seen the mountain until now.

Trying to re-orient himself, he looked to his left to where the hilltops were rolling past, framed inside the struts that were evenly holding the over-and-under wings apart out near their ends. Clouds were starting to form around them, and Kallie deftly maneuvered the aircraft through increasing turbulence and into the gap that led toward the rocky trail just beyond.

Twocrow swallowed hard, shut his eyes again for a few more seconds but snapped them open in a panic as the aircraft was jolted by another blast of turbulent air that seemed to be coming from directly below.

"Whoops!" Kallie shouted loud enough to be heard even over the combined engine and wind noise. "Looks like Mother Nature's going to give you the total flying experience on your first flight! Sorry, Alvin!"

As they sped into the gap she leaned over to her right and pushed her hand through the windscreen's opening on that side to get his full attention. Then she reached back and stopped the engine once again.

Pulling back slightly on the stick, she tapped the windscreen, and he looked back at her.

"Alvin, you still doing okay?"

"Yes! Where's the trail?"

"Just past these hilltops as soon as we clear the gap." She pointed to where the opening seemed to be dropping down between the rapidly approaching hills. "We'll glide straight across it in a line toward Old Baldy and then I'm going to fire up the engine again and make a quick turn back to the right. We'll go out of the valley the same as before. Okay?" She looked down. "About another hundred yards before I go into a dive glide. Get ready."

He gulped again as he watched the propeller blades continuing to slow from her stoppage of the engine. Where the propeller had once been just a spinning blur in front of him, it now looked like a scythe cutting backward through the air. Blade by blade the "cuts" switched from what appeared to be a counterclockwise motion into a clockwise one before finally coming to a complete stop.

For a couple seconds the plane and everything around them seemed to grow totally silent, the only sound coming from the wind rushing past. Then Kallie turned the nose into a semi-dive and the wind's rushing noise intensified as they picked up gliding speed. They popped out of the gap and the trail reappeared and started rushing up toward them.

Twocrow looked to his left and gasped. An Indian rider was reined up at the edge of the trees and hanging on behind him was a woman. He leaned further out and looked harder. Was that Minnie? He wanted to shout out her name but once again clamped his mouth shut, this time to avoid giving them away. He looked back at Kallie, who was holding tightly to the stick and "steering" them along the path she had set.

He pointed to his left before turning to his right side just in time to see a rider emerge from beneath the rocky shelf. Then he heard

Minnie's voice screaming, "Watch out!" Then she yelled something about a rifle before clearly repeating three times: "Gun! Gun! Gun!"

She? Gun? He looked back toward the rider, now further out into the open. It WAS a woman, and she was pointing something toward them. Rifle? He yelled back over his shoulder at Kallie. "Gun! They're going to shoot at us! Kallie! There's a gun! Go, go, go! They're shooting at us!"

Kallie pulled her head straight back, made a quick upward motion with her hand and yelled. "Hang on!" She hit the starter button just as Twocrow thought he heard the whining sound of a bullet going past. The plane's engine made a little cough and roared to life causing the craft to literally leap ahead. Then she jerked the stick hard right and over into a 60-degree angle, literally flying the plane on its side for about 100 yards as they picked up speed.

Her response flung Twocrow hard against the seat back, and now flying at the sideways angle he found himself looking almost straight down to his right. There he saw a second puff of smoke erupt from the rifle before another rider emerged from beneath the ledge and shoved the gun aside just as the woman fired for a third time. This time the shot went sideways, and dust kicked up from the top edge of a nearby rock wall as the misdirected bullet ricocheted off of it.

Continuing to fly in the evasive pattern, Kallie deliberately wobbled the plane sharply back to her left before once more turning it hard to the right. Then she leveled off and dived, now racing the aircraft into a different gap at the far end of the little valley. Literally skimming along just above the treetops, she guided the plane around two rock outcroppings before making another cut back to her right.

Finally out of the shooter's sightline, she nearly screamed her next words to make sure he could hear him through the windscreen.

Devil's Thumb

"I'll need to cut the engine as soon as I can and get the plane down on the first flat area we see! If one of those bullets hit us we need to land right away! So, hang on!"

Too frightened to say anything, Twocrow weakly held up his right thumb, turned his head and vomited all over the right side of his seat.

Chapter Thirty-One

Still weak and barely able to lift his head after the vomiting bout, Twocrow tried to look over the side as Kallie once again stopped the engine and took the plane into yet another glide pattern. Finally sure that he wasn't going to throw up again, he slowly straightened against the seatback and watched the landscape drawing closer and closer as Kallie guided the plane toward a fast-approaching grassy stretch in the next valley.

He shifted sideways to get a better look at what they were facing. While there were no trees on the line Kallie was taking, he could see boulders randomly protruding here and there. She rapped hard on the windscreen and pointed to the opposite side of where he had just vomited. Twocrow nodded and slid as far that way as the seatbelt would allow.

"Sorry! I couldn't stop myself from throwing up!"

"Don't worry about it. Okay?" She gave him a thumbs up and he gave one back. She pointed off to the left side of the propeller. "There's a pretty good stretch of grass coming up along this path and I'm going for it. Keep your fingers crossed that we can avoid any big rocks!"

Tasting the bile again in his throat, Twocrow gave another weak thumbs up and turned to sit as upright as possible as the plane continued on its downward glide. In seconds they were below the hilltops, then whisking along in line with the trees, and then they touched down. Prepared for a hard bounce, he was pleasantly surprised when the plane's oversized tires settled softly onto a two-foot-deep thatching of grass and rolled smoothly ahead for about a hundred yards before slowing the plane to a stop.

Devil's Thumb

"Get out quick and I'll check. If we're hit, the plane could catch fire, especially if there's anything leaking from the fuel tank. So, get unstrapped and get moving!" She was already tearing at her own safety harness and throwing her seatbelt aside as she spoke. Twocrow hurried to follow her lead. As he stood and started to step out onto the wing, he felt like he was still floating and reached up to grab the edge of the top wing.

Shaking off the weird feeling, he scrambled out onto the bottom wing, slid his legs forward and rolled over in the thick grass. Not looking back, he jumped to his feet and ran about 25 yards straight ahead before falling down and looking back. There, helmet in hand and curls bouncing up and down, Kallie was moving at full bore as she raced around inspecting the plane. She dropped to her knees, scrambled under the nose and propeller and disappeared on the far side.

After what seemed like an excruciating period of time even though Twocrow knew it was only seconds, he saw Kallie roll back beneath the tail end, just ahead of the rear wheel and jump to her feet.

"Nothing hit!" she called, waving for him to return. He started toward her, and she took a few steps away from the fuselage to greet him. "Well!" she exclaimed. "That was crazy, huh?"

"Yeah!" Twocrow took another step, reached the far outside edge of the wings and stopped. Everything suddenly seemed to be whirling around him. "That was crazy all right . . ." He stopped speaking and reached over with his left hand to grasp the edge of the bottom wing at the same time that a shocked expression filled Kallie's face.

"Sorry about that," he mumbled. "My head's still feeling a little whirly."

"No . . . Alvin, it's not that." She nodded past his right shoulder. "It's that!" Keeping her hand down near her waist, she gestured with her left hand toward the space behind him. "Who the hell is that? Riders coming."

Stabilizing himself against the bottom wing, he gave her a little nod and rested his right hand on top of the gun strapped just below his own waist. She gave him a little nod back and stepped further away from the plane, opening a space in between them.

"Hello!" She called out, now raising her left hand and making a more pronounced waving motion as Twocrow slowly turned sideways, sliding his shoulders along the wing's edge to help fight off the dizziness he continued to experience. Then he brought his head around to see who Kallie was calling to.

"Hell of a landing!" Even though the voice responding sounded familiar, Twocrow kept his right hand on top of his firearm, subtly using his thumb to flick open a clasp that was holding it in place. Finally, he turned his body sideways and leaned back hard against the wing to get a clearer look at where and whom the voice was coming from.

Then he smiled.

"Hello, major."

Major Goodman was riding toward them with Ben Black Elk riding along his left side and two other men that Twocrow didn't recognize trailing behind them. Both were wearing dusty brown Army uniforms, one with a corporal's insignia on the arm.

"Saw your plane coming out of that gap and when your engine went dead, we figured you must be in some kind of trouble!" the major continued. He pointed at the plane. "Everything okay?"

"Yeah. I shut the engine down. Glide landing."

Twocrow looked over to Kallie. "That's Major Goodman. He's leading the posse I was telling you about."

Kallie visibly relaxed and gave him a smile of her own. "Kallie Sinclair," she said. She stepped out in their direction as Goodman dismounted. "Major? You Army?"

He nodded and handed his reins over to Black Elk before walking toward them. "Engineers, but the marshal probably already filled you in on my being deputized to check into these shootings and everything else that's been going on." He pointed back at Ben. "That's Ben Black Elk. He's been acting as our guide." Then he pointed at the other two men who had rifles lying across the tops of their saddles and looked over to Twocrow. "Those are a couple of my men. Came back up here with Ben last night and then we decided to do a little recon in case those shooters might've gone over this way and . . ."

He paused as a frown crossed Twocrow's face. "I know, marshal, I know. You said wait for you. But I figured we'd be okay just checking along this trail running out front of Old Baldy. Those two are my best shooters and with Ben along, well." He stopped again and shrugged. "Anyway, we were just about to head back into Keystone to wait for you."

He pointed behind and to his left. "We were riding over that ridge when we heard rifle shots and saw your plane come through that gap and then lose power." He nodded appreciatively at Kallie and the plane. "Like I said before, hell of a landing. You both okay? And the plane? You get hit?"

"No. But I think the people you're looking for are the ones who were shooting at us. I cut the engine just in case one of their bullets hit the gas tank but far as I can tell they missed us." She stepped back and patted the side of the fuselage. "No better feeling than getting shot at and missed," Kallie said with a chuckle. "We're fine and so's the plane. Just gotta figure out the best way to get her back up in the air."

"Yeah, like Kallie said . . ." Twocrow paused, still feeling light-headed. "Glad you're here." He stopped and gulped. Everything was spinning again.

"Alvin! You okay?" Kallie rushed toward him, and he gave her a weak wave.

"Sure, no problem. I'm good." Then he turned his head away from her, dropped down on his hands and knees underneath the double wing and vomited once again.

Chapter Thirty-Two

Still seething over Jank's interfering with her firing at the plane and equally angry at Minnie, Clara rested her rifle across the top of her saddle as she rode silently behind Ghost Bear, who was now leading their procession— Clara in the middle and Jank bringing up the rear.

"The camp is just ahead," Ghost Bear said to them all before turning part way in Minnie's direction as if to say something further to her. Clara reacted by shifting her rifle toward them.

"Keep your trap shut and your face on the trail!" She rode up alongside of them as Jank continued on a steady pace behind them and appeared as if he were trying to ignore his irate partner. "She don't need to know nothin'," Clara continued as she waved the barrel of the gun toward the pair. "You got that?" The gun barrel narrowly missed hitting Minnie and she jerked her body to one side while Ghost Bear attempted to move further away.

"Leave them alone!" Jank commanded. "Let's just get into camp and out of sight in case that plane comes back."

"Still flying around and causing us trouble, thanks to Miss Goody Two Shoes here!" Clara jerked the rifle back in Minnie's direction. "Count your lucky stars I don't put a bullet in you right now and finally get you the hell out of our way. Do you know someone on that plane? I heard you shouting at them."

Minnie glared briefly at her antagonist before returning her gaze to the center of Ghost Bear's back and trying to not let her angry captor have any more reason to do anything that would harm her. She already had endured five minutes' worth of ranting and raving after the plane had disappeared over the horizon, and since she didn't hear anything that sounded like a crash, she was pretty certain that her warning had helped the plane's pilot avoid being hit by Clara's first shots.

As for knowing anyone on board, she didn't think that could be possible. She glanced over at the other woman and finally shook her head. "No. I just didn't want whoever it was to get shot or crash because you were shooting at them.

"That was an Army plane you know? If you had caused them to crash, you would have the Army after you, too."

"What? Army plane? What the hell you talking about?"

"I know an Army plane when I see one. Even wrote about one for my newspaper when they flew in for our new airport dedication down in Hot Springs. Probably a dispatcher."

"What the hell is a dispatcher?"

"Pilot's probably moving messages up and down between units operating around the Hills. I've seen them flying around here before. If you had been looking more closely instead of just shooting you would have seen all their military markings on the back end."

Now tuned into the conversation, Jank spurred his horse forward. "Army aircraft? You sure about that?"

Minnie nodded. "I've seen Army markings before. So, yes."

Jank glared at Clara. "Holy shit! Now we definitely gotta get our asses out of these Hills, and we can't waste any more time messing around. Those Army planes got two-way radios; you know? By now they've probably called it in that some lunatics are trying to shoot them down. Nice move Annie Oakley!"

"Oh, shut your damn mouth! Sometimes I wonder why I let you be my boyfriend." She reined in her horse and let the other two horses move on by before quietly moving into the trailing spot behind her partner. After a few more yards, she spoke again. "And you can drop the sarcasm because if I'd have shot them down like I wanted to there'd be no way they could call anything in. It's because of you they're still flying around. So, like I said Jank Kaufman, 'Just shut the fuck up!'"

Jank pulled back on his own reins as if to stop and say something, changed his mind and just made a little growling noise before continuing, now several horse lengths behind Ghost Bear and Minnie. "Ghost Bear, get us into camp as soon as you can!" he called ahead. "Let's move it!"

Minnie smiled to herself as Ghost Bear clucked to his horse to go faster. She leaned forward to hold on tighter and gave him a little nudge while softly speaking over his shoulder. "I guess maybe I really didn't see any military markings on that plane. What do you think? Did you?"

He made an ever-so-slight sideways movement with his head without turning and she smiled again, this time pulling her left hand up to do a fake cough and cover the little laugh that she was finding hard to control.

Chapter Thirty-Three

"Okay, we were definitely under fire from whoever robbed the Keystone Depot this morning and took my friend Minnie Thompson hostage because she was with those riders." Twocrow was sitting with his back against the biplane's left front wheel and taking sips of water from a canteen that Goodman had taken down from his saddle. "Did you know about the robbery?"

The major shook his head. "No. First I'm hearing about it. Must've gone down after I rode back out to where we found those bodies," he replied. "Anybody hurt in the robbery—besides your friend, I mean?"

"I haven't heard what happened to the stationmaster, or if anyone got shot or killed; anything like that, just that the conductor was clubbed over the head on board the train and that when he regained consciousness Minnie Thompson was gone. They found her travel cape out alongside the loading platform."

Goodman had a confused look on his face. "Why was Minnie Thompson riding on his train in the first place?"

Twocrow shrugged. "Beats me, but I've known her most of our lives and I'm not one bit surprised that she might talk her way on board to hitch a ride over to Hill City. She told me she was going to be doing some stories for the *Hot Springs Star* about the Mount Rushmore carving project. She was coming up here to interview folks in Keystone and Hill City, maybe even talking to that carver guy Borglum. But I thought she didn't have anything planned up here for at least a couple more weeks—maybe not even before that formal dedication ceremony they keep talking about. Guess she decided to come sooner."

"I actually met her yesterday when I was putting together the posse," Goodman said. "She's the one who gave me a heads up that you were out here looking for Bootleggers, and she was worried that you might have been the one that got shot." He grimaced. "Guess she never figured she would be in any kind of danger herself."

"Well, I heard about the robbery and that Minnie got taken from the Hill City Police Chief when I was up at the Harney lookout station this morning. That's how I got Kallie here involved. They were able to track Kallie down at the Army camp over at Custer Park and get her to fly up to Harney to get me. Long story short, we came from there to see if we could spot anyone and, well . . . you know the rest. Must've scared the crap out of them to see our plane come flying over the hilltops like we did. Anyway, next thing we knew they were taking pot shots at us."

"Alvin really saved us," Kallie was leaning against the wing as she spoke. "He saw the shooter and yelled out a warning. Gave me enough time to make some evasive maneuvers and save our butts." She tapped the plane. "Not to mention this beautiful government plane."

"Yeah, the Army might've wanted some money back from you if you'd damaged it," Goodman agreed. "Unless you were killed, of course. Hard to collect if you're dead." He grinned but she responded with a frown at his flippant remark, and he quickly sobered. "So?" he asked. "What's a plane like this go for anyway?"

"About five or six thousand dollars last I heard."

Twocrow gasped. "Five or six thousand! Holy Moley! Now I'm really sorry I threw up on the front seat."

"You threw up on the plane's front seat?" Goodman's amused look returned. "Thought you did plenty of vomiting under the wing just now."

"Yeah, both," Kallie said. "But it'll clean up in no time. Couple canteens of water from that stream over there and we can wash the seat clean. I've definitely seen worse. As for the rest of this beauty, I just gave it the once over and far as I can tell there was no harm done. And like I said, that's thanks to Alvin."

"Actually, I gotta say that thanks goes to Minnie," he answered. "I'm positive I heard her voice just before all hell broke loose. Someone—and I'm sure it was her—was yelling, 'She's got a rifle. Look out! And gun, gun!' That's when I saw a rider with the rifle and no question that it was a woman doing the shooting."

"So, there were two women riders. The shooter and Minnie?" Kallie asked.

"Minnie was riding double with some Indian. Couldn't get a clear look but I know it was her." Seeing a dubious look appear on the major's face, he added, "I've been listening to her yell at me for over thirty years now and I'd know her voice anywhere."

"And you're certain the shooter was a woman?" Goodman rubbed his hand across his forehead as he asked. "If that's true, then I'd say that it's a 90 percent possibility that we're dealing with the gang that robbed the Denver banks. The guard killed down there was shot by a woman with a rifle according to a second guard who was wounded but got away. He said it was cold blooded as hell. She just pulled the rifle up and shot him point blank."

"Well, shit," Twocrow said. "And now she and whoever's she's riding with—including whoever that Indian rider might be—are holding Minnie as a hostage and heading . . ." he paused. "Well, I guess I don't know exactly where they're heading, but I have a pretty good idea. It's probably northeast toward Rapid."

He leaned back and pulled his map out of the inside pocket of his vest and began opening it as Kallie and the major stepped forward to see what he was doing. Twocrow jabbed his right thumb at a circled area on his map that was out to the northwest of Old Baldy.

"This circled spot here is where the Fire spotters said they've been seeing that campfire smoke over the past few days. See, just northwest of Old Baldy." He looked up to his right toward the barren hilltop by that name. "If they had it right—and they swear they do—then it's almost straight north of here at a place all the native people know by the name of Katiyimo. That's Lakota for Enchanted Mesa."

He handed the map over to Kallie and she spread it out on the bottom wing to study it further. "I agree," she chipped in. "And that's right online with the direction those riders were following when we spotted them."

Goodman looked around toward the direction from which he and his own group of riders had come, and then back toward the northwest. "That's right about where I saw campfire smoke, too—a couple days back when I was up on the top of Mount Rushmore."

Twocrow extended a hand toward Goodman and the major obliged, reaching out to grab him and pull him back to his feet. While he still felt a little shaky, there was no longer any spinning or whirling going on and he felt ready to go again. "Guess it's like seasickness," he muttered. "You get it, then you get better."

"What?" Goodman asked.

"Nothing, nothing. Just feeling a lot better now, that's all." He looked over to where Black Elk was standing alongside the two horses and waved to him to come over to join them.

Checking to be sure the horses were both tied to a shrub there, Black Elk gave his mount a little pat on the nose before striding quickly across the open space. Twocrow greeted him with a quick "Hau, Kola."

"Hau, Kola, marshal," Black Elk answered. He started to say something further in Lakota, then spoke in English instead. "What can I do to help you?"

"Do you know that area north and west of here? Katiyimo?" He gestured in the direction that he and Goodman had been looking at before.

"Yes. My father and I have been there often."

"And that would be a flat place along a straight line going north of here? Could that outlaw gang be camped there? What do you think?"

The Indian guide frowned as he stood looking at the map for several seconds as if "picturing" the terrain, and then slowly nodded. "Yes. But if they are there, I hope they will move away soon. Katiyimo is a sacred place. It is the area surrounded by forests where our medicine men stay before ceremonies in the place we call Wanagi Yata." He looked at Twocrow for translating help. "You are Lakota. Do you know Wanagi Yata?"

Twocrow started to shake his head but then stopped. "I'm Lakota but a little out of touch with the sacred places. You're right, though; I DO know about Wanagi Yata. The Place of Souls. Yes?"

Black Elk nodded and Twocrow looked up to the others.

"It's a deep sort-of bowl depression beneath the enchanted mesa that Black Elk is describing. Lakota believe it's another place where our people's sacred spirits—like the spirits of the Six Grandfathers—sometimes reside. Did your father go there, too, during his vision quest?"

"No. After he saw and heard the Six Grandfathers, he was taken by the wind to the top of the Owl Maker—the peak the white men call Harney," Black Elk said. "But when he was taken away from there and back to his village, he said he passed above Katiyimo and saw Wanagi Yata glowing in the early morning light."

"I know it too!" Kallie excitedly jumped into the conversation. "I was flying over it once with another government pilot and he pointed it out to me. But he called it 'Moonlight Valley.' It's the same place, isn't it?"

Black Elk nodded. "The Lakota also know it as Ehani. But mostly we know it as the Place of Souls. It is only white people who call it the Moonlight Valley."

"Have you been there?" Goodman asked.

"Yes. I can lead you."

"And you know how and where to fly to go past it?" Twocrow asked.

"Yes," the pilot answered. "I know I can take you there. But if there's someone camping on the mesa it will be hard to see them through the trees, if we can see them at all."

"Sure, and maybe it's not even the right place, but I'd say there's way better than a 50-50 chance that it is, so we need to get there soon before they break camp and start to make their getaway. Agreed?"

All three nodded. Twocrow started refolding the map and Black Elk immediately turned back toward the tethered horses.

"Wait!" Goodman held up a hand and Black Elk stopped. "Lay that map down here again." Twocrow unfolded it and put it back on the wing. "If they are camped on the mesa top and planning to move out toward Rapid City, where would they have to go?"

Black Elk walked back and studied the map. "Here," he said, touching a spot about two miles further to the northeast. "From Katiyimo, they would have to go here to where there are two paths. One turns down into Wanagi Yata and continues straight north." He traced that line and touched a spot where the map's contours showed a natural trail down into the sacred valley.

"And here," he traced another line that ran northeast out toward where the gravel Route 16 showed up on the map. "Taking this trail leads to the roadway down toward Rapid City. Almost all of that trail will be under the cover of the trees so they probably will like following it. But there is a part of it that will be out in the open not far from where it reaches that roadway. It's where the water runs off Old Baldy in the Spring and washes away all the trees. By this time of the year, it is just a dry creek bed." He moved his finger further along the map.

"Then here—once they reach the gravel roadway—there will be two, maybe even three side trails that horseback riders can take. Two of those trails will stay in the trees even while they follow the main road down into Rapid City, so horseback riders can move quickly from there without being seen. And if they are riding with a Lakota guide like you say, I'm sure that he would know about those trails, too."

Goodman turned to Twocrow. "I think that's what they'll do, marshal. I think they're going to make a move toward Rapid and not risk riding out into that sacred valley."

Twocrow nodded. "Okay. Agreed. So, what are you thinking we should do?"

The major traced another route on the map, leading closer to Old Baldy before crossing back toward the gravel highway and the little open wash that Black Elk had pointed out before. "If we go on this upper trail from here, we could get ahead of them to the trail they might follow." He looked back to Black Elk. "Is this upper one a good trail?"

"Yes. Good and fast. Unless there are fallen trees from all the windstorms. If we follow it we should get to that wash in an hour. And even if there are trees down, it shouldn't hold us back."

"Then that's what we'll do." Goodman looked up at Twocrow. "We'll ride to that spot and wait. We're either going to surprise the shit out of them and take some prisoners or miss them completely." He gave a wry laugh. "If that happens, I'll probably be looking at a new assignment up in Alaska."

He gave them all a grim smile, but Twocrow could see he was dead serious.

"Okay," Twocrow answered. "And what about us?" He gestured to Kallie and back to himself.

"Well, we want to give them a little nudge in our direction and not out into that big valley, right? Nothing like a plane with an armed marshal on board to 'encourage' them to do just that. I think if you fly a nice little criss-cross pattern on this side of the mesa and out over the valley that ought to get them thinking that you're definitely looking for them and they need to go the other way. Just keep flying out over that valley, making a few turns and flying back to scare them into moving our way."

Kallie grinned. "So, Twocrow and I are just going to be glorified beaters for your little hunt, eh? Driving the game your way."

"Might not've put it quite that succinctly, but now that you've said it," he paused and grinned back. "Yep! That sounds about right." He nodded at Black Elk. "Okay, let's get the horses and get a move on before that gang gets out ahead of us and makes us all look like fools."

"And" Twocrow added softly, more to himself than the others, "before they do something bad to Minnie."

Chapter Thirty-Four

The first thing that greeted the procession as they entered the camp was a small, untended campfire with lean-to's set up in a semicircle to its north and west. With the prevailing winds being from the northwest, the small amount of smoke the campfire was generating was mostly being whisked off in the general direction of Old Baldy Mountain on a kitty corner line to the southeast.

"Let's get things ready to go," Jank said. "I'll go let Charley know what's happening. You go check on Chris and tell him we gotta ride out of here as soon as possible." Clara glared at him in return and started to say something back, but Jank ignored her, turned his back on her and rode off toward the far end of their campsite, not giving her the chance to speak.

Seeing the riders approaching, a young Lakota girl jumped up from one of the lean-tos and ran toward them. Jank's horse whinnied in fright, and he urged him on. Clara's horse snorted and took several steps back as she fought the reins to bring her under control. But Ghost Bear's horse just plodded ahead as before, already used to having the girl rush out to greet him and his rider.

She called out to her father in Lakota "Ate—Ah-tay—Father!" as she raced out to Ghost Bear's horse. Off to the side where Jank now pulled his horse to a stop and dismounted, a Lakota woman stood and also started moving out to greet them, but advancing at a walk and not in the excited run of her daughter.

As the girl drew near, Minnie leaned out from behind Ghost Bear and gave her a little wave and a smile. The sudden, unexpected appearance of a white woman riding behind her father caused the girl to literally slide to a halt. Clearly confused, she looked up at her father and simply asked, "Ah-tay?"

Ghost Bear pointed at Minnie. "Lela, this is our sister. This is Minnie. Cuweku Ki—Choo-way-ku key." He swung his arm back toward the girl and completed the introductions, this time addressing Minnie. "This is Lela, my daughter."

Minnie scooted her body away from Ghost Bear, pulled her right leg across the top of the horse and dropped to the ground. Her action startled the young girl and she took a frightened step back, almost falling into the arms of her mother, who had continued walking forward behind her.

"And Cricket," Ghost Bear started to say, but Minnie did not wait. Instead, she threw herself forward, arms outstretched, one going around the mother and the other reaching for the daughter.

Cricket gasped, looked fearfully at her husband and then heard him say. "It is KiKi. Cricket. It's our Choo Way. It's KiKi; our Minnie!"

The woman grabbed Minnie's shoulders and pushed her back in order to look into her face. Staring intently into the white woman's eyes, she made a little cry of joy and then bear-hugged her while shrieking. "Choo Way Coo Key! KiKi, KiKi! My sister! Oh!" Tears erupted and flowed down her cheeks as she continued to alternate between holding Minnie out to stare at her and hugging her so hard that Minnie found herself gasping for air.

Then both women burst into laughter while Lela extracted herself from between them and stepped closer to her father's horse to avoid being crushed by their actions. Cricket turned Minnie toward the girl, tears still streaking her face, and said excitedly: Lela this is my sister, my . . . my," she stopped as if unsure how to explain it to her daughter.

She gasped again and cried out her next words: "My dearest friend. My Minnie. We called her KiKi and she is the one who I have told you of before. Lela, this is Choo Way . . .!"

"No," Minnie interrupted and pointed to herself. "KiKi, darling daughter of my friend. "I am KiKi."

Cricket laughed at that and broke into a stream of excited Lakota while waving her arms and speaking so rapidly that Minnie only caught one or two words. Finally, she hugged Minnie yet again and said "Tanyan wacin yanke. Tanyan wacin yanke Cuwe."

"It means . . ." Ghost Bear started to say, but Minnie held up her hand to stop him and simply grabbed Cricket in response. "Tanyan wacin yanke Cunksi. It is so wonderful to see you again too, my dear little sister."

She started to pull the Lakota woman back in for one more hug just as a gunshot exploded to their side. Both women jumped while Lela screamed in terror and shrank tighter against her father's leg. Clara had ridden closer to them and was sitting staring at them with a sneer, her rifle still smoking from the shot.

She waggled the weapon toward them. "Isn't that sweet?" She pointed toward the lean-tos. "Take your daughter and go get your things!" Then she pointed the rifle at Ghost Bear. "And you get their horses ready to travel. Now!"

Finally, she pointed the rifle squarely at Minnie's head. "I'm done with you. I don't know why we even dragged you along in the first place. Party's over . . . Chewy!"

"Clara!" A man's booming voice cut through the air and a big man with the same hair color and facial features as Clara came striding from the lean-to where Jank had dismounted, and Clara had come from earlier. He held a rifle in one hand and had a pistol strapped in a leather holster beneath his left arm. It was a setup that would allow him easy access to the gun's handle with his right hand.

"What in hell's going on out here?"

"Hello brother dear," she replied with a sneer in her voice. She waggled her rifle back toward Minnie. "Jank brought you a little present but I'm about to dispose of her and dump her body over the edge of that cliff into that so-called spirit canyon if that's okay with you?" She glared at Minnie. "I'm tired of her smart ass talk and having to drag her around."

Clara's brother Charley kept up his rapid pace, reached his sister's side and slapped her rifle to one side. "Are you out of your fucking mind shooting like that? I don't give a shit who this woman is or why you don't like her, but you fire another shot without me giving you the okay and I'll hogtie you on top of your horse, stuff a rag in your mouth and drop YOU over the edge of that cliff. You got that?"

"Charley?" She started to speak but he pulled his hand up under her chin and toward his face. "I said, you got that sister? I'm tired of your sass and your being such a little bitch all the time!"

Clara swallowed hard, tears welling in the corners of her eyes at her brother's admonishment. She let the rifle sag in the crook of her left arm and gave him a weak nod of acceptance.

"Good. Now you take the Indian woman and go get Chris ready to travel. Jank says there's probably a posse coming and we ain't waitin' around for them to get here." She took a tentative step away from him and he grabbed her by the elbow and pushed her toward Cricket. "Both of you. Get Chris ready to travel. Now!"

Cricket turned and faced him with a defiant expression. "Your man Chris, he cannot travel. If you take him on a horse from here, he will die."

Charley looked over to the lean-to and back at her. "Die? I thought you said he was getting better?"

"Yes, but he cannot—he must not—be moved." She pointed to her stomach to explain to Minnie. "Their man Chris, he has a bad gunshot wound in his stomach. Lela and I have treated it, and he gets better. But if he goes with them now he will not live. He will die."

Regaining some of her bluster, Clara pointed her rifle toward the lean-to where Cricket had been sitting. "That's bullshit Charley, and you know it. They're just stalling and hoping someone will come for them." She turned to Cricket. "We're taking him. You don't know nothing. Chris is traveling so let's get him ready."

"No!"

Charley's face reddened at Cricket's strong reaction and all the others grew quiet as she squared off against the much larger man. He clenched and re-clenched both fists as he stared down at her. Not waiting for him to say anything she spoke again, this time in a more controlled voice.

"Your friend Chris is young. He has a life yet to live, but if you move him now, his life will end." She pointed an accusing finger at Clara. "Your sister says I know nothing, but this I know. If you move young Chris, his life's blood will forever be on your hands." She waved her hand. "And on your sister's head!"

Now Charley swallowed hard as he looked again at the lean-to where Chris was being treated and back to the defiant Cricket. "Okay. He stays. You stay with him. You and your daughter. But you fucking make sure he does live, you got that, or I'll come back and put both of you in the ground too."

He turned to Jank. "Leave the lean-tos and anything else that might slow us up and get the horses packed up and ready." He grabbed Ghost Bear's shoulder. "You and this woman are going to lead us down to

Devil's Thumb

Rapid City and then you can come back for your wife and daughter. But if you try anything; anything! I will shoot your friend here first, and then I will fucking shoot you." He pointed at Cricket and Lela. "And then no matter what it takes I will find them and kill them too. You understand?"

Ghost Bear nodded.

"Take Ghost Bear's family with you and leave me here with your friend," Minnie said. "I know my friends will be coming to find me and then he will be okay."

"What? No!" Charley was quick in his response. "We take them, they'll slow us down. They stay and you come along." He looked back at Ghost Bear. "She'll take your wife's horse, so get it ready. Right now! I want to get the hell out of here sooner rather than later. Everybody got that?" Jank nodded and started walking away.

Charley spun back toward where Ghost Bear and Clara were still standing, as if frozen in place by his sudden and decisive action. Charley threw his hands out wide, his next words erupting from him as he turned. "Then get your asses in gear! Now!"

The words had barely left his lips when a sound cut through the air. It sounded like a low growl followed by a sudden roar. All the horses whinnied uneasily and moved nervously from side to side.

Jank stopped in his tracks and turned back toward his boss. "Charley!" He warned as he pointed past Garrison's shoulder in the direction of the sound. "It's that plane. That Army airplane."

Chapter Thirty-Five

"We're going to get that mesa trail back in sight and then cruise along it for a ways before cutting down into Moonlight Valley!" Kallie called out as they leveled off following their second takeoff since Twocrow had joined her.

"If we can stay just beyond their range they shouldn't be taking any more potshots at us, and we can get them to start moving further northeast out along the top of the mesa. And that's right along the path toward where Black Elk and the major are headed and hopefully can intercept them."

"You think they can get out ahead of them?"

"Good question, but I think so. They've got a smooth ride through the grass and smaller trees up along the Old Baldy trail and they don't have to get anything ready to go. If that IS the gang camped out up on Enchanted Mesa then they've still got to get their things loaded onto their horses before they can head out.

"Our main job is to keep them from heading north through Moonlight Valley and get them to take the mesa trail northeast instead. If we can scare the crap out of them when we suddenly come up behind them again that should get them moving in the right direction."

They had leveled off now and were flying smoothly back across the valley on the other side of the hills that separated them from the second valley—the place where they had landed and taken off. Twocrow was still amazed at how easily the little plane handled the landing and takeoff in the place that Kallie had selected. Despite the deep grass and an occasional stick or rock, nothing seemed to slow its oversized wheels as they taxied and then came roaring back, quickly accelerating and literally jumping skyward after only a quarter mile or so.

She pulled back on the stick and the plane nosed up above the gap that they had flown into before. Twocrow felt better this time around and leaned back to enjoy the view. Treetops stretched out on the three sides he could see and at the higher elevation there wasn't as much turbulence from air drafts rising off the hills or from the gaps between hills that tended to create wind tunnels and even more bumpy air.

He felt Kallie's hand on his left arm and turned to see her leaning close to the side gap on the windscreen. "Can you hear me?" Sliding over further to his left he pointed to his ear and gave her a thumbs up, adding an emphatic "Yes!"

"Okay, once we clear this next line of hills coming up, we're going to be on a direct line toward the Enchanted Mesa and it won't be that far until we reach it!" she shouted. "If I remember it right there's going to be an open spot on the trail just before it disappears back into the woods that are covering the mesa's top. I figure that's where their campsite is located.

"As soon as we reach that open spot on the trail, I'm going to power up the engine and make it roar. I want them to know we're back and heading their way. Then we'll bank off to the left and head down into Wanagi Yata. Make 'em think we're watching that too. You said you know it, right?"

Twocrow gave her another thumbs up, still leaning over toward the windscreen gap to make it easier to hear what she was saying.

"It's just a big bowl-shaped area and sometimes the way the wind moves across it from northwest to southeast can make it a bit turbulent depending on the time of day. But right around now shouldn't be too bad. Still, you never know. You gonna be okay with that?"

He looked up toward her. "Yes!" he called back. "Now that I literally got everything else out of my system, I feel okay. Good actually. Even if you have to dip and dive again, I don't think it'll be so bad for me this time around."

"All right! Great!" She pointed. "Hey, look! There's that open stretch on the trail I was talking about. So, get ready!" He gave her another thumbs up and straightened himself against the seat back while she slid away from the windscreen and back to the center of her own seat where she began snapping a few switches. As they flew past the last stand of trees on either side of the trail and out above the open land, she pulled back hard on the throttle. The little plane's engine growled out a response and then, surprisingly, emitted what actually sounded like a roar. With a snap the plane banked hard left and zipped toward the edge of the mesa's rim.

Twocrow held both hands skyward. He felt okay.

They soared across the rim's edge, and he thought the gasp he emitted must have been loud enough for Kallie to hear even above the airplane's roar. Beneath them the ground had literally disappeared as the mesa's sheer rock wall turned straight down, dropping for hundreds of feet. Far below, he could see the ground reappear and swoop out toward the bowl-like depression that his people called Wanagi Yata—The Place of Souls.

They dived again and for the first time on either of the flights Twocrow felt something that he hadn't experienced before: Exhilaration! He held both hands higher above his head and let out a loud yell. Then he looked back over his shoulder at the pilot, and she grinned and gave him a huge smile in response. Controlling the stick with her left hand, she pointed off to her right and started to circle back for another pass across what they both were sure was the southwest entrance to the Enchanted Mesa's campsite.

"Get ready, you bastards," Twocrow muttered, now looking off to his left to try to see into the thick woods as they accelerated into their next climb and raced back toward the campsite location. Then he thought again of Minnie being held captive by whoever was in there and quickly sobered. He knew that he also needed to get ready for what could end up being a very bad outcome to this day.

Chapter Thirty-Six

Black Elk emerged from within a stand of heavy leafed, brilliantly gold aspen trees that were fronted at their base by two-to-three-foot-high bluestem grasses and tangles of wheatgrass. The grasses were growing so thick in among the trees that while they created a great cover, they also were an impediment to his movements.

He struggled to his left and finally maneuvered his way into a small opening a little southeast of where the mesa trail moved out across the completely open wash before bending back into the shelter of the wooded area that now surrounded him.

The trail crossed the open wash for at least a quarter mile from the point where it emerged on the southwest, heading straight ahead until it reached the wash's widest section. From there, as the wash area became narrower and narrower, the trail cut angled out toward the edge of the mesa until it finally reached a re-entry point into the woods on the northeast.

It was at that northeast entry point that Black Elk hunkered down into a spot where he could watch for movement across the wash while also signaling to Major Goodman and his men that he had returned.

He had left Goodman and the other men over on the opposite side of the open area, just beyond the spot where the tree-covered trail first came out onto the wash—a stretch of open ground that had no cover at all. Looking across the expanse he spotted the place where the three men had moved into the shelter of a pile of boulders. It was a well-protected area, visible from his position but almost completely invisible to anyone coming out of the woods from the other side.

Black Elk had left his companions about 15 minutes earlier to scout for several hundred yards further along the trail. Moving stealthily through the northeast side's stand of trees, he had stayed off the trail itself while carefully advancing along a course parallel to the trail, in case someone was already on it. And, if they weren't, he wanted to ensure that he wouldn't disturb it or alert the gang with his movements.

Convinced that no one else was directly ahead of them and that no one had traveled the trail for some time, he quickly retraced his steps until he reached the tangle of grasses and shrubs where he had settled into place.

Their small posse had arrived at the mesa trail's open spot—their destination to try to intercept the Garrisons—after following the unmarked Old Baldy trail from the spot where they had split up with Kallie and Twocrow. After riding for about a mile-and-a-half along this upper trail, which ran just below the front face of Old Baldy Mountain, they reached what appeared to be the obvious runoff "wash" area they'd seen on the map. From there he turned them downhill to follow the wash over to where the mesa trail ran across it.

Moving slowly but steadily, they finally reached the edge of a little arroyo branching from the wash and heading to the north. Tying up their horses on a tangle of brush that was blocking the arroyo's entry, they moved forward on foot to get a clearer view of both the wash area itself and where the trail passed across it.

Leading the way, Black Elk had crawled up to a small natural dam of rocks and logs that had rolled in to a spot less than 50 yards away from where the trail ran through. They settled briefly into this natural blind, then Goodman posted his two soldiers to watch in both directions. Then he and Black Elk crept even closer, edging up behind two larger boulders to try to get a better look.

From that point they could clearly see where the trail came out from the southwest woods and where it re-entered the wooded area on the northeast. "Do you think they've crossed already?" the major asked.

Devil's Thumb

"I can go up to those woods and scout the far trail," Black Elk volunteered. "If I stay further back in the trees I can still see if someone has gone through and listen for sounds of anyone moving on the trail." He pointed at boulders where the soldiers were positioned. "You should be safe here and be ready to give me cover if I need it when I return."

"Okay. Yes, that's good," the major agreed.

Black Elk pointed to the spot near where the trail left the wash and disappeared back into the trees. "When I return, I will go to that place and signal you—unless you want me to come all the way back here?"

Goodman looked over at the spot and then surveyed the entire open area that the mesa trail went across. "No, you're right. I think once you get back we should come to you if it's still clear." He held up his hand and moved his fingers. "Do this with your hand and I'll know it's okay for us to come over there. Then we can plan our next steps." He handed the Indian guide his rifle. "Take this with you. I've got one more on my saddle and I'll go back to get it."

Black Elk nodded, took the rifle and immediately moved back toward the arroyo and out of sight. In less than a minute Goodman saw him emerge about 30 or 40 yards below the trail's entrance point, give him a little signal and quickly move on into the woods. That had been twenty minutes ago and now he had returned and was ready to flash the signal.

From his new vantage point Black Elk looked out onto the broad open area created by the annual Spring runoff—or "wash"—that came down from Old Baldy. Because of the effects of those raging waters, nearly all the vegetation in the wash's path– trees, shrubs and grass— had been scoured away. Even most of the larger rocks were gone.

He knew that the annual Spring runoff and everything pushed within and out front of it would have washed over the mesa's edge and out into the valley fronting the northwest side. Perhaps, he thought, some had even been washed as far west as the sacred valley Wanagi Yata. Meanwhile this part of the mesa trail, so completely sheltered by the forests the rest of its way, had been "washed" wide open for at least a quarter mile.

Nothing but hard ground and low-growing scruff grass was left on either side of the trail, which nature long ago had hardened and left unscathed when the waters came crashing through. But here on the northeast where he was sitting, the open space had grown narrower and narrower until it once again was surrounded by the trees, shrubs and mishmashed tangle of grasses. Here, branches from both the low-growing shrubs and the trees jutted out from both sides, making the entry just wide enough to admit a single horse and rider at a time.

Crouching at his new spot for another minute and still catching his breath, Black Elk looked over to where the major and his men were waiting. From their pile of boulders, the wash area began its uphill climb stretching out past the arroyo and turning sharply uphill for 50 or 60 yards before continuing at a 60-degree angle toward the Old Baldy Mountain.

With one more look across the wash to make sure no one was coming, he finally signaled Goodman. From his vantage point he could clearly see them huddled together with their rifles at the ready, but they didn't seem to be seeing him. Finally, he half-stood and stepped forward out of the trees to show himself. Then he dropped back. Immediately, Goodman repeated the maneuver on his end to show Black Elk that he'd been seen.

The Lakota guide raised his right hand and made the special motion with his fingers followed by a little wave toward his left for them to come that way around the open space and join him. Goodman gave him a high sign in return, said something to the other two men and dodged out from behind the boulders, starting first toward another part of the dry streambed to a point about 50 yards left of where Black Elk was crouching.

Reaching that spot, which was sheltered by a little lip of land that probably was part of a "shoreline" during the runoff season, Goodman dropped down, got himself settled and looked again to Black Elk. Black Elk pointed from his eyes to the open space and trail, his assurance that he was keeping watch.

The major waggled his rifle to signal his men to follow his lead, then waited in his half-hidden spot until the others reached his side. Next, he pointed his rifle toward a pair of juniper shrubs as the next stopping point and they repeated the procedure. Within minutes they had leapfrogged their way over to the tangle of trees and grasses and crawled up to Black Elk's side.

"Well?" The major was panting as he wriggled his way through the heavy underbrush. He looked behind Black Elk to where the trail disappeared into the woods. "See anything back there?"

"Nothing that I could see or hear. I'm sure we are here first," the Indian guide answered. "I don't think there have been any riders on this trail for many days."

"So, no horses have gone through?"

"No."

"Or foot traffic?"

"No one has passed through here by horse, or on foot."

"Okay." Goodman re-surveyed the open space over toward where the trail emerged on the opposite side and slowly scanned back to where they were sitting. Then he turned to the others. "If all our reports are correct, there should be four of them coming. Plus, their Indian guide, whoever the hell he is. Oh, and Miss Thompson the newspaperwoman. Although Twocrow was pretty sure she was riding behind the Indian on HIS horse.

"If that's correct then there might be five shooters unless the Indian isn't armed. But if Miss Thompson is riding with him, we need to be careful because he might use her as a shield. So, let's figure there are four of them with guns. And remember, so far they haven't hesitated to shoot at anyone or anything that's gotten in their way."

He pointed toward the places on the far side where the trees fronted the edges of the wash. "We need one of us in or near the trees, kitty corner across from here. I need one of you to go back around—under cover of the rocks and trees—and set up on that corner, just above where the trail comes out of the trees. I'd say dig yourself in a couple yards back from the edge of the wash." He looked at his men. "Either of you want to take that spot?"

The youngest member of the group, who looked to be barely beyond his teenage years, nodded. "I got it sir."

"Okay, Private Grissom. You got it. Go now! We don't know how far behind us they'll be."

Grissom took a couple deep breaths as a bead of sweat formed and slowly trickled down his forehead and onto his nose. He swiped it away, his hand trembling slightly as he did so. As he started to stand, the major held up his hand.

"Grissom, remember, that's the spot closest to the trail and they're going to be riding right past you. So be patient and stay as quiet as you can. Like I said, I figure five horses. Once that fifth one's past you, be ready for us to stop them on this end and don't hesitate to shoot if you have to. But we really want to put them under arrest, not shoot them unless we have no other choice.

"And definitely don't shoot the hostage. She's a middle-aged woman and like I said, she'll probably be on the same horse as the Indian. So, if they come toward you, fire a warning shot first to try and get them to stop."

Devil's Thumb

Grissom gave him a little smile. "Got it, sir. Don't shoot the hostage." Still crouching, he saluted and reversed along the path he had just followed and took off. Within a couple minutes he reached the far tree-line, made a little wave, moved up across the trail and settled back into the woods.

"Okay Corporal O'Hara," he said to the man with the insignia on his shoulder. He aimed his rifle back at the same boulders where they had been waiting for Black Elk's return. "Sorry to do this now that you've come all the way over here, but I want you back over by the boulder pile. Settle in there as best you can.

"Black Elk and I will set up as the blockers on this side." He turned to Black Elk. "Keep the rifle and go just a little further over on this upslope side of where the trail re-enters the trees. Get yourself under cover there. Okay?"

"Okay."

He looked back to O'Hara. "I'll move down in a line with the boulders where you're going to be set up so that we'll have a good crossfire both going up the wash toward Black Elk and back along the trail if we need it. Once they come out of Grissom's woods and out into the open, let them all get past Grissom and clear of the woods. Once they do that, Black Elk and I can make a move to stop them. But you be ready to back us up and give Grissom any support he might need."

He gave the corporal a little smile. "There's probably going to be at least some shooting, so stay behind cover and make your aim true if you need to shoot back. And like I told Grissom, let's try not to hurt the hostage. She didn't do anything wrong."

He looked again from O'Hara to Black Elk. "Okay men, time for us to get set up. Lickety split!"

"Lickety split?" Black Elk seemed confused.

"Quick like a bunny! Okay?"

The Indian smiled at the bunny reference, gave a nod of encouragement to Corporal O'Hara and then was gone, almost seeming to melt into the underbrush as he quickly moved away.

"Well, shit," Goodman said to O'Hara as he gestured for him to get moving. "I didn't know their Black Hills bunnies moved like lightning, or I might've picked out some other animal."

Chapter Thirty-Seven

"Charley, you sure this is going to work? What's to keep that woman and her girl from just surrendering and turning Chris in to the law?"

Jank had ridden up alongside his boss, who was following directly behind Minnie, now riding on Cricket's horse in between him and Ghost Bear. Ghost Bear was another couple horse lengths ahead, leading the group along the mesa trail that he assured Garrison would take them out of the forest and down to the gravel road that went into Rapid City.

"That's exactly what I think she's going to do," Garrison answered.

"What?"

"Listen, Chris needed to stay there, and Ghost Bear needed to know that his wife and daughter were going to be safe by staying there with him. Now he's more than willing to get us down to Rapid so he can get his ass back up here and be with them again."

"But Chris will be arrested and taken to jail, won't he?"

"Yes, I'm sure he will. But if he had come along with us, he wouldn't even have that option. He'd be dead." Seeing the shocked look on Jank's face, he added, "That gunshot wound he's got is a bitch and it's not getting better. It's really only because of that Indian woman that he's still alive.

"I don't know what smoke and mirrors she's been using, but they're working. And I'm sure she doesn't want him to die on her now. But no matter what kind of magic she's been using, he needs a proper doctor or he's dead. Simple as that."

Jank nodded his understanding. "Yeah, I get it. Okay?" He rode on a bit further before adding, "So you're going to let Ghost Bear go, then too?"

Garrison made a little sound of affirmation. "Soon as we get to that train and have our horses on board, I'm sending him away."

"What about the woman?"

"What about her and what the hell, Jank? Why's she even here in the first place?"

"I just thought we might need some extra insurance, especially since she got herself into the middle of everything that we had going on with Palmer. And on top of that, Clara wanted to kill her on board the train." He held his hands out. "Sorry, but that's not me."

Even though they were a few horse lengths behind Minnie and the movement of their horses would make it hard to hear, he edged his horse closer and lowered his voice.

"Did you send Palmer's brother back today, too? Kind of figured you must have since I didn't see him, but you know?" He pantomimed a handgun being shot.

"Yeah, damn it! 'Course I did," Garrison seemed offended by Jank's action. "I'm not trigger happy like Clara, you know? I told him to get his ass back to Hill City and keep his brother in line if he knew what was good for him. Besides, with the Miller gang still hanging around there, I'm sure neither one of the Palmers will want to get on that bunch's bad side."

"Yeah, the Palmers are going to have their hands full dealing with Miller and his boys. You think he's really connected with Al Capone?"

Charley shrugged. "Maybe. I've heard he's one of Capone's new shooters. But once we're out of here it's not our problem. And shit, it shouldn't have been a problem in the first place. Clara and I are going to have to figure out a few things once we get the hell out of here and out to the Bahamas. Like I said, she's getting way too trigger happy for me."

He swung his horse to a stop and faced Jank. "First that guard—and there was no fucking reason to shoot him—and now your run-in with Palmer's boys down by Devil's Thumb. Why didn't you just ride away?"

Jank held his hands out again, this time in self defense. "Charley, she didn't give me a chance. Soon as those boys rode out to challenge us, she just started blasting away. I know she's your sister and all, and you know I love her! I truly do. And I think she might love me, too. But this 'Bobbed Haired Bandit' shit she keeps spoutin' is going to get us ALL killed."

They both started riding again as Minnie had now opened up a few more horse lengths ahead of them. "You know that Chris probably wouldn't have got shot in the first place if she hadn't started the shooting," Jank added. "Those guards were ready to just hand us the cash and let us go.

"And now we got that dead guard and those three dead guys over by that still on our record. And on top of that we got the Miller gang pissed at us. I'm glad we're getting the hell out of here, but I'm worried about what happens next time. Next time out somebody's probably gonna be shooting at us first and not the other way around thanks to Clara. Word gets out, you know?"

"Don't worry, I said I was going to have a heart to heart with her and I will. Now let's just get out to a safe spot, divvy up the money and lay low for a while. Far as I'm concerned, we'll be set for at least a year and by then everything will have blown over and nobody will even remember who we are. Especially if we're out of the country."

Jank raised his chin in Minnie's direction. "I'm a little worried about what happens if you just let the old lady go. Especially if she sees us get onto a train."

Garrison grunted. "She won't see us because she's going to be getting off her horse real soon now and start walking herself out of these woods. You said that was your original idea, didn't you?"

Jank nodded.

"It's a good one. I'm not in favor of shooting a woman, especially an older woman, but I'm not against letting her take care of herself. I figure it'll take her at least a couple days and maybe more to get anywhere on her own. Even after that she'll probably need a couple more days to feel up to telling anybody anything about us that makes any sense. By that time, we should be on board a boat heading out of the New York harbor on our way to the Caribbean."

Before Jank could respond, Ghost Bear reined his horse to a stop while holding up his right hand.

"Watch her." Garrison said, and he turned his horse over to the side of the trail and rode past Minnie to where their guide had stopped.

"What's the matter?"

"Nothing is wrong. But there is a place soon where the trail will widen and go out into an opening. Once we go through these trees we will be coming out to that open area."

"How big of an open area?" Garrison said with alarm in his voice. "I thought you said this was a good, sheltered trail all the way."

"Yes, it is," Ghost Bear replied. He sat stoically looking ahead. "It will not be a large open area, but we will all be out from under the cover of the trees for a short time. After that until we reach the gravel road to Rapid City there will be no more places like that. Just this one."

Charley looked up as the distant sound of the biplane's engine could be heard behind their left flank and out over the deep valley they had left far behind. "So that airplane?" he asked, pointing back. "If the pilot decides to start looking this direction? Could we be seen out in that opening?"

Ghost Bear said nothing; just continued staring ahead. Finally, he looked back at Garrison. "Yes. But that airplane is far behind us now. And if we go down into the valley they will see us."

"Are there any other ways?"

"No. This is the only trail. But we could turn into the trees and go down a steep hill on our right. But I have not heard or seen any other riders and if we stay ahead of the airplane, I think we are alone."

"Shit!" The outlaw boss glared at him and then looked at the sky behind them again. As if on cue, the plane's motor noise seemed to dissipate sounding as if it were flying away instead of closer. Then it seemed to disappear completely.

"Well, now that we're farther away from that camp, maybe we've finally lost that damn plane, especially if they think we're trying to go down through the valley. That might be why they keep flying back and forth out there." He glared up at the empty sky and back at Ghost Bear before repeating, "Shit!"

Clara rode around Minnie and Jank and up to where the two men were talking. She held out her hands. "Why are we stopped?"

"Ghost Bear says there's an opening on the trail ahead and we'll be riding out from the trees while we're moving through it," her brother answered.

Clara looked back down the trail they had been riding and then up at the sky. "Well, I don't think there's anyone behind us, and no sounds from up ahead. Besides, that plane doesn't seem as close. Don't hear the engine at all now and I've hardly heard it for over thirty minutes." She turned to Ghost Bear. "Have you?"

The guide shook his head.

She swung her horse around, so it was nose-to-nose with Charley's. "Let's just keep going. We can have our guns ready if we need them and move through the open space as fast as we can." She looked at Ghost Bear. "Is it going to be a long ride in the open?"

"No, not long. Maybe," he paused and picked out a rock formation with three trees on top and pointed at it. "From here to that spot where the three trees are on the rock. About that far."

"Charley, that's nothing. Quarter mile or so," Clara assured. "Let's just get up to the open area, have our guns ready and ride through it. You're too damn careful if you ask me."

"Well, I DIDN'T ask you and you're too fucking quick to 'get your guns ready' without thinking things through!" he snapped back at her. Turning past her, he rode up ahead of Ghost Bear and sat studying the trail, holding up a hand again for silence. All five riders sat quietly as he listened intently. Now with the plane's engine no longer buzzing the only sound in the air was the birds chirping.

"Okay. Okay. All I can hear are those damn birds and I doubt we'd be hearing from them if there was something or someone else on the trail." He pointed again at Ghost Bear. "You agree?"

Ghost Bear nodded.

"All right. Then let's get moving. But Ghost Bear, if you're planning to screw us over or we run into ANY trouble because of this, just get yourself ready." He extended his arm in Ghost Bear's direction. "Because the first shot I'm going to be taking will be the one I take at you."

And then, far in the distance, the sound of the plane's engine once again came cutting through the air.

Chapter Thirty-Eight

Their latest pass marked the fourth time since Kallie had first guided the biplane across the point where the mesa trail left the small open area and branched out onto the Enchanted Mesa. She banked the aircraft around in a big loop and headed out of the hills and crossed the trail one more time before they once again popped out above Moonlight Valley.

Twocrow was still in awe of the straight down view but this time he could feel a sudden uplift hit the front end of the plane almost directly beneath where he was seated. He looked back at Kallie, and she gave him a knowing nod in return then suddenly cut power to the engine. Just as before they were now gliding along with no engine power, but even more significantly they had eliminated any noise except for the rushing wind.

She leaned over to her right and spoke through the windscreen gap.

"We're getting a pretty strong updraft now so I'm going to glide out over the center of the valley this time before we restart the engine and head back. If I've got this figured right, they should've left camp and be well up the trail by now—probably getting pretty close to the open wash area where Goodman hoped to cut them off."

"You think he got there?" Twocrow was stretching out with his ear almost even with the gap as he looked back and spoke.

"We gotta hope! If not—and I'm afraid to even think it—they're probably going to get away."

He lifted his head, closed his eyes for a couple seconds and pulled his shoulders back against the seat. Rolling his head and neck to relieve the tension he was feeling, he looked straight up before turning back toward her. "So, what do we do next?"

"If they're on that mesa trail, I want them to think we're coming for them!" The volume and intensity of her voice increased as she said it and he looked back to see a determined and somewhat angry look on her face. "They've got Minnie and who knows who else. So, they need to be afraid of US and not even think that there might be someone else waiting to cut them off when they reach that wash! Agreed?"

"Yeah, agreed. What's your plan?"

"I'm going to stay out over the valley now and follow the ridgeline toward the wash. If they hear the engine noise they'll know we're out here and want to stay under the cover of the trees along that trail!" She pointed at his waist. "But if they try to shoot at us again you need to be ready to take a couple of shots back at them. I want them to know that we've got weapons too and we're ready for a battle if they want one."

She gestured toward where the seat butted up against the fuselage. "Do you think you can handle getting over to that side to shoot if you have to?"

Twocrow slipped his seatbelt loose, slid rapidly across to the fuselage wall and turned back in his seat. "Just don't 'fly' me out of the plane if I have to do it, okay?"

She smiled. "Okay. Promise." Then she sobered and pointed out the right side of the plane toward the mesa. "I want those bastards to think ONLY about us and that we're hunting them. If they make that mistake, they'll ride out into that open wash area without being cautious and . . ." She held her hands out wide, ". . . and then hopefully we put a stop to them once and for all!"

"Yes!" Holding tightly to the seat's bottom with one hand, Twocrow thrust his other hand toward her through the windscreen gap and she reached out to tightly grasp his wrist in response. They exchanged a deep and determined look before Twocrow pulled his arm back, slid back into position and re-locked his seatbelt.

Devil's Thumb

"Now let's go get Minnie!" he shouted. In response, Kallie hit the starter switch and the biplane's engine roared back to life.

* * * * *

Goodman sucked in a sharp breath and held it, trying not to make any loud breathing noises as he looked anxiously over to the spot where Black Elk was hidden in the underbrush. He wondered if the Indian guide was hearing some of the same "horses approaching" noises that he thought he had been hearing?

He had to admit that he almost hadn't heard the horses at all because the primary sound he had been concentrating on for the past 40 minutes was the steady buzzing of the biplane's engine. Then the plane seemed to start moving away, its engine noise growing softer as if it were headed out to look for the outlaws along a different trail. And then the buzzing had completely disappeared.

"Damn," he muttered to himself. "Where the hell are you, Two-crow? Did we screw this up?" He stared intently at the spot where the trail emerged out onto the wash at the open space's southwest side. Nothing was moving there. Had the gang turned and taken another route, and the plane followed?

Suddenly, as if reacting to his thoughts, the plane's engine noise resumed, this time coming from out over the big valley that ran along the mesa's northern side. The engine noise again started softly as if it was coming from far down in that valley but steadily grew louder and closer, definitely headed back their way.

In conjunction with the renewed sound of the engine, he clearly heard a horse make a nervous little whinny—as if spooked by that noise—and now Goodman was positive that what he had started hearing before was definitely the sound of horses' hooves grinding toward them along the rocky trail.

He looked again toward the spot where Black Elk was waiting in the shrubbery along the northeast side of the wash. The Lakota guide moved his head ever so slightly to remind the major of exactly where he had situated himself. Then he lifted his head and signaled to the major that he also was hearing something.

They locked eyes and Goodman made a motion with his right hand that he hoped would somehow translate as a horse's hooves prancing—even though the horse hoof noises he had been hearing obviously were not even close to prancing. They were just hoofbeats advancing along a trail.

Black Elk leaned his head back and smiled at the major's pantomime before responding with a little nod of affirmation. Seeing that response, Goodman finally exhaled. So, the Indian had heard horses moving too. Now it was just a matter of how close those horses were, how many riders they carried, and if they would move out onto the wash without their riders coming out ready to do battle—if they came out into the opening at all?

For the first time since they had reached the wash, the biplane came into view. Flying just above the ridgeline and moving fast, the plane roared past the open area and waggled its wings. The major could see both the pilot and her passenger clearly as they crossed alongside but before he could give her a signal that he was there she banked the aircraft sharply back down toward the valley.

The plane's sudden dive away from the wash almost instantly cut the engine noise to less than half of what it was before, and the horse's hoof noises grew louder. He sucked in another sharp breath as an Indian rode out into the wash from the trail's southwest entry point. Riding tentatively at first, the rider picked up the pace as he moved further out from the trees and across the wash.

Chapter Thirty-Nine

As the Indian rode, he slowly swept his gaze across the open space but didn't waver in his pace toward where Goodman and Black Elk were lying in wait on the opposite side: hidden where the trail left the wash and started to reenter the trees. As he watched the Indian riding ever closer, Goodman was surprised to see that the man didn't appear to be armed.

Maybe he wasn't part of the gang after all; just being forced to assist them.

The major looked across behind the rider toward where his other men were positioned and saw both were crouched and ready to close the pincers around whoever might end up out in the wash.

He grunted his approval just as a second rider—this one a younger man carrying a rifle and wearing a pistol strapped beneath his arm—emerged from the woods out into the opening. Behind him trailed the woman he knew to be Minnie Thompson, the newspaperwoman from Hot Springs. He was surprised to see her on her own horse but before he could give that much more thought a much younger woman rode out of the trees. She bore a striking resemblance to the man riding ahead of Minnie and like him she also was heavily armed.

The young woman pulled her horse to a stop and sat with rifle at the ready as she looked from side to side as if prepared to shoot in an instant. Seemingly satisfied that no one was there, she urged her horse forward into the crossing.

The four riders were spaced out about two to three horse lengths apart as they continued on their steady pace directly toward them. Goodman looked back toward the exit point from the woods then up and down the woods for a sign of any other riders, but none seemed to be coming. Had they figured it wrong and there were only these four? There was a slight movement behind the last rider and Goodman looked away from the line of riders toward it. Then he groaned.

Damn it! Grissom! The inexperienced, nervous young private had started to stir as rider after rider went past the brushy area where he was concealed. Now he was impatiently pushing forward with his rifle to get a clearer look at them. The bushes around him moved, and hearing the sound, the young woman pulled back on her reins and made a quick turn in his direction, once again raising her rifle.

"Grissom, watch out! Get back down!" The voice of Corporal O'Hara, who had a direct view of his fellow soldier, rang out from over on the Old Baldy side of the trail. The sound of his voice caused all four riders to rein to a stop and as Minnie turned back, she cried out a warning and pointed toward where the younger woman had turned around and was raising her rifle.

The young woman switched the rifle's aim and fired a round in O'Hara's direction before turning angrily toward Minnie, who pulled her own horse around and now called out to the Indian who had been leading their procession.

"Ghost Bear! Ride for help! Get away!" she cried. The Indian hesitated for only an instant before turning toward where the trail left the open area and returned into the woods. It also was where Black Elk had positioned himself and was lying in wait.

Hearing Minnie's yell to Ghost Bear, Corporal O'Hara now jumped up from behind his rocky cover and fired a shot back at Clara and she quickly returned his fire. O'Hara let out a little yelp as her bullet ricocheted off the top of the rocks next to him. The bullet's impact splintered off several granite shards in his direction with one seeming to strike him in the face.

Reeling away, he dropped out of sight for just a few seconds and then—as if to show the others that he was okay, even though blood was now running down his face—he leaned around the corner of his rocky hiding spot and fired once more toward the woman who had been shooting at him.

She turned away from O'Hara's shots and angrily looked again toward Minnie. The reporter flattened herself down on top of her horse in fear. Wrapping her arms tightly around the animal's neck, she tried to make herself as small as possible. Ahead of her, the Indian she'd called Ghost Bear reached the tree line's opening where Black Elk was positioned.

His horse let out a frightened whinny and Ghost Bear struggled to keep him under control as Black Elk stood up with rifle in hand and pointed it toward him. "Miyelo ca kola—Brother! Are you Lakota? I am Lakota," he called out in Lakota and English. As he called out the greeting, he cast a wary eye back toward the heavily armed man and woman riding behind Ghost Bear, both of whom seemed unsure about what they were going to do next.

"Emáčiyapi Black Elk (I am Black Elk)," he continued as he looked again to Ghost Bear. "Brother? Táku eníčiyapi he? Who are you?"

Before Ghost Bear could answer, the armed man riding nearest to them spun his horse in their direction and raised his rifle. He paused as a shouted "Charley! What's happening?" caused him to stop, and he turned to look toward where a fifth rider came galloping out of the woods. The new rider, who also was younger and equally well armed, advanced rapidly to the center of the wash, rifle raised and ready for action.

Turning his horse around in a semicircle to take in Ghost Bear, Minnie and the other woman, he once again called out toward Charley. "Charley! What's going on? Who's shooting?"

Ghost Bear looked back toward where Minnie was stopped between the two men. She was still flattened tightly against the top of his wife's skittish horse's neck that seemed ready to bolt. Then with a quick glance back to Black Elk he called out, "Emáčiyapi Ghost Bear. I am called Ghost Bear." He pointed at Minnie. "That is my sister Minnie! Cuweku Ki. KiKi. I must go get her now!"

Without waiting for Black Elk's okay, he pulled his horse's head around, dug his heels into the animal's flanks and galloped off toward the center of the wash. There, the two heavily armed men and Minnie were now swirling around, their mounts crisscrossing past one another in both fear and excitement.

"Jank!" Charley yelled over to the newest arrival. Then he waved at the young woman who had ridden back alongside the edge of the woods from where they all had first left the trail to ride out into the wash. "Clara!" He called as he motioned at her too. "That first shooter is over there by you. Take a couple shots over at those rocks on the southeast side! Keep him down."

Jank pulled his horse to a stop to look off in that direction just as Private Grissom reappeared from the underbrush on the southwest side of the trail aiming his rifle in their direction.

He yelled. "Hands in the air; There's another shooter aiming at you from this side, too! Give yourselves up! You're surrounded!"

Jank's reaction was immediate. Spinning his horse back in the young soldier's direction he fired his rifle from alongside his hip. "Ow! Goddam!" Grissom shouted, grabbing at his left forearm and dropping back down into the underbrush for cover. Jank pulled his rifle up to his shoulder and began sighting in on the spot where the young soldier had disappeared.

And then the biplane was back.

Rising up from the valley on the north it came straight at the riders, roaring across the wash from the point where its water dumped out over the edge of the mesa's ridge during the runoff periods. Spooked by the sight of this giant noisy bird coming his way, Jank's horse whinnied, kicked back and bucked him off as the aircraft roared past.

Still lying on his back, Jank took a shot at the plane before jumping to his feet to try to get behind his riderless horse for protection as shots rang out from the right side of the plane and back in his direction. Across from him and almost directly under the belly of the plane, he could see Charley's horse rear back and start circling in panic as Charley fought to get him under control.

From her spot near the woods, Clara also took a shot at the plane and kicked her horse forward to get into position for a better shot as the plane continued flying east and began climbing. But as she raised her rifle a bullet whined past her head.

"What the hell . . .?" She swore loudly and ducked as the sound of more shots followed. Beneath the spot where the plane had started climbing, Corporal O'Hara had come back out from behind the rocks and was moving toward her, yelling and shooting.

Fighting the reins as O'Hara's bullets kicked up dirt around her horse's feet, she spun the animal back toward the safety of the woods. Behind her Charley was calling out "Whoa, damn it. Whoa!" pleading with his own wild-eyed horse as the animal continued still spinning in total panic from the airplane's close pass.

Now with the plane gone, Jank jumped to his feet, slapped his horse on the rump to get him out of the way and turned again toward where Private Grissom was only partially under cover and holding his injured arm. He raised his rifle in the young soldier's direction.

Across the wash behind him, Major Goodman strode out several steps and fired a shot in the air. "Put down your weapons!" he commanded. "All of you put your rifles down and get your hands in the air! You're surrounded and you're all under arrest!"

Ignoring the major's command, Jank whipped around and once again fired from his hip, this time in Goodman's direction. The bullet made a loud "thwack" as it struck a fallen log next to the major and in one quick motion Goodman dropped to his knee and pulled his own rifle to his shoulder. As Jank aimed again in his direction, Goodman fired.

A shocked expression crossed Jank's face, and he turned to look over at Charley, who had finally gotten his horse under control. Seeing the strange look on his friend's face Charley simply asked, "Jank?"

Jank stood stock still for several seconds and then his rifle dropped from his hands as he slowly toppled to the ground. From the edge of the trees where she had dismounted from her own horse and was trying to find cover from O'Hara's shooting, Clara turned to see Jank fall.

"Jank!" She screamed. "Jank! No!" She dropped her horse's reins and started running toward him, stopped and fired twice at Goodman, and ran on still screaming Jank's name.

Goodman ducked back into his protected spot as one of the bullets whined over his head and the other one kicked up rocks and dirt off to his left.

With the shooting now away from her, Minnie lifted her head from her horse's neck and turned to look to where Jank had fallen. Clara reached Jank's side, tossed her rifle down and dropped to her knees beside him. Charley seemed stunned by everything that was happening until Ghost Bear rode past him and reached out to grab Minnie's horse's reins.

"KiKi! Hold on tight!" She nodded, rewrapped her arms around the horse's neck and held on for dear life as he jerked both horses around toward the northeast grove and headed back at full speed, riding straight past Black Elk and into the forested area of the trail, branches scraping the horses' sides as they wildly rode through.

"What the hell?" Charley finally seemed to break out of his reverie. Looking just briefly at where Clara was cradling Jank's head in her lap, he made a little angry growl, turned his horse toward where Ghost Bear and Minnie had disappeared and rode after them.

But he had only gone about 50 yards when an Indian holding a rifle suddenly stood up in front of him and fired a shot into the air. Charley's horse once again reared back in fear and the outlaw leader fell hard, dropping his rifle onto the rocky trail. Crawling to his right to retrieve the weapon from where it had bounced alongside the trail, he gripped it and jumped to his feet, turning to face Black Elk. The Indian guide slowly stood while continuing to point his own rifle in the outlaw's direction.

"Who the fuck are you?"

"I am called Black Elk."

"Get the hell out of my way, Black Elk!" He chambered a round and started to raise his rifle at the man who was attempting to block his path. "If you think you're going to stop me, you're crazy."

"He might and he might not stop you!" a deep voice accompanied by the sound of another rifle shell being chambered, interrupted. Startled, Charley looked over his right shoulder to where Goodman was standing looking down the barrel of a military rifle that was aimed at the young outlaw's head. "But I can guarantee you that I sure as hell will."

Chapter Forty

Twocrow and Major Goodman stood together in front of the Keystone Depot listening to a report from Carrie Swanzey, who had just disembarked from the Hill City to Keystone train with her husband David and stepson Harold.

As David Swanzey and a couple of railroad workers carried Harold on a stretcher over to where a military ambulance was waiting to take him down to Rapid City for a thorough examination, they stopped her to ask about what she had learned on her trip to the neighboring community.

"Well, first of all, Harold's much improved, but I think David will feel one hundred percent better if they can take that makeshift cast off his ankle and get his lower leg re-cast," she said. The men carrying Harold moved slowly past them and she reached out to give her stepson's hand a little squeeze.

"Sure, that's definitely a good idea, especially after all he's been through, although I have to say I'm very impressed with the treatment he got from Dr. Amundson," Twocrow said. He turned to look at where they were starting to get him on board the ambulance. "But like I told him and the major when we were up in the Hills: Better safe than sorry."

Goodman nodded his approval. "Glad we could arrange for his transport. Plus, it's good training for the medical team, too."

"And Minnie?" Twocrow asked. He was trying to sound unworried but the tremor in his voice was obvious.

"She's going to be fine," Carrie said. "She and her friend Ghost Bear are still being checked out at the Addie Camp's medical tent. When we made a brief stop there on our way back, I was able to leave the train to talk with her and the doctor. He said that aside from dehydration and some scratches and bruises, especially where she took a nasty whack on the side of her head, she was doing good. And she told me she was anxious to get on board this afternoon's train back to Hill City."

Twocrow scrunched up his face at that. "Oh, I was hoping she might be coming back over here so that we could go back to Hot Springs together in my pickup truck?"

"Well, I think she still wants to talk to some of the same people that she originally had planned on interviewing over there before all this stuff happened." Carrie held her hands out wide to indicate a general 'this stuff' as she spoke.

"Yeah, that sounds like Minnie, all right," he said for the major's sake as he gave Carrie a grateful smile. "Thanks for checking on her. I know she must appreciate it too."

"Did you get to talk to the Ghost Bear family?" Goodman asked. "They've had quite an ordeal, too, and Ghost Bear himself took a hell of a risk riding Miss Thompson away from all the shooting."

"No, I didn't. But Minnie said she also wanted to spend some time with them back in Hill City. I don't know if you know this, but she was very close to both Ghost Bear and his wife Cricket when she lived with the Yellow Feather Band in the 1890s? They call her Cuweku Ki."

Twocrow pulled back and stared at her. "What? Who? Yellow Feather . . . and Cricket? You sure that's who she said?"

"Yes, that's definitely what she said." She said Ghost Bear's wife is her friend Cricket." Carrie gave him a curious look. "Weren't you both out there living with Yellow Feather?"

He nodded. "Yes, but I was working with the tribal elders, traveling back-and-forth between there and the reservation and trying to reconnect to my own family roots. We kind of grew apart for a while. She was staying with a young woman's family and . . ." He stopped. "Ghost

Bear's family? No, it wasn't Ghost Bear. He was called Ghost . . . Dog, I think." He seemed to be puzzling over the connection.

"But she said Ghost Bear and his wife were the ones she was closest to when she lived out there? I have to admit I don't know that much about when you and Minnie went to live with Yellow Feather's Band. Just what she's shared with me over the years and the fact that you both were out there." She stopped and gave him an accusing look. "She said you left and went back to Hot Springs before she did. Later, she followed."

"It was only a very short time that I went back before she followed," he clarified. "We were with Yellow Feather for almost two years and then both ended up right back where we started." He shrugged. "Anyway, that was a long time ago and I don't want to mis-remember something and steer you down the wrong path. If the Ghost Bears are the same people, then I'll want to meet with them too, but only after Minnie and I get back together again and talk about it."

He held out a hand to Carrie. "Thank you, Carrie, for checking in with her and letting me know she's okay. We'll all definitely have a lot more to talk about once we come back to Keystone, or you make another visit to Hot Springs, whenever that may be."

Carrie took his hand and leaned over to give him a hug. "I've got to go with Harold and David. Don't be a stranger, okay?" Twocrow smiled.

Carrie held out a hand to Goodman. "And I'm sure you and I will have many more conversations in the months ahead now that you've been assigned up here. I think that with those shooters being arrested, the carving project will get right back on track. Nothing in its way."

"Yes. And I look forward to talking with you, David and Harold." He shook her hand, and she patted him on the arm before hurrying away.

"Oh damn," he said as he watched her get into the front seat of the ambulance. "I forgot to ask her if she saw that conductor Palmer over there anywhere. I thought he might be on this train, but maybe he's still healing up from his own attack by those gang members. Hard to say I suppose?"

"Yeah, I'll need to talk to him too," Twocrow said. "I need to get a written statement about his run-in with the Garrisons. But I guess we'll have plenty of time after we get that still broken down and moved out of the Calendar Mine, and we make damn sure there aren't any more bodies lying around."

Goodman smiled at that and was about to say something further when the ambulance fired up its engine and pulled away with the Swanzeys, barely pulling out as another car arrived and screeched to a halt only yards from where they were standing.

Gutzon and Lincoln Borglum got out of the vehicle and came walking toward them, the elder Borglum reaching out to give Goodman a heartfelt slap on the shoulder and a big smile. Then he turned and shook Twocrow's hand, too, adding a friendly "marshal, I don't know if we've met. I'm Gutzon Borglum and this is my son Lincoln." Twocrow released the elder Borglum's hand and reached over to shake hands with the teenager too.

"So glad you captured that gang," Borglum continued. "I feel very confident now that we'll get our dedication ceremony back on track and finally get this carving project moving. It's a big weight off my shoulders."

"Dad said you found a whiskey still up in an old ghost mine!" Lincoln Borglum piped up while giving Twocrow an admiring look. "What's going to happen with that? Can we go see it?"

"Well, I don't see why not," Twocrow replied looking back at Gutzon Borglum to make sure he wasn't speaking out of turn. But Gutzon just nodded his approval.

"Wouldn't mind seeing something like that myself," he said. "I haven't made it widely known, but I've had this idea that once the mountaintop is finished, I'd like to carve out some sort of Hall of Records, either beneath the faces out behind Mount Rushmore or somewhere nearby. It would be interesting to see if an abandoned mine like that might work. And even if not, I might get some ideas just by looking at it. Do you think it would make a good place to store documents and other memorabilia about our nation's history?"

Twocrow gave the major a quick glance, saw an encouraging look on his face, and said "Sure. But it's maybe too far back of the mountain itself to be the actual place you're thinking of. But like you say, it could give you some nice ideas. It's really well preserved and nice inside—especially once they get that liquor-making paraphernalia hauled out of there. Clean, dry, pretty wide open; two entrances, in fact."

He looked again at Goodman. "By the way, since the Calendar Mine's on government land, do you have any thoughts about getting that still torn down and hauling all that stuff out of there? It's not just the still, you know? There's probably 25 or 30 barrels of whiskey that have to be moved out too."

"I'm already way ahead of you," Goodman answered. "The CB&Q is going to let us put a couple of our wagons and teams of horses on board this afternoon and transport them out to the Addie Camp. My soldiers will camp out there overnight and then we'll follow that old logging road back down to the Calendar Mine tomorrow. That's the road that you and the Swanzeys took when you rode out of there with Harold."

"Sure. Figured that's what you meant."

"My teamster commander said he had reports from some of our survey crews about that old logging road being back in there. Said he figured he'd be taking me up there sometime soon to show it to me because it could work as one of our possible roadways. I'm planning to take the 9:30 train out there to join the troops tomorrow morning. Then we'll head on down and spend a couple of days clearing out the still and the whiskey. AND in the process, both going down there and coming back, I should be able to get a clear look at whether that old roadway might work for us."

Twocrow nodded. "Two birds with one stone, eh? Sounds like a very good idea. Be sure to tell your men that you're going to have to cut through a few trees and shrubs to get your wagons the last part of the way to the mine. That old road not only seemed narrow, but it was pretty heavily grown over the closer it got to the mine itself. When I was at the mine's east entrance—by that pond where I found Harold—I saw it, but just barely because of all the overgrowth.

"When we left you with that wounded man and started back up to Leaky Valley, we picked up the road okay but the first third of it had some trees and shrubs in it. It wasn't so bad for us being on horseback, but it'll be a lot tougher for horses pulling large wagons."

"Well, we'll have about a dozen, or maybe even fifteen men—a couple teamster squads—and they're all big strong guys. They should be able to cut their way through any growth so that we can get the wagons down there. And once we get there we'll camp by the mine until everything gets cleared out and loaded. So, if we need to do any more widening on the road before coming back some of the men can do that while the others load things up."

"What's your schedule once you get there?"

"Simple. Tear down the still and load it and the whiskey barrels onto our wagons and haul everything back up to the Addie Camp. Once we get it there, we can load it onto a flatbed car and then hook up to the train to bring it back here to Keystone. Then we can truck it down to the Army Depot in Rapid."

"Well, here's an idea if you're okay with it?" Twocrow said. "How about if I take Lincoln and his dad up there on horseback tomorrow morning and show them around the mine until you and your teamsters arrive? And if it's not too much of an imposition, we can spend tomorrow night camping with you all there. A little 'adventure' for the boy." He looked over at Lincoln and saw him beaming at the prospect. Gutzon Borglum also looked pleased. "Maybe an adventure for his dad, too, huh?"

"Wow, Dad! Can we? It sounds like loads of fun!"

Seeing how excited his son looked, Gutzon reached out and patted Lincoln on the shoulder. "Okay son, I agree, but not just because it sounds fun. I think it'll be a good way to unwind and see what the terrain looks like in the hills out behind Mount Rushmore. And of course, I can get a look at what might be the perfect model for my Hall of Records once we're finished with carving out the faces themselves."

He turned to Twocrow. "Marshal, if you're serious about that and Major Goodman is okay with it, I think we'd love to take you up on your offer." Lincoln looked over to the major, and the intensity of his expression caused the rugged military man to emit a happy laugh.

"Well, then that's the plan!" Goodman agreed. "And an overnight visit will give all of us a chance to get to know each other better, too."

He pulled out his pocket watch and checked the time.

"Guess I better go get my team ready to load up on the train so we can hit the dusty trail—literally, huh?" As the Borglums turned to talk excitedly with each other he added, "I'm afraid that when my men find out how much extra work is going to be involved in getting through those woods down to the mine, I might end up on their shit list for the next couple weeks."

"Couple weeks?" Twocrow snorted. "How about months if not more."

"Yeah, I know they weren't planning on an excursion like that when I told them we were going to take a train ride today and follow an old logging trail tomorrow to load up some bootleg whiskey from a ghost mine."

"Well, look major, I'm sorr . . ."

"No, hell marshal, you're right. That still needs to be torn down, and all that whiskey moved out of there sooner rather than later. The sooner everything is cleared out of that mine, the sooner I can report to the powers that be that there's no longer any illegal activity going on around here.

"And that's definitely going to make things easier for the Borglums and all those political types who have been pressuring us to get this mountain carving project underway once and for all. I can't tell you how many times I've been reminded that we're on a tight deadline to get this thing started."

Twocrow laughed. "Don't forget, I work for the government, too, so I know of what you speak."

The major extended his hand to Twocrow. "You go get everything ready to take that boy and his dad on an exciting ride and tour of the mine, and I'll go get my men ready to 'Hit the Dusty Trail' as we sometimes like to say in the good old U.S. Army. Hah!"

He turned and started singing "Over Hill, Over Dale" as he walked jauntily back toward the depot, continuing to whistle the old Army marching song "Caissons Go Rolling Along" as he walked further along.

"What have I gotten myself into?" Twocrow said, looking first at the father and son, then at the major's back. He shrugged and started toward the Borglums, finding himself involuntarily humming his own version of "Caissons" as he walked. "Oh great!" he said looking back in Goodman's direction. "Now I'm going to have that damn song stuck in my head all day."

Chapter Forty-One

"We really appreciate your bringing us up here, marshal."

Gutzon and Lincoln Borglum rode in a single file behind Twocrow, a formation they had used since making their way off the regular Keystone to Hill City trail and heading north along the much less-traveled trail paralleling Horsethief Creek.

"I'm glad to do it sir," the marshal answered. "I think you're both going to enjoy seeing the Calendar, although I have to admit that it looks way better than what most ghost mines look like. It's interesting to see what a bootlegging operation looks like, too, although by later today Goodman and his men will probably have it completely torn down."

"And that's definitely a good thing," Borglum said. "They'll make sure there's no reason for the Forest Service to hold things up because of some illegal operation going on anywhere near where my carving project is going to begin."

"Besides, if you're going to be working in the Black Hills for the next few years something like this might come up again and if it does you need to know what local folks are going on about or threatening to get in your way about. Right?"

Borglum laughed. "I have this feeling that I'm going to need to know more than just this when it comes to what local folks are going to be 'going on about,' as you so succinctly put it."

"Yeah, you're right about that. South Dakotans can be pretty persnickety when something rubs them the wrong way."

"Yes, as your friend Minnie Thompson so clearly explained to me when she was wrapping up our interview for her story about my plans. I feel like she's got a good understanding of what I hope to achieve here on Mount Rushmore. But I'm under no illusion that I'll ever break through to that boss of hers. And I suppose there are still plenty of others who feel like that Hot Springs woman does, too?"

Twocrow thought about the last conversation he had had with the *Hot Springs Star*'s editor-in-chief and emitted a little sigh. "True, but you know at least she's agreed to run Minnie's series of articles, and after talking with you and Carrie Swanzey, I get the impression that they're going to be pretty favorable toward yours and the Keystone populace's point of view."

Borglum didn't say anything, just nodded with a satisfied look on his face as Lincoln urged his horse forward and rode up alongside the two men. "Do we have a long way to go yet?"

His father and Twocrow exchanged an amused look at the boy's impatience before Twocrow pointed off to their left. "No. Not far. See that? That's the rock formation everyone around here calls Devil's Thumb. Once we ride past it, we'll come to a smaller creek called the Tenderfoot that empties out into this one. We're going to turn and follow that."

Lincoln raised himself up in his stirrups to try to see past Devil's Thumb.

"You can't see the Tenderfoot Creek from here yet, but you will soon. Once we get into it—and we're going to have to ride IN the creek and not alongside it—then it'll be about a half mile or so until we reach the Calendar Mine. I'd say we've got another thirty or forty minutes on our ride. How's your rear end holding up?"

In response, the boy lifted up in the stirrups again and rubbed his backside. "Okay, but I'll probably be sore by tomorrow. Can we stop to eat something soon?"

Twocrow tapped his saddlebag. "Carrie Swanzey and her sister Mary Ingalls packed us a nice lunch and I've got it right here. There's a really beautiful little pond out front of that ghost mine's back entrance and it has a nice sand beach. We can have something to eat there before we go inside to explore."

Lincoln nodded at that just as his stomach growled loud enough to be heard even over all the outside noise being created by nature and their horses.

"You sound like maybe you can't wait that long?" The marshal reached into the saddlebag and took out an apple. Tossing it to the boy he added, "This ought'a hold you until then." He looked at the elder Borglum. "How about you. Need an apple?" Borglum waved him off and Twocrow shrugged. "Suit yourself." He grinned at Lincoln, took another one from the bag and bit into it as Ice looked back at him, eyeing the piece of fruit as a possible treat for himself.

"Hang on partner," he stroked Ice between the ears, took another big bite and then stretched his arm out and held the rest of the fruit out to the right side of Ice's face. The steel grey mustang's reaction was immediate as he turned his head and lipped the apple out of Twocrow's palm and into his mouth.

"Wow!" Lincoln laughed at Ice's reaction. "He must be really hungry too?"

"Nah, he's just greedy, especially when it comes to apples." Twocrow rumpled the top of Ice's head. "Come on, let's get moving."

They splashed into the creek and headed upstream, trekking along without talking for about 30 minutes before finally exiting at a grassy valley that stretched out on the back side of the Devil's Thumb rock formation before sweeping up a hill into a large stand of ponderosa pines on the Mount Rushmore side of the creek.

"See that ponderosa grove over to our right? We'll need to go through those trees and then cut back to the left once we come out of them in the next opening. From there it'll be across another little meadow and into a grove of aspens and maples. The pond that fronts what I call the Calendar Mine's backdoor entrance is just beyond that second grove."

He started Ice up onto the bank, stopped and turned toward them. "The trees are pretty thick in there, but they shouldn't hold us back. Still, stay tight together and keep an eye out for snakes. It was right around here somewhere that Harold Swanzey's horse got spooked by one, and you saw how that ended up for poor Harold."

Borglum looked upstream and across to the dark stand of ponderosas. "How come we can't just stay in the stream until we reach the pond?"

"Gets too rocky and goes more uphill from here until it flattens out just before the outlet from the pond. Too many places where our horses might step into a hole or in between rocks and fall, or something even worse like breaking a leg. Don't want to take any chances. Besides, the ride through the trees ain't all that bad."

"And there's snakes?" Lincoln had a fearful look on his face as he eyed the open grassy area that they would be crossing next.

"Not out here in the grass, especially in the middle of the day," Twocrow assured him. "These are Timber Rattlers and they'll be hunkering down in the crevices or in the deeper tangle of trees. They're usually active early and late, not mid-day, but just be careful anyway. Your horse will probably see one before you do and if he pulls up at all, pay attention and let him back away."

The boy nodded and gave his mount a friendly rub alongside his sleek neck. Twocrow guided Ice back out into the lead and headed for the spot where just a few days earlier the posse had been taking care of the shooting victims. As they moved closer to the pine grove, he could still see the flattened-out grasses and stirred up gouges in the ground that they had created with their horses and themselves during their stay.

They advanced quickly across this smaller meadow riding away from the dense growth of evergreen trees and into the "airier" aspen grove with room for their horses to move. They had threaded their way more than halfway through the aspens when an unusual noise caused him to pull up. Quickly raising a hand for his companions to stop, the marshal sat perfectly still, hand still raised—and listened. Before either Borglum or his son could ask anything he turned sideways in the saddle and held his fingers in front of his mouth for silence. Then he cupped a hand alongside his ear and pointed back to show he was listening for something. They sat quietly on their horses and waited for his next move.

Then he heard the noise again. This time it was a distinctive creak coupled with the grinding sound of some sort of crank. Borglum edged his horse up closer to Twocrow and whispered. "I can hear something too. What d'ya think? Did Goodman and his men get here already?"

Twocrow shrugged just as they heard a little splash, followed by an intense round of someone swearing.

"Well, that doesn't sound like him, but it could be one of his men. Stay here," he whispered. "I'm going to take a look. If I get into a jam, I'll yell, and you and Lincoln get the hell out of here and ride for help. Go back on the trail we just came from, okay?" Borglum nodded and signaled to his son to stay put.

"Okay. Be careful!" He laid a reassuring hand on Twocrow's arm before turning his horse around and riding back toward his son. The marshal dismounted, tied Ice to a tree and reached down to unsnap the clasp over his pistol.

Pulling the Colt out of the holster he checked that it was fully loaded and looked back to where the father and son were waiting.

"If you have to ride, don't worry about Ice," he spoke to them in a normal, calm voice. "Besides, I'll need him for my own getaway."

The Borglums nodded.

He gave them a thumbs up for his approval and began cautiously advancing toward the noise that now was increasing in volume.

Reaching the edge of the same part of the aspen grove where he had found Harold, he dropped to his knees, checked around to be sure there weren't any snakes crawling through the brush and crept forward to where he could look between several of the larger drooping branches. At the mine's backdoor entrance, the vines he had found covering the opening when he was there earlier had been chopped down and pushed away. A pulley device hooked onto a round drum was filling the space and two men—one on either side—were turning cranks and drawing in a rope that led down into the mine itself.

Off to the far side, the opposite direction from where he had walked to find Harold, a narrow-bed logging wagon, its tongue hooked up to two Belgian draft horses, sat in among the trees. A smaller cart pulled by a pair of mules sat alongside it, the mules dozing as they stood.

It appeared as if most of the whiskey casks Twocrow had seen earlier inside the mine were already lashed onto the narrow but sturdy wood plank wagon, and two more men working there were maneuvering another of the small barrels into position to add to the load.

Perched at the edge of the pond halfway between the wagon and the mine's opening was one other man who sat splashing water up onto his face and across the back of his neck.

The two men sweating and swearing at the cranking drum device now emitted a shout of approval as another small barrel came rolling up toward them. The cask was firmly hooked onto the rope that they were reeling in with the drum. The figure of yet another man scrambled up behind this newly arrived cask, pushing on it with his shoulder and struggling to hold it level as the other two men continued to turn the crank. Finally, the little barrel reached their position, and they stopped cranking and hurried to stabilize it, helping the third man get it sitting upright while sliding the rope halter off the barrel's bottom rim.

Getting the barrel firmly stabilized, they half-carried and half-rolled it over to the side toward where the logging wagon was being loaded.

"This is it!" one of the men yelled over to the men at the wagon. "Last one." He looked over to the third man for confirmation. "Right?" The man, who was still bent over and catching his breath raised an arm to give them a little wave in return.

The men at the wagon made sure that the barrel they had just finished loading was firmly in place before jumping down and starting back toward the others at the mine's opening. The two men there finished setting the newest barrel on its end, removed the rest of the rope harness and thrust the rigging back in the direction of the man who was still half hidden behind the cranking device.

The man stood and stepped out of the mine's shadows and into the sunlight, causing Twocrow to gasp in surprise. It was the CBQ conductor, Sam Palmer. What the hell was he doing out here?

He was about to stand and yell something to him when the man kneeling by the edge of the pond splashed a hand onto the water's surface and brought another handful up to his face. All five of the other men, now standing together by the crank and drum pulley, turned to look in his direction. In the process they also were now all looking directly toward where Twocrow was hiding.

He scrunched lower while keeping an eye on them through a small gap between the branches. The man at pond's edge still had his back to the others so that he too was facing Twocrow across the pond. But, like the others, he seemed oblivious to the marshal's presence.

Getting his first clear look at the pond-side man, the marshal gasped again.

He had never had the occasion to cross paths with this man before, but he had seen his face so often on wanted posters he knew instantly who it was that was facing him. Standing there in front of him in the middle of nowhere was one of the region's most notorious criminals.

"Mister Miller!" One of the red-faced crank operators standing alongside the pulley called out in the man's direction. "This is it! The last keg of our whiskey. We should be able to take off as soon as we get it packed on the wagon with the others. Do you want us to load anything else?"

"Sounds like a question for your brother, Palmer. Not for me?" And then the outlaw Verne Miller, poster boy for almost every type of major crime in South Dakota as well as reputed to be notorious mobster Al Capone's newest favorite shooter, turned his back to where the marshal was hiding and began striding up toward the mine.

Chapter Forty-Two

Letting out a long slow breath to get his heart rate settled following the surprising appearances by Verne Miller and, especially by Sam Palmer, Twocrow flattened himself as close to the ground as possible and slowly pushed his body backward and deeper into the underbrush.

Pretty sure that he had moved completely out of sight of the group of men gathered at the mine's entrance, he got to his knees and crab walked deeper to a point where he felt secure enough to return to his feet and walk unseen. Moving cautiously to make as little noise as possible, he finally got to where he had tied Ice, loosened his reins and walked the horse back along the trail until he reached the Borglums.

The father and son's horses made a little snort of welcome to Ice who just shook his head in response and then stood quietly as the marshal held a finger to his lips again, remounted and slowly rode back on the trail with the others following. After about 40 or 50 yards and deeper in the grove he pulled to a stop.

"We've got a problem," he said softly. "There's a gang of men over there removing that bootleg whiskey from the mine. I don't know if you know him, but one of them is Sam Palmer. He's the lead train conductor for the CB&Q."

Borglum shook his head. "No, I don't think I've had the chance to meet him yet."

"And that's not the half of it," Twocrow continued. "I recognized one of the other men as a big time South Dakota criminal that we've been tracking. And he's not someone we want to have a confrontation with—not the three of us anyway."

Now both Borglums looked alarmed but said nothing, waiting for the marshal to give them direction.

"I don't want to put the two of you in any danger, but at the same time I hate to just ride off and let these guys out of my sight. So, here's what I propose." He looked at the elder Borglum. "I'd like to take you and Lincoln over to the trail we were following earlier, where it branches off and heads north alongside Pine Creek.

"From there you can ride north until it links up with that old unused logging road that Major Goodman and I were talking about yesterday. That's the road that he and his men are riding down on from that camp—the Addie—that the CBQ Railroad operates. They're bringing a couple wagons to pick up the whiskey and tear down the still. The men over at the mine are way ahead of them and I'm pretty sure they'll be heading up that same road."

He took out his pocket watch and checked the time. "But since it's already after 11, I know the major and his teamsters have to be well on their way coming down that road. If you start riding now, I would guess it'll take you forty-five minutes or an hour to meet up with them."

Borglum nodded. "We can do that. We WILL do that."

"But I don't want you to take any chances either," Twocrow said. "So, if you're concerned for Lincoln's safety, you can just turn around and ride back on the main trail into Keystone. Then send me some help once you get back into town."

"No!" Borglum was emphatic in his response. "Everything you and the major and all the good people from around here have been doing has been geared toward helping me get my project underway. And this is finally a chance for us to help with that too. Right, son?" He glanced over at Lincoln who looked excited at the prospect.

"Well, okay. Good. Thank you! Then let's get going and once I've got you started up that trail I'll come back here. Those men over by the mine have a logging wagon that's capable of going through some pretty rugged territory, but like I said and based on where they were loading it I'd say they plan to take it back on that same road that you'll be riding—headed right toward Major Goodman and his men.

"But I want to get back there and keep them in sight, just in case they do have another way out of here that I don't know about. Palmer probably knows about most of the back trails around here by now thanks to his job with the railroad. But I'd bet my last dollar that they'll be headed right back up to that same road because they won't know Goodman is coming.

"They'll be right behind you and headed straight at those Army boys, so you're going to have to get up there first to let them know who's coming."

"You think this Palmer might want to try to get that whiskey onto one of his trains?"

"No, I doubt even he'd be able to pull something like that off. But once they do get further up that abandoned road, they can take any one of the other active logging trails. The railroad is using several of them to haul out trees they've been harvesting. And Palmer would know all about those trails because they've been bringing the logs over to load onto the trains.

"I know for a fact that one of them runs out to the northwest toward a couple of old worked out mines just south of the Addie Camp. And I think one goes northeast. There's an old mine over that way, too, closer to Old Baldy. Actually, that'd make a great place for him to store the whiskey until they decide what to do next. He's probably thinking that, too."

"So once Lincoln and I meet up with Major Goodman, do you want them to stay and wait for these guys or ride down closer to here to stop them?"

Twocrow contemplated that. "I think they should leave their wagons to block the trail and come toward me with as many men as they can. Tell him I don't think these guys moving the whiskey are gunfighters, just workers. They're probably just a couple of wagoneers that Palmer found, someone needing a few bucks who can drive the loads. A show of force coming at them would probably stop them in their tracks without anyone getting hurt. Okay?"

They rode out of the aspens and back into the little valley and Twocrow looked over to where he and the Swanzeys had started north a few days earlier. "There." He pointed. "That's where the trail goes north through the woods. It runs almost parallel to Pine Creek, so you should be able to follow the creek if you have to get off it for some reason. But the trail should be pretty clear because it's probably still trampled down from when the Swanzeys and I rode it the other day.

"Just get on it and keep riding for about twenty minutes and you should connect to that old logging road. Once you're on that just keep riding until you find Goodman and his Army detachment. You still sure you're okay doing this?"

"Yes. We got it."

Borglum reached across and gave his son's arm a reassuring pat, pointed over toward the trail and started riding. Lincoln glanced over at Twocrow with what looked like a combination of fear and excitement on his face, then quickly turned to follow. Suddenly, he stopped and turned his horse back toward the marshal.

"Marshal Twocrow!"

"Yes?"

"Sorry to ask, but, uh . . . do you think we could have some of those sandwiches to take along with us? I don't know about Dad, but I'm still kinda hungry."

Twocrow grinned, reached into his saddlebag and extracted the burlap sack that had most of the food inside. He rode forward and handed it to the boy as Gutzon Borglum rode back, rolled his eyes and gave his son an exasperated look. "Be sure to give your dad a sandwich too. Okay? By the look on his face, I think he's hungry too." He gave a little laugh and added, "Safe ride, Lincoln. Safe ride to the both of you."

"Yes sir! And thank you sir!" Lincoln pulled out a sandwich.

"And listen to your dad," Twocrow added as the boy took a bite. "Do whatever he says. I'll be counting on you." He gave them both a quick wave, pulled Ice around and headed back west through the trees.

Chapter Forty-Three

"I think we should take this trail back over to the old, abandoned logging road and then go north from there. It's only about half-a-mile up to where the two come together and you saw when we rode down here that it's still in pretty good shape."

Sam Palmer gestured in the general direction he was talking about and back to where Verne Miller was sitting on the seat alongside the logging wagon's driver. "That was always Billy's and my plan—at least one of our plans—when we first set things up in that old mine, and I don't see any reason not to go ahead with it now."

"Yeah, and what was your other plan?" Miller asked. "By the time we finally get moving it's going to be dark. This has been a clown show since we got here."

"Sorry Mister Miller," Sam said. "Didn't know it would take us so long to get everything loaded and ready to go."

Miller held his hands wide with an exasperated expression. "So? Your other plan?"

"Well, we were just going to take the barrels out by mule, one or two at a time. A little slower, but then we figured we could negotiate through the trees if we did that. A lot easier than taking out the whole load on a wagon."

The man who had stuck a gun in the back of Palmer's neck on the night that he had met with Miller in Hill City rode up on horseback and stopped alongside his boss. "What do you think George?" Miller asked. "We been sitting here for too damn long already, but I don't want to risk anything. You're from around these parts and you know these trails, right?"

The man nodded. "Yeah. I think it's a good route since we got the wagon. And from what I could see earlier it looked like there'd only been a few horseback riders on that road and none for a while. Definitely no other wagons or anything like that. That road's been mostly unused for years, but when my old man worked in the Calendar it was the main route to haul out the ore—back 20 or 25 years ago."

Miller looked back to where the abandoned mine's opening was now completely torn asunder, its vines down and loose rocks and dirt pushed out from the men's extraction and loading of the whiskey barrels. The pulley-crank device had been taken apart and after being dropped several times was now tied down onto the smaller mule-team cart.

Another delay had come when the cart's driver had pulled the little cart around and into line with the big logger and the entire load had fallen off. Now, finally loaded and anchored, he had lined it up behind the bigger wagon. The Belgians hooked up to the logger stood blowing and pawing the ground, impatient to get underway after the long wait.

"What about some of those trees and shrubs that were growing out into that road?" Miller asked. He pointed off to the northwest toward an opening leading out through the trees. "And tell me again why just going through the forest isn't the best route out? Since that was what you were thinking of doing before? Definitely no chance of anyone seeing us—both on the ground OR from the air, right?

"I heard about what happened to the Garrisons with that Army airplane getting involved, and I don't want anything like that happening to us. Do you know for a fact that no one's going to be flying around up there today?"

Now Sam's brother Billy moved forward, riding on horseback like his brother Sam. He gestured in the direction Miller was asking about. "I've been up and down through there on horseback half-a-dozen times since we got the brewing operation started, and I agree it's pretty wide open and definitely sheltered. But there's also two or three—maybe more—spots where not even that donkey cart can maneuver. One mule with a barrel or two; but not this big baby."

He tapped the wagon.

"Palmer's got a good point," George agreed. "And Boss, we already brought the wagon down that road to get here in the first place. It was a little tight in spots but nothing we can't handle." He put a hand on the wagon. "This wagon's built to handle rugged roads like that and it's definitely high enough off the ground that if we have to cut down a tree and drive over the stump, no problem."

Now Sam Palmer continued. "And our original plan was to get that whiskey over to the old Ridgway Mine northeast of here. There's another—and better—road that crosses the old logging road going out there. It's maybe two-thirds or three-fourths of the way up toward the rail line. So, once we reach it, we'll just cut off on that road, take the whiskey and the still over there and offload them before the day is out."

"Yeah, maybe, but not if we take any more time." He looked at his watch. "Two hours wasted, and I don't want to waste any more driving this load to a place that isn't going to work for us." Miller's icy blue eyes seemed even icier as he stared into Sam's face. The conductor swallowed hard and gave a careless wave of his hand.

"Well, it's real close to where that gravel highway runs down to Rapid City—Route 16. From that mine we can get a couple of trucks from Rapid and bring them up there in a few days. Once we load them onto trucks you can take them anywhere you want to from there." He stopped and swallowed hard at the look he was still seeing on Miller's face, as if Miller was still debating with himself as to what he should do with the Palmers now that the whiskey was ready to move.

Billy hurried to fill the silence. "And . . . you know, once you drive out east of Rapid you can pick up the Yellowstone Trail. That's the route that goes all the way over to the Twin Cities; even Chicago."

Miller's eyes seemed to lose a bit of their intensity as he heard this new information. "Twin Cities? You mean Minneapolis and St. Paul?"

"Hell, yes Mister Miller, and if you think it might work out, THAT mine might make a real nice new location for us to do a lot more brewing," Billy said. "I know I speak for my brother in saying we'd be proud to work with you at that new location if you're interested? Gotta find somewhere new if we're going to make any money at all," he said with an off-handed laugh as if sharing something Miller already didn't know.

Sam Palmer jumped back in.

"Yeah, and that Yellowstone Trail is a good road, too. Hell, that's even their motto, you know. 'A good road from Plymouth Rock to Puget Sound.'" He laughed, too, then quickly sobered as Miller continued to stare silently off to the east.

"I thought the main highway going through South Dakota to the Twin Cities was Highway 14—the Black and Yellow?" he finally said. "That road ran right past where I was sheriff, and they said it went to the Black Hills one way and the Twin Cities the other."

"Where you were what?" Billy Palmer seemed taken aback by Miller's comment. "Did you say you were a sheriff?"

"Hell yes. Beadle County on the east-central side of the state. I closed down so many of these stills, like the one you boys have been running that I knew everything about them." His eyes glistened. "And I sure as hell could see that the money you could make in a month from bootleg whiskey would be more than I made in a whole year as sheriff." He held his hand up. "So, I switched professions. Onward and upward, eh?"

At that he finally gave a light-hearted laugh and pointed toward the direction Sam Palmer had originally suggested. "All right, then let's take your road, Mister Palmer. Get these barrels up that road and out to that other mine." He blew out an exasperated sigh and shook his head. "Been a hell of a day, but nothing's gonna stop us now. Right?"

Sam and Billy shared a worried look and Sam finally answered. "Right. Nothing can stop us now."

* * * * *

Twocrow gave Ice a reassuring pat as he turned the little Mustang away from the mostly hidden overlook where they had ridden up to observe what the six men at the abandoned mine were preparing to do. That had been nearly an hour-and-a-half ago, actually going on two hours since he had sent the Borglums up the adjacent trail to try to connect with Major Goodman and his men.

After watching them finish loading and tying down the last of the barrels of whiskey—a job that took them a full half-hour—he'd had all he could do from bursting out laughing as they tackled the job of disassembling and loading up the still itself. Over the better part of an hour, they had sweated, swore and nearly destroyed the precious whiskey-making apparatus with their incompetence. And now he had watched them have what seemed to be one final argument with the outlaw Miller before getting underway.

This so-called "gang," he thought, would be very lucky to get their cargo safely out of the woods, up the trail, and off to wherever they planned to either store it or ship it somewhere else. And from what he knew of Miller and his ruthless approach, he was sure Miller would be dispensing with the Palmers soon thereafter.

Twocrow watched the wagons and three horseback riders finally starting to move. He wondered if they could possibly reach whatever location they had in mind without losing any of those barrels, either by banging them into trees or having them fall off the rough-running logger. And the still itself, despite their efforts, was probably going to be unable to even function, let alone distill anything once they got it to that location and tried to put it back together.

And that would only be possible if the still's transport wagon didn't fall off one of the cliffs they'd be riding past on their trip out.

During the time he'd been observing them, the men had dropped parts of the still and the pulley-rope device off the wagon at least a half-a-dozen times. And then the entire load had crashed to the ground when the driver turned the wagon too sharply to try to line up behind the larger wagon. Finally, though, both wagons were loaded and on the move. And just as he had hoped, they were headed down the side trail toward the old, abandoned logging road.

"All that work but if the Borglums found Goodman it's all going to be for naught," he said to Ice. Per usual, Ice didn't seem to care one way or the other, seeming much more interested in snagging a few mouths full of the grasses they were now riding past as they moved down from the overlook toward the trail.

Twocrow's plan from here was easy. He'd stay a few hundred yards behind the little caravan and hope the men weren't smart enough to keep one of their number back to insure they weren't being followed.

That had been a worry for him earlier, but now after watching them in action he was less concerned about it. He rode out of the trees on the far side of the little pond, gave the torn-up front of the ghost mine a forlorn look and clucked to Ice to start moving toward the trail. But he had only gone a few yards before a steely voice stopped him cold.

"Hold it right there and get your hands in the air!"

Chapter Forty-Four

The marshal raised his hands and sat looking at the trail. Now what?

"Don't move." The voice sounded familiar, and he was tempted to look but didn't want to take a chance at getting shot. Then he remembered where he had heard it before. At the debriefing following the capture of the Garrison Gang.

"Corporal O'Hara? Is that you?"

There was a silence and then the voice answered. "Marshal Twocrow?"

"Yep."

"Shit. I'm sorry. Put your hands down." The side of his forehead still bandaged from where the rock shrapnel had hit him during the firefight with the Garrisons, O'Hara clucked to his horse and rode away from the edge of the aspen grove over to Twocrow's side.

"What are you doing here?"

"Looking for you, marshal." He sat back in his saddle as Twocrow turned toward him with a sour look on his face. "Yeah, sorry," O'Hara continued. "I thought you were further down toward Devil's Thumb so when I saw you I figured you must be one of the gang. We all rode down on that old logging road and when we reached the point where the two trails split off, the major decided to set up there to stop anyone coming out."

"So, the Borglums reached you?"

"Sure did, and now they're pissed at the major because he wouldn't let them ride back with us. He left them with our wagons and a few of the troops while the rest of the Teamsters and I came down to see if we could stop that gang before they got any further."

He pointed off behind them to the aspen grove. "I took the trail over to Devil's Thumb and the major said that if you weren't there, you probably would be over by the mine. He said the quickest way there was to follow a little stream from where it emptied out into Pine Creek. I got out of that stream at a little grassy spot and just rode over here through the aspen trees."

He shrugged. "I'm not much of a tracker, but I figured if anyone was over here, I'd hear them before they could hear me and then I could decide what to do. I had just come out of the trees when I saw you ride out ahead of me." He looked around. "So, what about the outlaws? Where are they?"

"Headed right for Goodman taking this other branch of the trail," Twocrow said. "So, we should get moving, too. They're about fifteen minutes ahead of us; maybe a little more."

"Sure thing. How many of them are there?"

"Six, but I think only a couple of them are anything to worry about. I'd bet the rest would give up faster than I just did when you got the drop on me." He chuckled. "I have to admit you scared the crap out of me because I was just patting myself on the back for having outsmarted them. I was ready to ride along behind them for a couple miles without them having a clue I was here. That'll teach me to be more cautious, so thanks for that at least."

"Always glad to be of assistance." He gave him a little salute. He looked around. "I don't have a clue where I'm at, by the way, so you're going to have to take the lead."

Twocrow nodded to where the trail picked up and then put a finger to his lips to which O'Hara nodded, and they rode into the woods. They'd only gone 15 minutes when the sound of wagons and horses, topped off by a sudden little bray of a mule, interrupted their mostly quiet advance. Twocrow reined in and waited for O'Hara to come up alongside him.

"We can't see them from here, but we must be close to them. And we're close to that spot where this trail and the road connect. So, Goodman's set up there to make the stop, right?"

O'Hara nodded.

"Okay, then let's split up to better cover the back side in case they try to turn around." He pointed off to his right. "See where those two trees make kind of a notch on that rock shelf? Go up there. You'll be about twenty or thirty feet above the trail. Good spot to see them and stop them if needed. And the trees will give you plenty of cover, too. In case one of those two shooters I was talking about decides to come this way.

"I'll take the left side." He looked ahead, located a little depression just off the trail and backed by a rapidly rising rock wall. "There. That's where I'll set up. No way they'll be able to turn those wagons around, so if they do come back, they'll either be on horseback or foot. We should be able to hear Goodman when he pulls them up."

"Yes sir, marshal," O'Hara answered and immediately headed off toward the shelf and pair of trees. He'd barely departed before shouting erupted ahead of them followed by several gunshots.

Twocrow jumped down, pulled Ice deeper into the woods and tied him to a pine tree. Giving him a reassuring rub on the nose, he scrambled forward to the depression and dropped down. The location gave him a ground level view of the trail itself, and a sweeping look up to his left through the mix of aspens and ponderosas.

Goodman's voice rang out loud and clear followed by another pair of shots and several men calling out to stop shooting, they would surrender. He smiled and looked over to where O'Hara was set up and raised his rifle to signal success. O'Hara responded in kind and got up from behind the trees and started making his way back down.

Twocrow took two steps up from the depression and onto the trail, rifle cradled and sucked in a sharp breath. Coming at him at a dead run was Verne Miller. The outlaw, who held a pistol in his right hand, skidded to a stop at the sight of the lawman and started to pull the gun up before a shot rang out and kicked up dust and pebbles at his feet.

"Since I don't recognize you and you're waving that pistol around like you might want to hurt someone with it, that's just a warning shot!" O'Hara called out. "And just so there's no misperception sir, the next shot ain't gonna be a warning and it ain't gonna miss."

The outlaw looked over to his left where Corporal O'Hara was aiming a rifle toward him. He slowly looked back toward Twocrow, who now held his own rifle aimed directly at Miller's chest.

"Unless you want to take your chances with two against one, our rifles against your pistol, I'd suggest you put your gun down and raise your hands now, Mister Miller."

Miller responded with a little smile. "Well shit," he said. "Since you're bein' so polite about it and all." He tossed his pistol aside and held his hands up high. "One thing I learned a long time ago is that when someone says something to you that makes a hell of a lot of sense, you probably shouldn't question it. You should just be happy to oblige."

Chapter Forty-Five

The Swanzeys, Twocrow and Black Elk stood studying Borglum's plaster model of the four presidents, while Major Goodman and Minnie chatted with the sculptor in the center of his makeshift studio.

"Miller and the Palmers are laying the deaths of those still operators directly onto the Garrison gang. And they're also going to be charged with the killing of the guard during the Denver robbery. There's little doubt they'll be charged, sentenced and sent to prison for a long time," Goodman said.

"But as for the Bootlegging itself, that's going to be charged against the Palmers, and more importantly against Miller. He's been in and out of jail for other things, but this would be a federal charge, and they really want to get him on something like that." Twocrow walked over to join them, and Minnie casually slipped her arm into his and gave him a quick smile.

"Have you heard anything more about the Bootlegging charges against Miller?" Goodman asked.

"The Big Marshal's office over in Sioux Falls is definitely going to file an indictment," Twocrow said. "He'll be charged and brought to trial and hopefully that'll mean he's done with all his criminal activities in the state—not only now but for the foreseeable future."

Borglum nodded enthusiastically at that. "I don't know that much about the man, but just what I've learned since all this began makes me more than happy that he's not going to be anywhere in the vicinity once we get things underway. Same with the bootlegging gang themselves. I can't imagine what we might've had to deal with if they'd been operating while we were trying to do our carving project."

"All the focus will be on your work," Goodman said. He turned to Minnie. "How were your articles received?"

"Good. There will probably always be those who don't believe in something like this, but after talking with you all as well as with the people who live here—and what it will mean to them—I've been convinced that this will be something good for the Black Hills."

Borglum turned to Twocrow. "And I promise you and I promise Black Elk that I will respect this mountain and all of the Black Hills as I move forward with my work."

Twocrow nodded but said nothing. Instead, he looked over to where Black Elk was still studying the model. Seeing that, Borglum said, "And I have had a conversation now with Mister Black Elk and his father, giving them my pledge to support and preserve their sacred land to the best of my abilities. And I've told Black Elk that they always will be welcome to come here, meet those who come to see the monument, and share their people's stories with all."

Black Elk looked toward them and gave them a little nod of his own. Borglum motioned for him to join them, but before he could make a move the door burst open and Lincoln Borglum rushed in, waving a telegram.

"Dad!" he called out, holding the paper high as he advanced with a huge smile on his face. "Approved Dad! We've been approved for the October ceremony!"

His father hurried over to the teenager, took the telegram and read it and then slapped it against his open palm.

"Well, ladies and gentlemen this is prodigious news, indeed. Especially since you're all gathered here together like this." He walked further into the room and waved for everyone to come and join him in front of the model.

"I wanted you to join Miss Thompson here—and Lincoln, of course—in being among the first locals to get a good look at my plans for the mountain carving. And now I have this approval as icing on the cake."

They moved in closer, and he held the telegram out to read it.

"From the Division of Forestry, U.S. Department of Agriculture. It is with great pleasure that we grant full approval for your October 1st Dedication Flag Ceremony to officially announce your new National Memorial in the Black Hills of South Dakota. Agents have deemed your proposed project fully approved, vetted, and ready to begin." He looked up with a smile. "And it's signed by the Forest Service Chief in Washington, D.C."

The small group broke into applause with the Swanzeys adding a little cheer.

"Thank you! All of you. Without your help in capturing those gangs, closing down that illegal still and solving those murders, who knows what would have happened? It might have been months, if not years, before such a special ceremony could take place." He handed the telegram back to his son. "Now, we can move ahead as planned and, of course, all of you are invited."

"Where will the Flag Dedication Ceremony take place?" It was Minnie with the question.

Borglum walked over and tapped the top of the models' heads. "Here. Right at the top of the mountain. Lincoln and I already have been thinking of how it will be arranged and will invite State and Federal government officials, but we believe the most important people to be invited are local leaders and all the good people of Keystone and the communities around us, including Rapid City.

"And while I believe this will be a day to long remember, I want to hold off on the Memorial's formal dedication until either the president or secretary can attend. And hopefully we can announce government funding and full support for the monument."

"You think that will happen?" Goodman asked.

"Yes, I'm positive. And it MUST happen. We've gotten donations, but the State of South Dakota seems to be holding back until they know that the federal government is also going to be on board. And" he turned to Black Elk, "I am glad for your support as well. Money is not everything. History and tradition . . ." he stopped, swallowed hard, and then lifted his arm back toward the model and then pointed out the window toward the top of the mountain.

"The figures I carve there will represent a new vision for the Six Grandfathers and for all of the Black Hills. Even for America itself." He looked intensely at the small group gathered before him. "America will march along that skyline. America will march along Mount Rushmore."

Afterword

Devil's Thumb - photo by Dan Jorgensen

Devil's Thumb—The Facts . . . and The Fiction

In 1923, South Dakota State Historian **Doane Robinson** came up with the idea for what ultimately would become the **Mount Rushmore National Memorial**. In hopes of promoting tourism in South Dakota, Robinson persuaded famed sculptor **Gutzon Borglum** to travel to the Black Hills in 1924 to study the landscape and see if a carving there could be accomplished. At the time Borglum was sculpting the Confederate memorial at Stone Mountain outside of Atlanta, GA. But he was in constant disagreement with officials there and ready to leave.

Robinson's original suggestion was that Borglum carve sculptures of famous South Dakotans, including a Sioux chief, into The Needles—granite pillars about 10 miles north of Custer. However, Borglum said

The Needles were too thin to support his sculpting and he thought a "grander" carving with a more national focus was in order. After visiting three other possible mountain locales he chose Mount Rushmore for his concept of four former presidents representing different elements and eras of United States history. After selecting Mount Rushmore—a location that faced southeast and enjoyed maximum exposure to the sun—he was reported to have said, "America will march along that skyline."

Because Mount Rushmore was located in the Harney National Forest, Congress had to approve the location. With South Dakota **Senator Peter Norbeck**'s and South Dakota **Congressman William Williamson**'s support, Congress authorized the carving, and then the formation of the Mount Rushmore National Memorial Commission on March 3, 1925. Exploratory trips up the mountain by Borglum and Robinson—accompanied by **Major Jesse Tucker**, wrangler **Ray Sanders**, and **Borglum's teenage son Lincoln**—took place in late August and early September 1925. Borglum planned to immediately dedicate the site, but with funding coming in more slowly than anticipated, he decided instead to do a "Dedication Flag Ceremony" on Oct. 1, 1925. One of the first speeches made at that event was by Robinson, who went on to serve as the de facto manager of the project during its early years.

The "official" Mount Rushmore dedication took place on August 10, 1927 when **U.S. President Calvin Coolidge** joined Borglum at the site, handing the sculptor a set of ceremonial drill bits and pledging much-needed federal funding, the support Borglum needed to keep the project on track.

Coolidge's support grew out of an invite from Norbeck to come and spend some time in the Black Hills in the summer of 1927. The President not only accepted the invitation but also established a "Summer White House" at the State Game Lodge in Custer State Park. He arrived there in June and resided there for about 10 weeks, both vacationing and conducting the nation's business. Coolidge brought with him a couple hundred staff members and attracted thousands of motorists—both from South Dakota and across the nation—eager for a glimpse of the President and his wife, who were sometimes fishing for trout along the newly named Grace Coolidge Creek near the Game Lodge.

While in the Black Hills the Coolidges participated in several events and programs, including a 4th of July/55th birthday (his) celebration. He also attended Deadwood's famed "Days of '76," drawing the largest crowd (up to that time) in the history of the event. And he was honored at a gathering of 300 Lakota tribal leaders, who ceremonially adopted him into the Sioux tribe while bestowing on him an elaborate war bonnet and the honorary Lakota name: **Wanblee Tokaha,** or **"Leading Eagle."**

On August 2, a week before the formal dedication of Mount Rushmore, he made the "bombshell" announcement to the nation that he would not be a candidate for re-election in 1928. That announcement appeared to come as a shock to his friends, colleagues and the political leaders from both major parties but did not interrupt any of the President's planned activities, including the Mount Rushmore dedication ceremony.

On returning to Washington, D.C., he simply said, "I have had a good time." That also might have been Borglum's sentiments following the dedication event. With crucial governmental support now pledged and no local impediments to his plan, Borglum began the mountain's **first drilling and carving on October 4, 1927.**

* * * * *

As noted above, Borglum's 13-year-old son **James "Lincoln" Borglum** accompanied his father to the Black Hills and was with Gutzon when he selected Mount Rushmore as the site for the carving. After working with his father on models and other small projects associated with the sculpture, he began unpaid work on the monument itself in 1933. He was officially put on the payroll in 1934, promoted to assistant sculptor in 1937, and promoted to project superintendent in 1938.

When Gutzon Borglum became ill and then died in March of 1941, Lincoln took over the carving and finished it by the end of that October, just over 16 years from the 1925 Dedication Flag Ceremony. Congress appointed him as the Mount Rushmore National Memorial's first Superintendent on October 1, 1941, and he served in that capacity for the next two-and-a-half years, until May 15, 1944. Like many of the men who worked on the Rushmore project, Lincoln's lungs were damaged from breathing in the granite dust associated with the blasting. Suffering from a form of emphysema caused by that lung damage, he died in 1986 in Corpus Christi, TX at the age of 73.

* * * * *

Going hand-in-hand with the start of the Mt. Rushmore carving was construction of new or improved roadways from Rapid City to Keystone and from Keystone to nearby communities like Hill City, Hermosa and Custer. Toward that end, the South Dakota National Guard and the U.S. Army Corps of Engineers led by people like **Major Jeremiah Goodman**, who is fictional but based on real members of the Corps, helped plan and carry out the new road construction.

But it was the visit of **President Coolidge** that really got the road projects moving—first in preparation for the President's use of them and then as a follow-up after Coolidge experienced the state's need for infrastructure improvement after bouncing over several ungraded (mostly dirt) roads that weaved throughout the Black Hills. Recognizing the tourism potential and wanting to help advance tourism in the region, Coolidge followed up on his support for Mt. Rushmore with federal support for infrastructure funding to build many new roads and improve others.

* * * * *

Everyone wasn't happy with the proposed project, and one of the earliest opponents to the carving was **Cora B. Johnson**, an environmentalist as well as co-owner and columnist for *The Hot Springs Star* in Hot Springs, SD. Johnson led a robust "anti-carving" movement, writing against what she viewed as "a desecration of the natural beauty of the Black Hills." She first spoke out after learning of Robinson's and Borglum's carving plans for The Needles, writing in an editorial: "Man makes statues, but God made The Needles."

Even after Borglum decided to focus his carving on Mount Rushmore instead, she continued to write against any such project, gaining support from several other regional newspapers and environmental groups in the process. Angered by Johnson's attacks, Borglum refused to refer to her by name, simply calling her "That Hot Springs person" and "An agent of evil."

* * * * *

A **Fire Spotting Lookout Cabin**—replacing an earlier temporary fire watch structure—was built on top of **Harney Peak,** the Black Hills' highest point, in 1919 and was operated by the U.S. Forest

Service. From this highest Black Hills vantage point, resident **"Fire Spotters"** could look out in all directions thanks to the cabin's walls being constructed with a combination of wood and heavy-duty glass panels. This provided the spotters with protection and clear views for spotting fires in order to help deploy firefighting crews. Until a phone line was installed, the spotters would have to ride on horseback down to Hill City to sound the alarm whenever a fire was detected.

One of the spotters' clearest views was to the northeast toward Mount Rushmore— "six miles as the crow flies and 12 miles and many, many long hours through rugged terrain by horseback, mule or on foot."

The Forest Service's ability to respond to fires and deploy firefighters got a major upgrade when the first phone line to Hill City was installed in the mid-1920s. By the 1930s, after a larger stone and glass structure was built to replace the cabin, a year-around phone line to Hill City followed.

Although the Forest Service was primarily a male bastion in its early years, female staffers—often part of husband-and-wife teams—had a major role as spotters in many locations. **Clarice Byers** and her husband **Ralph,** the spotters depicted in this book, are fictional but based on real people like **Helen and Paul Beard**, who served as fire spotters on Harney Peak.

The Beards were "in residence" at the Harney Peak Lookout Cabin for several years in the 1920s spending the "fire season" on the peak and the "off season" in Ames, Iowa, where they were students at Iowa State University.

The June 7, 1923 edition of **the weekly *Pioneer Times*** in Deadwood, SD, noted, "Mrs. Paul Beard, fire lookout at Harney Peak . . . (is) one of the few women in field work in the entire United States Forestry Service. The tiny glass house in which she lives, looking into four different states whenever she feels inclined, is lashed to the rock on which it stands by heavy steel cables. Her domicile can only be entered by climbing a 20-foot ladder.

"Mrs. Beard said one of the most important instructions she had, in addition to how to spot and precisely locate fires, was, 'During lightning storms, stay in the cabin and do not touch metal furnishings.'"

* * * * *

In 2016, **Harney Peak** (also called by the Lakota name **Hinjhan Kaga** - the Owl Maker) was renamed **Black Elk Peak** in the memory and honor of Lakota spiritual leader **Nicholas Black Elk**, father of **Ben Black Elk**, the character depicted in this story.

In 1872, when he was a 9-year-old boy, **Nicholas**—known then only by the name **Black Elk**—was gravely ill and in a comatose state when he had a great vision. In his vision he said he had been visited by Thunder Beings (*Wakinyan*), kind and loving spirits full of years and wisdom much like human grandfathers who took him on a journey to the sacred Black Hills.

Black Elk said that he first came to a mountain where he saw six grandfathers appear. They were atop a peak that 15 years later would become known as **Mount Rushmore**. But from the time of Black Elk's vision the Lakota would only call the peak **The Six Grandfathers**.

He said he also was transported to the top of a much larger peak called **Hinjhan Kaga** (the Owl Maker) before finally being returned to his village, looking down into a deep bowl-like valley he called **Wanagi Yata**—the place of souls—where the spirits of the Lakota reside.

Lakota medicine men said they were "astonished by the greatness of the boy's vision."

Revered as a Lakota spiritual leader from that point forward, Black Elk became known to a worldwide audience after doing interviews with the poet **John Neihardt** about his religious views, his visions, and other events from his life.

Neihardt published his Black Elk interviews in the 1932 book ***Black Elk Speaks,*** which is still in print with more than 1 million copies sold.

* * * * *

Nicholas's son, **Ben Black Elk** was born in 1899 on the Pine Ridge Reservation. He was friends with many Keystone area residents and with **Lincoln Borglum** and after Mount Rushmore was completed, he became the Lakota people's "unofficial greeter" at the mountain. Wearing traditional Lakota clothing and a single Eagle feather, Black Elk greeted visitors for nearly 30 years until his death in 1973. Ben shared stories and posed for many thousands of photos. He also traveled extensively, testified before Congress on the importance of teaching Indian history to Indians, and appeared in a number of Hollywood movies. Locals and state tourism officials alike affectionately knew him as "The fifth face on the mountain."

Since 1980, South Dakota's Tourism Bureau has presented the annual **Ben Black Elk Award** to a leader or leaders in the industry to recognize "Lifetime Achievement in Tourism" in South Dakota. **The Gutzon Borglum Family** was one of the first recipients of this prestigious award.

* * * * *

The Lakota characters in this story—**Al Twocrow, Ben Black Elk,** Nelson, Cricket and Lela Ghost Bear—are depicted with "first" and "last" names, which were just becoming the "norm" around this time in the Black Hills area. Traditionally the Lakota did not have Family Names, or surnames before the early part of the 20th century.

Nicholas Black Elk, for example, was simply known as Black Elk until he was baptized in 1904 or 1905, and it was at that time that his son **Ben** took the name **Black Elk** as his own surname. The widespread use of surnames came about because of the requirement by the U.S. government that all Native Americans "register an official first and last name" in order to receive land on the reservation or to obtain other assistance from the U.S. Government.

Many of the Oglala Lakota—the tribe residing on the Pine Ridge Reservation east and southeast of the Black Hills—took the names of tribal leaders or of their parents or grandparents. Names like Red Elk, Yellow Boy, Wounds Plenty or Little Hawk became "family" surnames for many. Others took on or were given surnames of white ranchers and farmers living in the area. And still others had names chosen for them by the Indian Agent or by census takers or interpreters. Thus, names like Nelson, Watson, Buckman and James also were among the "family" names registered on the reservation.

The 1920 United States Federal Census for Shannon County (today known as Oglala Lakota County), home to the Pine Ridge Indian Reservation, includes the names Ghost Bear and Black Elk but not Twocrow since the Two Crow family had relocated to Hot Springs. **Albert Twocrow**, a friend of the author, is the inspiration for the **Alvin (Al) Twocrow** character, not only in this book but also in the two earlier historical novels—*And The Wind Whispered* and *Rainbow Rock*—mentioned above.

The Two Crow family name dates to a mid-to-late 1800s Lakota tribal spiritual leader and chief known only as **Two Crow**. Unfortunately, when smallpox and diphtheria epidemics swept the reservation and surrounding area in the 1880s, most of the Two Crow family died. That's when the remaining family members moved to the newly established (in 1882) town of Minnekahta—the Lakota name for what officially became Hot Springs in 1890. There, some surviving family members adopted the "combined" version of the name—**Twocrow**—as their own.

* * * * *

David Swanzey, **Bill Challis** and **Ted Brockett** achieved considerable fame among Keystone and Hill City area residents for their friendship with **Charles Rushmore**, a New York City attorney whose name was the basis for labeling the Black Hills peak **Mount Rushmore**.

The men did many rides with Rushmore into the hills west of Keystone as he checked on land titles for clients back East. On one of those rides in 1885 they unofficially named the massive granite peak Mount Rushmore even though the Lakota and Cheyenne people still called it **The Six Grandfathers.** Up to that point, Black Hills ranchers and miners referred to the granite peak by various names, including "Cougar Mountain," "Sugarloaf Mountain," and "Slaughterhouse Rock," seemingly unable to settle on one name over another.

Despite the three men having re-named the mountain Mount Rushmore as a lark—after Rushmore told the others that they ought to name the mountain for him since he had ridden past it so many times—their new title stuck. After Borglum began carving the **Four Faces on the Mountain** memorial—also called **The Shrine of Democracy**—the

Mount Rushmore National Memorial became its "official" title through a 1930 Act of Congress.

While not widely known, since most of the project's funding came from the federal government, Charles Rushmore was monitoring Borglum's efforts to carve the mountain and made a personal contribution of $5,000 to the effort. His would be the largest individual gift given to the project.

Despite the "official" Mount Rushmore designation, many Native American people still refer to the mountain by its Lakota name **Thunjkasila Sakpe** or **The Six Grandfathers**.

Before the carving—The Six Grandfathers
(Photographer unknown but likely William Cross, a well-known Hot Springs-based landscape photographer and character in the book *And The Wind Whispered*)

In addition to his local "celebrity" for his part in naming Mount Rushmore, in August of 1912 **Swanzey** was married to **Carrie Ingalls**, the younger sister of **Laura Ingalls Wilder**, author of the "Little House on the Prairie" books. They honeymooned in the resort town of Hot

Springs where she first met journalist (and book character) **Minnie Thompson**.

Carrie had moved to Keystone in 1911 as a reporter and bookkeeper for Keystone's newspaper *The Recorder*. Two days shy of 42 years old at the time of her marriage to Swanzey, who was a widower, Carrie also became stepmother to Swanzey's children **Mary Elizabeth** and **Harold**. She lived in Keystone until her death in 1946. At her request, she was buried in the Ingalls family plot in DeSmet, SD, the **"Little Town on the Prairie"** locale.

Known as a generous and caring person, Carrie led fund-raising drives to help with everything from saving a local church to building a fire station. She also made arrangements to donate land and money to other local causes after she died.

Carrie's stepson **Harold Swanzey,** 19 years old in this story, worked as a miner and then went to work for **Gutzon Borglum** as a carver on Mount Rushmore. His name can be found among the list of carvers on the granite walls below the monument. He was killed in a car accident near Hill City in 1939. Harold and his father David, who died in 1938, are buried alongside David's first wife (Harold's mother Elizabeth) in the Keystone Cemetery.

Carrie's stepdaughter **Mary Elizabeth** married Miciah Monroe "Monk" Harris in 1921. By 1925, at the time of this story, the Harris's were ranching between Keystone and Hermosa and soon to move to a ranch near Scenic, east of Rapid City.

After Mary Elizabeth and Harold had moved out of their childhood home, Carrie and David took in and cared for Carrie's blind older sister **Mary Ingalls** following the death of the two women's mother **Caroline Ingalls** in 1924. Mary lived with the Swanzeys until her death from pneumonia in 1928.

Laura Ingalls Wilder, who was working as a columnist and editor at the *Missouri Ruralist* magazine at that time, visited Keystone often, discussing her ideas for journalistic stories with Carrie and sharing her plans for a memoir (later instead becoming the *Little House* books) that she was hoping to write about the girls' childhood days in Wisconsin, Minnesota, Kansas and South Dakota.

* * * * *

Maxine Grimalski and her husband **Matthew Grimalski**, along with Matthew's brothers **Merle** and **Howard**, are fictional but are representative of the families who populated Keystone and worked at the local businesses and as miners at that time.

Hot Springs Star reporter **Minnie Thompson** (as noted above) was a real person and newswriter friend of Carrie Swanzey. Minnie's uncle **Col. Jack Thompson** was editor and publisher of the *Buffalo Gap News* where Minnie and her older sister **Laura Thompson** began their journalistic careers in the 1890s. Minnie was an accomplished feature writer and news reporter for both the *News* and the *Star* while **Laura** went on to become a reporter for several East Coast newspapers.

Both women were influenced by the writing and reporting of the famous *New York World* reporter **Nellie Bly**, who the girls' met when Bly vacationed in Hot Springs—and helped bring an outlaw gang to justice—in 1894 (and depicted in the author's historical novel *And The Wind Whispered*).

Bly was a protégé of the *World*'s equally famous publisher **Joseph Pulitzer**. It was money from Pulitzer's estate that helped establish both the world-renowned Columbia University School of Journalism and The Pulitzer Prizes, which have been awarded since 1917.

*****

Otto "Red" Anderson also was a real person, representative of the local miners who became an integral part of the Mount Rushmore carving project. And Anderson was a member of Mount Rushmore's famous baseball team, made up of members of the carving crew. **The "Mount Rushmore Nine"** were contenders for South Dakota state amateur baseball championships in the late1930s and early 1940s when Lincoln Borglum served as their team manager.

*****

Pilot **Kallie Sinclair,** while fictional, is based on the brave young female pilots who were making their mark as early leaders in the fledgling U.S. air flight industry. By the mid-1920s when **Amelia Earhart** was becoming known worldwide for her long-distance flying exploits, other female flyers like **Kathleen Simpson**, **Kitty Stinson** and **Nellie Wilhite**, South Dakota's first known woman pilot, were flying U.S. mail routes, carrying dispatches for the military, and joining in barnstorming visits to communities around the nation. These fearless young women laid the groundwork for the many women flyers who were instrumental in helping the U.S. win World War II. They also paved the way for generations of women pilots in both the military and the growing civilian aviation industry.

Kallie's biplane in this story, the single engine **Kinner Airster**, was a workhorse plane of the 1920s in both one- and two-seat open cockpit models. Earhart, in fact, owned an Airster that she named *The Canary*. The Airster was powered by a variety of 60 horsepower engines that gave it a maximum speed of nearly 100 miles per hour and a range of over 300 miles.

Dan Jorgensen

* * * * *

Mail carrier Joseph Parker is fictional. The "regular" carrier referred to in the story—**Lewis (Louie) Mills**—was a real Keystone Mail Route carrier. His father **Jesse Mills** was the first mail carrier in the community of Keystone when it was established in the late 1800s. Lewis's grandson **Rick Mills,** who provided valuable background information for this book, is curator and historian of the South Dakota State Railroad Museum in Hill City.

* * * * *

The Baldwin Steam Engine was a workhorse train engine for many railroads in the 1920s, and its use in this story is imagined by the author. One of the big engines—Engine #7, built by Baldwin Locomotive Works in 1919—has been part of the **Black Hills' 1880 Train** since 1962. The engine, on display in Hill City, is called a Soaker, a non-super heated engine that uses a lot of water. The additional water needed was stored in a Tender that could weigh as much as 75 thousand pounds. This extra weight sometimes limited the number of train cars that could be pulled by the Soaker. The engine itself weighs over 200 thousand pounds, operating on a 2-6-2 wheel base.

* * * * *

The Calendar Mine is fictional, but its description is based on a combination of the **May Gold Mine** in Custer County and the **November Mine** near Black Elk Peak. Both mines produced a wide variety of minerals and still exist as "ghost" mines in the hills west and south of Mount Rushmore. None of the mines have a "front" and "back" entrance with a pond on either end as depicted here as imagined by the author.

* * * * *

Moonlight Valley or **Wanagi Yata,** the site located below the outlaws' campground, later became known as **The Stratobowl**. A compact natural depression northwest of Old Baldy Mountain and southwest of Rapid City in the Black Hills National Forest, it was regarded as a sacred Place of Souls by some Lakota Bands. Surrounded by wide, flattop cliffs, the primary one called **Katiyimo** or "Enchanted Mesa" by the Lakota, it was only known to a few locals as "Moonlight Valley" while the overlook mesa had no title at all. It was a place for small-scale mining until 1934 when an enterprising Army Air Corps captain named Albert W. Stevens decided it was the place to launch a balloon in the name of high-altitude exploration. In 1934–1935 it housed a stratospheric balloon launch site initially known as **Stratocamp** and sponsored by the National Geographic Society and the United States Army Air Corps.

Camping still takes place on the flattop mesa overlooking the site, especially when hot air balloon launches are scheduled. Every year in September, Black Hills Balloons hosts a hot air balloon launch from the Stratobowl. Each August, Hot Springs hosts The Fall River Hot Air Balloon Festival with launches taking place near the Hot Springs Airport.

* * * * *

The Denver Bank Robbery—basis for this story's bank robbery by the Garrison outlaw gang, which then escaped into the Black Hills—is a mash up of two 1920s robberies of Denver financial institutions.

One of those robberies was alleged to have been carried out by the infamous **"Bobbed-Hair Bandit"**—a petite New York woman named **Celia Cooney** who was linked to or blamed for a number of robberies in New York and across the country.

While a "bobbed-hair bandit" (the title taken from Denver newspaper headlines) and her companions were sought for the armed robbery of the Denver Bank, it was never actually proved that the woman was Cooney, and no one was ever captured.

Cooney eventually WAS arrested in Florida and did time in prison.

The second, and more deadly, robbery was carried out by a gang who attacked a Federal Reserve Bank transport truck. The gang—one of whom was a woman—killed a bank guard and stole more than $200,000 (nearly $3.6 million in today's dollars). That gang escaped to northeastern Colorado and was last seen in western Nebraska although "sightings" also were made in the Black Hills.

The bank robbers eluded a massive manhunt by regional sheriff's departments and federal marshals until a hint of their whereabouts came from a report by a Nebraska rancher's wife. She said the men held her hostage while she treated the wounds of one of them. She thought that when they left her family's ranch they then drove north toward the Black Hills. But despite months of searching and hundreds more "sightings," probably sparked by promises of a big reward, the gang disappeared, and the stolen money was never recovered.

The four **Garrison Gang** members as well as the brothers **Sam and Billy Palmer**, leaders of the whiskey bootlegging operation depicted in this story, are fictional.

* * * * *

Devil's Thumb

The airplane/horseback pursuit of the outlaw gang in the story is based on a similar real-life pursuit in the hills and mountains of Wyoming in July of 1924. A banner headline in the July 16, 1924 *Rocky Mountain News* reads: 'Cashier Is Pursued By Airplane Posse', with a sub headline reading: 'Sleuths take to sky in hunt for missing man'.

The story is datelined in Rock Springs, WY and tells of the pursuit of an 'outlaw' cashier who had stolen large sums of money and was trying to escape through the hills and mountains. The story notes that two airplanes carrying sheriff's deputies are pursuing the robber through the air, while on the ground a posse of "hard-riding deputized cowboys on horseback also have taken up the chase and are combing the hills."

In two of my own experiences while writing feature stories for the *Hot Springs Star*, I flew with the FBI in pursuit of a cattle rustling gang and a second time with a private detective to take photographs from his small plane of an area where a crime had been committed. The "diving" and "sharp banking" scenes in this book, as well as the "gliding" with no engine noise, come directly from my own experiences flying "in pursuit of the bad guys."

* * * * *

The Whiskey Still and bootlegging are based on a reported bootlegging operation led by notorious South Dakota outlaw **Verne Miller**. Miller was a native of rural South Dakota (although some records have put his birth in Illinois) who went from a planned career as a lawman to one as a criminal, beginning in the mid-1920s.

A decorated World War I veteran, Miller was elected Beadle County (SD) Sheriff and had a stellar two-year record before running afoul of the law by embezzling money to help pay for his wife's medical bills. Ironically, in his early years as sheriff, he was devoted to destroying illegal liquor operations and the so-called "Stills," confiscating so much bootleg whiskey at one point that he was using it as antifreeze in his Sheriff's Department vehicles.

Miller's growing knowledge of how bootleg whiskey was made led him to set up his own still after being released from prison following the embezzlement conviction. In October of 1925, he and several of his bootlegging partners were captured without a fight while trying to transport a batch of illegal whiskey. Ultimately, Miller was indicted for the bootlegging operation that some said stretched from the Black Hills to St. Paul, MN. It also was said to be connected to **mobster Al Capone's** organized crime operation, headquartered in Chicago. But after being released on bail for the bootlegging arrest, Miller disappeared from sight for several years before resurfacing as a much more hardened criminal having honed his skills working as a "shooter" for Capone.

From 1928 on, he was linked to everything from bank robberies to the illegal trafficking of drugs and alcohol to kidnapping and as many as 12 murders. His involvement in a June 1933 shootout known as "The Kansas City Massacre" led the FBI to conduct a nationwide manhunt for him. It ended with the discovery of his bullet-riddled body in October of that same year.

The identity of his killer or killers has never been determined.

About the Author

Born in the Mayo Clinic's St. Mary's Hospital in Rochester, MN, Dan Jorgensen grew up on a South Dakota farm, was educated in a one-room country school and after high school at Viborg and Parker, SD, became the first member of his family to attend college. He earned both his bachelor's and master's degrees from South Dakota State University and studied creative writing and film classes at Colorado State University where he wrote his first novel *Killer Blizzard*.

He has won awards for his creative writing and newspaper feature writing and for his work in educational public relations.

In addition to writing many hundreds of news and sports articles and feature stories, both as a journalist and in public relations, he is the author of 10 books, including the award-winning *And The Wind Whispered, Rainbow Rock* and *Killer Blizzard*. He also has written 3 songs, and a one-act play "The First Day"; contributed to 2 anthologies; and writes the several-times-a-week Blog "A Writer's Moment." He is a frequent speaker on "The Writing Life" and "Storytelling."

Among the professional organizations with which he has been affiliated are Rotary International, National Association of Science Writers, Kappa Tau Alpha (the national journalism honorary), The Society of Professional Journalists (Sigma Delta Chi), Historical Writers of America, The Historical Novel Society and the Veterans of Foreign Wars.

Dan and his wife Susan are the parents of two adult daughters—Kari Diener, her husband Obie Diener and their sons Theodore and Cyrus of Harrisonburg, VA; and Becky Yeager, her husband Evan Yeager and their sons Joshua and Nolan of Longmont, CO. Dan and Susan make their home in Milliken, CO.

Now Available!

MYSTERIES FROM MASTER STORYTELLER DAN JORGENSEN

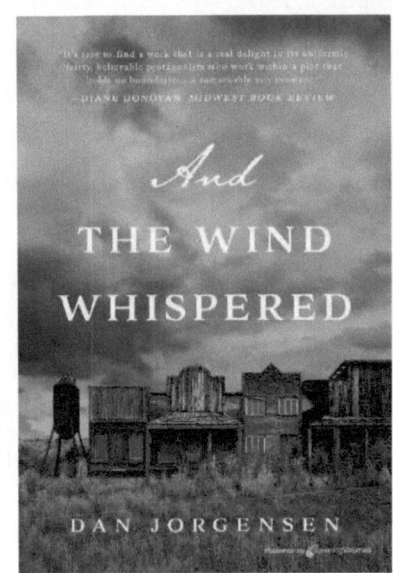 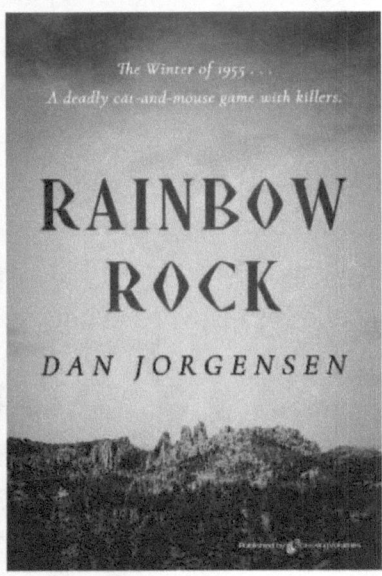

For more information visit: www.SpeakingVolumes.us

Now Available!

AWARD-WINNING AUTHOR
DICK BROWN

UNDER THE CANYON SKY
Books 1-3

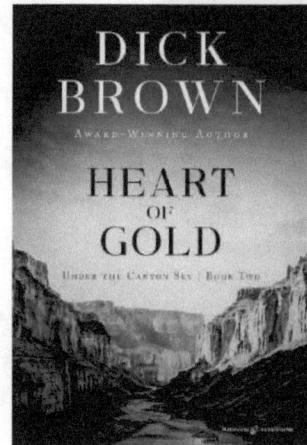

**For more information
visit: www.SpeakingVolumes.us**

Now Available!

AWARD-WINNING AUTHOR
MARK WARREN

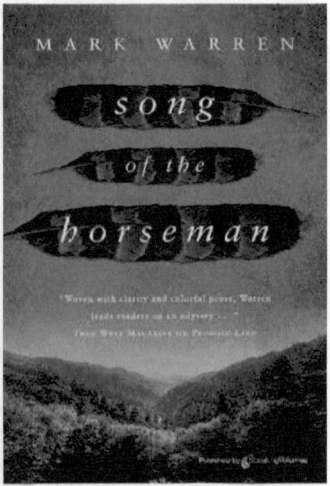

For more information
visit: www.SpeakingVolumes.us

www.ingramcontent.com/pod-product-compliance
Lightning Source LLC
LaVergne TN
LVHW041657060526
838201LV00043B/464